Praise for the N

How to Bake a Perfect Life

"Mothers and daughters are at the heart of this beautiful novel by O'Neal. . . . Highly recommended."

—*Library Journal* (starred review)

"Absorbing . . . O'Neal's tale of strong-willed women and torn family loyalties is a cut above the standard women's fiction fare, held together by lovingly sketched characters and real emotion."

—*Publishers Weekly*

"Envelops you like the scent of warm bread, comforting and invigorating, full of love and forgiveness and possibility."

—Erica Bauermeister, bestselling author of *The School of Essential Ingredients*

"This book will have you smiling and crying and pining for an old love, or just a hunk of really good fresh-baked bread. I loved every single delicious bite."

—Jennie Shortridge, author of *When She Flew*

The Secret of Everything

"O'Neal has created a powerful and intriguing story rich in detailed and vivid descriptions of the Southwest."

—*Booklist*

"Readers will identify with this story and the multilayered characters. . . . And with some of the tantalizing recipes for dishes served at the 100 Breakfasts Café included, O'Neal provides a feast not only for the imagination but the taste buds as well."

—*Romantic Times*

"Barbara O'Neal has masterfully woven local culture, the beauty of nature, her love of food and restaurants, and a little romance into this magnificent novel." —*Fresh Fiction*

The Lost Recipe for Happiness

"*The Lost Recipe for Happiness* is a delectable banquet for the reader. . . . This book is as delicious as the recipes interspersed throughout an incredible story."
—Susan Wiggs, *New York Times* bestselling author

"*The Lost Recipe for Happiness* is utterly magical and fantastically sensual. It's as dark and deep and sweet as chocolate. I want to live in this book. . . . A total triumph."
—Sarah Addison Allen, *New York Times* bestselling author

"Beautiful writing, good storytelling and an endearing heroine set against the backdrop of Aspen, Colorado, are highlights of O'Neal's novel. A tale that intertwines food, friendship, passion, and love in such a delectable mix is one to truly savor until the very last page." —*Romantic Times*

"Will appeal to women's fiction fans and foodies, who will enjoy the intriguing recipes . . . laced through the book."
—*St. Petersburg Times*

The Garden of Happy Endings

By Barbara O'Neal

The Lost Recipe for Happiness

The Secret of Everything

How to Bake a Perfect Life

The Garden of Happy Endings

The Garden of Happy Endings

A Novel

Barbara O'Neal

BANTAM BOOKS TRADE PAPERBACKS
NEW YORK

This is a work of fiction. Names, characters, places, and incidents are the products of the author's imagination or are used fictitiously. Any resemblance to actual events, locales, or persons, living or dead, is entirely coincidental.

2012 Bantam Books Trade Paperback Original

Published in the United States by Bantam Books, an imprint of The Random House Publishing Group, a division of Random House, Inc., New York.

BANTAM BOOKS and the rooster colophon are registered trademarks of Random House, Inc.

Originally published in mass market in the United States by Bantam Books, an imprint of The Random House Publishing Group, a division of Random House, Inc., in 1989.

LIBRARY OF CONGRESS CATALOGING-IN-PUBLICATION DATA

O'Neal, Barbara

The garden of happy endings : a novel / Barbara O'Neal.

p. cm.

ISBN 978-0-553-38678-3

eBook ISBN 978-0-345-53446-0

I. Title.

PS3573.I485G37 2012

813'.54—dc23 2011036881

Printed in the United States of America

www.bantamdell.com

2 4 6 8 9 7 5 3 1

Book design by Mary A. Wirth

To all mis chicas peregrinas
who walked the Camino with me,
especially
Anne Pinder who led us,
Betsy May, who got it all rolling,
and Mary Strand who corralled me into walking.

Thanks to Bethany Barber, who sang the most glorious
Ave Maria at Monte do Gozo, bringing us all to tears,
and her mother, Brenda, for long talks about writing and love,
and Sharyn Cerniglia who walked on bloody feet
just like a medieval pilgrim.

Love to Jean and Chris, Caroline and Rhonda.
I'm honored to know you all.

Acknowledgments

Some books require an army to be born. This one certainly did.

A tremendous amount of research was required for me to understand the lives of ministers and priests. I'm grateful to Reverend Lawrence Palmer, Unity minister, and one of the most influential teachers on my own journey, and to Father Ben Bacino, in Pueblo, for helping me to understand the day-to-day lives of ministers and priests, the great power of a calling, and some of the challenges of a life of service.

To say I am grateful to Reverend Ahriana Platten would be a gross understatement. It is impossible to express how providential and illuminating her arrival in my life was—and remains. This book would be a shadow of what it is without her. Thanks for showing, through example and conversation, so much of what makes a woman's calling so different from that of a man. I am honored to now call you friend.

Other women who shone with spiritual beauty in my thoughts as I wrote this book: my grandmother Madoline Putman, as always; my dear friend Heather Stocker, who has brought joy and a certain sanity into my world; also Noreen McGregor and Christina Ahlen, who have taught me so much. And last, but certainly not forgotten, the fellowship team who had my back through the intense, crazy year I was writing this book: Virginia Clark, Julie and Brad Poulson, Ann Luciani, Pam and Brenda and John Rogers. Thank you, thank you, thank you.

Much gratitude to Aphra Caraballo, a natural and elegant cook whose soups inspired me—and many of the recipes in this book. All mistakes are my own.

Without my publishing team, my books could never arrive in the world. Deepest thanks to Meg Ruley, who saw the potential in the early, early stages, and to Shauna Summers, who encourages me to do the work that inflames me—that's rare and I'm grateful—but also pushes me to give it all I've got. Deep thanks to Jane von Mehren, who creates such excitement for the books, and to the entire art and sales departments at Bantam who create the beautiful packages and get the books into the world.

Y mil gracias a Santiago, por supuesto.

The Garden of Happy Endings

Prologue

MANY YEARS AGO

The second time Elsa turned her back on God, it was raining.

She had imagined that they would end their pilgrimage by walking from the Camino right into the Cathedral de Santiago de Compostela, which she had seen in pictures. It was one of the largest cathedrals in the world, and in her mind, the Camino was a red carpet leading directly to it.

Instead, there was first a long slog through the city itself. It was pouring, a relentless deluge that soaked them as they walked suddenly on sidewalks instead of gravel, trudging through the large and thriving metropolis, complete with noisy cars, and planes roaring overhead, and the cacophony of thousands of people. After forty-three days of walking from one quiet hostel to the next, where the noisiest things in the world were roosters and frogs, the city jangled her nerves.

Joaquin, her fiancé, was deeply quiet. They had begun the *camino* as a lark, one last adventure before they started graduate school, but it had become much more as they traveled, one foot in front of the other.

They should have known better, Elsa thought, shoulders

hunched in misery. *She* should have known better. The *camino* called you for a reason. Secretly, she had hoped to find some indication of the way to express her vocation. From tiniest girlhood, she had wanted to be a priest. That idea had been shattered when she was fourteen, but she had still focused on comparative religions as an undergrad.

"Are you all right?" she asked Joaquin.

He took her hand. "Yes," he said, but his throat betrayed him, showing his Adam's apple moving in a big gulp.

At last they made their way to the square and into the vast, ancient cathedral. And there they stopped, dripping rain from hair and ponchos and packs, their mouths open in astonishment at the gold. *Oceans* of gold, mountains of gold. Gold slathered over statues and walls and candlesticks, gold enough to feed all the poor in the world for a century at least. Gold and adornments and Santiago overseeing it all.

Joaquin walked to the altar and knelt, and she saw that he was sobbing, his shoulders shaking. He had always been deeply faithful; it was one of the things they shared in a world that was increasingly underwhelmed by the old practices. To give him time and privacy, she knelt and crossed herself and entered a pew. Pilgrims with dusty feet and grimy packs milled around, along with tourists in tidy skirts who had arrived by bus, going to kiss the saint. Some of them looked sideways at Joaquin, but not as many as you might have thought.

At last, he rose and turned to her. Elsa left the pew to meet him. He took her hand. His eyes were red from crying, and she had a terrible feeling. She thought of the way he had made love to her that morning, with both fierceness and tenderness, and a burning began in her heart.

"Don't say it," she said, and backed away from him, closing her eyes, covering her ears with her hands. Water dripped down her back from her wet hair.

"Elsa," he said, and caught her hands. "Look at me."

She did.

"I am going to be a priest."

Elsa stepped away from him, and looked up at Santiago, draped in gold. "All that way I walked," she said, "and this is what you give me?"

She spat on the floor and stormed out of the cathedral.

Autumn

October is nature's funeral month. Nature glories in death more than in life. The month of departure is more beautiful than the month of coming—October than May. Every green thing loves to die in bright colors.

—Henry Ward Beecher

SEATTLE, PRESENT DAY

Chapter One

Six days before she turned her back on God for the third time, Elsa Montgomery went to the harvest festival at her church.

It was a bright orange Saturday in October, possibly the last sunny day of the year. She parked her car beneath an old monkey tree and let her dog, Charlie, out of the backseat. A long-legged black rescue with exuberant energy, he knew to mind his manners in crowds, keeping to her right side as they wandered toward the booths and tents set up on the lawn of the Unity church.

Just as they rounded the edge of the fair, ducking beneath the low arms of a pine tree, Elsa caught the scent of rotten apples. For a moment, she thought it came from an earthly cause, an apple that had fallen behind the booths or lay in the thick grass, forgotten in the rush to get everything ready.

There were certainly plenty of apples. Apples in baskets and apples in pies and apples floating in a tub filled with cold water for bobbing. Washington State was one of the premier apple-growing states in the nation, and local orchards had contributed heavily to the annual church festival.

It took place on the second weekend of October, when the leaves in the Seattle area hung on the trees like construction paper cutouts in shades of red and orange and yellow, and the worst of the winter gloom had not yet set in. The church, a small and humble building that boasted the stained glass art of a now-famous former parishioner, sat unassumingly in the midst of an arts-and-crafts neighborhood, where the houses—and thus the land the church sat upon—were commandingly expensive even after the real estate debacle.

The harvest committee rented booths to local farmers and craftspeople. It attracted a cheerful crowd of well-tended parents, their scrubbed children, and obligatory golden retrievers. The families played games and ate caramel apples and plumped up the church coffers better than any other single thing they did every year.

Elsa loved the fundraiser. It had been one of the first things she had created upon her arrival here as minister nine years ago. This year, the sun was shining, but the air was sharp enough that she wore a pink wool sweater and a pair of jeans with boots. She'd left her hair, crazy as it was, loose and curly on her shoulders, and she walked along the tables that were set up outside. Tents were erected over them, just in case.

As she moved down the center aisle, again she smelled the sulfurous odor of rotten apples. Insistent, dark. She paused, recognizing the warning.

Something was coming. Something dark and wicked.

She turned in a slow circle, looking for clues. Apples of ten varieties spilled out of baskets, along with pumpkins and squashes and piles of freshly baked bread. In the face-painting booth, Kiki Peterson carefully painted dragons on the face of a little girl wearing a fairy tutu. Next to them was a table set up to serve crepes made by Jordan Mariano, a vegetarian chef who attended the church. The menu offered roasted pumpkin and tomato crepes, apples and sugar, or classic chocolate and cream. Nothing seemed amiss. No one who looked out of place. No—

"Reverend!"

Elsa turned, still half seeking. A tall man dressed in khakis and a gold shirt strode toward her. He was a member of the finance committee.

"How are you, George?"

"You have a minute, Rev? I want to talk to you about the shortfall in fundraising last week."

"Let's talk about that at the meeting on Wednesday, shall we?" She peered over his shoulder, seeking a possible escape. "It's on the agenda—"

"But I don't think the committee is taking it seriously."

She touched his arm. "That may be, but let's enjoy this beautiful day and talk about it on Wednesday."

"But—"

"Excuse me." She headed toward a bent old man sitting in the sunshine. "How are you, Eddie?"

He turned his nearly blind eyes toward her, wispy white hair springing out in Einstein fashion around his head. "If I was any better, I'd already be in heaven."

She let him take her hand, and squeezed it. "Glad to hear it. How are the new digs?"

"Fine, fine. I have me a cat and some television, so what more does a man need, huh?"

He was eighty-nine, suffering from terminal cancer, asthma, high blood pressure, and crippling arthritis, but he put his love in things beyond himself, and that kept his spirits high. "I'm glad to hear it. I'll be over to see the new place sometime this week, and we'll say a blessing. How's that?"

"Wonderful."

A trio of girls in plaid shorts and T-shirts swirled over. "Reverend Elsa, we made you some dragonfly wings!" The smallest of the trio held up the tissue-paper-and-coat-hanger wings, pale purple with green and purple glitter. Their faces, too, had been painted with dragons. She looked over to Kiki and winked.

The teenager smiled. "I can paint your face, too, if you want."

"Oh, that would be so pretty!" the smallest of the girls said. She took Elsa's hand and pulled her toward Kiki and the face-painting booth. "Please, Reverend Elsa?"

Elsa capitulated, and let them pull her down into the chair, their cool little fingers and hands touching her arms, her shoulders, her neck. Someone pulled her hair away from her face, gently, pressed it to her temple. "I'll hold it so you don't get paint on it."

"Thanks, Alice." She gave the tiny redhead a kiss on the wrist.

Alice wiggled happily. "You're welcome."

Charlie slumped onto Kiki's foot. "Do you want a dragon or a rose or something else?" Kiki asked.

"I don't know. What do you girls think it should be?"

"A flower!"

"A dragon!"

"A castle!"

Kiki laughed. "A castle? How about a unicorn?"

"Oooh, yeah!" Alice traced a spot on Elsa's cheek, the touch as light as gossamer. "Right there."

"Can I fix your hair?" Davina asked, tilting her head sideways. "I have a brush. I'll be careful so Kiki doesn't mess up."

"I won't mess up," Kiki said. "I can do this in my sleep."

"Sure, then," Elsa said. "You can fix it."

Kiki dipped her brush into a pot of iridescent white paint. Her extraordinarily long brown hair, straight and glossy, fell in a silky wash over one thin shoulder and she tossed it back. "Ready?"

"Ready." Elsa closed her eyes as the liquid touched her cheek. The little ones fluttered their hands through her hair, and one hot plump body leaned into her, probably sleepy. The child suddenly bent over and rested her head in Elsa's lap. Gently, Elsa touched her back. The pink bubble gum smell of girl wafted around her.

"You're going to be such a good mom," Kiki said. "You're so patient."

"She's not married!" Alice said, standing on one foot. "You have to be married to have a baby."

Kiki smiled, a twinkle in her dark blue eyes. "Well, then she needs to get married."

Elsa gave her a rueful grin in return. Kiki's mother, Julia, had been trying to matchmake Elsa for months, one very nice man after another, but so far, there had not been a single second date. Julia said she was too hard on men, that Elsa needed to relax a little, but what was the point in that? Why spend your life with someone who wasn't just right?

Except . . . she wanted children. She'd always wanted them, at least four, maybe six. It was beginning to seem as if that might not happen. She was thirty-eight, and running out of time. And as much as she loved her work, the congregation, and the children of others, she would really mind if she didn't have a child of her own.

This, please, she said, a soft prayer sent out above the heads of the sweet-smelling girls, whose hands touched her, patting her hair, painting her face.

This.

It was only as she stood up that she again smelled the reek of disaster, deeper now, worse, like bloated fish. She swayed.

"You okay, Rev?" Kiki asked.

Elsa touched her arm. "Fine, thanks. Tell your mother I'll see her tomorrow."

"I will." Kiki screwed the lid of the paint back on. Blue stick-on stars decorated her fingernails. "I think she's lining up a new one for you."

Elsa shook her head and left, putting a hand over her upset

stomach. She made her way through the crowd and walked into the church, to duck into the haven of her office. She closed the door, as if to leave the threat behind.

It was a small room, with a single window overlooking the grass and trees and a square of earth planted with chrysanthemums. The décor reflected her simple tastes, with airy white curtains that blew on summer breezes, and only a trio of simple photos on the walls, all in a line, memories from her travels. Glastonbury Tor, pointing into a dark heavy sky from the top of an English hill; a shot of a mile marker on the Camino de Santiago, with an abandoned boot on top of it; and a shot of an old man painting a canvas by the sea.

Below the photos stood a small altar table with a pillar candle and a vase she filled with fresh flowers. Today, they were striped pink and white carnations, and their peppermint aroma lent a sweetness to the air. Elsa lit a candle, asking for protection, for goodness to blow this miasma away. She asked for insight to assist those who might need her, and patience, and stillness.

When that was finished, she picked up the phone and dialed Joaquin, her oldest friend, who had once been her fiancé. He answered on the second ring. "Father Jack."

"Walking, it's me," Elsa said. "I'm getting one of my warnings. Will you say some prayers?"

"Absolutely."

"Thanks, I have to get back to the harvest festival. I'll call you later."

"It's the fundraiser for the soup kitchen tonight. I won't be back until about ten." He said something over his shoulder, and Elsa imagined him talking to his secretary. "Your sister contributed a quilt. It's amazing. She really needs to show them."

"Which one is it?"

"It's a garden, which makes it sound ordinary, only it isn't."

"Shoot a cellphone picture and send it to me." Someone tapped on her door. "I've gotta go. Talk soon."

* * *

A thousand miles away, Elsa's sister, Tamsin, knelt in a flower bed, using a hefty pair of garden shears to prune the frost-killed plants. In the high desert of Pueblo, Colorado, the sun could be very hot even so late in the season, but a giant old elm protected the backyard at high midday. Even so, Tamsin wore a sun hat and long sleeves and gloves to protect her pale white skin.

Any day she could spend in a garden was a good day in Tamsin's book. She had restored every inch of the 110-year-old garden beds herself, reviving ancient peonies and climbing roses; Naked Lady lilies and a bed of poppies that bloomed like lush courtesans each June. Just now, there were only seedpods and withered flowers, so she gave the plants their haircuts, leaving coral bells and intriguing stalks to stand for winter interest. She pruned the roses mercilessly, trimmed the irises to fans of three inches, yanked up annuals and tossed them into the compost heap. It was hard work, sweaty and dirty, but that was what it took to make beauty.

Her husband, Scott, called to her from an upstairs window. "Tamsin, do you know where my black dress shirt is? I can't find it."

Tamsin rocked back on her heels, and pushed her hat off her hair so that she could see him. Her husband was a big man, tall and broad, and lately a little stout, though she didn't mind. He worked hard as an investment banker, a career that had given Tamsin more luxury than she'd ever dreamed of. He played hard, too, with an epicurean lustiness that made her worry sometimes that he'd give himself a heart attack.

He was packing for yet another business trip, this one to Memphis. They were more and more frequent lately. Some, she suspected, were mainly gambling trips, high stakes poker games in back rooms in big cities. He loved gambling, and the black shirt was his favorite for poker.

None of her business. As long as he kept his head, what did it matter to her? "Check the dry cleaning in the downstairs closet." She straightened, slapped dust off her jeans, and her mind drifted back to the garden. Maybe she should divide the peach irises next year. They were looking a little crowded.

"Hey, Tamsin," Scott called again, and she looked up.

He leaned from the window and tossed her a small, colorful cloth bag, the kind you could buy at shops that sold Tibetan goods. It landed at her knee with a plop of dust. "What's this?"

"A little something, that's all."

Smiling, she thought he must have made a good deal. Through the years both she and her daughter, Alexa, had become accustomed to surprises like this. The strings of the bag were tied, and she loosened them, pouring the contents into her hand. A pair of diamond solitaire earrings winked at her. Each was the size of a fingernail, and they glittered even in the shade, sending out rays of yellow and blue and violet.

Holding them cupped in her palm, she looked up. He was fond of surprise presents, but not this big. "What's the occasion?" she asked in some bewilderment.

For a minute, he looked too sober, then his usual twinkle returned. "Maybe I just want to get lucky before I have to leave."

She laughed, because it was acknowledged between them that Tamsin was by far the more sexual of the two. And lately, he'd been very stressed and busy with work. "Is that so?"

His hands hung loosely over the windowsill on the third floor of the red sandstone Victorian, one of the most beautiful in the city. Her pride and joy, this house, this garden, the tower room where she created her quilts. "Come upstairs, Tamsin," he said.

"I'll be right there." She headed inside, tucked the earrings into the secret drawer in her bread box, and dashed into the downstairs shower. Clean, still damp, she wandered through the house naked and feeling deliciously wicked about it. There were benefits to an empty nest.

He waited on their enormous bed, tucked demurely beneath the sheets. His bearish chest showed some gray hair lately, and he had started shaving his head because he was balding. He was fifteen years older than she, but she still found him attractive. Loved his size, his twinkling blue eyes, his wicked sense of humor.

Tamsin took her time walking toward him, knowing her body was still in great shape, that he was immensely proud of her, and that this would be good, hot sex.

"God," he said, holding out a big hand toward her, "I'm the luckiest man in the world."

"You are," she agreed with a chuckle, and dived in beside him.

Across the world, Tamsin's twenty-two-year-old daughter, Alexa, wore a blue dress and stood on a rooftop garden in Madrid, sipping a glass of Rioja. Around her, sibilant Spanish rose and fell, a perfume for the ear, the most musical of all the languages. There was nowhere in the world she would rather be than in Spain. She inhaled the air of it, dry and light.

Spain.

Again.

At last.

She had first fallen in love with Spain through her aunt Elsa's stories. Elsa and her boyfriend had walked the Camino de Santiago when they were young, and they had met bandits and ghosts and angels, and travelers from all over the world. Elsa spoke of cows wandering up a street in front of an old woman with a stick in her hand. She told stories of black dogs that seemed to appear out of nowhere, and cidra, a hard cider that was cold and refreshing after a long day of walking. Elsa had seen the enormous censor swinging from the rafters in the cathedral at Santiago de Compostela.

Curled up in her arms, with her aunt's warm voice pouring over her, murmuring words in lispy Spanish, Alexa fell in love with the magical far away. Spain became a siren to her, calling and calling. The yearning drove her to study Spanish in a serious and focused way, and to learn about the history and culture of Spain.

Not *Mexico*, as many of her friends in Pueblo had, but Spain. Sometimes they thought she was being arrogant by dismissing the new world in favor of the old; they cited the bloody stories of the Inquisition. She countered with tales of the Moors and the high degree of medical knowledge that had been their legacy, and the flamenco, and the great cities and cathedrals.

Mostly, she didn't care what anyone said. Only Spain would do.

In her senior year of high school, she was an exchange student in Madrid. Her host family had been cold and unfriendly, but Alexa loved the city, the people, speaking Spanish all day long. She made friends and had a string of sweet boyfriends, and promised herself she would be back.

Sometimes, it felt like she had been born in the wrong country. How could she have been born in America, when she clearly belonged in Spain? It was the most fanciful thought she ever had, and she was not a particularly fanciful girl. Her mother always said that Elsa was mystical enough for the whole family, so she was free to focus on the beautiful, beautiful world. Alexa loved the world of the mind.

When the opportunity to return to Madrid arrived in college, Alexa leapt. Honestly, the opportunity didn't just show up. She'd had to track it down and then beg her parents to let her go, and she still didn't get to spend her junior year abroad, but instead had to finish her course work and achieve her degree before they would let her spend the year there. Her parents were worried that she would not return. They were worried about terrorist attacks.

Mainly, she thought, they were worried that they would lose her to the far away. And perhaps that was not so far off the mark.

But she had at last succeeded, as she usually did with her parents, who doted on her, both of them. She tried not to take advantage of it too much, but in this case, it had been important. She'd had to get back to Madrid. *Had* to. Her life was waiting. She could feel it, ripe and ready beneath a thin skin of distance.

And this time, her host family was much kinder, a wealthy family with connections. They liked her manners, her excellent accent, her knowledge of Spain. Tonight, they had brought her along to a dinner party that began at ten p.m., with cocktails on this elegant rooftop garden with the stars overhead.

It was warm. Alexa wore an aqua dress with a loose empire skirt that floated over her body, and a beaded shawl. Her hair was her pride, long and thick and shiny, and she'd left it loose, curling over her shoulders.

One of the brothers of the host family came over, bringing with him another man. "Alexa," David said, "may I introduce my friend?"

He rattled off a string of names, but all Alexa caught was "Carlos." He had the long face and bedroom eyes of a Spanish actor, but his eyes were bright, bright blue, and his beautiful mouth smiled at her.

Alexa thought, *Oh! Here is the reason I have come to Spain. To meet my husband.* It made her cheeks flush, but not with embarrassment. With anticipation. She smiled, meeting his eyes directly. "I am pleased to make your acquaintance."

He took her hand and kissed it with courtly grace, and there was a smell of sugar in the air, and a fine blue ring of enchantment that fell down around them. For a moment, they only hung there, suspended in the magic—*at last!*—and he asked if she would sit beside him at supper.

"I'm afraid I am dependent on what our hostess has planned," she replied.

David laughed. "Oh, I think she will allow him to make the choice."

"Well, then, I would be honored," Alexa said.

It was only several days later that she understood he was a count, in line for the throne, obscenely wealthy and much too much for a girl like her to want.

By then, it was too late.

Chapter Two

The phone call from Julia Peterson came in at just past eight the following Wednesday evening.

Elsa had been to the YMCA for a long swim. She tried to get there every day. It was a moving meditation, a way of shaking off the world. In the pool, the world was silent and there was only her body, the water, her breath. Gliding. Tonight, she'd practically had the place to herself, so she felt good as she walked into her small house and dropped her gym bag on the floor in front of the stairs so she would remember to stick the wet towels and suit in the laundry.

When the phone rang, Elsa reached for it automatically, and then halted, feeling the miasma seeping out of it. Her body went cold.

She closed her eyes, let it ring one more time, trying to stay on this side of the change for one more minute. Automatically, she sent out a prayer for assistance—*Give me what I'll need for this*—and taking in a single breath, picked up the phone. "Reverend Elsa."

"Kiki's missing," Julia said without preamble. The Petersons, mother, father, three teenaged daughters, and a seven-year-old son who'd been a happy "oops" baby, were one of the solid cornerstones of the church. Allen served on the board, and Julia taught the middle schoolers Sunday school, never the easiest job. Kiki was the fourteen-year-old who had painted Elsa's face with a unicorn. "She never came home from school."

"You've called the police and her friends, all that?"

"Yeah." Julia's voice was breathless. "Her English teacher saw her leave school at four, with her backpack. She was by herself. She'd been working on a chemistry project for extra credit. You know she wants to be a doctor, right, so . . ." Julia made a small, pained sound. "I'm so worried!"

"I'll be right there."

"Thank you. I'm freaking out so badly I can barely hold the phone. Allen took the other kids to stay with his mom and I'm just not sure what to do with myself."

"Hold tight."

By the time she arrived, there was a detective in the living room of the Petersons' home. Evidence of supper was still on the table, and the carpet, which had once been very expensive but was now showing the wear of such a vigorous family, was scattered with books and toys. Elsa paused on the threshold, feeling a dense, dark energy swelling from somewhere, through her. Dizzy, she closed her eyes and put a hand on the door to steady herself.

Bad. This was going to be very bad.

And yet, in this ordinary room was a mother still on this side of the worst day of her life. Elsa sat down and took her hand. The long thin fingers, so much like Kiki's, were ice cold.

"The police say that a bunch of kids saw a guy hanging around the school grounds the past few days," Julia said. "They think—" She halted, her fingers tight on Elsa's. "One officer let it slip that there was a sex offender released from prison a couple of months ago."

She made a small moan, covered her mouth with two fingers. Her eyes looked triply blue against the red of weeping. "What do we do?"

"What we need is to be out looking for her," the detective said. "Can you give us something of your daughter's, something that has her scent?"

"Her scent?"

"For the dogs," Elsa said gently.

"Oh." The word came out on a waver, barely a sound at all. "Of course. Her coat is . . ." She tried to rise but couldn't.

Elsa stood. "I'll get it. What color is it?"

"Yellow," she said.

When the detective left, Elsa sat with Julia. They prayed. They waited. They prayed again. But nothing was discovered that night.

Or the next.

Or the next.

On the fourth day, an army of community volunteers joined the police and state patrol and other professionals to sweep the woods behind the school.

Elsa joined the search party, along with her dog. Charlie wasn't a bloodhound or a trained beagle, just a mixed-breed black dog with a solid helping of flat-coat retriever. He had glossy, thick fur and patient, intelligent eyes. He'd been more than a handful as a pup, and now he was so tall he stood nearly to her hip, but she'd worked with him a long time and he behaved well as they combed through the bushes and undergrowth.

They had been at it for an hour when Charlie caught a scent at the edge of a ditch and practically yanked Elsa's arm out of the socket, pulling her toward a thicket. A pulse leapt suddenly in her throat.

Elsa gave him the lead. He snuffled through wet leaves in a zigzagging line that probably broke all protocol, pulling so hard she could barely keep up with him. When he ducked under the protective branches of a pine tree, Elsa ducked with him, barely missing a slap of needles to the eye.

Charlie halted at the body, tenderly sniffed her naked thigh, and sat down hard. He whimpered softly.

Elsa did not move for a long, long moment. Kiki's slim body lay naked in the leaves, her hair twisted and tangled with twigs. She barely had any breasts at all. Her skin was a waxy shade, and there were marks all over her—puncture wounds and blood and bruises. One hand was clenched into a fist, the earth marking the place where her nails had scraped across it. They still had blue star stickers on them. Her eyes were open to the sky, as if looking for help.

Elsa fell to her knees and wished for something to cover the damage, the unholy evidence of a long slow death, and knew she could not. "Over here!" she cried, and her voice was too hoarse to carry. She staggered to her feet, vomited into the trees, and felt something shift in her belly.

Strike three, you're out.

Her knees straightened. She cleared her throat and called, "I found her."

On the morning of the funeral, Elsa stood on her back porch, smoking a contraband Kool from a pack she'd bought at the local gas station. Rain poured in a hard gray sheet from the sky, making lakes in the yard and rivers in the streets. It had been at least a decade, maybe more, since she'd last smoked a cigarette. She'd bummed one from a detective at the scene and had smoked it with hands shaking so badly she couldn't even light it, not caring who saw her.

She'd taken up smoking late, when she was twenty-three, the year she spent wandering around England after walking the Camino de Santiago. With other illegal immigrants, she worked under the table at restaurants, where she was badly paid, and slept in hostels, pretending she was a carefree backpacker. Everyone smoked, all the European youths she wandered with, and she took it up to be friendly, just as she drank to anesthetize her wounds, and slept with some of the men to ease the howling loneliness that had once been filled by Joaquin and God.

A long time ago now. She smoked and stared at the gray rain, wondering what she would say when all those faces turned to her for some semblance of reassurance, some sense of hope or possibility in a world where something like this could happen. At the moment, she had nothing.

Last night, she had pored through dozens of writings from every spiritual tradition she had studied over the years—and there were a lot. She'd culled quotes of bewilderment and howls of sorrow and a dozen platitudes that only made her furious, but none of them seemed right.

She kept thinking of Kiki at the harvest festival, so long-limbed and pretty, sweet with the little ones, coy over the man her mother had lined up for Elsa's next date, and it seemed impossible that she was gone.

But gone she was, and Elsa's job today, the *only* thing she had to do, was offer some tiny kernel of healing to the girl's mother, her father, her siblings. She had to offer some small branch of hope to the congregation, which was stricken and horrified and deeply unsettled by the swath of violence. They were depending on her.

It was going to be the hardest thing she had ever done.

She inhaled the last acrid breath of smoke and put out the cigarette and thought of bubonic plague wiping out half the earth. It had seemed a visitation of evil, but it had only been a terrible accident of nature, a tiny, tiny bug. But what had those spiritual leaders thought? What must they have struggled with?

The death of one small human seemed very small in comparison. Going inside to have a shower, she focused on that.

And on Kiki. For Kiki, she could do this.

* * *

Every single member of the congregation came to the funeral, nearly all of them dressed in bright spring colors at Julia's request. The sanctuary was filled with carnations, which had been Kiki's favorite, and Elsa had woven some pink ones into her hair.

The day before, Elsa and Julia had gone over the service, what Julia and her family needed. Julia had been adamant that it needed to be an uplifting celebration of Kiki's life, rather than a dark, dour, howling marker of loss. "That isn't who we are," she said, and paused to keep her voice clear. "It isn't who Kiki was."

It was never easy to preside over the funeral of a young person. Kiki's friends looked stunned or raw in their bright Easter clothes, and they had all brought mementos and cards to pile on the coffin, which was, of course, closed.

Complicating this funeral were the throngs of media outside the church. They gave lip service to the grief of the attendees, but in fact, the story was violent, mysterious, and tragic. It also played hard on the fears of every mother and young woman in the Seattle area. In all, a winning formula for news. Elsa had set strict boundaries on how close the reporters could come to the church, and had asked for the burliest members of the congregation to enforce those boundaries. They had gladly agreed.

Elsa sat in her chair on the dais as the music team led the mourners in song, a traditional favorite that Kiki had loved singing. For a moment, Elsa was overcome, thinking of her standing on the dais to sing with the youth group, and it seemed to strike others, too, especially her friends, who sat together in a tight huddle right behind the family. They leaned on one another, pressing tissues to their faces. They had a presentation planned, which Elsa had encouraged.

When it came time for her to speak, Elsa looked out at the expectant faces. She walked to the podium, entirely empty, and stared into the sea that blurred in front of her. Light fell through the windows in red and blue and yellow bars, touching faces, the coffin, and Julia.

At last a sentence came to her. "Spirit fashioned Kiki Peterson out of dragon dust and unicorns, belly laughter and a graceful paintbrush." In the faces, she saw a sudden wash of tears in many eyes, but also ease, and she continued without even knowing what she said. Continued with the words that came from some other part of her, speaking them with a sturdy voice and laughter and even some tears. She would never remember a word of it.

It was not until the evening that she collapsed, alone in her little house, with the great darkness of a black hole sucking her soul into it so she could not even feel. She fumbled with the cigarettes and took them outside to the cold night. It was not raining, and the sky was thick with stars. They gave her no comfort.

She lit a cigarette, inhaling deeply, feeling the chemicals ease her panic almost instantly, leaving behind a depth of loneliness that nearly brought her to her knees. The vast, empty universe mocked her with light from stars that had been dead a billion years, and a darkness that held no life at all.

No life. No spirit. Nothing but unfeeling dust, formed by accident into life on this tiny planet in a far little corner of the universe.

Alone.

Twice before, she'd felt this engulfing recognition that God was only a construct to help humans make sense of their short, tragic lives. Twice she had weathered it and come back. This time, she saw the truth all too clearly—there was nothing.

Finished with the cigarette, she put the butt in a coffee can and crossed her arms, looking up. Emptiness looked back.

But God or not, there was a congregation of humans who needed her. She would not abandon them, no matter what her personal feelings were.

She would not abandon them.

Chapter Three

Joaquin Gallegos, known to all as Father Jack, liked to run in the early morning to prepare himself for the day ahead. He'd been a devoted runner since winning his first blue ribbons on track days in elementary school. His fleet feet had snared the scholarships that had made college possible. Made his *life* possible.

This Thursday morning in late November, his heart was heavy as he rolled from his bed and washed his face, then pulled on his running pants and a warm fleece jacket one of his brothers had given him a couple of Christmases back. The shoes were his one indulgence, a new pair every three months that provided his long narrow feet and high arches with serious support.

From the top of his bureau, he picked up the rosary beads he'd bought so long ago in Roncesvalles, Spain, before beginning the pilgrimage that had changed his life.

The world was still covered in eggplant shadows as he loped out the front door of the rectory and ran through the sleeping streets. It was snowing lightly, but with a certain steady intent that made plain there would be piles of snow by evening. It was good to be back in Pueblo, after so many years away. He'd been deeply pleased when the bishop offered him this church in a challenged neighborhood in his hometown two years before. He loved Pueblo, loved being close by his siblings and large extended family, who were so proud of him, the priest.

With his thumb, he caught the first bead of his rosary and began to quietly chant the Lord's Prayer, then the Hail Mary's and the Glory Be's, sliding the beads around his wrist, each one worn smooth by his touch over the years. Sixteen years, to be exact.

His usual run was six miles, a long loop down the levee, around the ditch, and through a sleeping old neighborhood of tiny houses in the shadow of a church, and back to San Roque. He prayed the rosary through the first half, then simply held the beads in his fingers, sliding them comfortingly back and forth across the back of his knuckles, and listened for anything God had to say in return.

Sometimes it was prosaic, a nudge to check the toilet in the men's restroom in the basement, or to ask Mrs. Marelli about the lasagna she usually cooked for the monthly potluck. Other times, it was more mysterious, a whisper to look up a passage from the bible, or a visual of a person who needed prayer. He made no claim to getting these communications perfectly right every time, but he did his earnest best.

It was Elsa who was on his mind this morning. He had dreamed of her last night. Several times over the past few weeks, he'd caught something hushed in her tone, as if she were using her voice to compress something she could not say. In his dream, she was smoking, looking at the moon.

Joaquin and Elsa had been friends since childhood. They had both been nerdy kids—Joaquin skinny and tall, Elsa one of those invisible girls with braces and crazy black hair and knees that were too big. He at least had had track, but she'd nothing to redeem her in the cutthroat waters of elementary school.

Today, he rubbed his thumb across the beads and prayed to see the shadows obscuring her faith. To see how to help her heal.

A warning moved through him. *Be ready.*

Be ready. He frowned.

When he was seven years old, Joaquin had had the measles, a terrible case that nearly killed him, at least by some accounts, and left him with scars on his body, face, arms, chest. Even at the end of grade school, he still wore a T-shirt to the swimming pool. His legs tanned and covered the marks, and anyway, who cared if you had scarred legs?

At his very sickest, when he'd been limp with a fever that made him delirious, and likely should have had him in the hospital, an angel came and sat with him. He'd been painfully isolated, quarantined from the other children, and his mother was afraid of contagiousness so she barely visited his room.

The angel didn't have big white wings or even any wings at all. She wore a long green gown. Light emanated from her skin, and she had very dark clear eyes. She took his hand, cooling the heated, itchy flesh, and said, "Joaquin, you can't die yet. You have important work to do. One day, you will be a priest and save many lives."

He had been delirious, but not that delirious. "No," he said. Not a priest.

She just smiled. "You'll see," she said, and started to sing the most miraculously beautiful song, as if harps and birds and guitars and the sweetest voices in the heavens were joined together. As she sang, she stroked his forehead and neck, her hands smooth as silk, and he smelled something that even now he couldn't describe, like brown sugar or simmering cherries.

He fell asleep, and when he awakened, his fever had broken. His mother brought him food. She asked who he'd been talking to, and Joaquin only shook his head. Obviously he had imagined it.

But so many years later, he could still close his eyes and see her, exactly as she had been, that angel. Her name was Gabrielle, she said. *I will see you again.*

It had been a long time later, but she had returned. And he was a priest now, just as she had said. He did not tell the story, though Elsa knew it. It had marked a breach between them, the loss of the union they had imagined. He had not been able to be there for the crisis of faith she experienced that year, long ago. He had, in part, been the cause of it.

A bible verse from Ecclesiastes came to him:

> Two people are better off than one, for they can help each other succeed. If one person falls, the other can reach out and help. But someone who falls alone is in real trouble. Likewise, two people lying close together can keep each other warm. But how can one be warm alone? A person standing alone can be attacked and defeated, but two can stand back-to-back and conquer.

He wiped a droplet of sweat from his forehead. *Someone who falls alone*. He would call her again this afternoon, make sure she was all right. Push, if he had to, past the barriers she sometimes erected.

Bring her home.

He scowled his resistance, a wall of resistance, enormous and hard as brick. No. That was his imagination, the wrong side of him. Instead, he would ask Tamsin to go see her.

As he looped back up the hill toward the parish, a whisper moved through him one more time.

Be ready.

Tamsin swung by Father Jack's office in the rectory of San Roque Catholic Church. He had called last night to ask if she would come see him.

It was a blustery day, the sharp wind giving lie to the bright sunlight, and drying out any remaining life in the grass in the lawns, turning the city a uniform pale brown. It would be ugly until it snowed. As she parked, Tamsin shook her head over the vacant lot between the church and a block of three-story apartment buildings. Trash and tumbleweeds blew into the lot, catching on junk of various kinds—discarded tires, unidentifiable wood, a couch where two young thugs sat sharing a joint. They eyed her with faintly hostile expressions as she locked her car—luckily she was driving the ordinary Subaru and not Scott's BMW—and hurried up the walk.

Mrs. Timothy sat at the desk, a sixty-something professional secretary who guarded Joaquin as if he were the pope himself. "Is he in?"

Officiously, she rose and smoothed her gray pencil skirt. "I'll check. You are?"

Tamsin smiled. Mrs. Timothy knew very well who she was—she and Scott were enormous donors to the church, and Alexa had been here every Sunday of her life, thanks to Scott. But Tamsin didn't care for Mass. Didn't care much for the Catholic Church, or *any* church for that matter, and she didn't attend. Mrs. Timothy liked to rub that in. "Tamsin Corsi. He'll know who I am." She did not add, *as we've been friends since childhood*. Technically, it was just Joaquin and Elsa who had been friends back then. Tamsin was eight years older, forty-six to their thirty-eight now.

"I'll tell him." She sniffed and knocked on the door of his office.

A pair of pigeon-breasted Italian women stuck their heads into the office. Sisters, by the look of them, and judging by their aprons, they had landed the plum duties of caring for Father. "Where is Wilma?" one of them asked. "We need to put coffee on the list! He's almost out!"

"Do you want me to tell her?"

The sisters exchanged a worried look. "We'd better wait."

Mrs. Timothy came back out, waved a hand. "Father will see you now."

Hiding her smile, Tamsin headed for his office.

Father Jack sat behind the desk and stood up as she came in. He was, they all said, too handsome to be a priest, despite the scarring on his skin from a terrible case of measles when he was a child. Black hair fell in a glossy swath across his forehead. He had large dark eyes that could be sympathetic or furious or inscrutable. "Good morning, Tamsin. I'm so glad to see you."

"I have to tell you," she said, "that field is an eyesore and dangerous and I think we need to do something about it."

He raised his eyebrows. "We? If you'd like to head a research committee to see what can be done, that would be terrific."

"Ha-ha."

"'We' doesn't always mean somebody else. I can get you a few volunteers."

"I don't even come to church."

"That's all right." He gestured for her to sit down and took a seat himself. "Lots of other people don't come to Mass, either, but they do work around the church. What would you like to see done with the field?"

"I don't know, I haven't thought about that. It's just ugly and not very inspiring. Maybe it could be—" She paused, running through possibilities "—a community garden! Wouldn't that be great?"

He inclined his head, a quizzical expression on his brow. "Do you think it's possible?"

"Sure, why not? We'd have to raze it and bring in some topsoil and, I don't know, make little plots." She stopped. "Oh, no you don't, Mr. Machiavelli. I know you."

"You don't have to commit to anything right now, but what if you just looked into what exactly would be required, and got back to me?"

Tamsin thought of the garden, the flat-eyed boys, and then the transformation. Maybe she did need a project. "I'll look into it."

He smiled. "Thank you," he said with emphasis, then sobered. "I asked you here today to talk about Elsa."

"Are you worried, too? I can't put my finger on it, but she just doesn't sound right."

"She's stopped taking my calls. We usually talk at least once a week, sometimes more."

Tamsin blinked. "You do? Even after all this time?"

As if he saw nothing strange at all in that, he nodded. "We've been friends for twenty-seven years. We share a calling." He shrugged. "It feels very natural."

"So when was the last time you talked to her?"

"She sent me an email about a week ago, but before that, it was at least a couple of weeks. I call, but she doesn't call back."

"That's not making me any happier." Tamsin frowned. "She just sounds . . . weird. Flat. Like she's not all there." She made a decision on the spot. "I'm going to fly to Seattle." She stood. "I'll let you know what's going on."

"Please. And ask her to get in touch with me. Tell her I'm worried."

Elsa had loved Sunday mornings her entire life. As a child, she'd even liked the ritual of a good long bath on Saturday night, and having her hair washed. Of course, she'd hated the pins and curlers her mother had put it up in, hated the way they interfered with sleep—her mother had been at war with Elsa's hair from babyhood, when she was born with a headful of black corkscrews. But she'd endured even the discomfort of sleeping in rollers for the pleasure of church.

On Sunday mornings, she liked getting dressed in special clothes, held just for this one sacred day, and then having a better breakfast than usual, after which she went to Sunday school. There she learned about the saints and Jesus and the Blessed Mother, who was always her favorite, with her pretty face and kind eyes. Jesus was good, but he seemed like a teenager, a little aloof and far away, as if he'd want to be with his friends and would be annoyed if she bothered him, as her sister, Tamsin, often was.

Although no one else in her family had particularly stuck with it—her parents had only gone out of duty—Elsa loved church even when she went alone. She never missed Sunday school, which was where she had met Joaquin in the first place. They were in the same Sunday school class in the fifth grade. He loved it as much as she did.

Since becoming a minister, Elsa had grown to love Sunday mornings even more. She still had rituals. Her Sunday clothes had become simple linen slacks and tunics in neutral colors, paired with bright scarves. People brought her scarves from their travels now, beautiful things in amazing fabrics and textures. She also had a massive collection of bracelets, but only wore one at a time, since she gestured so much giving her sermons. Gestured and paced and paused and stopped.

She adored it. Part teaching, part theater, part pure love offering, a way to serve the world and the people in it.

This gloomy November morning was the first Sunday of Advent. She rose at five, as was her habit. Usually she spent time in meditation before she took a shower, but lately she couldn't bear to sit in silence in the small room she had set aside for the purpose.

Instead, she took Charlie for a long walk in the drizzle. He never minded. She had a good raincoat, and the repetitive motion, breathing in the cool air, the stillness of early morning were as steadying for her as meditation.

When she returned home, she had her shower and let her hair dry, curly and long, over her shoulders. She chose a deep purple scarf of thinnest, airiest silk, in honor of the vestments priests wore at the beginning of Advent. Her bracelet was an enameled purple cuff.

She could do this.

It was her habit to eat a good breakfast, oatmeal or eggs, along with strong milky tea and some cheery rock music to raise her energy. Salt-N-Pepa and Cyndi Lauper, Motown and The Cars. Light, happy songs to get her heart into the right space. Her sermons were woven of the challenge of being human and the pleasure of being one with the Divine, and joy was always her goal. Uplift. Happiness. Joyful people could overcome trouble and illness and sorrow. Joy could blot out darkness.

And this was a powerful, beautiful Sunday, one of the best of the year. Advent. Light arriving in the darkness of the world.

But she felt no light, anywhere in her, anywhere in the world. It was always a challenge to adjust to the rainy season, but this year it was even more difficult. They had not seen the sun since the harvest festival, almost two solid months before. The deep gloom, the eternal, endless sound of rain falling and falling and falling, and the constant cold damp were taking their toll.

Focus, she told herself, drinking tea and poking at a bowl of oatmeal. She went over her notes for the sermon. *The light coming into the world. The beginning of the most sacred season for Christians. Advent. The birth of Christ. In metaphysical terms, a new start for all.*

An R.E.M. song wound through her head, mocking. *Losing my religion.*

Lost. It was lost.

And yet, she had an obligation to her congregation, who were still reeling. A web of soft despair had fallen over them, like a people enchanted in an old fairy tale, and they were looking to Elsa to help them shake it off.

This morning, she would give them the first Advent candle. She would sing the first Christmas carols of the season and would act *as if*—as if she believed, as if she still loved this season with abiding passion, as if there was healing if they would only reach for it.

At her feet, Charlie whined softly and licked her shin. "It's all right, baby," she said. But it was hard to fool a dog. "Let's go to church, shall we?"

He leapt to his feet and they drove over in the rain.

The church was tucked into a neighborhood full of monkey trees and firs and hemlocks, the ground thick with ferns and moss and greenery of a thousand varieties. Elsa had grown up in the high, bright deserts of southern Colorado, and she never ceased to marvel at the number of things that grew here.

She had learned to carry an umbrella, which she opened now before she left the car, keeping it angled so that her hair and clothing stayed dry. Charlie leapt out of the car behind her, padding into her office, where he would stay until after the service.

It was dark enough that she had to turn on the lamps. She closed the door behind her so that random people would not disturb her before she grappled with this morning's lesson. She could hear the small choir practicing in the sanctuary, and women talking and laughing in the kitchen. It was a church filled with artists and massage therapists, professors and students, a vibrant, energetic—and often eccentric—crowd. They arrived at Unity through metaphysics and Wicca, fallen away Catholicism or old-school theologies that no longer served modern, questing populations. There were meetings for mothers and children, for Abraham adherents, for Reiki sessions, and studying Lessons in Truth. The bulletin board held flyers for masseuses and jewelry makers, for psychic readings of many varieties and lessons in shamanism.

She loved them, every single one of them. How—

A strong knock shattered her thoughts, and Elsa scowled. They knew better than to disturb her on a Sunday morning when her office door was closed. Who in the world . . . ?

She opened the door, prepared to deliver a firm correction. Instead, she gaped at her sister, Tamsin. Tall and sleek, as long-legged as a Barbie doll, she was as pretty as Elsa was plain. Their mother used to say that Elsa was as ordinary as peas, while Tamsin was a dinner plate dahlia.

"Hi," she said. "Surprise."

Elsa blurted out, "What are you doing here?"

"I came to see how you are." She looked Elsa up and down. "Turns out I was right to be worried. When was the last time you ate?"

Elsa held up her hands. "Look, I can't do this right now. You're going to have to come back after church." She gestured behind her to the lamplit office, her desk, scattered with paper. "I-I have work to do. I have a sermon in an hour."

"That's fine." Tamsin took a step back. "I'll go find the kitchen and get a cup of coffee, leave you to it."

"Okay. I'll see you around one."

"Can't I stay and listen to the sermon? I've never heard you preach."

"Teach. We call it a lesson."

Tamsin shrugged. Her hair was long, down to the middle of her back, and although she was eight years older than Elsa, she looked younger. "Teach, then. You know I'm not that big on sermons anyway." She blew Elsa a little kiss. "Get back to it. I'll see you in a while."

Elsa closed the door, airless. If her sister had shown up, Elsa wasn't covering her crisis as well as she'd thought. She turned back to the desk, looking at the papers stacked up there, the things she'd left undone. What was she doing with her time, anyway? It was like she lost hours each day to nothing at all.

None of that mattered right now. She had a lesson to deliver, and come hell or high water—both of which seemed likely this morning—she would give it. She kicked off a shoe and rubbed her foot along Charlie's side. He thumped his tail against the floor.

Elsa focused on her task.

She could do this.

* * *

Tamsin sat through the sermon with a brick in her belly. Elsa had lost weight she could not afford to lose, and she had dark circles under her eyes. The worst was how her sister's hands shook when she tried to light the Advent candle. It took her six tries. Six. The congregation sat in quiet agony as their minister dropped match after match, grimly determined to finish the task even if she burned the building down.

But as Elsa began to speak, Tamsin forgot all of that. How was it possible that she'd never heard her little sister give a sermon until now? She'd been a minister for more than ten years.

Elsa was transformed as she stepped forward, as if she had stepped into a new body. Her voice was vibrant and strong, her face radiant with love. She made her congregants laugh, and told them stories, and circled around to deliver a spiritual and emotional punch that had many of them reaching for tissues, including Tamsin. "Wow," she breathed.

"Isn't she amazing?" the woman sitting next to her said. "I'd just about given up on organized religion, when I came here and heard her talk."

Tamsin nodded. After the service, she wandered down the hall to the fellowship room, where coffee and snacks were spread out on the counter. People greeted her, shook her hand, welcomed her, as she wandered around the room, mainly eavesdropping. The mood was subdued. "I like to think we'll all feel better once winter is over," one older woman said to her friend.

Elsa came into the room. "Everybody," she called, lifting her hands in the air. "I want to introduce someone to you. This is my sister, Tamsin." She pointed to the corner where Tamsin stood. "Raise your hand, sis. Isn't she beautiful?"

Tamsin raised her hand, feeling a flush of pride in her relationship to this tiny woman with her beautiful hair and beaming smile. "Thanks."

"We are so lucky to have her," said a man standing near Tamsin. "It's been a terrible time here, but she's getting us through it."

Tamsin squeezed his arm. "I heard. I'm so sorry."

"Spirit will see us through," he said. "Now, you take her out and get her something hearty to eat, why don't you? She's skin and bones lately."

Tamsin had been imagining that she would take Elsa back home to Pueblo with her, at least for a few weeks, but she saw now that wouldn't happen. No way Elsa would leave them, not when they were in such dire straits.

So, for today, Tamsin would do just what the man had suggested—feed her sister, make sure she was eating. She would listen if Elsa would talk. She would keep a close eye on her.

Maybe Elsa would come home at Christmas, just for a week or two. Or right after Christmas, since the church would want its minister on the holiest days of the year. She would talk her into it.

Chapter Four

On the darkest day of the year, four days before Christmas, Elsa awakened long before dawn and made a pot of tea. As the tea bags steeped, she checked her phone messages and saw that Joaquin had called twice. She didn't listen to the messages. It would be the same thing. *Call me. Call me. Call me.*

But she couldn't talk to him right now. He with his mighty faith. How could she tell him what she was thinking? It was humiliating, in a way, to suddenly be one of the lost, instead of one of the leaders. She kept telling herself to pull it together, to find a way to get over all of this, to stop being a big baby, but it wasn't working.

Even thinking about it, she had to go outside to smoke. Which was insane, too. She knew it. She just couldn't stop.

She had grieved before—grieved her father most sincerely, and a friend who had died in a car accident when she was in college, as well as many others since becoming a minister. She understood, both emotionally and intellectually, the process of grief.

But no amount of understanding was doing any good this time. Yesterday, the board had called her in to a meeting and gently, firmly told her that she had to take a sabbatical. They were contacting an associate pastor at a Unity church in Portland, who would be more than happy to take the position until Elsa "felt better." A semi-retired minister who had sometimes subbed for her in the past, Reverend Harris. He was a fatherly man, and kindly, a good choice to lead the bruised congregation during her absence.

She had resisted, insisting she was fine, that she'd be okay in another week or two, but the board had been immovable. They'd dismissed her, for six months. At the end of May, they would reassess.

Objectively, she could see that she was in crisis. She hadn't slept more than two hours at a stretch in the ten weeks since Kiki's murder. She had to set reminders on her phone to make sure she ate at regular intervals. Her dog followed her around with a worried expression, never leaving her side for longer than he absolutely had to.

For that, at least, she was grateful. Even now, he slumped on the kitchen floor, looking up at her dolefully. "I'll be all right," she said, sinking down beside him to kiss his head and nose. "I promise. Sooner or later, this funk will break and I'll get answers."

His feathery black tail thumped the ground.

When the doorbell rang, Charlie barked sharply, and Elsa jumped a foot. She glanced at the clock—it was only six a.m. Who could possibly be here?

Warily, she went to the door and called through it, "Who is it?"

"Joaquin, Elsa. Let me in."

She swung the door open. He wore his clerical collar beneath a heavy winter coat. His hair was too long, as always. "How did you know?"

"Your friend called me. Julia?"

Elsa bent her head, ashamed and stung. "Don't try to rescue me," she said.

"Wouldn't dream of it."

But as if she had been waiting for him, Elsa suddenly felt herself give way. She sank to the floor and began to weep. "I just can't keep pretending," she said. "I can't."

"I'm sorry I didn't come sooner, my friend." Joaquin sank down beside her, and put a steadying hand on her shoulder. Charlie nudged his face into the space beneath her arm. They held her so that she would not fly away into that dark, cold, unfeeling universe and be lost for all time.

"I am going to take you back to Pueblo," he said.

Elsa nodded. It was the only answer.

March

No winter lasts forever;
no spring skips its turn.

—Hal Borland

PUEBLO, COLORADO

Chapter Five

On the day of the spring equinox, Elsa sliced big yellow onions on the counter of the kitchen at San Roque Catholic Church in Pueblo. She was volunteering in the church soup kitchen, serving humanity without serving God. When Joaquin breezed into the room, a sheaf of papers in his hand, she was blinking away onion tears.

Outside, a blizzard was whirling. She was tired of snow and wet and dark days and she ached for spring. Her sister's garden was beginning to sprout little shoots of daffodils and tulips, but now they would be buried by the snow.

"Hey, Walking," she said, calling him by the nickname she'd given him long ago. "Want to chop onions?"

"No, thanks." He leaned on the battered faux wood counter. Then without preamble, he said, "I want you—and maybe Tamsin, if she'll do it—to run the community garden this summer."

"What are you talking about? There's a community garden?"

"It was your sister's idea, last fall. We're starting it in the vacant lot." He passed her a sheaf of papers.

Elsa wiped her hands on the thin cotton apron she wore and took them. On top was a map, with a check paper-clipped to it.

"The finance committee released some seed money," he said, and snorted. "Ha-ha."

"Ha-ha." She frowned at the drawing, which showed blocks of gardens, illustrated with curlicues that were meant to be plants. Broccoli, she supposed. Tomatoes and corn. "The lot behind the church? The one between the back door and the apartment block?"

His dark eyes glittered. "Yep."

"*This* year?"

"Yep."

She handed back the sheaf of papers. "You're crazy."

"O ye of little faith."

Slicing an onion in half with a big knife, she gave him a look. "It will take a year just to clean it up." The lot had long been abandoned, and it was littered with everything from old mattresses to tires. Drug deals transpired there in the dark of night. Not long ago, a stabbing had sent a youth to the hospital.

Which was, of course, the moment Joaquin the Crusader had had enough. "It's a good project," he said now. "Creation. Community." He gestured with a clean, open palm toward the soup pot. "Food. Fresh and sustainable, just the way you like it."

In that moment, Elsa caught the vision. She saw the garden in full green summer, corn tasseling beneath the apartment windows, children plucking tomatoes they'd grown themselves. A breeze blew through her hard, dark soul, just for a second.

Joaquin smiled. "It will be good for you."

"Don't try to save me," she said.

He shook his head. "Never."

She took the sheaf of papers back. "I'll do it for the kids."

"I know." He pointed one long brown finger at a name at the top of the sheet. "That's Deacon McCoy. He's got the heavy equipment we'll need, and he'll be a good second in command. Nice guy. Big Brother, runs the AA meeting."

"On Thursdays." Elsa blinked. "I've seen him around. He comes to get the coffeepot."

"Good, then. He should be here today." He headed for the door. "We on for breakfast in the morning?"

He liked to make waffles, or sometimes blueberry pancakes, to fortify himself for the weekend. Since she'd limped home just before Christmas, she'd never missed a Friday. She nodded. "I'll bring the eggs this time."

He gave her a thumbs-up. "Gotta go. See ya later."

If you were going to do a thing, Elsa believed, there was no point wasting time. When she had the soup simmering on the stove, she washed her hands and headed down to the basement. It was Thursday, so Deacon McCoy was already there, unfolding chairs and setting them down in neat lines. The meeting started at ten-thirty, and many of the attendees wandered into the soup kitchen afterward. It worked out well.

"Hi," she said. "I'm Elsa. Do you have a minute?"

"I do." He flattened the seat of a chair and straightened, a tall man with sun-darkened skin and an accent as southern as his name. "How can I help you?"

She stepped off the last step and waved the papers she was holding. "Father Jack wants to turn the vacant lot into a community garden. I seem to have . . ." She pursed her lips. "Er . . . volunteered to help get it going."

He chuckled. "He has that effect on people."

"Tell me about it."

"Don't you already run the soup kitchen?"

She nodded.

"Can't pay much."

She brushed hair out of her eyes. "He gave it to me as a kindness and it's been helpful."

He nodded, waiting.

Elsa took his measure. He bore the faint weariness of so many recovered alcoholics—a weight of unresolved regrets still dragging at his ankles—but he was also a good-looking man by any standard, fortyish, with long limbs and wavy dark hair. A lusty sort of man, she thought unexpectedly.

The combination would ensure any number of women would be happy to volunteer in the garden if he was part of it. "Joaquin said you might be willing to help with the heavy equipment. Is that right?"

"I might be persuaded." He glanced at the clock. "Do you mind helping me set up chairs as we talk? Meeting starts in a half hour. Still need to make the coffee."

She laid the papers on a nearby table and grabbed a chair, set it in the next row. "What do you think we'll need?" Elsa asked.

"I run a landscaping business, so I've got earthmovers and—well, pretty much all the necessary equipment."

"That helps."

"Before, though, we're gonna need a Dumpster. A big one. Volunteers will throw all the trash into it."

"Right." She placed a chair at her end.

"A cold frame to get the seeds going." He grabbed two more chairs. "And then we'll till it, get ready to plant. Probably want some topsoil."

Elsa halted with a chair flat against her body. "I have no idea what I'm doing. I grew a garden as a kid, but nothing this big."

"Ain't nothin', sweetheart," he said, and it was impossible to be annoyed with an endearment that was so plainly automatic. "Big or little, it's dirt and water, sun and paying attention."

"So you'll help?" she asked, putting the chair in place. There was one more space, and he carried a chair forward, meeting her in the middle of the row.

"Is that bean soup I'm smelling in the air?" he asked.

"Beans and ham hocks."

"Magic words. Save me a bowl, will you? And I'll come help you clean up later. We'll map out a plan."

"You've got it." She stuck out her hand. "Thanks, Mr. McCoy."

"Deacon." His palms were leathery with hard work, his grip strong and sure. "You're welcome . . . what's your name again?"

"Elsa Montgomery."

"Elsa. That was the lion in *Born Free*."

She grinned. "Gold star. My mother loves cats."

His eyes crinkled. "Are you really named for that lion?"

"Yes. At least I'm not Thomasina, which is my sister's name."

"Is that a lion, too?"

"No—a cat. You mean you've never seen the movie?" Elsa covered her heart mockingly. "It's a Disney film from the sixties, about a cat that gets lost and finally found."

"Missed that one."

A man wandered into the basement wearing a ragged coat. She recognized him from the soup kitchen, an old man with a greasy baseball hat pulled over his hair. He only had his bottom teeth, which made him look like a pug. Seeing Elsa, he waved. "Good morning, Reverend."

"How are you, Hank? How's your foot?"

"Better, thank you." He lifted it as if to show her.

"Glad to hear it."

Hank yanked off his hat and worried it in a circle. "Coffee made yet?"

"I'm just about to get on it," Deacon said. "We'll talk later," he said to Elsa. "Don't forget to save me some soup."

"Done," she said. "I'll see you after lunch."

The church served soup and bread every Thursday, taking up the slack from the main soup kitchen downtown. They served between seventy-five and a hundred lunches, depending on the time of the month, to a mixed group. There were the homeless, of course, wearing too many layers of clothes, none too clean, and the young drifters and runaways, pierced and tattooed, their eyes hungry.

But there were also women and children from the rent-assisted apartments on the other side of the vacant lot. The church had set aside a special area at the back of the fellowship hall for the family groups, to keep them apart from the more unstable population, and the children loved the corner that was filled with books and toys. They drank milk instead of the tea and coffee served to adults, and Joaquin made sure they had cookies, too.

It took a small crew to make it work. Elsa created the menus, organized the volunteers, and did much of the cooking. A rotating pair of men in their forties and fifties from the men's fellowship group provided security. A team of mostly retired seniors assisted with cleanup, service, and preparation.

Although other places offered more variety of food, the menu at San Roque was simple and plentiful. They served soup, vats of it, with bread they made from scratch, and then whatever dessert or bakery goods might have been donated by the local groceries or parishioners. It was day-old or more, all of it, but it was gobbled up eagerly.

On a snowy day like this, people lingered over their empty bowls, eyeing the dark skies, and as always, Elsa wondered where they would sleep. Many would go to local shelters. Others would camp beneath a bridge or in a protected copse of trees somewhere. As a young and idealistic woman, she would have worried about every single one of them. Maturity had shown her you did what you could. She fed them.

A crew of volunteers cleaned up, banging pots and gossiping about a marriage that was in trouble, and why. Not knowing the players, Elsa let the gossip wash over her as she bent over an egg and tried to balance it on the counter. According to legend, it should balance on one end at Equinox. "Is it supposed to be raw?" she asked the room at large. "Or cooked?"

"Raw," called out one of the guys.

"Cooked," said another volunteer.

"It's raw," said a ragged, southern voice. Elsa looked up to see Deacon, carrying the coffee urn up from the basement. "But it's not Equinox, it's Solstice."

"Are you sure?"

"Is it working?"

The egg rocked sideways. "No."

"There you go." He set the urn on the counter, and waved away a volunteer who scurried over to take it from him. "I'll wash it out. You've got enough to do."

The woman was middle-aged, her hair fading from red to orange. She brushed at invisible crumbs on her chest, and took possession of the coffeepot. "Don't be silly. We're doing dishes already."

"I saved your soup," Elsa said to him. "Cornbread?"

"Absolutely." He ducked between two of the women and washed his hands quickly. They made room for him with indulgent smiles. "Thank you, ladies, for all you do."

"It's our pleasure."

He gestured toward a table in the back and said to Elsa, "Come sit with me while I eat?" He tapped the clipboard under his arm. "We're gonna have to get moving pretty fast if we're going to have a garden this year."

Elsa grabbed a cup of coffee and followed him.

He was already eating when she sat down. "Damn, this is really good, sweetheart."

"My name is Elsa."

He looked at her. "Got it." Taking her cue, he flipped open the clipboard. "I wrote some notes, and I can send them to you in an email. We'll need to get that Dumpster first, and organize a cleanup day. I'll get the Dumpster. You organize the volunteers, the sooner the better. I want to plant by tax day."

"I thought Mother's Day was traditional."

"You've been away awhile, haven't you? Not in Pueblo. It's warm enough here that we should be able to get away with planting earlier, and that'll give us more yield at the end of the season."

She wrote notes of her own. "I'll talk to Joaquin in the morning about getting the call out for the garden volunteers. Let's aim for two weeks from Saturday?"

He buttered the cornbread lavishly. "Too late. One week from Saturday."

"We won't have enough people."

"Sure we will. Get the kids to paint some signs, put them up on the boards, and at the apartment buildings." He mopped the bottom of his bowl with the bread, ate the last bite, and closed his eyes. "Mmm, mmm, mmm," he said, and licked a finger. "That sticks to my ribs."

Elsa took some pride in cooking, and eyed his empty bowl with a sense of satisfaction. "It's meant to." She made a couple more notes. "Sounds like you've done your share of community organizing."

"A bit." He drank from his coffee cup. "How do you know Father Jack? You're the only person who calls him Joaquin, you know."

"Yeah, it's hard to make the transition." She skirted the vast history she shared with Joaquin Gallegos, and said only, "We grew up together, right here in Pueblo."

"It's good to have a young priest."

"Young?"

"Well, not old."

"I suppose that's true. Are you Catholic?" Elsa asked.

"Oh, no. I'm a plain agnostic. My church is the outdoors, but I like Father Jack a lot. He's the real deal."

A sting of regret needled through her. She'd once believed herself to be the real deal, too. "He is that," she said, and stood. "I'll get this going. Let you know."

"I might need some contact information, sw—Elsa." He winked.

It was not the kind of thing she ordinarily responded to, and she hadn't exactly been in touch with her emotions lately, but something about that single wink, the direct way he met her eyes, and the slight, charming quirk of his mouth caused a stir at the base of her neck.

She made her expression blank, then reached for his clipboard and scribbled her email address and telephone number on the page. "There you go. See you soon."

He put his palm over the information, as if to keep it from jumping up and running off the page. "Nice to meet you, Elsa Montgomery."

"You, too, Deacon."

Once she made sure the kitchen volunteers had things under control, Elsa headed for her sister's house, anxious to pick up Charlie and get home before the roads got too bad. Tamsin lived in an exquisitely updated Victorian made of enormous blocks of red stone, complete with a tower and a deep porch. It was Tamsin's joy.

Elsa wanted to like it more than she did. Despite the beautiful lines and the detail work Tamsin had poured into it, Elsa always felt as if there was some evil presence looking out of those tower windows. A ghost. A demon. Something noxious.

Charlie greeted her at the door, barking his big, deep bark, wagging the whole back half of his body. "Hey, buddy," she said, and held her hands out, waiting.

He sat politely, his black tail sweeping back and forth across the hardwood floor. "Good job." She gave him the reward of her hands on his body, scrubbing his back, rubbing his ears. "You're the best. And I missed you every single second."

"Hi," Tamsin said, fastening an earring. "I'm glad you're here. I was going to have to start worrying. The weather is supposed to be terrible tonight. Do you want to just stay with me?" Tamsin's husband was away on business, her daughter in Spain for the year. "We could open a bottle of wine and find something to watch on Netflix. I'll even cook."

"Thank you, but I really need to get home." She kissed her sister's cheek. "You can come to my house if you want."

Tamsin shrugged. Shook her head. "I'm just kinda bored. I haven't heard from Scott for days and my daughter can barely find time to write three lines to me."

"Where is he now?" Elsa tried to skitter away from the bleat of warning that ran over her nerves, a picture of Scott in a dark bar, with soccer on the television and a drink—

She blocked it.

"Europe. Working with some bank presidents on investments." Tamsin shrugged. "At least it's not Argentina for three months, like last year. Alexa saw him for dinner a few nights ago, not that I got many details."

"Oh, you know how it is at that age. She's in love. And you'll have her all summer." Charlie leaned on Elsa's knee and let out a heavy sigh.

"For now." Tamsin put her hands in her back pockets. "I guess I do need to think about what to do with my life now that she's finished with college. I love being a mom, but I guess I'm kind of redundant now, aren't I?"

"That's a good thing. It means you did your job well." Glancing out the window at the increasing snow, she shifted slightly, unwilling to leave when Tamsin was feeling so blue—it lit the air around her like a halo—but concerned about the roads. "I know one way you can stay busy—we're going to be pulling together the community garden you suggested to Joaquin."

Tamsin crossed her arms. "Did he rope you into that? He tried to get me to do it last fall, when you—"

Elsa looked down, threaded one of Charlie's ears through her fingers. *Lost it*. "I know." She tossed her hair out of her eyes. "But

I need your help. You love to garden, and I know next to nothing." She thought of Deacon. "There's a good-looking landscape guy you'll be flirting with in ten seconds."

"I'm not a flirt."

"Yes you are, and so is he. You'll get along famously. C'mon. You know you want to do it."

"Maybe." She peered at Elsa. "Does this mean you're not going back to Seattle?"

Elsa shrugged. "There's still time. They won't let me come back until the end of June no matter what happens."

"I'll think about it. When are you starting?"

"We'll clear the lot next Saturday. Now, I love you, but I don't want to sleep in your haunted house, so I have to get out of here."

Tamsin waved a hand. "I get it. I'll be fine. I have a quilt I'm working on. You get your baby home." She bent and took Charlie's face in her hands and kissed him, one two three. "See you next time, sweetie."

"You could get a dog yourself, you know."

"Maybe."

Chapter Six

A dog wasn't going to help.

Tamsin stood at the big front window and watched her sister's car disappear into the blizzard. Loneliness fell on her like a shroud. She went to the kitchen and poured herself a glass of wine.

What she had not told Elsa was that she had not heard from Scott in three *weeks*, not three days. He was on a business trip in Europe, and the time zones were sometimes difficult to work around, but still. Three weeks? He wasn't responding to emails, either.

The only thing that kept her from total panic was the fact that he had stopped in Madrid to see their daughter only five days ago. Alexa had been thrilled to take him to a restaurant she knew, to be the adult showing her father around. Tamsin hadn't wanted to say, *Hey, did he mention that he hasn't returned any of my phone calls?*

A blast of wind slammed into the windows, and upstairs something rattled. She glanced in that direction, but really—this house was the warmest, most loving place she had ever been. She did not understand why Elsa disliked it so. If there were any ghosts—and in a house this old, there probably were one or two—they were friendly. She'd never had a sensitive bone in her body, unlike Elsa, who'd imagined seeing ghosts and angels and demons their whole lives. Tamsin had never seen one thing to evidence any kind of life beyond this one, and frankly, all that devotion seemed like a waste of time. More practical to be a good person and try to make the world a better place while you were in it.

She cut some cheese and bread and carried the plate and her wine up to the third floor of the tower. The room had windows in a circle all the way around it and a big table in the middle. Shelves with piles and piles of fabric in a thousand colors and patterns filled the space beneath the windows. She protected the fabric by drawing the shades whenever she left the room, but tonight she tugged the strings to raise them. It wasn't possible to see much, only snowflakes swirling and turning in the darkness. Beautiful.

And lonely. She sipped her Sauvignon Blanc.

"I'm tired of winter," she said aloud into the silence. "Tired of the quiet."

A computer in the back of the room was hooked up to a good set of speakers, and she turned Pandora radio to a Celtic list, cheerful, upbeat music to keep her company as she worked.

On the table was a quilt just beginning to take form, a collage of bright reds and yellows and shiny gold. It was a woman, of sorts, with long hair and a triangular skirt. Some days, Tamsin thought it was her mother. Other days, it made her think of her daughter. There was whimsy to it, falling stars and dancing shoes. A woman dancing in a forest, like a fairy. She tilted her head. Or a princess under a bad spell, like the girl in the red shoes.

Hmmm. She squinted, forgetting about the cheese, and fell into the emerging story.

The sky and trees were next. Tamsin picked up a grayish green patterned square and cut it in half to make two equal triangles, and placed them loosely on the table.

Why hasn't he called?

She cut long narrow rectangles of three different shades of brown fabric—sienna and mahogany and tan—and stacked them unevenly against the background, making a tree trunk. A cottonwood, with that wild depth of texture. Whenever she saw a cottonwood she wanted to stop and press her whole body against it, tuck her fingers into the rivers of the trunk. When she quilted it, she would add deep dimension. The idea gave her a skittering sense of excitement.

With long stickpins, she fastened the rectangles to the base, then stepped back and narrowed her eyes to test the layout. Last year, Scott had sometimes been out of touch a lot, too. It was an unfortunate part of his travels, and it was nothing to worry about. She was being silly.

Everything would be all right.

She took another sip of wine, turned the triangles this way and that, testing them.

Everything would be all right.

Chapter Seven

Elsa arrived at the rectory at eight on Friday morning. She had walked the two miles from her small house to the church with Charlie, who loved snuffling along the Bessemer Ditch, which carried irrigation water from the reservoir to the dwindling farmlands on the eastern plains.

It was a quiet, overcast morning. Until she'd returned to Pueblo, she had not really realized how much she minded the endless gray in the northwest. This little gloom would burn off by lunchtime and the sun would arrive to coax new tendrils from the earth, even now poking up through the muddy ground along the route. Globe willows, like lollipop trees in a child's drawing, showed the first glaze of green. She inhaled, exhaled, thought of the garden. Broccoli and lettuce and peas before it got too hot, cantaloupes and honeydew melons, carrots and corn, potatoes, and, of course, tomatoes. Lots and lots of tomatoes—little yellow cherries, striped heirlooms, a bunch of romas for the Italian dishes the church loved. It was a heavily Italian and Spanish parish.

The church was over a hundred years old, built in 1889 of large blocks of the same red sandstone as Tamsin's house. On one side was the levee, built to keep the Arkansas River in place. A railroad bridge crossed it, bending angled industrial knuckles into the sky.

The church's front doors faced a block of houses, narrow and tall, middle-class Victorians with deep front porches. Other houses had been built later, filling in the lots between—a few pale brick with arched windows that had been built in the twenties; a handful more that dated to the postwar fifties, utilitarian boxes with picture windows. All of them had seen better days, as had the neighborhood. The place wasn't exactly run-down, just weary. Most of the houses could have used a fresh coat of paint. Many needed some lawn work.

Tall trees and wide sidewalks gave the area grace in the summertime. Now, in the last days of winter, it wore the downturned mouth of an old man. Doors stayed tightly closed. All activity was carried out indoors.

The church, however, was well tended by its parishioners. The bricks were tuck-pointed by a mason, a man who also made sure the trim stayed a pristine white. The lush lawn and carefully tended flower beds were looked after by another volunteer. It was a healthy parish, a solid thousand families who loved the old wood and famous stained glass windows.

Walking around the side toward the rectory, Elsa paused at the edge of the vacant lot behind the church. Charlie immediately sat on her foot, looking up at her for instruction.

"I'm just wondering what I've gotten myself into," she said, scratching his big solid head. It looked like a dump, overgrown with last year's weeds, cluttered with tumbleweeds and junk of all kinds, much of which she didn't want to examine too closely.

This, she thought, was the kind of place you'd imagine a young girl's body would be found. Not in a sylvan forest.

At the other end of the lot was a bank of unremarkable apartment buildings, three in a row, three stories tall, all rent-assisted.

Elsa wondered why city housing always had to look so gray. At least the garden would improve the view from those windows.

"Come on, Charlie. Let's get some breakfast."

He jumped up and trotted toward the back door of the rectory, and before she could knock, Joaquin opened it.

"Good morning!" His voice was deep and hearty, exactly the kind of voice you'd want a priest to have. This morning, however, he did not much look like a priest. He wore a dark gray sweater and jeans, and his shiny black hair had grown a little long, so that it fell over his forehead. She knew every inch of that face, the scar across his left cheekbone that he'd received when Ricky Carleo hit him with a rock in a seventh-grade game of war; the heavy dark brows that could signal wrath or disapproval or amusement with the slightest shifts; the prominent eyetooth that had never been fixed.

Elsa pulled off her pink wool hat and kissed his cheek. "I brought eggs," she said, because he'd been eating only egg whites for a couple of months and Elsa couldn't bear them by themselves.

Joaquin took the eggs. "I'm way ahead of you. We're having tortilla España this morning."

"Really?" Elsa loved the potato and egg dish, a standard in northern Spain.

"You can peel the potatoes."

The rectory kitchen was generous, a leftover from the days when two or more priests lived on the premises. A multi-paned window looked over the rose-filled courtyard where San Roque himself presided, then toward the stained glass windows of the nave. Sparrows and wrens fluttered around a feeder in the crabapple tree. Elsa rubbed her arms. "I can't wait for real spring to get here."

"We don't actually have spring, remember? You're going to wake up one morning and it will be full summer." He poured a cup of coffee and handed it over to her. "Sugar there behind you."

Elsa stirred in the sugar, and milk. The radio played quietly, a ballad by Sheryl Crow, and Joaquin hummed along as he stirred baking powder into flour. "Are we having biscuits or pancakes?"

"*Tortillas, mi amiga,*" he said, and flashed his wolf grin, filled with big white teeth.

She shook her head. "Don't make me speak Spanish. I'm too tired, *amigo*." Opening a utensils drawer, she found the potato peeler.

"Bad night?" he asked lightly, not looking at her.

"Yeah." She started peeling the potato. "I'm worried about my sister's husband. There's something not right there."

"Like what?"

"I don't know." She moved her shoulders, forward and back, up and down. "Just have a feeling that there's trouble coming."

"Ordinary feeling or *feeling* feeling?"

She met his eyes, raised an eyebrow.

"Oh. Sorry. Anything I can do?"

"No. I guess we'll just be here for her whenever the shit hits the fan." She rinsed the potato, set it aside. "Didn't we figure out last time that we could microwave the potatoes and then take off the skins and they'd be done faster?"

"Aha! It's true." He pointed with a spoon. "Go for it."

Elsa scrubbed the potatoes and put them in the microwave. "Do you think we should grow potatoes? I love red potatoes, but I've never grown them. How do you know when you're supposed to dig them up?"

"Good question." He added water to his tortilla mix and stirred vigorously. His forearms showed ropy muscle, born of a hundred tasks he undertook in the church—moving benches, tables, chairs, desks; helping to wash windows, changing lightbulbs. He took seriously his responsibility to visit the homebound, and he also did household tasks for shut-ins on a regular basis. In this light, it was possible to see the ghosts of his measles scars. "I've never had a garden, so it's all new to me."

"Never?"

"Where would it have gone?"

"True." He and seven siblings had grown up in a house on a tiny lot not far from here. "My mother liked her fresh tomatoes," Elsa said, "and I did garden when we went back East to stay with my grandmother."

A knock at the back door surprised Charlie into a rough bark. "Shall I?" Elsa asked.

"Sure."

When Elsa swung the door open, she saw the quickly hidden dismay on the face of the woman standing there with a casserole dish. A trim woman in her forties, wearing jeans and a red sweater. She said, "Oh, good morning! Is Father here?"

"Yes. Come in." Elsa stepped back, and waved the woman into the kitchen.

Joaquin turned, brushing flour off his hands. "Good morning, Mrs. Rivera!" he said in his hearty voice. "What a nice surprise! What have you brought me?"

"I hope I'm not interrupting anything." She glanced over her shoulder at Elsa with the faintest frown of censure, then offered the casserole up to Joaquin. "I just brought you some home-baked chicken pot pie. I know how much you like the crust when I bring it to potluck dinners."

"That's very nice of you. I'll just put it in the fridge." He relieved her of the dish and gestured toward Elsa. "Have you met my old friend Reverend Elsa?"

"Oh. Reverend." The woman held out a long elegant hand. "Pleased to meet you."

"Elsa and I have a standing meeting for Friday breakfast. Would you like a cup of coffee? We can hold off on our discussion of theology for a while if that's not to your taste."

"No, no. Heavens." Waving her hands, she backed toward the door. "I'll just . . . I wanted . . . well, you know, Father, we're all so grateful to have a young priest here in this parish. We're so lucky and we want to make sure you always feel well taken care of."

He smiled gently. "I'm not going anywhere, Mrs. Rivera. But thank you so much for your thoughtfulness." He saw her to the door, waved again, and closed it behind her.

Elsa plucked the potatoes out of the microwave. "Still got it."

He shook his head. "This is not a part of the vocation I ever foresaw."

"Yeah, yeah, Walking. I know."

On his way past her, he touched her back, high between the shoulder blades.

"Men are definitely turned off," she said, "when they find out I'm a minister. Why are women so excited by you being a priest?"

"Forbidden fruit," he said matter-of-factly, plunging his hands into the tortilla mix. "Women want to be the one who brings a priest to his knees with desire."

Startled, Elsa paused to look at him. "You've thought about this."

"Yes." Pinching off a piece of dough, he rolled it in his palm. "I am young as priests go. It's something I've had to work out." The dough became a perfectly round ball between his palms, and for a moment, it made her think of a breast. She looked away. "Has it really been so hard to find men to date?" he asked.

"Sometimes." She pulled out the cutting board and skimmed thin sweaters of skin from the microwaved potatoes. "It doesn't matter. It's not like either of us was given a choice."

"God doesn't force you to do anything," he countered. "We both chose."

She wanted to say, *You chose*, but she was unwilling to go there this morning. "I know," she said. And that was true, too.

"It's good to have you back, Elsa."

"Just another woman to adore and spoil you."

He gave her his best grin.

* * *

"All right, everybody, listen up!" Deacon stood in the bed of his pickup truck in the vacant lot, calling through a megaphone. The snow had melted in two days, leaving the landscape muddy. "Father Jack wanted to be here, but he had to conduct a funeral in Rocky Ford."

The milling group gathered at the back of the church turned toward his voice, Elsa among them. She wore a ratty sweater and old jeans with boots and gloves, her hair tied back beneath a bandanna. Everyone around her was similarly attired in the cool morning. The sun shone, but winter lingered in the soft purple shadows. People sipped coffee out of paper cups, steam curling around their noses.

It was a better turnout than Elsa had expected, probably forty-five or fifty people. A Teens for Christ group, some volunteers from the high school who would get community service hours toward graduation, the usual church regulars who showed up for everything. Every church in the world had that little knot at its solid center, and if they dispersed, a church would die, plain and simple.

There were also a surprising number of people from the apartments lining the lot. Mothers and children, mostly, eager to have a garden they could call their own. Each family who helped wouldn't have to pay the registration fee for a 4 x 6 plot.

"We have gloves and shovels and rakes over here—use them," Deacon said. "Everything goes in the Dumpster, and I do mean everything. Careful when you scrape things up—there's liable to be needles and broken glass and God knows what else. Parents, supervise your kids, all right?"

A boy of about eight raised his hand. "What if you ain't got your mama with you?"

Elsa stepped forward and took his hand. "You can work with me. Anybody else?"

A couple other boys, also around seven or eight, peeled away from the crowd and came toward her. So did Tamsin, bundled up in jeans and a turquoise fleece jacket, her long hair tugged back into a swingy ponytail. "Sorry I'm late," she said, and handed over a pink-frosted doughnut. "I brought you this."

"That was nice," Elsa said, eyeing the hungry eyes of the boys next to her. How to split a single doughnut three ways? "Do you have any more?"

"No," she said. "But I could get some. It would only take a jiffy."

The first boy who had spoken up laughed. He had two enormous front teeth with the edges still rippled, and two missing spaces on either side. His nappy hair sparkled with early morning moisture. "Jiffy? What's that?"

"In a minute, in a second, quick as a wink," she said, and illustrated winking. "You want me to go get some?"

"Later." Elsa split the doughnut into bite-sized pieces and offered them in her open palm. "One per customer, please."

Tamsin sipped her coffee, finally noticing that Deacon was still giving instructions. "Mmm. That's him, huh? The hottie?"

"Do you have to talk like you're nineteen?"

Tamsin grinned. "You like him."

"Don't be silly. That's Deacon McCoy, the heavy-equipment guy. Runs a landscaping company here in town."

"And he's *my* Big Brother," said one of the boys. He was chubby, with long black hair braided into a rubber band at his nape. His coat was too big for him, the grubby sleeves hanging down to his knuckles. "He takes me all kinda places."

"How'd you get a Big Brother?" the first boy asked.

"I dunno. My mom put me on the list, I guess because she says my dad is a dickhead." He sidled his glance at the women to see if they'd freak.

Elsa shook her head. "No swearing. I don't like it. What I do need are names. You," she said, pointing to the first child.

"Calvin."

She pointed to the boy with the braid. "You."

"Mario."

A dusky, skinny boy who would be very tall one day. "Tiberius."

Elsa paused. "Really?"

He nodded sadly.

She mentally pinned names to details, and herded them over to the truck to put on gloves. The small size fit most of them pretty well, and she put on a pair of smalls herself. Tamsin chose the large, and shaded her eyes to look up at Deacon. "Hi!" she said. "I'm Elsa's sister, Tamsin." She stuck a hip out, and Elsa felt a twinge of annoyance. Ridiculous.

But Deacon didn't fall under Tamsin's blue-eyed spell. He only gave her a polite nod. "Good morning." He jumped down from the bed of the truck, and greeted the children. "Tiberius, my man," he said, slapping his back. "Mario, we on for supper tonight?"

Calvin tugged on his sleeve. "Hey, how do I get a Big Brother? I want to go out to dinner."

Deacon chuckled. "Is that right? Tell you what, I'll look into it for you, kiddo. How's that?" He patted him on the back, and called out at a pair of volunteers struggling with a mattress. "Put it all the way to the back!"

"Come on, kids," Tamsin said. "Let's get to work."

"How are you this fine morning, Miss Elsa?" Deacon asked, pulling on his own gloves. "Pretty good turnout, wouldn't you say?"

"I'm amazed. You're a natural at community organizing."

"Nah, that's you." He waved a finger at the people. "Father Jack told me that you'd called everybody, got all this in motion. I knocked on some doors, that's all." He eyed her. "That color red looks good on you."

Elsa flicked her fingers over the hem of her sweater. "This is the oldest, raggediest sweater I've ever owned."

"I don't care. It's still a good color." He held her gaze steadily, and in the bright clear morning, his eyes were as blue as the sky behind him. "Say thank you."

"Save all your charm for the others, my friend," she said. "I like you just fine without all that embroidery."

He laughed. "I meant it!"

She nodded, waving as she walked toward the children. "I'm sure you always do."

Elsa gathered the children just after one. Most of the debris had been cleared, and people were bringing dishes into the kitchen, a potluck arranged by the San Roque knitting club. "You guys hungry?" she said to the boys. "I need to get into the kitchen and help."

"I'm starving!" Tiberius said. "I could eat a horse!"

"I could eat a horse and a cow," Mario said.

Calvin rubbed his belly. "I could eat a horse, a cow, and a *pig*."

Elsa laughed. "C'mon, guys. Let's go get washed up. Not sure there will be any horses, but if I know this group, there will be plenty of pie."

Tamsin slapped her dirty gloves together. She had a smear of dirt across her forehead, and a sweaty ring around her neck. "I'm just going to run home and grab the salad I made. You want me to get anything else?"

"Doughnuts!" Calvin shouted, poking a fist in the air.

She laughed and put a hand on his shoulder. "You got it. I'll be back in twenty minutes."

Elsa herded the children into the boys' room and ordered them to wash up. After they came out and showed her their hands, one by one, they all trooped into the kitchen, where the knitting club was setting out the feast. "Not yet, young man!" one scolded Calvin as he reached for a deviled egg. "Let the adults get theirs first."

"He's done an adult's share of work this morning," Elsa said, stepping forward. "They all helped. The adults are on their way, too."

"I'm sorry," the woman said. She had a pair of rectangular blue glasses perched on her nose, and she peered over them. "Do I know you?"

Elsa stuck out her hand. "I'm Reverend Elsa Montgomery. I'm running the garden project for Father Jack."

"Oh." She shook hands limply. "The ex-minister. Not Catholic, though, are you? Something metaphysical or the like, isn't it? Unitarian?"

"Go ahead, kids," Elsa said, putting paper plates in their hands. "Not ex, actually. I'm on sabbatical, and it's Unity."

"Huh."

Elsa moved on, filling her own plate with the bounty—the eggs, of course, but this was a heavily ethnic community, Italian, Mexican, and African American, so there was manicotti and lasagna, tamales and a pot of green chile, pulled pork and lemon cake. By the time she reached the end of the line, her plate was bending in the middle. She sat down with the boys.

Tiberius popped his eyes. "You gonna eat all that?"

"Yes, I am," she said. "Look at you."

"Yeah, but I'm a boy. Girls ain't s'pposed to eat like that."

"Girls who work hard get to eat just as much as boys who work hard."

"My mama's always trying to lose weight," Calvin said, and slurped the meaty center from a tamale. "She don't eat no meat and no sugar. She say they bad for you."

"Not my mom," Mario said. "She cooks everything so good you couldn't help but eat."

Elsa let their conversation flow around her, realizing it had been a long while since she'd been in the company of children. It was one of the things she missed about her job, the kids.

One of the many things.

Firmly, she clamped down on that line of thinking. She would eventually have to sort out her thoughts in order to be ready to go back when the board allowed it. But not today.

Not today.

Tamsin drove to her house, thinking she might change her shirt as well as pick up the salad. She was sticky and a little stinky after the morning's work. Her blood fizzed with the unfolding summer—gardens, gardens, gardens! A chance to create beauty in a very ugly spot.

As she came around the corner, she was humming under her breath, so it took a long, long minute for her to comprehend something was wrong.

Very wrong.

At first, it just didn't make sense. There were several cars parked in front of her house, two more in the driveway. Two of them were patrol cars with lights blinking on top.

Cops.

Tamsin parked crookedly at the high curb and slammed out of the car, crying, "What happened? Is someone hurt?"

No one paid her any attention. She hurried toward the front door and came face-to-face with a man in a black suit and that little squiggly thing going from his ear down into his coat. Black sunglasses masked his eyes. He carried a box of papers and files. Behind him came a man awkwardly carrying a computer monitor. Post-it notes were attached to the side, and she recognized that it was the computer from the family room.

"What are you doing?" Tamsin cried. "Stop right now!" She lunged for the cord, trying to grab it. The man easily swung away from her. There were others behind them, and she heard the staticky sound of a conversation on the two-way radios. "What do you think you're doing?"

"Step aside, ma'am. Official police business." He pushed by her.

"Stop! These are my things!" She grabbed his arm. "Stop!"

Again he yanked away as if she were a ghost. "Sheriff. A little help here."

A man in a brown uniform took her arm, not ungently. "I need you to step out of the way, ma'am," he said in a rumbling voice. A broad-brimmed khaki hat shaded his face.

Tamsin hauled her arm out of his grip, spying another man carrying more things. She ran toward him, planted herself on the steps of the porch, and pointed. "Put that back! It belongs to my daughter!"

"Sheriff!"

"Give me a minute, ace." The brown-uniformed man held up a hand. "Let me talk to her."

"No!" Tamsin cried. "I don't want to talk to anybody!" Adrenaline pumped into her body and she made a running tackle at the man on her porch, wresting the box away from him and diving back into the house. She smashed into the body of another giant bug-eyed man and dropped the box, spilling Alexa's school papers and notebooks all over the floor. She cried out in frustration, tears running down her cheeks as she scrambled to gather the mess, keep all this history *safe*—

She was suddenly and forcefully hauled to her feet by hands on either side of her. Two big men picked her up and carried her outside, kicking, crying, trying to wrest herself out of their grip, until they dumped her on the lawn.

The sheriff had handcuffs in one dark fist. "If you don't calm yourself, ma'am, I'll have to arrest you for obstruction of justice, and that's just going to make a bad day worse."

She suddenly became aware of a cluster of neighbors standing on their sidewalks, watching her. The grass beneath her bottom was wet, soaking her jeans, and she was as snotty-nosed as a two-year-old. Lacking anything else, she used her sleeve to blot her face. "What's happening? Why are they taking all of my things?"

"Are you the lady of the house?" he asked, and flipped open a notebook. "Thomasina Corsi?"

"Tamsin. Yes." She stood up, watching men carry out box after box of her belongings. Rage and terror boiled in her chest, insisting she do something, *anything*, to stop it, but she forced herself to cross her arms and stay put. "How can they do this?"

"Do you know how to reach your husband?"

"He's on a business trip in Europe, changing locations nearly every day." She crossed her arms, suddenly feeling a cold shadow move over the top of her head as she thought of all of the days he had been out of touch. "I have an email address for him."

"No cellphone?"

"He doesn't like to carry a cell in Europe. He says the roaming charges are too expensive." She shivered. "What *is* all this?"

"Your husband is being indicted on criminal charges related to a Ponzi scheme," he said. "I'm afraid we have orders to seize your house and everything in it."

She heard the words, but they made absolutely no sense. "What do you mean? I *live* here. I need to go change my clothes and get some food for the church potluck. My sister is waiting for me."

"I understand. But I'm afraid you won't be going into your house for a few days at least. Can you stay with your sister?"

"No." Tamsin shook her head. "This is ridiculous." She wasn't about to be kept from her house. *Her* house, the house she had worked for years to bring to perfection, one of the most beautiful Victorians in the city of Pueblo. Every year, it was on the Christmas tour, and it was always a favorite. "This is my house. Mine. I'm sorry, I really am in a hurry." She started for the door. She would just go in and—

Again, he caught her arm. "Mrs. Corsi—"

With a rush of terror, she yanked her arm. "Leave me alone! This is my house. Those are my *things* they're carting away!"

His grip was immovable. Not painful, but not about to be shaken off. "I know this is difficult, but your husband has stolen millions of dollars. It's possible you can get the house back, but for now, it's being seized. We're taking everything."

"But what about my clothes? My computer? My daughter's things?"

He shook his head. "We can probably let you in to get some of your personal things with an escort, but not today."

"When?"

"I don't know."

For a long moment, she simply stared up at him. He had a pointed nose and very dark eyes. "A Ponzi scheme?"

"Yes."

Tamsin blinked. "He wouldn't do that. We have lots of money."

"We'll need to know exactly where you are for the next few weeks, and we'll need to interview you and find out what you know."

"I don't know anything about his business. It's finance. Numbers bore me to tears."

"That's fine. You can tell that to the investigators."

She whirled suddenly. "What about his office? Downtown? His employees?"

"His office has been seized as well. His employees will all be interviewed, and we suspect that at least a few of them had some knowledge of the scheme."

"I'm sure there's been some mistake," she said, feeling suddenly winded, as if she might faint. "I'm just . . . it's so . . . I think I need to sit down." She plopped down to the wet grass and put her head on her knees, trying to breathe.

"In through your nose, out through your mouth," the sheriff said.

Tamsin followed his instructions, her brain whirling insensibly. After a moment, she raised her head. "What now?"

"Will you come with me to the Sheriff's Office to be interviewed?"

She shrugged. "Yeah. I mean, of course." She brushed hair away from her face, feeling empty and shaky. "I need to stop and tell my sister, over at San Roque. She's expecting me."

"That's fine."

Tamsin got to her feet. "Do I have to ride with you or can I drive my own car?"

"You can drive," he said. "The Subaru, though, not the BMW." He nodded toward a tow truck hooking up the sports car.

His heart will be broken, Tamsin thought. And then, *What if he really did it?*

"I'll meet you at your office," she said in a dull voice. She picked her purse up from the grass, put back all the things that had spilled out, her little brush and a pair of lipsticks, and some gum wrappers, and slung it over her shoulder. She put her glasses on and walked straight to her car without looking at her neighbors, still assembled on their lawns, afraid of what she would see if she did.

Chapter Eight

Elsa and the boys were finishing their lunch in the fellowship hall when Tamsin materialized at the side of the table, wild-eyed, her bangs in a sweaty tangle on her forehead. "Can I talk to you?" She pointed. "Outside."

"What is it?" Elsa asked, alarmed. "Is Alexa okay?"

"Sorry, yes, nothing like that."

Elsa eyed the children. "Boys," she said, "I'm going to have to go. Thanks for your help—come see me next Saturday, okay?"

They nodded, feet swinging, and waved their hands. "Okay, Miss Elsa," Calvin said.

She touched each of their heads as she walked by, carrying her dishes to the sink. Tamsin headed outside and Elsa followed her out to the front sidewalk. "What's up?"

Tamsin started to speak, lifted a hand, palm to the sky, and closed her mouth again. "There's . . . I went to my house . . . I'm not sure . . . They wouldn't let me in."

"Who wouldn't let you in?"

Her sister swallowed. "Federal marshals. The Sheriff's Department. They said that Scott's being indicted and they're seizing everything in the house. Maybe even seizing the house itself."

Tears ran, unchecked, down her face. "That doesn't make any sense, does it? I mean, there has to be some mistake. Right?"

"Yes. I'm sure it's a mistake." Elsa took her sister's hand. "When was the last time you talked to Scott?"

She took a deep breath, squared her shoulders. "Four weeks. Yesterday."

"Oh, Tamsin. Why didn't you tell me?"

Her eyes rolled wildly, almost like a horse's. "I don't know! What would you think of me?" She pushed her hand through her bangs, leaving them standing on end. Elsa reached up and smoothed her sister's hair. "I have to go to the Sheriff's Office. They want to interview me." She looked down at her grimy T-shirt. "They wouldn't even let me go in to get a change of clothes."

"I'll come with you. Just let me make sure there's someone to cover the bases around the kitchen, and I'll be right back out."

"No." Tamsin pulled her hand from Elsa's grip. "I'll be all right. I'm just going to talk to them."

"Don't be silly. I'll be right back out. Don't move."

Tamsin grabbed her hand. "Elsa, what am I going to *do*?"

"One thing at a time. Let's go downtown."

The interview lasted just over an hour. Tamsin didn't know anything. It was that simple. Not that they necessarily believed her, she could see that, but in the end, they simply let her go.

What they did not do was tell her when she could get back into the house, or even get her things. Her bank accounts and credit cards had been frozen. She had exactly seventeen dollars in her wallet.

Also, she smelled like a goat. That had probably made a very good impression.

They advised her to get a lawyer. Which, she pointed out, she had no money for.

Again, they were very sorry.

Shaken, Tamsin walked on wobbly legs to find her sister, who was reading a very tattered *Field & Stream* in the waiting room of the Sheriff's Office. "I'm done," Tamsin said.

"Have you had anything to eat?"

"No. Just a doughnut this morning."

"Let's get you a hot dog and take a walk around the Riverwalk."

The hot dog vendor was on the corner. Tamsin automatically pulled out her wallet, because her sister was the poor church mouse, and then remembered that the bills inside were all she had.

"I've got it," Elsa said.

As she stood there, Tamsin could not stop the tears streaming down her face. Not noisy. Not dramatic. Just open faucets, pouring over her cheeks, dripping off her chin. A wind came up, carrying the bite of lingering winter.

Elsa handed her a hot dog and a root beer. "Come sit by the waterfall."

They settled on a bench and Tamsin forced the food down, even though it stuck in her throat like a cork. "I have absolutely nothing," she said. "What am I going to do?" A jumbled list of losses spilled out. "I don't have fresh underwear. I can't even buy a bottle of wine."

"We have to get you a lawyer. I'm sure we can find someone who can help you. You should be able to get into your house to collect your personal things eventually, and in the meantime, you'll stay with me." Elsa rubbed her sister's arm. "And I'll buy you a bottle of wine."

This shift in their roles was almost more disconcerting than anything else that had happened today. Tamsin was the older sister, born to their parents when they were thirty-eight, a surprise after twenty years of marriage. They were amazed by the pretty little princess they had miraculously produced. When Elsa, too, showed up eight years later, when their mother was forty-six and had thought herself almost finished with the messiness of her female body, they had been a little less thrilled.

That younger sister now took Tamsin's hand in her own. "Things will sort themselves out in a day or two, Thomasina. You can't let panic overwhelm you."

"I'll try." Suddenly she remembered something. "Oh! I just realized that my Kindle is in the car. And I might have some clothes at the gym."

"That's the spirit. Books and underwear are all a woman really needs."

"And wine. Don't forget the wine."

Elsa smiled. "I won't forget the wine."

One did not enter the ministry with the goal of making a lot of money. Elsa lived frugally, however, and had for many years, so she'd managed to save a bit of a cushion. But not even those savings would have lasted long through this unpaid sabbatical if she hadn't owned the small house where she and her sister had grown up.

It was just two miles from San Roque, in a pocket neighborhood known as the Grove, which had once boasted a Guinness World Record: the largest number of parishes in the smallest area. There were also a handful of grocers in small shops, though most of them sold little more than lottery tickets and beer these days. A union hall stood proudly on the main entry corner, where wedding receptions and wakes were still held. And bars, of course, neighborhood bars that had served generations of steel workers. One of them, the Star Bar, was famous for its Slopper, an open-faced hamburger served with green chile poured over the top.

Like most of the houses in the area, Elsa's was modest—a two-bedroom bungalow with a deep backyard, and a good front porch shaded by elm trees. The kitchen was tiny. The living and dining areas were combined into one room, and a bathroom sat between the two small bedrooms. The bedroom windows looked over the driveway, which was lined with tall juniper trees where entire nations of birds nested—singing and twittering and tweeting.

The house still technically belonged to their elderly mother, who lived north of Denver with her second husband, but Elsa had been overseeing the rental for years. She had also overseen a handful of upgrades—a new stove, a better fridge, new carpets. That the house had been recently vacated when she returned in December had seemed like a sign.

If she believed in signs.

Now Tamsin dropped her gym bag and eReader onto the bed in the guest room and tugged at the bottom of her shirt. "Weird," she said. "It's just so weirdly tiny, isn't it? How did we not notice that then?"

"Everybody else lived in houses like this, too." Elsa gave her fresh towels. "You can have a bath if you want. I need to make a few notes about the garden before I forget."

Tamsin sat down abruptly. Her arms fell loosely between her knees like noodles. "And what am I going to tell Alexa?"

Elsa put a hand on her sister's shoulder. It was trembling faintly. "First take a bath. Then we'll take the next steps. How about a cup of tea?"

Tamsin nodded and picked up her towels. "Bath first."

In the tiny kitchen, Elsa put the kettle on. Outside, a blustery wind had begun to blow, tossing the junipers back and forth, and it made her wonder for the twelve-millionth time how birds managed to stay in their nests. Sometimes they fell out, but mostly they didn't. It was miraculous, if you thought about it. Standing with the heels of her hands against the sink, she imagined a clutch of little birds huddled together, wings around one another, eyes closed tightly as their house swayed side to side.

The water started to run in the bathroom, and Elsa blew out a breath.

This was terrible. If Scott really had been involved in a Ponzi scheme, chances were good Tamsin was about to lose everything. Her husband, her comfortable life, the ease of having no financial worries, and—painful for a woman who'd grown up with so little—the house she loved and had spent so much time restoring.

Surely they would be able to rescue her personal belongings and clothing, her quilting supplies and such things. How did this all work? Would they auction it off to pay the bills? Would it just sit there, getting dusty, while the courts sorted it out?

Elsa closed her eyes, reaching for the comfort she had always relied on—the peaceful depth of spirit that reminded her this life was only one sliver of everything. Once, she had accessed that velvety peace at will, had found courage and sustenance in it.

Now, nothing was there. Only a dead cold emptiness.

And yet, from force of habit she wanted to pray. She wanted to ask for assistance, to say, as she had so often, *Help me help her*, but the words stuck in her throat.

Instead, she took a breath and gathered all the tools she had learned as a counselor over the years—listening, reflection, compassion, non-judgment. Even without prayer, they could be helpful. Humans did not have to rely on God—or be in service to him—to be helpful to one another.

Charlie padded into the room, snuffled at his empty food dish, and looked up at her.

She chuckled. "Sorry, my man." She filled one stainless steel bowl with kibble, the other with his minuscule portion of canned food mixed with a tablespoon of yogurt, which had cured a gassy problem that had sometimes driven her outside in desperation. He waited politely, his feathery black tail swishing over the floor, spreading out more debris than she would have thought possible.

When she put the dish down, he still waited patiently, until Elsa said, "Okay, go ahead."

As the water boiled, she remembered that she still needed to send a note to Deacon and Joaquin about the garden. The thought of it blew like a fresh green wind through her dark, worried mood, and she found she was even smiling a little as she composed the email.

To: deaconmccoy@tinmail.com,
fatherjack@sanroquepueblo.org
From: lionelsa@catmail.com
Subject: Garden ideas; monthly meals and kids

Hey, guys. The cleanup was a smash success and we had such a great turnout that I think we're going to have a lot more applications for the garden plots than we first anticipated, which gives us a great opportunity for community building.

Two ideas.

#1 A communal meal in the middle of the garden once a month (once a week if it gets going?). It would be great to have a place set aside in the middle for that. So we could bring out chairs and tables or even just spread cloths on the ground (though some older folks will have trouble with that).

#2 I want a kids' garden for the children in the apartment buildings (and those in the church, of course). They can grow magic beans and carrots of gold and scarlet runner beans in teepee shapes. I'll go to the library tomorrow and see what they might have on that. We won't need any extra funds (I'll finance that myself—it's only seeds and a handful of bedding plants).

What do you think? Walking, thanks for pulling the funding together to get us in motion. Deacon, I knew you'd be great at organizing volunteers, and you were.

Next step is to put a calendar in place and start the planting. Are you both free at some point in the next couple of days? Tuesday, maybe, since Monday is Father Jack's day off. Tamsin has some challenges at the moment, so I'm not sure she can be there, but I'll keep her in the loop.

Off to a great start!
Elsa

When the kettle water was boiling, she made a heartening pot of strongly scented tea. On the table, she spread an old, worn-soft cloth embroidered by some unknown hands long ago, and linen napkins, and two cups from the collection she had amassed, china in all sizes, in colors of blue and pink and gold. The cup she set at Tamsin's place was one of the best she had, blue on the inside with a rim of gold, and a matching saucer. The spoons were antique English teaspoons, gathered on her travels when she was young and heartsick. No flowers were blooming outside yet, so she put a potted African violet in the middle of the table, along with a plate of ordinary shortbread cookies and some chocolates in foil wrappers.

Tamsin emerged a little while later with wet hair hanging down her back. She wore a YMCA T-shirt with long sleeves and a pair of yoga pants and some socks. Her face was washed clean of makeup. She had always been a beauty, from smallest babyhood when photos showed that she'd had a crown of soft blond curls to frame her eyes, the color of the inside of the china cup. As an adolescent, she'd grown coltish and radiant, with slim hips and generous breasts, and silky blond hair that tumbled over her shoulders. Even now, exhausted by the worst day she'd probably ever had, she was gorgeous, her skin still smooth at forty-six, her eyes the same electric blue, her mouth full and plump. Elsa suspected she had begun fillers and lasers long ago, and the result was a face as lovely as it had always been. Elsa was so much plainer, it was hard to believe they had the same parents. Perhaps if they were closer in age it would have been an issue, but Elsa had worshipped her big sister when they were growing up.

"This is so pretty," Tamsin said as she sat down. "You have such a knack for setting a table."

"Thank you." She picked up the pot and poured a cup of deep red tea. "It's an herbal blend. Caffeine didn't seem like a good idea." She pushed a little crystal bowl of sugar cubes across the table.

"Do you have any Equal or Splenda?"

Elsa smiled softly. She didn't believe in artificial ingredients. "You know better."

Tamsin lifted her cup and sipped, made a face, and reached for the sugar. Elsa simply waited as she stirred it in, watched it dissolve, and took another sip.

"I feel shell-shocked," Tamsin said, finally. "Like I'm in a dream. I don't even know how to begin to make a plan. Like, how long will it be before I can get some clothes out of the house? And if it's a long time, what should I do in the meantime? I can't go around like this forever."

Elsa nodded.

Tamsin stared into her tea for so long that the silence in the room took on a noisy rustling depth. "He's gone, isn't he? That's why I haven't heard from him." Her eyes filled with tears.

Elsa paused before she answered. "I don't know. Maybe he is. From a practical standpoint, it might be best to move forward as if that's true."

Tears spilled from her sister's lovely eyes. "He disappeared to some faraway place so he doesn't have to face the music. He probably stashed a big pile of money in some Swiss bank account and left me to deal with this mess on my own."

"Do you have any idea where he might be? Favorite places? People tend to do predictable things even when they're in trouble, maybe even more so then."

"You know how smart he is. He won't do anything predictable."

Scott *was* almost freakishly smart. But it was also true that an animal run aground usually found a way to reproduce the familiar. "Just for the sake of argument. What if he did?"

"He loves anywhere they speak French, since that's the only other language he really knows, so France, Canada . . . where else? Switzerland, maybe."

"For someone who only speaks English and French, he sure

spends a lot of time in the Spanish-speaking world—Chile, Central America, Spain, even, right?"

"I guess he might have learned some Spanish by now. There are a lot of places he could be." She dropped her spoon, leaned back in the chair, and stared across the table. "Elsa, really? What the fuck am I going to do? What if they never let me have my house back? Or my stuff?"

For a long moment, Elsa was quiet, listening just in case some angel wanted to step in and handle this for her. But she was on her own. "You'll start over. Just like somebody who has been in a fire or an earthquake or a terrible accident."

Tamsin put her head down on her arms. "I don't know how to do that." It came out muffled.

"I know." She put a hand on her arm. "But you aren't alone, I promise you that. We'll get through this together."

"Shit!" Tamsin's head jerked up. "What am I going to tell Alexa? I don't want to ruin her last month in Spain, but what if this is all a big mess when she comes home?"

"Let's just leave that alone for now. You don't have to decide tonight."

Tamsin nodded.

She looked so exhausted that Elsa slid the laptop over to her. "Why don't you check in with your quilting people and have a glass of wine. There isn't anything more we can do tonight."

Across the world, Alexa Corsi stood stunned in the middle of a one-bedroom flat in an old neighborhood in Madrid. The flat was tiny in every way, tiny stove and fridge against the back wall to make a tiny kitchen and dining area, tiny salon, tiny bedroom almost filled by a double bed, teeny-tiny bathroom barely big enough for the door to open. But the windows, three of them, two in the salon and one in the bedroom, were giant, floor to twelve-foot ceiling. They overlooked a quiet, out-of-the-way plaza still in shadows this morning. It would be scorching hot by afternoon.

A package had come for her three days ago, containing a deed and a key and instructions to contact a real estate agent. She knew it had to be her father who had provided it, but when she asked the agent, the man only shook his head—it had all been managed long-distance, through a third party.

Clearly, he thought she was the mistress of a rich man, and Alexa had let him think what he liked. The apartment was exactly right for her—old and darling and a little bit weary. She would replace the drapes with something lighter, and order a sofa that did not smell of old dust and dogs, but the rest—

She spun in a circle, laughing. Perfect!

The agent gave her the key and the papers with a courtly bow, and left her to it. Her own flat. In Madrid.

She carried a simple kitchen chair over to the window and read through the paperwork. The price of the sale was staggering for such a small space, and Alexa shook her head. Her father had been extravagant with her before, when he'd made a big deal or won big at his games, but this was unprecedented.

She laughed. In the square, a woman tugged a wheeled basket with groceries through the shadows, and Alexa could hear the sound of a fountain splashing somewhere nearby. The woman looked up, spied Alexa, and waved.

Her first home, Alexa thought.

Giddy, she leapt up and looked through the cupboards, opened the fridge, peered inside the narrow oven. She used the toilet and opened the medicine cabinet.

A postcard was taped to the inside. A picture of a church in Madrid graced the front of it. Alexa pulled it free and turned it over, finding her father's distinctive handwriting. *Baby*, he'd written, *this is your pied-à-terre, for always. Your first home. Our secret, ok? Don't tell anybody. You'll realize why later. Burn this card. <wink> When things hit the fan, remember I love you.*

No signature. Alexa frowned. Her dad liked to stir up drama sometimes, but this was over the top, even for him. A little ripple of worry crossed her shoulders, and she turned the card back over, thinking he must have picked it up the day they had supper together last week. He'd embarrassed her a little with his hectic color and slightly-too-loud voice. Now she thought she understood. He'd known he was setting this up for her. He'd also given her an envelope stuffed with cash—a lot of cash—which wasn't entirely unusual.

Another ripple of unease moved through her body. "*When things hit the fan*"? What did that mean? She sucked on her lower lip for a minute, wondering if the price tag had been too high. Was there some trouble attached?

No, she decided. It was just Dad being Dad. It was entirely in keeping with his larger-than-life gestures, and it was deeply touching that he'd given her something so meaningful to her. She couldn't wait to thank him.

She also couldn't wait one more minute to call Carlos. Taking her phone from her envelope of a purse, she punched in his number. "Guess where I am?" she said, and started to laugh in wonder all over again.

Home! Her own home in Madrid!

Chapter Nine

Deacon McCoy loved dogs, every dog on the planet, even the little yappy ones with no hair and those ugly bug eyes, for one reason: They were true. They were honest. They might have some issues but only because some asshole had beaten them or mistreated them or trained them to kill or be killed. (And if Deacon had *his* way, he'd go out and shoot every last one of *those* bastards clean through the heart, which was a lot more than they deserved.)

After he'd been released from prison, his soul dry as salt, Deacon went straight to the humane society to see about finding a dog to rescue him. All through that long last year, he'd had in mind a pup of some kind, a midsized dog with some fur to run his hands through, smart and not too crazy. It didn't matter what kind, a mutt was a mutt, and he just needed dog loving. So he wandered through the aisles of the shelter, holding his hand out, looking for somebody who needed him.

And damned if it turned out not to be a pup at all, but an old black Lab mix with white all around its muzzle and the kind of sadness in its eyes that Deacon recognized clear to the bottom of his heart.

"Well, hell, buddy," he said, kneeling so the Lab could come over if it had a mind to. "What's your story?"

The dog just looked at him. Deacon stayed where he was, waiting, talking quietly. When the dog sighed and hung its head, showing that it'd given up all hope, Deacon damn near cried. He went and found somebody to let him into the cage. The girl, skinny as licorice, walked with him. "He's a good dog," she said, and he saw that she had one rotted tooth in front. "Family got divorced and neither person could keep him."

"Couldn't keep him," Deacon repeated, rubbed the dog's solid ribs. "How old is he, do you know?"

"He's eleven," she said, and hurried to add, "but he doesn't have anything wrong with him."

"Aside from a broken heart, that is."

The girl looked at him in surprise, and her eyes teared up. "Right."

"Give us a little time here, will you, sweetheart?"

When she walked back toward the building, Deacon sat down and faced the dog. "Here's the thing. I'm worn out and don't know what I've got left inside. But I'll give you a walk every day and make sure you have a good bed, and I will find out what kind of bones make you happy. You don't have to do nothin' but lay around and look at the sky. What do you say?"

The dog looked at him a long time, considering, his whiskey-colored eyes searching Deacon's face. Deacon scratched him under the chin and the dog lifted his head, then put a paw on his forearm. Deacon smiled. "All right, Joe. Let's go home."

That was four years ago. Joe had been joined by Sasha, a fourteen-year-old terrier whose owner had been killed in a car accident, and much to Deacon's complete surprise, a ragamuffin of a Shih Tzu, a three-year-old whose owner had surrendered him at a pet fair. Deacon had never had a little dog, but he had to admit it wasn't so bad when Mikey would sit in his lap and stare up at him adoringly. Like a cat, maybe.

But two real old dogs and a crazy little Shih Tzu meant he didn't spend a whole lot of time trying to find a nice house. He lived out east of town in an old ranch house, not a rancher, but an old ramshackle cottage with a big fenced yard where the dogs were safe from predators. Joe was fifteen now, and arthritic, but happy. He loved to ride in the truck in the front seat and still liked going for walks in the mountains when Deacon could get him up there. Sasha was in diapers when she was in the house, and not much went on in her mind these days, but she still liked a bone so he wasn't going to rush her off this plane. She had the sweetest brown eyes you ever saw, and a sandy Fu Manchu mustache he loved.

Tonight, he fed and watered them all, put down a fresh blanket over a trash bag for Sasha, and let Joe waddle behind him into the truck. He kept a stair step for the old dog, and even so he had to help him into the cab, but Mario, Deacon's Little Brother, loved the old critter, and Joe purely adored getting out, so that was that.

He drove back into town and parked in the lot in front of the apartment buildings. Eyesores, all of them, completely neglected by the landlord. Screens were missing from the windows, where mini-blinds with broken slats didn't quite rise the way they should. The bones of the place were sound—it just needed painting and sprucing up. He heard somebody was trying to buy it, so maybe that would help. Just because you were poor didn't mean you had to live like trash. The gardens would offer some dignity and self-sufficiency to the community, not to mention beauty. He liked Father Jack for pursuing projects like this. He was a good priest, selfless and smart and compassionate.

Haunted, too, Deacon sometimes thought.

Mario lived on the third floor. The boy was waiting by the door of his apartment when Deacon walked out of the stairwell. His long hair was washed and combed back into a shiny black braid the way his grandfather Joseph, the medicine man who lived with his daughter and grandson, wore his. Mario wore a clean shirt and jeans and bright new tennis shoes. "Hi, Deacon!"

"Hey, kid. New shoes?"

"Yeah, my mom got a bonus. She said you should come in for a minute if you have time."

"All right." Gingerly, he stepped into the apartment, a sunny place filled with houseplants he remembered from childhood—purple Wandering Jew, coleus and Swedish ivy and spider plants. Nothing strange or exotic, but simple, robust, and easily propagated. The walls were covered with Native American art—calendar pictures in cheap frames from Walmart; a woven blanket in red and white and black; a poster of a beautiful young man with long hair, sitting on a horse. Mario's mother was in the kitchen, a pretty, plump woman with dark eyes and long hair as black as her son's.

"Hey there, Deacon," she called. Her cheeks were flushed from the steam. "I saved you some good bones for that old dog of yours."

"Thank you kindly." He picked up the package she pointed to with her chin. "Where's your papa tonight?"

She waved a hand. "Drumming away evil spirits or something."

"I see." He breathed in, smelling spice and onions. "What are you cooking this evening?"

"Oh, just suppers for the week. Some beef stew, some enchilada mix, a pot of posole."

He thought of the rich hominy stew, studded with tomatoes, and his stomach growled. "Smells good."

"You're always welcome to stay and eat," she said, and inclined her head, sending her long hair down her back in a fresh, glossy wash. She couldn't be thirty yet; her skin still held that fresh rosiness that started to fade as a woman got older. Her mouth was plump and pink, her breasts generous, and he thought she would taste like cinnamon and coffee. As a young man, he would have thought she was fat. Now he knew better.

He also knew she was about six lifetimes too young for him. "I appreciate your generosity, Ms. Padilla, but I reckon me and Mario are going to head on out. We'll be back by nine."

"No problem. Thanks for being there for him. He loves it."

Deacon waved, and gathered Mario with an arm around his shoulders. In the hallway he said, "I was wondering if you'd mind if we asked Calvin to go along with us? Would that interfere?"

"Calvin's my *man*," Mario said. "Let's go ask him."

The other boy lived in the next building over, on the middle floor. His mother answered the door, a woman as thin as a paper clip, her hair covered tightly by a bright scarf. She was hard and pretty at once, her mouth tired. "Hey, Mario," she said. "What's up?"

"Ms. Jennings, this here is Deacon McCoy, and he's my Big Brother. He takes me to dinner most Saturday nights and we was wondering if Calvin could come with us."

She looked at Deacon's face. "I don't know you." Now he could hear a southern accent, softer than his own. Kentucky maybe, or Tennessee.

"You could call my mom," Mario said. "Deacon's the one getting the farm ready out there. Father Jack and him are friends."

"Y'all come in for a minute, let me call."

"No problem."

The rooms were painfully utilitarian. Couch, chair, coffee table; an old television with a converter box balanced precariously on top. A pickle jar of wildflowers, including two bright yellow dandelions, graced the dining table under the window. He and Mario sat on the couch while she went to get her phone.

Calvin came out of a bedroom carrying a comic book. He wore a white golf shirt three sizes too big for him and a baggy pair of khakis. "Hey, Mario. What's up?"

"Wanna come to dinner with us? We're going to Village Inn for pancakes."

The boy's face blazed. "Yeah! Hold on. Let me get my shoes."

"We're asking your mom's permission first, son."

In the kitchen, Calvin's mother was on the phone. She came out and said, "You want to go, baby?"

"Can I please?"

"Go get your shoes." The woman looked at Deacon, her gaze smart and clear. "He's the most precious thing in my world. Make sure you keep him safe and sound, hear?"

Deacon smiled. "You bet." He held out his hand. "What's your name, honey?"

"I'm Paris Jennings."

"Deacon McCoy, ma'am. And I promise I will treat him like the young prince he is." Her fingers were cold in his own and he thought maybe he'd order an extra meal and send it up with Calvin when they got home.

"Come on, boys," he said. "Let's get some grub."

Elsa was flung out of sleep in the cold predawn. She must have made some noise of protest as she hurtled through dream space to land with a hard crash in her own bed, because Charlie leapt up and nosed her palm.

In the dark stillness, her heart raced. She stared upward into the night sky, haunted by a shard of an image, Kiki's blue-starred fingernails digging into the earth.

This was the worst of it. She could not stop thinking about the details. What sound had come from the girl's throat? What tool had made such terrible marks on her young skin, her sweet young belly?

It made Elsa feel sick to her stomach, how she kept returning to the violence.

With a groan, she shook her head back and forth, trying to dislodge the images. But in the darkness, in the middle of the night, they always came back at her. Wearily, she flung her legs over the side of the bed and set her feet on the cold floor. If demons existed, she figured this was the form they would take. Horrific thoughts.

She padded softly into the hallway, wrapping her robe around her. Tamsin's door stood open, and Elsa peeked in on her sister, who looked like a teenager, with all her long hair spread out around her. Gently, Elsa closed the door.

In the kitchen, she put on water for tea. The clock on the stove said 4:07. Not even the slightest bit of light yet broke the night. Somewhere, she'd read that more people died at this hour than any other. The dark before the dawn.

She had begun to hate Sundays. Rubbing her hand over the top of her belly, as if she could scoop out the lump of tangled emotions that lived there, she wished it were a different day, at least. That there was something she could do that would replace all her years of Sundays in church. The ritual of it. The punctuation to her weeks.

The joy of it.

Yesterday, she'd had an email from a congregant, a woman whom Elsa could never love no matter how hard she'd tried. The letter was bitterly angry, accusatory—and probably fair. Elsa *had* left them at their moment of greatest need. But she had truly been falling apart, and without confessing the truth of her own crisis of faith, which would be worse for all of them, she'd had no alternative than to let them think it was her decision, rather than the board's. As it was, she'd hung on for six weeks longer than had been wise.

Better to leave the flock in the chubby, fatherly arms of Reverend Harris, who could gently nurse them through their year of grief. She had tried. She had failed.

But she missed them. Missed the congregation and the church and Sunday mornings and standing up to deliver a lesson. She missed fellowship hall afterward, catching up on the tidbits of news from everyone, being present for the lonely, the devout, the children.

Water boiled in the kettle. Elsa poured it over a strong English tea bag, and was transported back to the days when she had learned to drink it, in England. For a moment, she felt the press of cold damp air on her skin, air that had made her hair into such a kinky mass that she could do nothing with it at all.

She'd fled to England after Joaquin had announced his decision to be a priest, without any plan in mind. She knew only that she could not return to the States or linger in Spain. At least in England, they spoke English. She got off the train in London with a horde of other backpackers, who swept her up into their midst, teaching her the ropes of working under the table, finding the crap jobs that nobody else wanted.

After a month, she knew she wasn't going to go home for a while. She left the noisy, crowded landscape of London, however, and began a pilgrimage on her own—a quest to find her own purpose. If she was not meant to be Joaquin's wife, then what?

Back in her house in Pueblo, Elsa took her fresh cup of tea to the front porch and shook out one of her contraband cigarettes. It could be tricky to hide the fact that she was smoking now that Tamsin was staying with her. At the moment, however, she lit a Kool and blew out the smoke with a gusty sigh of satisfaction. Huddled in her robe, with strong caffeine at her side and a cigarette burning, she felt the world set itself aright again.

In England, she'd gone on a quest for the feminine side of God. The idea had come to her in a forgotten little church in a village along the Camino. Its graveyard lined the street. Elsa liked the idea—it would be so nice to have your loved ones close by, right around the corner instead of a long drive away. Joaquin disagreed. He thought it was sad.

But they had both loved the church, tiny and ancient. It was noted for the lusty carvings that decorated its exterior, but it was inside that Elsa experienced one of the most profound moments of her journey. Praying beneath a shrine dedicated to the Blessed Mother, she felt enveloped in the Divine. For the first time, she experienced God as a woman, with long dark hair and a ripe goddess smile.

Of course, Elsa thought.

In England, it was as if that Divine Feminine, that Goddess energy, had laid a trail for Elsa to follow, whimsical at times, heartbreaking at others. She wandered through cathedrals and tiny chapels, north to Scotland and the old goddess islands, through the ruins of cloisters, where women had been sheltered and freer than many of their compatriots. She visited an ancient rowan tree that was rumored to hold the spirit of the Divine and slept there. As she slept, she was prompted to go to Glastonbury.

Taking a sip of tea, Elsa smiled to herself. Glastonbury. It was equal parts hippie side show, tourist central, and genuine spiritual center. She sensed the power of the place the minute she stepped off the bus, and shivered in anticipation and worry.

It was an old, old place. Sacred to the pagans before the Dark Ages, then central to the tales of King Arthur, and later still, the site of a vast, thriving cathedral and monastery.

Elsa at first thought she had been called to the Tor, a lonely, much celebrated spire at the top of a hill, but though she found it beautiful, it had not spoken to her. Below, in the wells of Mary, she had felt stirrings of truth and spirit.

But it had been in the ruins of the cathedral village that she'd found herself overcome. Once it had been a lively, beautiful place, filled with monks and nuns and pilgrims and ordinary citizens lucky enough to find themselves attached to it. Elsa wandered the grounds, imagining a medieval world full of riches and comforts, imagined herself as an abbess with keys on her belt, devoted to study and God and the women in her care.

She saved the ruins of the cathedral itself for last, looking for what many thought was Arthur's grave. A band of tourists had been there, but they wandered away as she came into the space, leaving her entirely alone to look at the roofless walls. She wandered, hushed, shocked that so beautiful a space had been wantonly destroyed by King Henry in his selfish quest to balk the Catholic Church.

One man, she thought then, could build or destroy, could change time and history, for better or worse. One man.

Or one woman.

Standing in the green, green grass in the ruins of Glastonbury Cathedral, Elsa suddenly knew that she still wanted to preach. She could not be a priest in the current Church. But there were places she could be a minister.

As if the Goddess herself applauded Elsa's decision, a flock of butterflies sailed into the space, dancing in fluttering waves around her, their wings flashing blue.

Elsa laughed. And she went home to study with Unity.

Now, as dawn peeked over the eastern edge of the world, she thought of that healing time and wondered if there was some pilgrimage she needed to make now. Did she need to walk away her grief and loss of faith?

She didn't know. She certainly had no peace at the moment. She had no idea if God was a lie she'd told herself all these years, or if she was just on strike.

She drank the last of her tea, found a pair of wool socks, a heavy sweater, and Charlie's leash. He jumped down from the couch and trotted over eagerly, tags clinking. She left a scribbled note for her sister, still sleeping. Dog and woman headed out into the misty morning.

This, too, had once been her meditation time. Charlie tugged on his leash and pulled Elsa toward some massively fantastic smell, yanking her out of her reverie. He snuffled across the weeds, nestled his nose into the depths of the damp yellow grass.

Once upon a time, she would have prayed during this walk. Started a friendly conversation with God, about this and that, problems and joys, concerns and excitements. It had been such a joy, to reach out and feel that constant, loving presence.

All those years, such a long habit, her prayers. She felt like she was going through detox. Detox from prayer! The thought made her laugh. There could be twelve-step programs, only instead of recognizing the *presence* of a Higher Power, they could recognize the fact that humans were alone in the universe, condemned to brief lives, then snuffed out. No more than bees or moths.

Fleeting. Forgotten.

As she continued walking, she realized that she was heading for the soon-to-be garden. Skirting the church, where the first Mass would start in an hour, she headed for the field in back.

The rectory windows glowed yellow in the low light. She thought of Joaquin, preparing himself for the day, washing and shaving and praying, and blinked away sudden tears of longing. She missed it, the sense of purpose, that immovable, solid knowledge of why she was on the planet. A fierce stab of jealousy burned in her lungs.

God had always loved Joaquin more than he loved her.

The fog deepened, casting a deep hush over the space, swallowing the church behind and the apartments ahead, and she felt suspended in a cloud, alone in the entire vastness of the universe. She stopped and bent down to let Charlie off his leash, then stood there as he ran off, her hands loose at her sides, breathing in the cool mist.

A young man emerged from the gloom, head down under a dark blue hoodie, his hands tucked deep into his jeans. Elsa had seen him around before, and she waited for him to look up so she could say hello, but he shuffled by without speaking, lost in his own thoughts, his mouth working as if he was talking to himself. In a moment, he was swallowed again, and Charlie came bounding from the other direction, carrying a stick. With great ceremony, he dropped it at her feet and waited for her, bounding out of sight as she threw it.

The gloom lifted ten feet or so, revealing a glimpse of the open field, and Elsa blinked, amazed all over again at how much work they'd done yesterday, how the hands and backs of all those volunteers had turned a dump into this level, waiting place of potential. Stakes had been set up at intervals. Curious, Elsa paced between two of them, ten feet or so.

Into the hush came the sound of a Native American flute, floating, eerily, as if it were being played by a ghost. Elsa blinked and peered into the mist, goose bumps rising on the flesh of her arms and her scalp. In her quest for truth, she'd spent a summer with the Lakota once upon a time. The wistful, haunting sound tugged at her now, but she didn't want to disturb whoever it was.

She whistled quietly for Charlie. He did not come, and she walked the way he'd gone. His form emerged from the fog, sitting in cheerful expectation in front of an old Native American man Elsa recognized from the soup kitchen. His eyes were closed as he played. She stopped, closing her own eyes to let the sound move through her, loosening something in her shoulders, easing through her belly. Almost without thinking, she took in a long, slow breath, tasting the cool morning, the promise of spring in the scent of fertile earth, sweetened by a faint grassy note.

The song ended. Elsa opened her eyes to see the old man looking at her with a smile. "Aho," he said, a twinkle in his eye. "You're the soup lady."

"That's right. And you're Joseph, Mario's grandpa, right?"

"Yep. A good boy." He gestured toward the cleared field. "I was calling the ancestors to bless this land." He frowned. "They say there's some trouble here, but they'll help us."

"Are you a shaman?"

"I do what I can," he said. His voice was raspy with age, and his braids were silver shot through with threads of black. "This is good, to grow things. It brings people together, makes a spirit whole, to put your hands in the earth. It makes the Mother happy." He put his finger on his nose, like Santa Claus, and with a teasing glint added, "That's Mother Earth, you know."

Elsa chuckled. "Thank you."

He said, "I could use some help drumming. You think you could drum while I play?"

"Um, sure."

He gestured for her to follow him and he picked up a big round drum from a tree stump. Using a stick covered with hide, he pounded it with a firm, powerful hand. "Like this," he said, nodding his head each time. "Like your heart. Can you do that?"

"I can try." Charlie trotted behind her, curious. Elsa gripped the drumstick and brought it down somewhat gingerly. It whispered.

"Harder!" Joseph cried.

She brought more force to it. A powerful *dum* came from it, sending a wave of energy up her arm. The man nodded, spun his hand. *Again*.

She hit it again, and tried to find a rhythm, counting under her breath, one two three *four*, one two three *four*. He seemed to approve, because he picked up the flute and started to play, weaving sweetness around the rumbling throat of the drum.

Without warning, she was suspended in the otherworld, feeling the ancestors or ghosts, or whoever they were, rustling around them. She imagined that they were bringing blessings and cleansing energy to the field, preparing it for the miracle of food.

What is true? What is real? The silent prayer slipped from her almost without her notice, and she let it stay and hang in the foggy air only because this old shaman needed her for his own form of magic, and even if she didn't believe, he did. It was something small her hands could do this morning.

* * *

Paris Elaine Jennings was named for the city she was born in, which she had left in the middle of the night when she was fourteen. Not Paris, France, but Paris, Kentucky. It was a silly name, she thought, and it made her sound like somebody she wasn't, which was why she had named her own son Calvin, a solid name. A name that a boy could grow into. A Calvin could be anything. Calvin Jennings, CPA. Judge Calvin Jennings. President Calvin Jennings.

And he was a beautiful boy, too, with that perfect hair that mixed kids so often had, and his daddy's big brown eyes. She could see his daddy in him in lots of ways. Not that he'd been around for a long time—he'd shipped off to Iraq only ten months after they'd started living together. She was pregnant when he left, though she didn't know it, and when she found out, she thought she'd wait to tell him. For a while. She didn't know when. He wrote her emails and clung to her in a way that made her feel so good, not like other guys. He was true and real. He loved her.

And he got himself killed. They weren't even married, so she was up a creek. Neither her folks nor his would have wanted anything to do with their baby. Not a mixed-race baby in Kentucky, and not in Georgia, either, where Calvin's daddy was from with his pretty, soft drawl. She was on her own.

She worked, yes she did, as a grunt in a nursing home for eight dollars an hour. Hard, dirty work. Sometimes the old people were mean to her. One old man always tried to pull her hair, but she knew he was just out of his mind with age and sadness. The apartment was rent-subsidized, and she got food stamps from SNAP, the Supplemental Nutrition Assistance Program, but it wasn't but $162 a month. That didn't buy as much as you would think. It always made her laugh when the politicians started complaining about abuses of the system. She'd like to see them live on

$162 a month in groceries. Some of them probably ate at restaurants that cost twice that for a single meal.

Muttering under her breath, she poked through the cupboards, wondering how she'd feed them both for the rest of the week. She'd had to fix her raggedy-ass car and it had taken just about everything she had. She'd even taken her jar of change over to Safeway to cash it in. All that was left was five dollars. She'd had to do it; the car was how she got to work.

But that left almost two weeks to get through before the next SNAP payment. She didn't have two weeks of SNAP left, and they'd have to eat careful. She took stock. There was most of a gallon of milk left. One can of tuna. Some store-brand Cheerios, and rice. They could eat rice, but not all week. She'd maybe get some eggs for two dollars, and leave the milk for Calvin, and send him over to the church to eat at the soup kitchen on Thursday. That was one good thing, having the church right here. After the twelve o'clock Mass on Sunday, they served coffee and pastries and little bits of meat and cheese. She and Calvin made a big feast of it. She didn't mind going to church if it meant they could eat. Father Jack told her God didn't care if she was Catholic, and that she was welcome at Mass.

Outside her window was the freshly turned field. It had been an eyesore before they cleaned it up, all kinds of junk and weeds growing in there, and the gang boys smoking and talking till late in the night. It was a dangerous place. Haunted, she sometimes thought. Her bedroom window looked out that direction, too, and sometimes she thought she saw blue lights dancing around. Somebody at work told her that it was swamp gas. Maybe it was.

Now, though, the field was clear and open, and she had claimed one of those plots, you better believe it. She and Calvin would grow their own plants, just like she had as a child. Collards and beans and tomatoes, fresh and juicy. Squash because it was easy, and she liked yellow squashes, especially, steamed with just butter and salt. Corn, because Calvin wanted it. And of course, his magic bean seeds, which his teacher had given to all of the children on Valentine's Day. He was sure he'd grow a beanstalk to find a giant, and she'd let him discover on his own that it was miracle enough to grow something in the earth to feed yourself.

The idea of so much food, all free except for the seeds, made her dizzy. She wouldn't waste one single bit of it, either. She knew how to put food away, in the freezer and into jars. Her mama had taught her that, and although Paris had hated it at the time, now she was grateful.

Behind her, Calvin came into the kitchen. "What's for breakfast, Mama?"

"How about Cheerios?"

He climbed into his chair and she kissed his head. As she poured the cereal, her stomach growled. Later, they could eat at the church, and this afternoon, she'd take that last five dollars and buy some eggs and bread, maybe a tiny bit more milk if she could squeeze it out. Eggs and bread and milk could keep body and soul together pretty well.

Chapter Ten

When she looped back home, Elsa could see the news vans from two blocks away. Antennas stuck into the lifting clouds, and even at this distance, she could see a handful of reporters in long camel coats milling around, coffee cups in their gloved hands. She paused on the sidewalk and tried to think of an alternative to plowing right into the middle of them. She ducked left and headed down the alley, cursing under her breath when it set all the dogs on high alert. Charlie loped along, ignoring them in his superiority. He looked over his shoulder at her, as if to say, *Do you hear these cretins going insane?*

"You are so supercilious, Charlie-Man."

One intrepid reporter had set up camp in the alley and he whistled loudly as she appeared, moving forward to shove a mic at her. "Can you tell us where Scott is? When's his wife going to spill the beans?"

Elsa held up a hand and hurried by him, letting herself in through the gate and closing it firmly behind her. She didn't have the key to the back door, so she knocked on it, calling loudly, "Tamsin, it's me! Let me in!"

Her sister appeared at the door, hair an uncombed tangle, her eyes swollen from sleep or wine or crying. Her phone was pressed to her ear and she raised a finger to her lips. *Alexa,* she mouthed.

A hubbub erupted in the alley as Elsa closed the door behind her and drew the curtains over the windows of the sunporch, an unheated space at the back of the house, lined with windows. In high school, she'd grown plants of various sorts out here, and her mother had kept small appliances on the shelves—a blender and a mixer, and all the things that wouldn't fit in the cramped kitchen. There was nothing here now but the view of the backyard, which thankfully no one had yet breached.

Privacy secured, Elsa headed into the front room. Tamsin was making listening noises to her daughter, her tone upbeat and utterly unconcerned. Elsa caught her eye. Tamsin shook her head, again putting her finger to her lips. "That sounds like a great weekend, honey." She laughed, lightly. "Not everyone can say they swam with royals."

Elsa went to the kitchen to make a pot of coffee—clearly Tamsin had only just rolled out of bed for Alexa's call. She would need something heartening. When the coffee was going, she pulled out a skillet and the ingredients for pancakes, eavesdropping shamelessly.

Tamsin said, "I just haven't had a chance to check my email for a couple of days." Not *strictly* a lie. "I'll read it after a while. I have plans with your aunt Elsa this afternoon." Also sort of true.

From the freezer, Elsa took a package of blueberries, and poured some into a bowl to run under cold water. In the living room, Tamsin was finishing off her conversation. "Don't worry about anything for this last month, honey, just enjoy every single second, okay? It'll be back to the real world before you know it."

Still holding the phone, Tamsin leaned on the threshold to the kitchen. "She called because she hasn't heard from her dad since he was in Madrid," she told Elsa. "He's not answering emails and his phone goes to an error message." In the early morning, without makeup, she looked suddenly older, her mouth pale, her eyes ringed in smudgy shadows. "I didn't know what to say. I don't want to lie, but she's only there for another month, and I'd hate to see that ruined."

Elsa broke eggs into a dish, nodding. Privately, she was pretty sure Alexa would hear the news before much longer, but she'd let Tamsin come to that conclusion herself. It wouldn't hurt to let her have her delusion for a few hours.

"Do you think that's going to come back and bite me, that I'm protecting her from the truth? What is she going to do differently? I mean, nothing, right? And there's the possibility that it will all be sorted out by the time she gets home."

"Sure. That's possible."

Tamsin looked at the phone and a long hank of hair fell down in her face. "You think I'm deluding myself. I don't actually think it will be sorted out, either, but there is the *possibility*."

"You know your daughter better than anyone, Tamsin. You know the right thing to do."

She raised her head, hope giving new light to her blue eyes. "You think so?"

"Good grief, who *are* you? Where is my mighty sister? The mistress of all she surveys? The queen of all things?"

She shook her head, balancing the phone in the middle of her upheld palm. "I feel winded. Like I can't breathe."

"Well, go wash your face and then we'll eat breakfast."

Shouts came from the front of the house and there was a knock at the door. "What are we going to do about them?"

"I don't know if there's anything we can do. You're part of the story. They're going to do what they can to get something out of you."

"Should we watch the news?"

"No. Breakfast first, then we can decide on a plan of action. Seriously, sis, go brush your hair and wash your face and we'll eat. It will make you feel better."

"I need to go to church," Tamsin said firmly. She looked at the clock. "There's a Mass at ten. I can get a shower and go to that one."

Elsa raised her eyebrows. "Mass, Tamsin? Seriously? Since when do you ever go to church?"

"I have to do *something*! I feel like I'm right on the brink of a panic attack." She put her palm on her throat. "Like I'm going to throw up."

"So say the rosary from here," Elsa said. "Or, better yet, make something beautiful. That's your worship."

"No! Those, those . . . nosy *pigs* out there aren't going to keep me locked up in this house."

Elsa thought of Kiki's memorial service, all of the reporters, the sensitive and the crass all mixed up together, their prurient curiosity creating a wedge and an unwanted distraction for those who were earnestly grieving. Their presence had interfered with what might have been a pivotal healing point for a great many of them.

Including, perhaps, Elsa herself.

"I get that, but you can't go to church," she said to Tamsin. "You have an obligation to do what you can to minimize the trouble this is going to cause for other people. You can't do a lot to spare your neighborhood or even mine, but you can keep it away from San Roque during services. It's only fair."

"How is *any* of this fair?" Tamsin's red-rimmed eyes filled with tears. "And why do *I* have to be the noble one? I've lost everything."

"No you haven't. You have more than a lot of people. You're healthy. You have your daughter. Your life. Even if everything else is gone, you've got a lot of advantages."

Tamsin bowed her head. "It doesn't feel that way right now."

Elsa hugged her. "I know, sweetie, but it will get better." Releasing her, she said, "Now, go take a shower. Wash your hair. We'll eat breakfast."

"And say the rosary."

Clearly Tamsin expected Elsa to participate. Whatever. She didn't have to believe it to do it. "Yes. That, too."

At a little past seven that evening, Joaquin came over for a late supper at Elsa's house, at her request. She watched from the window as he wove calmly through the little knots of newspeople, holding up a hand and shaking his head as he made his way to the door. She cracked it open and ushered him in. "I wasn't expecting that," he said.

"Tell us about it." From the table, Tamsin rolled her eyes. Her hands were cupped around a mug of tea. "Things aren't crazy enough without them, right?"

Elsa took his long black coat. He held a small package. "Come on in. We're having chicken and dumplings because it's Tamsin's favorite comfort food and she needs a little comfort."

"Smells great. And you know I love it."

"Yes." She hung up his coat as he went to Tamsin's side and put his hand on her shoulder, that big, steadying hand.

"How are you?"

She shrugged. "I feel trapped."

"Well, I brought you the sacraments, if you like. Perhaps it will help."

Tamsin nodded.

As he chanted the words, Elsa stepped back, giving them space for the rite, watching as he carefully poured wine and wiped the chalice, as he offered it to Tamsin. Funny, Elsa never saw him in this role, as priest and confessor. It seemed to give him height, breadth. She listened to the words, loving as always the timbre of his voice, the depth of his reverence.

But her stony heart did not soften. Or crack open.

When he finished, Elsa took dishes out of the cupboard, wide shallow bowls, and ladled chicken and soft, biscuit-style dumplings into them, making sure there were enough carrots and celery to brighten each serving.

The bowls did not match. One was a *Titanic* replica she'd found at a yard sale, another was deep cobalt and gilt, which she put in front of Joaquin, and the third was a delicate china bowl with flowers at intervals along the edge. With a secret little smile, she put the *Titanic* bowl down in front of her sister. The ship's name was hidden under the food.

"How were your sermons today?" Elsa asked, sitting down.

"Very good. There were a lot of people this morning."

"And it's not even Easter."

Joaquin grinned, his hair falling down his forehead. "True. That always brings them in." Capturing a dumpling, he admired it for a moment. "I think it's the garden that's bringing more people in. They feel included, like they matter."

"That's the whole point, right?"

"I thought it would take longer." He tidily ate the dumpling. "Do you think it would make sense to have chickens?"

"To eat?" Elsa asked. "Or for eggs?"

"Both, I guess. I've never had them, so I don't really know what's involved, but maybe having fresh eggs and the odd old hen for the pot would be a nice addition. Teach the children about sustainable food, get some fresh eggs for the soup kitchen. What do you think?"

"Ew!" Tamsin cried. "How can you eat them after you've made friends with them, fed them? That will totally traumatize those kids."

"Don't be silly," Elsa said. "Kids are sturdier than that."

"Who's the mom here?" Tamsin snapped.

Elsa looked at her.

"Sorry."

"I haven't had chickens, either," Elsa said, "so I need to look into it, gather some facts. It might not even be allowed in the city."

"But what if it is? What do you think of the idea in general?"

"Not sure, really." She put down her fork and spoon and picked up her napkin, imagining plump black hens clucking around the gardens, speckled brown eggs still warm from the bodies of the birds. "I like the *idea*. You know, fresh eggs and teaching the children about where food comes from in a real, honest way." She scowled. "But what about roosters? Do you have to have one to get eggs?"

"I have no idea!" Joaquin admitted with a big grin. "I guess we'll need to find that out, too."

"They're really noisy."

His eyes glittered. "Are you thinking of the roosters in Spain?"

"Yes! I am." A memory of a cock crowing all night long somewhere along the Camino came to her—his voice ragged by the time the sun came up. "Where was that really obnoxious one? Estella?"

"Maybe. It's been a long time. I remember they woke us up a lot, and the one I remember most is the guy at the end, right after everyone finally went to bed following that all-night fiesta."

"Oh, I remember that! It was some festival for the dead and they had a band that started playing at eleven o'clock at night. We were exhausted."

"Lavacolla." He glanced at Elsa, then away. "The last day."

She remembered, too. They had an unspoken pact to keep certain things off the table, some painful, some joyous, some—like this one—carnal. She tried to think of something to say, but the memory of the big open window of the hotel room, the stars shining, Joaquin's skin against hers, was powerful.

In the silence, their spoons clicked against their bowls.

"Jeez," Tamsin said. "You two sure got quiet. What happened that day?"

Joaquin shook his head. "Nothing. That just brought back a lot of memories. Do you still have your shell, Elsa?"

"Yes. And my passport."

"Was the *camino* hard?" Tamsin asked.

Elsa glanced at him. Their eyes caught and tangled for the

most fleeting of seconds. "Brutal, actually. We thought we were so tough, and we were whining within a few days."

Joaquin carefully cut a piece of chicken, noticeably silent.

"You guys never really talk about that trip. What happened to you?" Tamsin asked. Her tone was flat, and she was barely eating, pushing food from one side of the plate to the other, which would undermine Elsa's *Titanic* joke.

"It was a big adventure," Elsa said lightly, and reached for the bowl. "If you're not eating that, maybe I should pour it back in the pan."

"Sorry. Not very hungry."

"It would be good for you to eat," Joaquin said gently, and touched her hand.

She looked at him for a minute, then picked up her spoon and ate a bite. Two. Elsa thought again of the *camino*, of a rainy day and the way her feet felt after fifty-six days of walking, and how her heart and spirit seemed to grow lighter and lighter with each new blister.

"Did Elsa tell you that they wouldn't let me in my house today?" Tamsin said to Joaquin.

"No," he said.

"They told me I'd be able to get in there, but then they wouldn't let me go after all, not even for my personal things. The investigation is under way or something." She tucked a long lock of hair behind her ear. "I don't know what they think my underwear is going to tell them."

"I'm sure they're worried that you'll take something else," Elsa said. "We'll talk to the lawyer tomorrow, and if they don't let us in then, we can go to Target and get you some underwear and things."

"With what money, Elsa? I don't have anything. Not even one little bitty credit card or secret stash or anything. Nothing."

"I have some savings," Elsa said calmly. It wasn't a lot, but it would stretch that far. "I'll take care of you, I promise."

Joaquin said, "We have a benevolence fund for emergencies. I'll talk to Wilma in the church office tomorrow and she can order a check. It'll cover a few clothes."

She bent her head. Nodded.

"Eat," Joaquin urged quietly. She obeyed.

Again, the thick ticking of the clock. "Maybe we need some music," Elsa said. She pushed back her chair and turned the radio on to a pop station. But it was too jangly and she turned it off.

Joaquin finished his dumplings, placed his napkin neatly on the table. "'All things work together for good for those who love God,' Tamsin," he quoted. "You asked what happened on the *camino*. In a way, I did. That's when I was called to the priesthood."

Tamsin raised her head, intrigued. "How did you hear a call? Like a voice?"

"People hear it many different ways, but for me, it was an actual voice."

Elsa leaned on the table, pushing away her bowl. *Let him do his work.* Her sister needed him.

"What did it say?" Tamsin lifted a hearty bite of stew. Ate.

"That's private, but I can say that it was unmistakable, and true. I knew from the time I was seven that I was meant to be a priest, but I had been running away from it."

"Why?"

Elsa watched his face, the weariness that moved over his temples, his mouth. He didn't look at her. "Because it is not an easy road. Because I wanted the ordinary joys of a family."

"And you were engaged. You guys were like the most solid couple ever."

Elsa took a breath. It had been a long time, almost two decades, but in her current raw state, these memories could still sting. She had to fight a powerful urge to stand up and fuss with the food or do the dishes, start some coffee.

"We were," he said. "From the eighth grade, there was nobody else for either of us." He folded his hands, as if to keep them to himself, and Elsa smiled gently, a sudden softening in her chest making her breathe more easily. She rested her own hand on his forearm briefly.

"We were," she echoed.

"I don't see how God could want to take that away from you."

"I knew what I was supposed to do from the time I had the measles, remember." He lifted a finger, pointing it toward the heavens. "If I had been faithful to the first call, I would not have—" He cleared his throat. "I would have done things differently."

"So would Elsa. It wasn't very fair to her, was it?"

He started to speak, but Elsa held up her hand. She could spare him this, at least. "All things work together for good," she said, and something rippled through her, a softness. "I had things I needed to do, too."

Tamsin inclined her head. "I wish I felt that. Not the call, the God thing, because honestly, I don't think there's anything out there."

"And yet you accepted the sacraments today." Joaquin smiled.

She shrugged. "Maybe it will help." She took a breath. "A sense of purpose would be nice."

"You need only ask," Joaquin said.

"But then watch out, right? What if I get called to do something I don't want to do, like you did?"

"Oh, but I love being a priest," he said, and put a hand on his heart. "It gives my life meaning, and shape, and purpose. I am honored every day to be so called. That's how it works. You're called to do work that's right for you."

She bent her head. Her glittery hair fell forward. "I'll think about it." She took another bite of dumpling and it cleared the bowl enough that the *Titanic* flag and emblem showed through the pale yellow broth. She burst out laughing. "Very funny, sister dear."

"I thought you would appreciate that." Elsa stood, clearing her bowl and Joaquin's. "Who wants a cup of tea or coffee?"

"I do," Joaquin said. "That cinnamon tea you made last time?"

"Absolutely. Tamsin?"

"No thanks. I'll have a glass of wine."

After Elsa went to bed, Tamsin stayed awake, playing on her sister's laptop, drinking box wine. Not bad. It lasted longer, that was all. Maybe by the time it ran out, she'd have some money from somewhere. Surely they couldn't expect her to live on absolutely nothing, not when she hadn't known anything about Scott's business.

The wine sealed the sucking hollow in the middle of her chest, at least for a while. For the first time all day she was able to stop thinking for more than three minutes about Scott, about the house, about what it was going to mean for herself and Alexa and . . . well, everything. Her own *Titanic*, and she was now clinging to a life raft in the freezing waters of the Atlantic, waiting for help.

For now, cozy on her little raft, she checked the quilting websites and waved at some friends, answered a few questions on the boards she moderated, and read the comments on the photographs of her latest quilt, which made her feel equal parts pleased, furious, and bereft. Pleased because the group was responding as she had hoped—with awe and respect and high compliments. A couple said things like, "This is the best you've done yet, Tamsin!" She agreed.

Which wasn't vanity. She had made her first quilt, a doll blanket, when she was seven, and she'd been making them ever since. She was a devoted gardener, a cheerful cook and hostess, but only a true expert at this one thing.

Her pride over the praise gave way to fury. The quilt was locked up in the house, along with all of the supplies she'd collected over the past three decades. All of the fabrics and notions, the Bernina sewing machine, the pattern books, and the piles and piles and piles of quilts. Some simple, some elaborate. Some had won prizes at local shows, and she'd been urged to enter a couple of them in the art show at the State Fair, rather than entering them in the home arts. She had friends who were weavers who had done that, but she hadn't yet had the nerve.

Until this one.

When rage leaked into her eyes, she took another gulp of Sauvignon Blanc, blinking hard to keep the tears at bay. Right now, if she started crying again, she'd kill herself. Her eyes already looked like somebody had punched her a few times.

Alone in the quiet room, with only the sound of the keys clicking to keep her company, Tamsin wondered how she would continue. What she would do. Listening to Father Jack tonight, she had wondered what her own calling would be. If she had the nerve to ask.

At last she checked her email, hoping in some bizarre way that there would be something from Scott to explain all this, something that would say, *Hey, sorry I left you in a bad place, but I'm just trying to get things together to get us out of this hot water.*

Would he ever come back? Or had he completely disappeared from her life forever? The thought was so enormous on top of everything else that she shoved it away. She had to believe that somehow, some way . . .

What? That he'd get a message to her? What would it even say? *Sorry, babe, I screwed up?*

But of course there was no email from him. Instead, there were three emails from her daughter. One said only, *Where are you? I've been calling and can't get through.* The other two had photos.

She opened them and scrolled through the pictures with a hushed sense of pleasure and sorrow. Her daughter was remarkably beautiful, with a long, lean body and milky skin, her hair as black as Elsa's but as straight as Tamsin's. Her face was a triangle of wide brow and cheekbones and narrow chin, her mouth a full pillow over it.

It was no surprise to Tamsin that Alexa had attracted the eye of European royalty. Her boyfriend was a count or a duke or something, but in a secondary line of succession, which Tamsin didn't really understand. There had been some schism in the royal family decades ago and Carlos was in very distant line for the throne.

A count, and incredibly handsome. He was in his late twenties, to Alexa's twenty-two, a fit-looking man with tumbles of curly black hair and an aggressive nose. He and Alexa were almost exactly the same height. They'd met in Madrid, at a dinner party in mid-October, and had been seeing each other ever since. In all of the pictures, it appeared to be mutual adoration. He was sometimes captured gazing at her as if she were a princess herself.

Heartbreak was imminent, of course. Alexa would come home and they would write emails and make phone calls and maybe even try to see each other a few times, but long-distance things never worked out.

She clicked on *reply*.

> Hi, honey. You look more beautiful than ever, and boy is Carlos good-looking! I hope you're enjoying every single second of this time, and sucking up all you can about Spain and Europe and everything else. It's such a fantastic opportunity to really live, and you will look back on this time with happiness. Wish I could have done a European tour at your age. I'm sure I'll get to it in good time, but there is something really special about doing it when you're young.
>
> Sorry I didn't check email for a few days. There was a lot going on here, but I'm back online. Did you get the picture of the quilt I finished? I'm so pleased with the way it turned out.
>
> Oh, and this—I know one of the reasons you studied Spanish was because Auntie Elsa had traveled there and told

you all those stories. Tonight, Father Jack was here, talking a little bit about their walk on the Camino, and it made me curious. Have you and your friends considered doing something like that? I think I might be intrigued! It changed both of them profoundly, which I somehow never think about. I never thought about it even when they were there, and now I wonder why. You were probably six or seven. Elsa was the same age you are now, so I had to have been about thirty. You were in school and your father [she managed to keep typing even though the word sent a pained electric shock through her system] was building his business. I must have been in the house by then, so I guess that's what occupied me.

At any rate, that's enough babbling. Send me more pics and maybe a little bit of narration on them next time, huh? Where are you in the boat (yacht?)? What does Carlos do, anyway? Does he work at something?

Love,
Mom

By the time she finished, the glass was empty and she'd probably had enough to be able to sleep. Turning off the laptop, she carried the glass into the tiny kitchen and thought suddenly of her own kitchen, every detail designed and carried out to her own standards.

She bent her head, then took a breath, steeled herself, and placed the glass in the sink. She went to bed before she could cry.

Chapter Eleven

On Tuesday morning, Elsa headed for the meeting with Joaquin and Deacon at the field. She brought Charlie with her, heading out the back door to avoid reporters. They walked several blocks down alleyways, heading for the levee and San Roque. Only a couple of dogs were awake so early, and they gave desultory warnings, but no one followed her.

So many reporters! Elsa had discovered via a stealthy search of the Internet that millions and millions of dollars were missing, thousands of people victimized.

And where was Scott, anyway? She had always liked her brother-in-law, his big laugh and hearty manner. It was almost impossible to believe that he could have done such a thing.

After a couple of blocks, she took up her usual route. She wore her winter coat, but the morning was tinted blue and bright yellow, and it tasted suddenly of spring. By the time she made it to the field, the air was so mild she'd tied the coat around her waist. She was the first to arrive, and she let Charlie off his leash to run.

The field still looked pretty scruffy, like an old man who'd lived too long, ears and jaw and nostrils tufted with scruffy grass and low-growing weeds, head bare and empty. She kicked at a clump of evil-looking goat heads. Surely they would not be able to turn all of this by hand? They'd have to plow it.

Not that she knew anything about that sort of thing. Luckily, Deacon and Tamsin did. She'd wait for their input. She picked up a stray bit of trash and a bottle cap, pulled a handful of weeds, and tucked them into a poo bag she had in her pocket.

Yesterday, she'd gone with Tamsin to see a lawyer, who had agreed to take her case pro bono. Not to defend her pro bono if she ended up as part of the criminal investigation, he clarified, but to help her get her personal belongings. Tamsin had asked if the government would free some money, something to get her through until she could get a job, and he shook his head. Doubtful.

They would see the judge in the near future, as soon as it could possibly be arranged. In the meantime, Tamsin had to make do, find a job, try not to get on the nerves of those working the case.

Charlie galloped toward Elsa, stick in his mouth, ears flying backward, and she laughed. He pretended he was going to drop it, but kept running, even faster, to the opposite end of the field, then turned around to race back to her. He dropped the stick at her feet and backed away with an enormous grin, body practically shivering in excitement.

Elsa said, "What? You want me to throw this or something?"

He woofed happily, tongue hanging out, and bowed.

She picked up the stick. "Ew." She looked it over, taking her time. "This stick?"

He ruffed.

"Are you really, really sure?"

He yipped.

She laughed and flung it hard. He dashed after it, paws kicking up mud. He was going to need a bath. In Seattle they had a shop where she could wash him, but she hadn't bothered to track one down yet in Pueblo. They'd been making do with the bathtub and a hair dryer, which Charlie thought was fine, but it made a huge mess. She'd look around this afternoon, bring Tamsin along. It would be good for her to get out and do something different.

She caught a flash of blue from the corner of her eye and swiveled toward it, expecting Deacon. Instead, a trio of boys, maybe fifteen or sixteen, swaggered toward her. They were dressed in gang regalia, oversize coats and pants and a bandanna tied around a head or a wrist. Tattoos wound around their wrists and necks and even over the face of the leader, a hard-eyed boy who stared at Elsa without friendliness.

She met his eyes, standing her ground. "Good morning, boys."

"We saw youse guys cleaning the field. It don't belong to you."

Elsa whistled for Charlie. "No, it doesn't belong to me. Doesn't belong to you, either. We got permission from the owner to plant it. Do you live in the apartments?"

"None of your business."

"Mmm." Charlie raced to stop at her side, dropped the stick, but did not smile. He sat close to Elsa and she leashed him. "The thing is, if you live there, you're free to have a plot for yourself or your family. Fresh vegetables." She grinned. "You look like you could grow some mean chiles."

The boy laughed, putting his hand on his chest. "You hear that? Vegetables? You want to grow some carrots, Toby?"

Toby was skinny, the youngest, with pale cheeks and enormous dark eyes. He snorted, on cue. "Maybe if I could grow me some herb, man."

"This is all that crazy-ass priest's doing, I know it is," the leader said. "He comes in here like some Mother Teresa or some shit and thinks he's gonna save all of us, like he *knows* us. But he don't know nothin'." He stepped closer to Elsa, pointing a finger at her chest. "You tell him he don't know us, and we don't need him."

"He grew up in this neighborhood, you know. Right around the corner."

"I don't give a shit. You think that makes him some homey or something, bitch?"

Elsa looked up at him, strangely perfectly calm. He could not be more than sixteen. Sixteen. What was his life like that this was the best he could come up with? "No. He's just not a stranger. He gets it, this neighborhood."

One of the other boys snorted. "He's a priest, *chica*. He don't know nothing."

She reached for that place, the deep well of calm that had served her in her ministry. "Maybe not. But maybe he knows more than you think. He's a good man. He's been my friend for a long time."

"A good priest!" the leader said with a whinnying laugh. "Ain't no good priests, *chica*, ain't you heard?" He stepped forward, and in a flash of movement produced a knife with a gleaming blade, which he held in Elsa's face. She instantly realized that if she gave off any sense of fear, Charlie would attack, and they would hurt him. Maybe even kill him.

The petition emerged automatically. *Help, Mother*.

She met the boy's eyes. He leaned in close, and slid the flat of the knife down her cheek, over her jaw, then put the edge against her neck. It could only have lasted a few seconds, the boy leaning in so close their noses nearly met, his blade cold and light against her throat, but it seemed to go on for a very, very long time.

It was the thought of Charlie that kept her still. She thought of him and reached for the essence of calm, trying to imagine a column of white light descending to protect them. Her hand loosened on the leash. She felt Charlie sit down.

She held the boy's gaze steadily, noticing the edge of amber that rimmed his dark chocolate irises. His eyes were almond-shaped, with very long, downward-sweeping lashes. She thought of his mother, putting him in a crib when he was a baby, and his girlfriend perching on a chair with an oversize T-shirt pulled down over her knees, watching him sleep, those eyelashes laying like a feather fan across the sharpness of his dark cheekbones.

"You ain't afraid of me," he rasped, "but you should be."

"*Ese,*" said one of the other boys. "*Vamanos.*"

The leader backed off, pulling his knife away, his mouth bunched up into a sour expression. "You tell him, your priest"—he spat the word—"what I said."

She nodded, not moving, not giving Charlie a reason to do anything. The boys turned and sauntered off. She didn't see Deacon or Joaquin. Only a young man carrying a little white cat. "You okay, lady?"

"Yes." She took a breath to see if it was true. "Thanks."

He scratched the ears of the cat, his fingers blunt and not terribly clean. Now she saw the tattoo of a rose beside his eye and recognized him as the boy she'd seen the other day, the one in the hoodie.

"Watch out for that guy," he said now. "That's Porfie Mascarenes. He's the leader of the Wilson Street Thugs. He's killed people."

"Hmm." Elsa sank to the ground beside her dog, a tremor of aftershock moving through her limbs. Charlie's big body braced her, and she leaned into him, smelling sunshine in his fur. She closed her eyes and pressed her cheek against his furry neck. Let go for a minute. "That was scary."

For a long minute, she held on to him. Breathing. Feeling him pant.

"Elsa?" Joaquin's voice said. He touched her shoulder. "Are you okay?"

She turned her head to look at him, still not letting go of Charlie. Sun made a halo around Joaquin's head, and it broke through her sense of suspension.

"I'm fine." She stood up, brushed off the knees of her jeans, and looked around for the boy to thank him, but he was already down the block, walking toward the church. "I just had a little run-in with a trio of gangbangers. We might have some problems."

His face blanched. She'd never seen that happen before—every drop of color drained right out of his skin, leaving his flesh the color of a worm. He took her arms. "What happened?"

"Nothing. Don't worry. I was fine."

"Who was it?" His fingers were uncomfortably tight.

"I don't know. Three boys. Somebody said they were the Wilson Street Thugs. That one of them is the leader of that gang."

Joaquin let her go, putting his hands on his hips, turning his body away. He cursed, softly. His fear made her feel tender and protective. "I'm fine, Walking."

He closed his eyes, bent his head. He was so very thin, she thought, his shoulders like a shelf. "You are running too much, my friend. You need to either eat more or cut off some miles."

"Maybe this was the wrong approach."

"Don't be ridiculous. They're bullies."

"Dangerous bullies."

"They're also kids, Joaquin. Really young. Isn't it partly the duty of the church to reach out to them?" She put her hand on his sleeve. "Help them change?"

"Maybe." He scowled into the distance. "Not like that's ever been tried before."

She smiled, shaking his arm a little. "C'mon, Father Jack. I know you can come up with something."

Deacon drove up in his truck, and she waved. A big black dog had his nose hanging out of the window, his face nearly entirely white. "Go say hi, Charlie," she said. He bounded away. "Walking."

He looked at her. "I couldn't stand it if one of them hurt you. If one of them *had* hurt you."

"You *could* stand it," she said without sentiment. "But as you see, I'm fine."

He patted her hand. "You're right. I'll think about ways to reach out."

Deacon came toward them, walking at the same slow pace as his dog. His head was bent toward the black Lab, as if he was offering him encouragement. At this distance, the weariness in his face was blurred. His hair was thick and wavy, the dark streaked with blond from his long days in the sun. Appealing, she thought, those long legs, his tanned forearms, the kindness in him. The nerves at her inner elbows and the base of her throat rippled ever so slightly.

Charlie picked up a stick, tossed it in the air, raced ahead, raced back, offered the stick to the dog, then the man. Elsa chuckled. "I wish I had that much energy."

"'Joyful, joyful, joyful,'" Joaquin said, quoting Pablo Neruda, "'as only dogs know how to be happy.'"

She punched him in the arm. "It's all good, old man. Have faith."

"Right." He gave her a half smile.

"Good morning," Deacon said. He reached out a hand to shake Joaquin's. "Father Jack. How are you this fine morning?" He tipped an imaginary hat toward Elsa. His eyes were startlingly blue against his sun-weathered face. "Miss Elsa."

She laughed. "Don't call me that."

"Huh. Not 'sweetheart,' not 'sugar,' not 'Miss Elsa.' Any others I should know about?"

"How about 'Reverend'?" Joaquin said.

Elsa glanced at Joaquin, scowling a little at the obvious ploy to make her less attractive.

Deacon raised his brows. "S'at so? What flavor?"

"Unity."

"My daddy was a preacher. Did Father Jack tell you that?"

"No." She smiled. "What flavor?"

"Oh, hell fire and damnation, independent tent variety."

"Red hot, then."

He chuckled. "You betcha."

"And the Catholics are . . . what flavor would you say, Joaquin?" she asked, needling him back.

He didn't miss a beat. "Umami, sister. The flavor that is all flavors, bitter and sweet, salty and sour, for all souls in all the world."

Elsa laughed outright, and high-fived him. "Father Jack takes the gold."

"Hey, Rev," Deacon said, "are you aware that you're bleeding?" He pointed to his own neck, along the side.

"Am I?" She put her fingers to the place and they came back smeary red. "Oh. Must not be much, because I don't even feel it."

"Here." Joaquin took a clean white handkerchief from his pocket and moved toward her. "Let me."

She tilted her head, giving him access, and he was not gentle as he showed her the smear of blood on the snow white cloth. "He *cut* you."

Elsa took his wrist, waited until he met her eyes. "He meant to intimidate me . . . and you. All of us. But this project is important, and you know it. Keep your eye on the prize, Joaquin."

He stared at her, his mouth sewn into a thin line. She shook his arm slightly. "Hear me?"

Finally, he nodded, stuffed the handkerchief back in his pocket. "Let's get this plan going. I only have an hour." He strode out ahead on his long legs.

Deacon inclined his head, raising one eyebrow in a question.

Later, she mouthed, and shook her head. "Have you ever had chickens?"

"Sure."

She tucked her hand into the crook of his arm. "Just the man I need to talk to, then. Tell me about chickens."

He leaned into her, covering her fingers with his palm. "I'll tell *you* anything you want to know."

An almost forgotten sensation of pleasure spiraled through her body as she smelled his skin, man and sunlight and line-dried cotton. It gave her a vision of his bed, covered in plain white sheets.

How curious, she thought, and did not push it away. "Just tell me if we could raise them on this field, if it would be a good idea."

When Elsa returned to the house, Tamsin was sitting at the computer, drinking tea, her hair tied carelessly in a knot at the back of her head. She looked like hell, Elsa thought. "We need to get you some clothes, sister, dear," she said lightly. "Ready to brave the milling beasts?"

"I don't have any money, and I'm not letting you spend any more on me."

"Well, I can't buy you what you're used to, but we can get some bargains at Goodwill or the Salvation Army. We can pick up new underwear and things like that at Target maybe."

Tamsin stared at her, bright blue eyes brimming with tears. "Goodwill? Really?"

Elsa sat at the table. "It's just to get you through until you can get some things of your own. You can't keep wearing the same sweats and shirts."

"Why not? Wash one set, wear the other." A shrug. "Not like I have anyplace to be."

"You have to find a job, Tamsin. I don't have enough for us both to live on for any length of time. I'm not paying any rent, of course, so you don't have to worry about that, but we'll still need food and gas money and wine. I'm very frugal, but even I can't stretch my little purse for very long if we're both using it."

"I am so sorry." Tamsin covered her face with her long, narrow hands. "I've been so thoughtless! The reporters, the money, the—" She stood up, her hip bumping the table and sending tea sloshing over the edge of the cup. "I can't impose on you this way. I should . . ."

Elsa let her ride the welling anxiety for a long moment, then said gently, "Sit down. I want you here, and I want to help you, but we have to be smart about it."

"What am I going to do if this isn't resolved by the time Alexa comes home?"

"You really are going to have to talk to Alexa, before some reporter gets to her."

"That's not going to happen."

"All right, let's table that for today. We have enough to think about, I guess. First, we need to get you some clothes and figure out what kind of work you might be able to do."

"God. I haven't worked in *decades*."

"One step at a time. Finish your tea and go take a shower. Put on your makeup and do your hair so you feel good, too."

"You don't have makeup on."

"I have a little on, but I don't really wear much. You, on the other hand, have always been as vain as a fashion model, so it's important to your self-esteem."

"Very funny," Tamsin said, but she got up to follow her sister's orders.

At home, Tamsin had at least forty pairs of shoes, in every possible variety. Only one pair was foolishly expensive, a pair of Christian Louboutin heels she'd bought for a ritzy dinner Scott's firm had hosted for a presidential candidate. But she missed her collection of boots—flat heels and high, brown leather and black and even maroon. She also had hiking boots for trips to the mountains and running shoes for the gym and sandals in many different styles, both for beach vacations and the long hot summers in Pueblo, but the boots were a sore spot in her cache of losses.

She also had excellent taste in clothes, if she did say so herself. Her colors were turquoise and hot pink and white. She was still the same weight she'd been in high school, give or take a few pounds, not that she could really take credit for that—she didn't much care about food and ate, as everyone always said, like a bird. A nibble of this, a taste of that. Since all of this had happened, she'd had a hard time eating much of anything at all. Nothing sat well.

Which was just to say that she looked good in clothes and liked them and had a lot of them. When she and Elsa walked into the Goodwill, the smell almost overwhelmed her. Nothing was unclean or anything, but there was that tired smell of old cotton, clothes that had been worn a long time. "Oh, Elsa, I don't think I can do this. How can I wear things that other people used to have on?" She clutched her sweats in both hands. "On their bodies?"

"We'll take them home and wash them. Come on. You have to find a couple of nice pairs of pants, and maybe a few blouses. We can get new underwear and socks and bras at Target."

Reluctantly, Tamsin followed Elsa, who flipped through the racks with speedy efficiency. "No, no, no. Yes." She pulled out a sweater in a soft rose and put it in Tamsin's hands. "No, yes, no, no." She grabbed a white blouse and handed it over, then paused, hand on a hanger. "You can look, too, you know."

"I'll look for jeans." Tamsin pointed to a rack with pressed ones hung neatly over hangers. Quite a few had good labels, and her spirits lifted the tiniest bit. There was a pair of Calvin Kleins in her size, practically brand-new, and a little more worn pair of black jeans that looked very good. She'd try them, too.

She carried a pile of clothes into the grim, dark dressing room and closed the door. The overhead fluorescents cast light in a thin green hue, making her eyes look even worse, and her nose about six miles long. She hung the clothes on a half-broken hook and leaned her forehead on the wall, suddenly airless.

How could this be happening to her? How could everything just disappear in a single moment?

If she had to live this way, shopping at Goodwill, surviving hand to mouth, for the rest of her life, she would kill herself. She and Elsa had been working-class children. Tamsin had hated being the girl with the out-of-date clothes, the cheap shoes, the raggedy backpack she'd carried for three years. By the time she got to high school, she'd figured out how to employ her sense of style and flair to turn old clothes into something more attractive, but she'd vowed never to do it again.

And here she was.

Where the *fuck* was Scott? Sitting on some beach drinking Mai Tais? Holed up in some mountain chalet in the Swiss Alps while his wife tried on clothes at Goodwill, and his daughter would never be able to hold her head up around here again?

Once she *knew*, that is. Tamsin still didn't know whether to tell her or not. Which would be worse? Every hour Alexa did not know was a gift of ignorance Tamsin could give her.

With a vicious yank, she pulled the jeans off the hanger and held them in front of her. If it was the last thing she did, she would hunt him down and make him pay. Somehow. Someway.

Shedding the gym clothes, she stared critically at herself in the mirror. Too thin, for sure. Arm bones showing. Hip bones sticking out. The size four jeans would be a little too big.

They looked okay, though, once she got them on. The sweater was a loser, shapeless and wrong. The simple button-up white shirt was decent, and the price was right, three dollars.

By the time she came out of the dressing room, she'd approved three pairs of pants and four shirts that were bearable. Price for all seven pieces, thirty-four dollars.

Elsa gave her a smile. "Good work. And fast."

She nodded.

"Let's amble by the dishes," Elsa said. "You never know when you might find some beautiful china."

"You seem to find good stuff like that," Tamsin said, "but I never have."

"China karma?" Elsa laughed. As she tilted her head back, Tamsin saw an angry scratch on her neck. "What did you do to your neck this morning?"

"Nothing big. It looks worse than it is. Ooh!" She pointed to a table piled high. "Look at all of those fabrics!"

There were piles and piles and piles of them. As if she had turned a corner into a garden, Tamsin suddenly felt better. She moved her hands over them slowly, tracing the curves of a green and blue paisley cotton, the edges of a pile of squares in a palette of pinks and reds in stripes and prints and even gingham. "You go ahead and look at dishes," she said. "I'm going to browse here for a minute."

As she plundered the piles of fabric, Tamsin felt potential rise within her. The promise of that pink against a deep magenta suggested Martha Washington geraniums. She saw them pieced in her imagination, with tubes of that green calico.

Around the table she moved, using her thumb to shuffle the corners of neat stacks, pausing when one whispered to her, or sang, or shouted in a gruff voice like the black and white checks. A wisp of aqua organza caught her, mid-throat, and she tugged it out, putting her hand beneath it and admiring her skin against it. She heard the sea and saw the way ocean water moved over her skin, hiding and revealing a knuckle, a fingernail. There was at least a yard of this fabric, maybe two.

She held it loosely, and mentally wandered the stacks in her tower studio, high above the earth, like an aerie. She had installed shelves in an arch beneath the windows. The fabrics were arranged horizontally by color, in a rainbow hue, red to green to violet. Vertically, the colors moved from lightest to darkest. Sometimes she would just sit and look at that arrangement of color and pattern and feel eased.

In her imagination, she halted at the stacks of greens and held up the gossamer aqua, pairing it with—

As if she had fallen from that nest so high above the earth,

Tamsin slammed back into the reality of where she stood and why. She made a little sound, as if the wind had been knocked out of her. That room was lost to her now.

What if she could never go back there again? What if all of those fabrics whose stories had yet to be explored were just stuffed in a box and lost forever?

"That's beautiful fabric," Elsa said next to her. "Maybe you should get some quilting supplies. It would be something to do, right?"

"I was thinking that, and then I thought about my studio, that beautiful, beautiful room! I worked so well there. Just last week, I finished—" She dropped her hands, spread her fingers over the stacks of cloth.

Elsa touched Tamsin's back, between her shoulder blades, and made a circle of comfort. "I know. It's a beautiful room. But it's beautiful because it's a reflection of you, of the way you see the world."

"You think so?"

"Yes. How much are these remnants?" She looked at the tag. "Cheap! Let's grab a bunch and bring them home." She picked up the organza. "This one for sure. What else?"

Tamsin took a deep breath, reached for the pinks, the green. Paused, narrowing her eyes and reaching for the organza.

Elsa handed it over. "Do you need time?"

"A little."

"There's no hurry."

Tamsin was already lost in the tug of memory suggested by a scrap of yellow satin, a sunny afternoon when her daughter was small. Lost in her dreams, in that other world, she tugged it out, moved on, let the voices of the patterns and colors speak her name, raise their hands.

Tell my story! Tell mine!

Chapter Twelve

Elsa rose at four on Thursday mornings, which were soup kitchen days. The alarm went off, yanking her from a surprisingly deep sleep. She climbed out of bed, stepping over her conked-out dog, who lifted his head, peered at her, then fell back asleep, his head hitting the carpet with an audible *thump*. She chuckled softly in the dark. Crazy dog.

Nestled into a warm chenille robe, Elsa padded silently into the kitchen and made a pot of tea. While it brewed, she opened her email. There was a Daily Word, which she read every morning out of long habit. This morning's word was "healing."

Ha-ha-ha. Very funny.

There was also a note from the interim minister, asking for some clarification on an ongoing class she taught. At the end, he added,

> There are some issues I'd like to speak with you about. Will you kindly give me a call at your earliest convenience?

Elsa typed,

Absolutely. I'm working at the soup kitchen this morning. Will call you late this afternoon.

Aside from a half-dozen advertisements and department store circulars, that was it. Elsa sipped her tea, thick with milk, and listened to the roar of silence, broken only distantly by Charlie's intermittent snores. The lack of email was hard to get used to. In the past, it had often taken her a full hour to sort through it, morning and night.

Bored, she opened the news websites and scanned the headlines. Nothing of interest.

Except—there, in a small headline on cnn.com:

COLORADO FINANCIER SOUGHT IN CONNECTION TO PONZI SCHEME

In the accompanying photograph were Scott and Tamsin, dressed for a formal function. Tamsin was draped in jewels and a designer dress, looking like a movie star. Beside her, Scott was a little shorter and balding, but good-looking in a Stanley Tucci kind of way, that clean Italian robustness. The photo showed his adoration of Tamsin, the pride and delight that was on his face whenever he looked at her. Always.

"Scott, Scott, Scott," she said aloud. "Where have you gone? And what have you done to my sister? Couldn't you have at least left her something in a secret stash?"

But of course, he couldn't have, not if Tamsin was to escape without criminal charges.

The reporters had pretty much disappeared, but this would bring them back again. Tamsin would not be able to find a job easily with them trailing her every move.

Insane. But staring at the picture, she noticed the earrings. Emerald earrings the size of almonds, which Tamsin had worn all the time. She said it was safe because people just thought they were fakes. She often forgot she was even wearing them. Elsa couldn't remember seeing them since the first day Tamsin had arrived, so maybe she'd taken them off before the work in the garden. Or perhaps Elsa had grown used to them, too, a part of Tamsin like her hair or her long legs.

If not, they could probably carry Tamsin through. But who would buy such emeralds? Quietly and quickly. Someone had to know.

Her email dinged, and absurdly pleased to have a distraction, Elsa clicked back to the email program. It was from a name she didn't recognize, but the subject seemed sincere. She opened it.

To: elsa@unityseattle.org
From: margaretreims@gmail.com
Subject: A thank you note

Dear Reverend Elsa,

I've been thinking about this for a long time, how very much you have influenced and helped me, and I thought you should know. Even though you didn't say so, it's plain you're questioning your abilities as a minister, or maybe you're questioning your faith.

Far as the first goes, as you always say, we have the work we're supposed to do, which is what makes God's ways work. I would hate it if I was quiet and didn't say what I was supposed to say and you kept feeling despair.

Wow, that's a tangled-up sentence, but I hope you get what I mean. I'm not a good writer.

"Despair" is a good word, right? That's where I was when I came to the church, five years ago. I was going through my second divorce, even though I got sober after the first one, and it just seemed to me that I was not a very good person if even stopping drinking couldn't help me make my life whole. I was very down on myself, hated just about everything about me, from my crazy hair to my belly to my fingernails, which I bite. I had a lousy little job in a convenience store, which was honestly one of the only good things, not the money, but the fact that people came there in even worse shape than me and it was good for me to be nice to them. My mom always said you should do something nice for people when you're feeling sad or depressed or whatever. I never went to college, never had any kids, never did one single thing that would make a difference in the world, and I was already past 40, so most of that wasn't gonna happen. There used to be this lady who came into the store before church on Sundays, and she was always really friendly and . . . I don't know, glowy? And one time I heard her talking about her church, which was Unity, and I knew where it was because I lived pretty close by. Like close enough to even walk. But I worked most Sundays, so I didn't go for a while.

And then, when I had a very bad week with my ex, who had taken pretty much everything already and wanted to take my house, which I was trying so hard to keep and keep nice, it was the one good thing in my life, and I was so mad and so lost and so sad that I was afraid I might go back to drinking if I didn't do something, and I remembered about Unity and that lady, so I looked up the times on the computer and went that very next Sunday.

You won't remember, of course, but you talked that day about love. How could God love me less than I love my dog? Which I don't have a dog, but I have a cat and he is my best friend in the world. (His name is Jordan and he's a giant creamy tabby with blue eyes. The prettiest cat you ever saw.) And you talked about animals and how they love us and something in me just gave way, like I never thought of loving myself the way Jordan loves me, which is a lot, you should see the way he looks at me, and he comes running when I get home from work, and purrs on my chest. I'm his favorite thing and he's mine, but I'd never thought about it the way you said it that day, how God loves us like that. Always I thought about God being this big judgmental president kind of guy, and what you said made me imagine that if I could see him, he'd give me a hug. Because no matter what, he'd love me like I love Jordan and Jordan loves me. I started to cry right then, and I knew I'd come back. I loved the way you looked up there on the stage or altar or whatever it's called, with your hair all curly and your pretty scarves and your bracelets rattling on your wrists. You have a voice that's easy to listen to, too. Like music.

And I guess I'm getting embarrassed now, that you'll think I'm a crazy stalker person, but I wanted to let you know that. And I know I'm just an ordinary person without any skills or whatever, but if you ever want to talk, I'm sure willing to listen.

Your friend,
Maggie Reims

Elsa didn't recognize the name Margaret, but she knew who Maggie was, a time-worn woman in her forties. She volunteered with the cleaning committee and the library and, just before Elsa had taken her sabbatical, she had stepped forward to be an usher for the coming year. It would be good for her to greet the congregants as they came in, giving hugs or handshakes.

Abruptly, Elsa exited the program, stinging. *The work we are meant to do.* If she wasn't going to be a minister anymore, what would she do?

Who would she even be?

No time to worry about it now. She had to take a shower and get over to the church. It was the end of the month and the soup kitchen would be busy.

She left a note for her sister.

Don't forget! Come to the church by 8:30 and there's wine in it for you tonight. We really, really need your help today, so please come.

When she peeked out of the front windows, there were no reporters, thank heaven. She leashed Charlie and zipped her coat, pulling on a wool cap and gloves. It wasn't light out yet. Not unusual—she often walked to the church before dawn on soup kitchen days—but something lingered from her forgotten dreams, something dark and bloody and evil. For a moment, she paused on the step, listening. Charlie waited with her, looking up with a puzzled expression on his snout, his tail sweeping slowly side to side behind him.

"I know, you're right. Let's go."

She walked briskly, only realizing after several repetitions that she was chanting the rosary under her breath, a very old habit. *"Hail Mary, full of grace, the Lord is with thee . . ."*

How she had loved Mary as a teenager! It made her feel slightly foolish to chant the rosary now, but—even so—she imagined a capsule of blue light falling down around her, making her invisible to those who would cause her harm, keeping her warm and safe. Just as she had when she was a child.

What could it hurt? She highly doubted Mary was there, either, but if the image of blue light made her feel better, that was fine, too. On the far distant eastern horizon, the sky had begun to lighten, and just the promise of light made her feel less anxious.

Maybe the encounter with the gang boys had unsettled her more than she realized.

As she and Charlie approached from the back of San Roque, she saw that Joaquin's lights were on. Maybe they could have a cup of coffee before the day began. With that in mind, she cut in a diagonal across the internal courtyard, and startled a white cat at the base of the statue of San Roque. It dashed away, and Charlie made a small yip of yearning.

There were lights in the field, or at first she thought there were, soft little balls of blue light bobbing along the ground. When she took a step toward the field, peering into the darkness, they disappeared, and she heard the distant sound of laughter.

"Must be fairies," she said to Charlie, who looked up at her with his head cocked, perplexed. Elsa rubbed one uplifted ear. "Don't look at me. I have no idea where it went."

As she passed the statue of the saint, she touched his foot. "Bless the dogs," she said, and brushed the head of his dog, "and those who love them."

She unlocked the kitchen door, let Charlie off his leash to go see Joaquin, and turned on the lights. Grocery bags sat on the counter, and she peeked into them, finding day-old cinnamon rolls and cookies and bags of clementines that would be very cheerful to look at. Someone had donated carrots that had gone a little soft and she pulled them out to be washed. The soup today was one of her favorites, a split pea with barley, which stuck to the ribs and had a great solidness in the mouth from the grain.

The thing that took the most time every soup kitchen morning was the bread, which they made from scratch, always the same seven-grain, which volunteers started the day before. She pulled the loaves out of the fridge and lined them up on tables to begin to warm to room temperature and rise a final time. There were three ovens in the room, and she turned them all on to 350°.

She glanced at the clock. The first volunteers would arrive around seven, another hour and a half. She started a pot of coffee in the little pot, not the giant-sized one they would use at lunch, and pulled the dishwasher open. It was full of clean dishes, so she put them away, checking the stores of spoons and bowls.

All routine. As she worked, the email echoed through her, earnest and so kind. Impossible not to think about her little church tucked away from the street in its grove of firs and monkey trees. The first time she'd seen it, Elsa had fallen in love. It looked like a chapel at church camp, cozy and welcoming, never judgmental. The sanctuary always smelled of cedar and old carpet and the candles that were part of the altar table. They changed colors through the seasons, replaced by the women who kept the altar beautiful.

Arms crossed, she stared absently through the window at the predawn sky, letting it in. Letting *them* in, all the people who filed in on Sunday mornings to the upbeat sound of piano or flute or whatever the musicians were playing that morning. The church was blessed with musicians—a cellist from the local symphony, a blues singer from Mississippi, a classically trained opera singer who could blow the windows out of the place when she was on full power. Elsa smiled, remembering the high drama that could erupt over music when so many talented people were involved.

The woman who had sent the email, Maggie, had begun by slinking into a seat next to the wall at the back, but as time went by, she claimed a spot near the middle, on the aisle, where fingers of sunlight sometimes touched her hair. She was as ordinary as grass, with her dishwater hair and round figure. Before Elsa left, Maggie had begun to wear a red jacket to church, or sometimes a bright blue sweater that made her look like a piece of stained glass.

Homesickness swamped Elsa. That sea of faces, turned expectantly in her direction, waiting as she rose to take the lectern each Sunday. Her ritual was to breathe in Spirit in the instant before she stood, letting go of what *she* wanted and trying to become a conduit for light and hope and help. For whatever they needed.

"Hey, are you all right?" Joaquin's voice broke her vision.

She straightened. "I was thinking about Sunday mornings, just before you stand up to begin speaking. All the faces."

"Mmmm." He leaned on the opposite counter, arms crossed over his black shirt, mirroring her posture. "What brought that to mind?"

Elsa shrugged, recognizing that she didn't want to tell him about the email. *Interesting*. He was her prime confidant, and had been for years. "I guess I just miss it a little."

"A lot."

She nodded. "Yes. A lot."

"Will you go back, Elsa?"

"I have no idea." She struggled with the tangle of emotions. "I don't know if I don't believe or if I'm just mad or—" She broke off. "I kinda feel like I'm mooning around now, like there's some action I should take, but I don't know what it is."

"And I suppose it's foolish to suggest that prayer might help?"

"No, of course not." She scowled at him. "I think about it all the time, but when I get ready to do it, something blocks me."

"You really are angry." His dark eyes rested quietly on her face, without judgment. "I keep feeling like there's more to this than the murder."

"Of course there is," she said. "It was walking all that way to Santiago only to lose the life I wanted. It's that bastard Father Michael dismissing my passion for the priesthood and making me feel like a worm. It's God favoring men so much."

Two hectic patches of color burned on his cheekbones. "What did you do the other times?"

She shook her head. "No." She waved a hand, pushing away the anxiety the conversation raised. "I have work to do this morning. I don't want to talk about this."

"Okay." He gave her the beneficent priest version of his smile, which was low key and meant to be kindly. "God is patient."

She waved that away, too. "Have you eaten?"

"I was waiting for you. Oatmeal?"

"Very good." She poured them each a cup of coffee and they wandered down the hall toward the rectory kitchen, which was friendlier than the vastness of the church kitchen. Charlie thumped his tail at her and she gave him a perfunctory pat.

Joaquin said, "I've been up for hours, thinking about those gang boys. There was another confrontation between two rival gangs yesterday. I'm concerned."

"About the garden?" She took a saucepan out of the cupboard as Joaquin pulled out a glass measuring cup and filled it with water.

"Maybe we're going to need security. Fencing. Something." He handed the water to her and she poured it into the pan.

"Security sends the wrong message." From a salt shaker on the stove she poured a tiny pile into the center of her palm, dumped it into the water, and turned on the stove. As she pulled out the metal measuring cups, Joaquin found the oatmeal, and set it on the counter, by her elbow. She said, "I think you're letting that encounter get under your skin too much."

He spread cloth place mats on the table. "And I don't think you're taking it seriously enough."

"There's always a rough element in a poor neighborhood." She took spoons from the drawer and handed them to him. "One of the reasons you wanted to start the garden in the first place is to create a setting for grace."

"Yes." He paused. "Grace will not be compromised if there is a security detail."

"You know better than that, Joaquin." The water started to boil and she stirred in the oats. "People don't like to feel they're being watched. That won't heal things."

He turned away to retrieve a carton of milk, and poured some into a small metal pitcher. Placing it carefully at the exact center between the two settings, he said quietly, "I feel uneasy."

"Walking," she replied in a firm voice, "look at me."

He obliged. Elsa touched her neck. "I'm okay. Nothing happened."

"He cut your throat."

"Yes. But you can't let that stop this project. You know it's the right thing to do. It will bring food and beauty and life into the neighborhood, and especially into the lives of the people who live in that apartment complex."

As a boy, his eyes had been much too large for his face, with the shiny liquidity of a lake. Time had whittled his cheekbones and jaw and given proportion to the size of those eyes, but they were still grave and thoughtful, almost unreadable. She waited. Behind her the oatmeal bubbled.

At last, he nodded. "You're right. I know you are."

"Maybe we can brainstorm things to help address the gangs themselves, those boys."

He sighed. "It's a big problem. I don't know the answer."

"Let's just think about it."

"I will. Do me a favor, will you?" He pulled a chain from his pocket, and on it was a saint's medal. "Wear this."

She recognized it, a St. Christopher medal his mother had given him as a child. He'd worn it through his nearly fatal bout with the measles and often through high school. She held it in her palm for a moment, then remembered the oatmeal and turned around to take it off the burner. Joaquin put the bowls beside her. "Just wear it," he said. "It's no big deal. It'll make me feel better, that's all."

The medal was warm from his body, and she rubbed a thumb over the worn shape of the saint, then kissed it and pulled it over her head, letting it drop below her shirt. "Done."

He smiled. "Thank you."

"Let's eat, worrywart."

Tamsin awoke with a soft feeling of well-being. Last night, she'd spent an hour talking online to her friends in the quilting world. They had no idea that anything in her life had changed—that part of her didn't matter to them. On the quilting boards, she was admired and liked for the work she did with fabric, for the insights she could offer others, for her good color sense and talents. It eased her heart.

When she finished, she'd taken out the fabrics she purchased at Goodwill and spent a couple of hours spreading them on the dining room table, humming along with her iPod. A quilt was brewing, though she didn't see its shape yet. The organza spoke to her, and the magenta satin. Intriguing. What story would they tell?

The peacefulness she felt upon waking lasted until she heard the noises outside. Voices calling out to one another, static and electrical sounds from the equipment, a motor running. The journalists had returned. She groaned and covered her head with a pillow, then flung back the covers and marched into the kitchen. They were *not* going to rule her life. She would have a shower, make some coffee, and march right over to the church to honor her commitment to Elsa. They could all come right into the soup kitchen with her if they wanted.

But she couldn't stop fretting as she braided her hair and put on the gym clothes so it wouldn't matter if they got dirty. Why had they come back? Had something else happened? She was torn between turning on the news and clinging to the peace she'd felt upon awakening.

Her body was tired of being on high alert. Just for today, she would be an ordinary person, her sister's helper in the soup kitchen.

She was grateful for her enormous sunglasses, and a baseball hat she took from a hook in the back room. Even so, as she stepped off the front porch, the reporters surged toward her. "Tamsin, where's your husband? Where's Scott? What are you going to do?"

The questions pinged against her ribs, each one like a tiny arrow. The answer to all of them was "I don't know." She missed her husband, or at least the man she had imagined him to be. She missed her house and studio and the easy cadence of her days.

Head up, she kept walking, and they left her alone, more or less. Somebody followed behind in a little car, parking across the street when she got to the church.

Tamsin went over and knocked on the car window. "We have a soup kitchen going today. We can always use extra hands if you feel like pitching in."

"Is this a publicity stunt, a way to get sympathy?"

"No," Tamsin said, and left it at that.

The long church kitchen smelled of yeast when she entered.

There were already six or seven volunteers in place, washing dishes, talking, chopping. Others were setting up chairs and tables in the adjacent fellowship hall. Elsa was nowhere in sight, so Tamsin pulled off the cap and glasses and approached the first person in the row, who chopped carrots on a big white cutting board. "Hi, I'm Elsa's sister. What can I do?"

"Over here, honey," called a black woman with a high voice. She was plump and freckled, with a short reddish Afro. "You're helping me with the dishes for now. Elsa wants you to serve later, if that's all right."

"Sure."

"I'm Alberta," the woman said. "You can start with these pans, if you would."

"Tamsin," she said, and tugged up her sleeves.

"Hey!" said a girl with tattoos circling her arms and growing across her chest. She had black hair and blue eyes and was extraordinarily pretty. "Are you that lady I've been seeing on TV? Your husband is the guy who disappeared with all that money, right?"

Tamsin was not given to blushing, but judging strictly by the burn, her ears must be the color of cherries. She glanced at the girl. "Yes."

"He's gone completely, huh? You don't know where at all?"

Tamsin shook her head, focused on scrubbing the bottom of a deep pot.

"That must suck. You must—"

The woman with the Afro said, "Crystal, hush. It's none of your business. You want people asking you all kinda questions about your ankle bracelet?"

"I don't care. I'll tell you. I was the getaway driver when my boyfriend tried to rob a bank." She stirred the soup she was tending. "That's how stupid I was. Men make women do some stupid shit sometimes."

"Language, Crystal," Elsa said, coming into the room. She carried a bag of apples. "And no man can make you do anything you don't want to do."

"Sorry!"

Behind Elsa came Father Jack, carrying more bags of supplies. He smiled at the volunteers, showing off those wolfishly white teeth, his slightly scarred skin adding to the appeal. "Good morning, ladies," he said. "What's on the menu this morning?" He poked his nose in the pots, lifted a lid. "How are you, Crystal?"

"I'm good, Father. And my baby boy is growing like a weed, you should see him!"

"Bring him to church when you come."

She rolled her eyes, cheerfully.

Tamsin wanted his attention, too, she realized as he stopped and talked to each of them. The old woman painstakingly peeling potatoes with her gnarled hands got a quiet joke about angels, and he asked after her cat. Finally he stopped between Alberta and Tamsin. "Come see me later, will you, Tamsin? Let's talk a little."

She nodded, weirdly relieved. Father was safe, a calm port, who would be able to guide her if she listened. As he listened.

"Thank you."

An hour later, she was manning the soup pots as people filed into the room. Tamsin had expected the ragged men with their dirty fingernails, and had braced herself in case they might smell. She wasn't her sister, with a heart ready to embrace all the lost and lonely people in the world. Some of them scared her, like the gang boys she saw at Safeway, smoking cigarettes. Homeless men on street corners begging for change. Crazy old women with shopping carts.

But this morning, it was different. It was safe in the church, for one thing, making it easy for Tamsin to say "Good morning" over and over, and ladle up the soup, feeling something like kindness or honor fill her chest. The men met her eyes, one after the other, almost in challenge—*Do you see me?* It was hard at first, to meet those slightly hostile eyes, blue and brown and hazel and black. Some just stared at her with hostility when she spoke, saying "Good morning" and "How are you?" and "Would you like soup?"

Others spoke in return. "This is my favorite," said one.

"You're new," said another, frankly appraising her. "You get in trouble or you here because you want to be?"

She laughed and pointed to Elsa, passing out bread. "My sister made me."

"Mmm. Elsa's good people. Good for her." He held out his bowl and his thumbnails were black, as if they'd been hit by a hammer. It gave her a pang of worry—what had he done? "Good for you, too. Do you like us?"

"So far, so good."

"I want a different spoon, please," said another. "This is a baby spoon. I'm a man."

There were others, too, who she had not expected. The teens, filled with bravado, coming in knots of two and three. A young girl with her hair chopped raggedly, a boy with shoulders hunched in an Army jacket, another boy with ashy dark skin who barely spoke. Runaways? she wondered. Crackheads? She wished for combs, for warm showers, for beds for them.

And then there were the families. Elsa said they were busy the last week of the month, always, because people on public assistance had run out of food and money and wouldn't get any more until the first. Tamsin had imagined that would mean a lot more men, but of course it didn't. There were painfully young mothers with toddlers, and tiny family units, mom and dad and little kid, washed and humble, waiting for bowls of soup. A three-year-old boy with a cowlick in his blond hair showed her his shoes—two left boots. "I just got these at the basement!" he chortled.

"Amazing," Tamsin said, but she wanted to cry, too. His quiet mother gave her a sidelong glance.

She recognized one of the boys who had been at the church for the cleaning of the fields, a mixed-race boy with his skinny blond mother. "Hey there," she said. "Calvin, right?"

He peered up at her. "Hey! You're the lady who was supposed to bring back doughnuts!" He held out his bowl. "How come you didn't?"

"It was kind of a bad day for me. Sorry about that." She ladled soup carefully into his bowl.

He waited for a second ladle, his eyes canny beyond his years. He knew, and she knew, that she wasn't supposed to give it to him. She did. He grinned.

His mother grinned, too, shyly. "He's incorrigible."

"Adorable."

"Thank you." She touched her boy's back as they moved down the line. Tamsin ladled again. And again.

An old Native American man stopped in front of her. He hardly looked homeless. His hair was tidy in braids, and he wore a clean shirt with a vest over it, and silver bracelets around his dark wrists. "I saw you on TV," he said.

She nodded.

Next to him was a plump boy Tamsin also remembered. He said, "Hey, I remember you! You were going to get us doughnuts last week, and you didn't come back!"

She laughed. "Your buddy Calvin already said that. Sorry."

"Maybe you could bring them some other time?"

"I'll see what I can do." She thought of her frozen funds. "But don't hold your breath, okay?"

"If you do get some, will you get the kind with sprinkles on the frosting?"

"Now, that I *can* promise. I absolutely promise that *if* I can buy doughnuts, I'll buy the kind with sprinkles."

He gave her a thumbs-up.

In that moment, Tamsin realized she hadn't thought about her problems for at least an hour, maybe more. Even now, it all seemed a million miles away, like something that was happening to somebody else.

She turned to the next man in line. Maybe this was why Elsa did it.

Because it felt good.

Chapter Thirteen

It was so warm after lunch that Elsa wandered into the field, where Deacon was supervising a crew of two volunteers, middle-aged men, who were laying rubber pipe for the garden's irrigation system. The water would come from the church and the apartment buildings—the owner had been more or less shamed into it when Deacon pointed out how many city codes the buildings were violating.

In the bright light, the field stretched luxuriously, arching her back, her belly and legs beginning to sprout a pale green fur of elm seedlings. Elsa and Charlie strolled through them, and she imagined how it would all look later in the season, with hardy plants growing tall, and family plots boasting their own unique mixes.

She spied Deacon sitting on the open bed of his truck, legs swinging, talking on the phone, and a little flower of pleasure bloomed in her throat. She didn't often meet men with his kind of outdoorsy good looks; his lean body, the sun lines by his eyes, his tanned skin were all very appealing.

He was plainly a man with a big heart, and she loved that he had adopted an old dog, and volunteered as a Big Brother. If she was honest with herself, though, it was the sheer physicality of him that kept drawing her closer. She had considered, more than once, what it might be like to kiss him.

Which told her that she hadn't been so ridiculously picky before when she had resisted all of those blind dates. While it would be perfectly possible to arrange a nice match in order to have children, Elsa was a bit too lusty for that. From the first time she'd had sex at age sixteen, after nearly two years of foreplay with Joaquin, Elsa had loved it. When they broke up, sex had been one of the few things to ease the agony for a little while, and she had probably slept with a few too many guys during that lost year in England. Since then, she'd tended toward longish relationships with one man. One at ministerial school, another at her first church. One with a local cop in Seattle that had seemed as if it might lead to marriage and children, until they had both realized their values were simply too different.

He'd been the last one. And it had been several dry years since then.

Deacon was relaying instructions to someone on the phone as she approached. "All right, then, my friend. Call me when it's done." He ended the call, palmed the phone, and gave a nod toward Elsa. "Afternoon, Rev."

She smiled slightly and jumped up to sit beside him. "You're moving right along." The plots were all divided neatly by two-foot posts at each of four corners. Rolls of low fencing waited for the gardeners to erect around their plots. "How many families have signed up so far?"

"Thirty-four," he said with satisfaction.

Elsa dropped her mouth open. "Get out!" She smacked his thigh. "That's fantastic!"

"Yep. Almost all of them are from the apartments. Nine are from the church and two are neighborhood people."

"I can't wait to plant. It's going to be such a great community builder." She pointed at the center, left open for her picnic idea.

"I think we should have our first meal there after the planting, depending on the weather."

"We should do it no matter what the weather."

Elsa pursed her lips. "You've obviously never experienced a Colorado thunderstorm."

"I have, actually. But it's not thunderstorm season yet."

She nodded. "How long have you been here, then, Deacon?"

"I've been in Pueblo four years, since I got out of prison."

That would account for the extra weariness in his face. "Were you there for a long time? In prison?"

"Three years and some change. Vehicular manslaughter." He brushed at a patch of dust on his jeans. "Drunk driving."

"I'm sorry."

He glanced at her. "Thank you. Me, too. But you can't undo a thing once it's done. I'm making amends the best I can."

She nodded.

In quiet, they watched the men connect piping. "How about you, señorita? How long have you been in Colorado?"

"I grew up here, then left for college, and now I'm back. I came here only a few months ago." He'd been straight with her, she thought. She would tell the truth, too. "I left a church in Seattle. I'm trying to figure out if I'm going to go back."

"Anything in particular weighing into that decision?"

"A lot of things." She smiled up at him. "I'm feeling a little sick of my own story today, though, if you don't mind."

"Tell me something else, then, why don't you?" he said, and bumped her arm with his. "I'd like to know a little more about you."

"Well," she said, "I . . ." She stopped, at a loss for something to say that wasn't connected to the church or her ministry, her identity as that person. "Wow, I'm stumped."

He chuckled. "Do you like to roller-skate?"

Elsa laughed. "Yes. Do you?"

"Nope. I broke my arm in two places when I was eleven. Haven't put on skates since. You ever break any bones?"

"My nose. A baseball hit me in the face when I was in fourth grade."

"Oooh. Let me see." He peered down at her, touched her chin to move her face side to side. "Can't tell at all. That's a cute little nose."

She gave him a wry smile. "You're flirting with me."

"You came over here to flirt with me, don't lie."

Her blood bubbled. "I would never lie."

"Good." He dropped his hand. Paused. "So, what's with you and Father Jack?"

Elsa frowned. "Nothing. We're old friends, that's all. Since the fifth grade, actually."

"Huh."

"What does that mean?"

His mouth worked a little, a southern thing she liked. "Just that I would have said it was a tetch more than that, at least at some point."

"And you would be right," she said. A lock of hair blew into her mouth, and she pulled it away, trying to catch all of it in a scrunchy she pulled off her wrist. "We were . . . almost married. Once upon a time."

Deacon's attention was quiet, his face turned toward hers as he listened. Sun angled across one deeply tanned cheekbone with its fan of laugh lines, pierced the collar of his shirt, and landed on his collarbone. "And then what happened?"

"He was called to be a priest."

"I see."

She studied his face and he studied hers back and there was suddenly a lot blooming in the formerly empty space between them. She jumped off the truck. "I guess I'm going home for a nap. It's been a long day."

"I didn't mean to run you off."

"You didn't. I've been up since four."

"All right, Reverend. Sweet dreams."

Elsa couldn't resist looking over her shoulder as she walked away, toward her house, Charlie trailing behind.

Deacon waved.

Elsa napped for a couple of hours, cocooned in the quiet of her bedroom at the back of the house, low dog snores a comforting lullaby. In the late afternoon, a commotion from outside awakened her. Blinking, she got up to see what was wrong, and Tamsin slammed inside, hat askew. "Argh!" she cried when she saw Elsa. "They're so rude!"

"Yeah, they are. So sorry you have to go through this." Yawning, she headed for the kitchen and poured herself a glass of water. She drank deeply and turned around. "Are you okay?"

"Fine." She threw her hat on the table. "I'm afraid to turn on the news to see why they're back. Do you know?"

"I saw a headline on CNN.com this morning, nothing new, but it was national. The story is catching on. Everybody loves to hate a rich guy."

Tamsin sank down on the couch and rubbed her face. "I know. I get it. It's a good story—the disappearance, the big house, the younger wife." Her hands went flat on her thighs. "You don't think they'll bother Alexa, do you? I mean, how would they know where she is?"

"You still haven't told her?"

"No! I'm not going to!"

"Tamsin, she's going to hear."

"I know that. But every hour she doesn't know is another hour she keeps her innocence."

"That's pretty shortsighted."

"Mind your own business. This is my decision."

Irritated, Elsa waved a hand. "You are stubborn as an ox."

"And you think you know everything."

"I'm going on record as your sister and Alexa's aunt that you might need to prepare her for what's coming."

"Her boyfriend is a count, did I tell you that?"

"And? What does that have to do with anything?"

"Oh, I'm sure all those wealthy nobles would love to know Alexa's father is a criminal!" She made a low moaning noise and banged her head on her wrists. "If I ever find Scott, I'm going to kill him. How could he leave Alexa destitute?"

"How could he bilk thousands of people out of all their money?"

"I know." She kept her hands over her face, tips of her fingers pressed to the delicate skin of her eyelids. "It's all so insane. I can't believe he would do this to us. To himself. To all those people."

"Do you think he had some weird midlife crisis or something? I wouldn't have thought he had it in him."

"I don't know. I keep thinking back, wondering if I missed something. He's been traveling a lot, but he always has." Her eyes filled with tears. "I'm never going to see him again, am I?"

"I don't know." Elsa reached for her sister's hand, rubbed it between her own. "I'm sorry."

"I'm sorry for calling you a know-it-all."

"I am, kind of." Turning Tamsin's hand in hers, she touched her palm, traced the lines there. "How did you like the soup kitchen?"

"Honestly, I loved it."

"Yeah? What particularly?"

Tamsin raised her shoulders, pulling her hand back to herself. "I don't know. I mean, I guess I should say their problems made mine look small, but that's not really true. I'm pretty scared. But I forgot about all my stuff while I was there. And it felt good to feel like my being right there was important. Meant something."

"I'm glad." She remembered that the interim minister had

asked for her to call him. "I have to make a phone call. You okay for the moment?"

"Of course."

"And that reminds me of something else. Where are your earrings?"

Tamsin pulled her hair back to show a pair of small opal studs. "These?"

"No, the big emeralds you always wear."

"Probably on my dresser."

"Too bad."

"Why?"

"I saw them in a photo on the web and thought you might be able to sell them for money to live on for a while. But if they're in the house, I guess they're part of the seized property."

"Maybe I should sneak in there and steal them."

"No, that's a really bad idea."

"You're probably right." She fell back against her chair. "Go make your call. Do you want me to cook supper?"

"I'd love it." Elsa found her phone in the pocket of the jeans she'd shed in favor of her baggy cotton pajama bottoms. The church office phone number was engraved in her brain. When Reverend David answered, she said, "Hello, it's Elsa. How are you?"

"I'm so glad you called. I've been praying for you."

"I appreciate that. How are you doing?"

"Well, I have some bad news, I'm afraid. I have injured my knee again and they're going to have to do surgery within a couple of weeks."

Elsa's breath gusted out of her. "Oh, I'm sorry."

"So, the board will be in touch, and you might want to petition them to let you return sooner than planned. Otherwise, they'll have to hire another interim minister."

"I see." A hurricane of conflicting emotions sucked the air from her lungs. "Do you know who they'd ask?"

"Allen Tall Pine."

"Oh." Reverend Tall Pine was a charismatic, long-limbed Lakota who'd entered Unity, as Elsa had, as a fallen Catholic. Elsa knew him through various regional meetings and committees, and also knew he'd had an eye on the Seattle church for a long time. His wife's family lived in the area and she wanted to come home. "Will he do it for only a couple of months?"

"I seriously doubt it, Elsa. That's why I'm calling. Just thought you should know."

"Thank you, David." She paused, thinking. About her yearning for her congregation, for Sunday mornings. She had not wanted to leave in the first place. Maybe it was time to—

Behind her, Tamsin clattered pans and dishes, the homey sound of dinner preparation. "There are some complicating factors here," she said quietly. "Do you follow the financial news?"

"Some."

She told him about the Ponzi scheme and Tamsin's connection. "She's staying with me. I don't think I can leave her for at least a month." Worry moved through her belly. "But if Reverend Tall Pine gets into that church—"

"Exactly."

Elsa nodded. "Thank you again for letting me know, David. I'm sorry for your injury, and I'm deeply grateful for everything you've done."

"I understand."

"How are they? The congregation?"

"They miss you, of course, but we're hobbling along all right." He chuckled at his joke. "I've encouraged them to write to you, to let you know they're thinking about you."

"I got an email this morning. It was beautiful."

"I'm glad. You do good work. Don't forget that. Will you let me pray for you?"

"Of course." She stared into space, letting him offer a prayer on her behalf, a prayer for clarity and guidance and truth. She steeled herself against it, but prayers could still get to her. She found it seeping into the back of her brain, easing something along her neck, urging her to close her eyes. A soft buzzing peace, wide as an ocean, filled her for a fleeting moment. *Enough for today*. "Thank you."

"God is always there, Elsa."

She thought of Kiki, looking skyward for help, which had never arrived. "I do want to believe that," she said, and left it there.

Tamsin hummed under her breath as she cooked. She was surprised that she wasn't tired of food after handling it all day, but she felt even more pleasure in it, not less. Charlie watched her from the doorway, his feet just touching the threshold he was not allowed to cross if someone was cooking. She was charmed by his focus and the sense of companionship he offered—she'd never had a dog before and had never even known she liked them until Elsa owned her first one. "Stick with me," she said to him now. "I'll see to it that you get a treat or two."

The first step was a pot of rice steaming on a back burner. At home she liked using a wild rice mix, but this was ordinary long-grain white. Traditional. Once that was bubbling, she washed a single plump chicken breast and cut it lengthwise into narrow, even pieces that would cook quickly. One strip she cut into smaller pieces for Charlie, who took a tidbit from her fingers with the most delicate of mouths, his tongue clever and not at all slobbery. She sliced long thin strips of red pepper and slivered a small yellow onion and then opened a hideously expensive carton of grape tomatoes. Elsa indulged in her passion for tomatoes the way Tamsin indulged in wine; her sister didn't care if they were expensive, they were necessary to her happiness and she'd give up a lot to keep them.

Tamsin halved the small red fruits, thinking of the yellow

cherry tomatoes she'd grown last summer in a pot on her patio. She had called them her grenade tomatoes, so explosively full of flavor that even a handful overpowered a salad. She'd grown lavender in big pots, too, so their leaves would fill the night air with scent. Often she and Scott had sat out there in the evenings and sipped wine, listening to the whirring softness of crickets and the tick of sprinklers watering the grass. Her own grass was lush and thick, cared for by a lawn company Scott had hired, and it gave off a damp coolness that offset the dry Colorado air. In the summer dark they would talk, about politics and the stock market and Alexa, about where they hoped to next travel and what they would do on the weekend.

Ordinary, all of it.

Gone.

Her lungs pinched hard enough that she had to cough, like an old lady, to get air. *No wallowing*. She picked up the remote control from the counter and turned on the small, blocky television that sat on top of the fridge. She would watch the news.

At home, she had a wok, a beautifully shaped thing like a Chinese field hat, but here she made do with an enormous cast-iron skillet, letting it get very hot before she measured in vegetable oil that would tolerate high heat. When it was not quite smoking, she poured the mixed vegetables and meat into the pan, sprinkled them with salt and pepper and some ginger that she'd found in the cupboard. She stirred it all together, letting the flavors blend and add to one another, sending up a cloud of fragrant steam. It was the simplest of dishes, rice and chicken and vegetables, but so very nutritious, something she used to make once a week. Alexa loved it.

Elsa came into the kitchen. "Mmm! That smells wonderful. I'm starving."

"Set the table. It'll be ready in just a minute or two." She focused on turning, stirring, making sure everything touched the oil and the heat and the spices but never long enough to scorch. The chicken browned lightly, and she pulled the pan off the burner, still stirring. Elsa put out the plates and silverware, filled tall glasses with ice. Tamsin lifted the lid to the rice, seeing the small holes and dry surface that meant it was properly cooked. "You can put the rice in a bowl," Tamsin said, and poured the stir-fry into another bowl, which she carried to the table.

Elsa brought the rice, steaming and mounded into a slightly off-color china serving dish with a border of blue flowers and gold piping. The television played in the kitchen. "Do you mind if I turn that off?" Elsa asked.

"No, I just turned it on as a distraction."

"From?"

Tamsin waved a hand. "Things. My backyard."

Elsa smiled gently. One of the best things Tamsin liked about her sister was that gentle, understanding smile. It lit her eyes, made her look like a pixie with that tumble of black curls. "Right."

Tamsin dished out rice for both of them, finding she was beginning to like the mismatched dishes. Elsa had a cobalt plate with a flower in the center. Tamsin's was ivory with a winding vine. Her fork was a heavy ornate thing, her knife a slim elegant blade. She picked it up and stabbed the air playfully, and then felt Elsa's presence again, standing motionless at the threshold of the kitchen.

"You need to see this."

Tamsin jumped up and joined her, and there on the screen of the national news was her face from this morning, scrubbed and tired-looking as she walked to the church. The anchor said, "No news yet on the whereabouts of Scott Corsi, who is wanted for questioning in the scheme that some investigators say may have cost investors over three hundred million dollars."

"Wait. Three hundred *million*?" Tamsin said. "I've had a very nice life, but I never saw anything like that kind of money."

"It might be exaggerated, though he might have hidden a lot of it, too. Or done any number of things."

Tamsin thought of Scott at the crap tables in Vegas, at poker games in Argentina. "Or gambled it all away."

"Does he gamble?"

"I'd say this is all a big gamble, wouldn't you? He bet that it would work out before he got caught, and it didn't." She swallowed, feeling a knot of truth in her throat. "Yes," she said. "He gambled. Sometimes it scared me. That's one of the reasons he liked traveling so much—he had a bunch of rich guys he liked to play cards with. Poker."

Elsa nodded. Took her sister's arm gently. "Let's eat. I don't want it to get cold."

They returned to the table, but the bubble of forgetfulness had broken, and Tamsin looked at the table with despair. "I wish I'd figured it out sooner."

"Eat," Elsa said, dishing stir-fry onto her plate. The vegetables and chicken spilled perfectly over the rice. It did look pretty. Tamsin picked up her fork. "At home, I would have added toasted sesame seeds. They're really tasty."

"It's fantastic just the way it is, Tamsin. No one ever cooks for me, you know, not an ordinary meal in my own home. I love it that you're doing that here."

"You're welcome. I've missed being able to cook for other people, with Alexa gone and Scott on the road so much." She took a bite, and took the time to really taste it. The peppers. The onions. The rice. The subtle touch of ginger. "Good."

She let the food nourish her. Light tumbled in through the windows, carrying the lemon glaze of spring. She wished she could appreciate it, wished that she was planning her garden, not couched here at her sister's house, lonely and afraid. If she started to think about her future, it was so chaotic and overwhelming that she started to feel sick to her stomach.

"I don't even know what steps to take, Elsa, to the next part of my life. I feel like I'm in an airplane, circling the earth. What do I do?"

Elsa put down her fork and touched her lips with her napkin. "Maybe the first step should be getting a job. It will help you feel grounded. And maybe they'll let you into the house soon, too. Didn't they say maybe this weekend?"

Tamsin nodded. "I'd like to get some kitchen stuff. Will they let me get my wok, do you think?"

"I can't see why not." Elsa lifted a pepper to her mouth, ate it delicately. "You also need to tell Alexa what's going on, Tamsin. The world is a very small place. What if she sees it on the news or something? She'll be devastated."

Tamsin closed her eyes, tried to imagine that phone call. "I don't even know what to say. 'Alexa, I have bad news. Your dad turned out to be a crook. And oh, by the way, the house you've lived in all your life now belongs to some government process.' What do you think of that?"

"I know it will be hard to say, but you're a good mother and you'll find some way of breaking it to her that's not so bald. How much worse will it be for her if she finds out some other way?"

Tamsin took a breath. "I'll think about how to tell her and call her in the morning."

"The sooner the better."

"It's the middle of the night there right now."

"Tomorrow, then." Elsa pointed. "Now, eat your dinner. And thank you for cooking."

It was well past midnight in Madrid but Alexa was not asleep. She and Carlos had been out with friends, eating dinner and watching a small band play mediocre pop music. The only reason the band landed gigs, Carlos whispered to her, was because the woman was so beautiful. And well endowed.

"Is that so?" she asked, leaning into him.

"Not so beautiful as you, of course," he said, laughing. It was the thing she liked the most about him, that he was so full of laughter. He made her laugh, and she tended to be very serious. A serious student, a serious person. She had just been born that way. They had pictures of her as a baby, not giggling like other babies, but staring with curious intent at the camera, her eyes too big for her face.

He kissed her neck, right at the nape, knowing that it made her shiver, and she slapped at his hands. "Later," she whispered, and nipped his earlobe, which was the thing that made him crazy.

And so they had come back to her tiny apartment with its big windows and made love. Now they were lying in a tangle of sheets in the warm night, legs flung out, sharing a cigarette. One of the many habits she would have to change when she headed home next month.

"I cannot bear the thought of you leaving," Carlos said. Her head was cradled on his chest, and she blew out smoke and handed the cigarette back to him. "How long will it be before we can be together again?"

"I have the apartment now. It will be all right."

He kissed the top of her head. "It won't be the same. You'll grow apart from me and some other man will catch your eye and then Carlos will be a poof of smoke."

She laughed, lifting her head to kiss his chin. "No other man on this earth could hold a candle to you." She tucked her cheek into his shoulder, brushing her hand over the black hair on his chest. "Far more likely that you will forget all about your little American fling and find yourself a nice countess and settle into the life you were meant to live."

"Never say that!" He gathered a fistful of her hair and kissed it, tugging her face up to his, so he could kiss her mouth. "I love you. I love you. I love you. Do you hear me?"

She closed her eyes. "Yes," she whispered.

He kissed her again, and again. "I love you," he chanted. "You love me, too. We will find a way to be together, I promise."

Chapter Fourteen

On Friday morning, Deacon got his men working on the two big landscape jobs they had in motion, and then headed for the church. This week, he'd brought in a tractor and spread truckloads of topsoil. The volunteers had finished laying irrigation tubing.

Tomorrow was the official blessing of the fields, and the potluck supper they'd share together, and then the planting would begin. Officially, anyway. Many of the residents of the apartment houses had to wait for their SNAP funds on the first to buy seed.

Pulling up in the bright morning, he felt a deep sense of satisfaction. Nothing had felt this good to him in a couple thousand years. As he stepped out into the field, slamming the door behind him, his phone rang in his pocket, and he tugged it out, expecting one of the crews to have questions.

Instead, it was his ex-wife's name on the screen. "Hello, Lucinda," he said, perplexed. "Is everything all right?"

"Fine, fine. Nothing to worry about. I just need to talk to you about something. It's a little delicate. Are you able to talk?"

"Yeah, sure. What's going on?"

She paused. "Deacon, I'm sorry, but you need to stop writing letters to Jenny."

He held the phone to his ear, thinking of his sixteen-year-old daughter, whom he had not seen since she was eight. He wrote letters to her about once a month, just to stay in touch, which he'd started doing when he was in prison, grappling with the enormity of his sins. He didn't burden her with any of that, of course, just sent chatty, sometimes thoughtful letters that he wrote by hand. Reaching out. "I see." He cleared his throat. "That coming from you or her?"

"It's her. I know you're trying to make amends, but she isn't interested."

"I see," he repeated. "Is that . . . ever?"

"Deacon, I can tell you've got your life together now, but some things aren't fixable. She doesn't want to know you. She has a father."

"Stepfather."

"Father," she said, more emphatically. "We've been married for half her life."

Standing in the gravelike silence of the field, he croaked, "Right."

"Isn't there something in the AA principles about making amends unless it makes things worse?"

"Yep."

"You can't fix this. She's not interested, and I think you have to leave her alone. Maybe someday, when she grows up and has kids of her own . . ."

He swallowed. "Good enough. I won't write to her again."

"Thank you. I hope you won't take it too hard."

"Don't worry I'm not going on a bender anytime soon."

"That's not what I meant."

"I know, Lucinda. It's fine. I'm going to go now. You take care of yourself, all right? Give her a kiss from me, even if she doesn't know who it's from."

"I can do that."

He ended the connection and held the phone, bending his head blindly. "Damn it."

"You all right, Deacon?" said a voice. Father Jack.

"Yeah," he said, but tears welled in his throat, hot and dangerous.

The priest stood there patiently, wearing his black shirt and white collar, a pair of jeans and tennis shoes. "You don't really look all right."

Deacon toed a weed, his hands on his hips. "No," he amended. "But I will be."

"Do you want to talk about it?"

Deacon considered. A hole had opened up in his chest, sucking goodness and holiness and light into it, and he knew from long experience that was never a good place to be. Better to talk than try to wrestle the demon into submission on his own. "It's my daughter," he said. "Her mother just asked me to stop writing to her." His voice all but broke on the last syllable, and he looked over the fields, blinking, until his emotions subsided.

"How old is she?"

"Sixteen. Her mother divorced me when she was seven. I don't blame her. She'd put up with me binge drinking for thirteen years, and just finally had enough." Again that heat in his throat. Too much. "God damn it."

Father Jack waited. "Have faith, Deacon. In time, she might come around."

Deacon cleared his throat. "I reckon." Rubbing his jaw, struggling to hang on to his dignity, he croaked out, "I can't talk about it right now."

"It's all right. You know where I am if you change your mind."

"Thank you." He dropped the phone into his pocket. "What's on your mind, Father?"

Father Jack paused, and Deacon felt the priest's eyes on him. After a long moment, he said, "Couple of things. I've been wondering if we need to have an instructional class or two. Talk about the various crops and what they do, so people can make good choices. Maybe something on companion planting?"

"Elsa has organized a group of experts to volunteer here a few afternoons a week, and I've printed up some packets to pass out, with particular instructions for various crops, tomatoes and corn and whatnot."

"Good. I like that. What happened with the chickens?"

"Probably isn't a good place for them. Too many coyotes coming up the river. We might be able to find some ways to build good coops over time, in a year or two, but that's beyond the little budget we've got right now."

"Understood. It was worth a try."

Deacon narrowed his eyes, imagining the coops, the chicken yard, the valuable lessons they would provide for the children—and even the adults—on the source of food. "All in good time."

Father Jack nodded. In this light his black hair shone like a raven's tail, the ends too long and splitting into sections like feathers. "Joseph Whitetail wants to drum, and I told him he could do it this afternoon, so give him some space if he asks for it, if you don't mind."

"Good man." He cocked an eyebrow. "Kinda outside the realm of the church to let a Native American drum away evil spirits, isn't it?"

"He's an elder, and a lot of the boys respect him." He crossed his arms. "They need role models other than the gangs. There are some fathers in the homes here, more than other places, but not enough. Still too many mothers trying to raise boys into men on their own. You're a Big Brother, aren't you?"

"That I am, but don't make it anything noble, now. It's my way of making amends."

"I'm wondering how to get more men in the church to take up that mantle. Will you think about that?"

"Sure."

"The last thing I am concerned about is the gangs, about the possibilities of vandalism."

"Any ideas?"

"A few. I've asked the police to make more trips through the neighborhood, but that's only going to provide a little help. We need to get some on-site, internal protection."

Deacon raised a brow in curiosity. "Where are you going to raise this force?"

"Haven't worked that out yet. Maybe recruit some of the homeless or some of the toughs to be the patrol at night."

"Maybe not the most reliable, Father."

"Right." He sighed. "I'm not sure of the logistics, but we need to do something." He sniffed. "Elsa's against any kind of guard."

"Is that right." He nodded, looking across the field. "Floodlights might help, motion-detector lights."

"Expensive, though."

"Maybe not as much as you'd think. How about if I look into it?"

"Do that."

Across the field trooped the three rascals, as Deacon called them, Mario and Tiberius and Calvin. Mario was the sturdy one, an ox, while Tiberius was an ostrich, all legs and neck and big eyes, taller than the other two by nearly a foot. Calvin was the smallest, but strong. With his streaky brown and blond curls and wide eyes, he was a cheetah, fast and pretty.

Before they reached the men, Father Jack said, "Those gang boys were just like these three, seven or eight years ago."

"Yep."

"Elsa wants to find ways to address the gang issue directly."

"No small problem there."

Father Jack nodded, arms crossed over his chest. "Hey, guys," he said to the trio. "No school today?"

"Teacher in-service," Mario said. "My grandpa's gonna drum and he said we could help."

Calvin leapt closer. "I'm going to help him, too! We're going to chase away bad spirits."

"And bring good ones," Mario said. "And we're kinda hungry, Deacon. Can you take us to get sandwiches?"

He chuckled. "Do I look like Mr. Moneybags to you?"

"Yeah!"

"It's okay," Tiberius said in his high, thin voice. "I had a good breakfast."

"But look how skinny he is!" Calvin protested. "He don't *need* no food. I'm always hungry! My mama say she don't know where I put it all."

"You got a hollow leg," Deacon said.

Calvin laughed, his back arching, and his missing teeth showing. "No I don't!"

Deacon bent and knocked on Calvin's knee, making a plonking noise with his tongue as he did so. "There it is, right there."

The boys all laughed.

"Tell you what, I'm going to put you to work here, and you can *earn* you some sandwiches, okay? You help me out and I'll pay you with a trip to Subway. How's that?"

"Okay!"

Father Jack said, "Do good work, gentlemen. Deacon, I'll speak with you later."

He halted when a dog raced toward them, Elsa's big black retriever, ears flying, mouth wide open in a smile.

Calvin cried, "Charlie!" and the dog bounded right toward him, grazed his leg with his long back, as if to say, *You're it!* and bounced away again. Calvin hollered and raced after him.

Elsa emerged from the courtyard, as calm as her dog was wild. Her hair was pulled hard away from her face, though no amount of scraping could catch all the curls, and a few sprang free around her forehead and neck. She waved when she saw them, but didn't hurry.

She was no beauty, yet Deacon liked looking at her. There was something appealingly healthy and calm about her movements, her easy ways, her small compact body.

And yet, this morning, what he noticed was the way Father Jack did not hurry away after all, but waited, his face carefully blank, as Elsa approached. "Good afternoon!" he said. "You're later than usual."

"Long day yesterday," she said, leaning forward to kiss his cheek. Father Jack closed his eyes, a split second of quiet coming over his face, then stepped back. "How are things going here?"

"Good," Deacon said. "You here to help?"

"Sure. What are we doing?"

"A little of everything. Fencing, mainly. I promised the boys some sandwiches at Subway if they helped." He slapped a pair of work gloves together to get the dust out and offered them. "We'd love to have you join us."

She inclined her head, smiling, almost coquettish, and took the gloves. "You're on."

Father Jack lifted a hand and headed toward the church. Deacon watched his stiff back until he disappeared into the courtyard. Of course, it wouldn't be appropriate for a priest to be jealous, but Deacon would swear that's exactly what he was.

Curious, he thought. Curious indeed. "Come on, crew. Let's get to work."

On the way to the church, Elsa had been turning the dilemma of returning to Seattle over and over in her head. She clearly could not desert Tamsin at the moment, but Reverend Tall Pine had been eyeing her church for a long time, and if he got a foot in, she might lose it to him.

Could she bear that?

Yet, could she bear to return, still feeling so lost? Even if she could, it would be impossible to leave Tamsin for at least a little while longer.

It was a relief to find Deacon and Joaquin and the boys in the garden, allowing her to avoid introspection. She loved the physical work, loved the feeling of warm sunshine on her head and her hands in the earth. Loved being part of something that felt so healing, when the rest of her life felt so chaotic. The boys raced around with the dog, performed short tasks as Deacon directed, raced around with Charlie some more.

They set up the area for the shared children's garden, fencing it off with heavy green recycled plastic made just for this purpose. She helped Deacon hold it and he used a staple gun to fix it to posts. It was nice that he didn't seem to have to chat the whole time, that he was capable of being quiet. She also liked the way he kept an eye on the boys at all times, as if they were his charges. Which in a way, she supposed, they were.

"Father wants us to have a class after the blessing of the fields tomorrow," he said, fixing a staple to the post. "We can do it after the first meal. What do you think?"

"Is everything really ready for planting?"

"Not yet. We had a couple of setbacks that called for the need of fencing, but it will also help keep animals out, so it's worth it." He straightened. "We can have the official planting date moved to next Saturday."

"If people want to start early, that's okay, though, right? I think some are chomping at the bit."

"You know, I'm a little worried about frost. There's a storm coming in early next week that might bring snow."

"That's the kind of snow that soaks the ground in the best way. Good to have the seeds in the ground, right?"

He gave her his amazing half smile. "You anxious to get started, sister?"

Elsa laughed. "Yes. Tamsin and I have mapped out a grand plan for the kids' garden. We'll have a garden of our own, too. How 'bout you?"

"Absolutely." He hauled the roll of fencing down to the next plot and Elsa followed, holding it up for him. "What are you putting in the kids' garden?"

"We'll make a teepee of scarlet runner beans at the center, a pretty good-sized one, so they can go inside. Also pumpkins and corn, of course, and some really early crops, like radishes and lettuce, so they get the payoff of seeing things grow and eating them right away."

"Great idea." He put her hand on the plastic, which had holes all through it to imitate metal fencing. "What about your garden?"

"I mainly want a fajita garden—tomatoes, onions, peppers. Tamsin wants some herbs. She's an excellent gardener."

"Well, she's the lady of the manor. She's had the leisure to polish those skills."

"Lady of the manor? Not anymore."

He clutched the staple gun, *clack clack clack*, and they moved to the next post. "Maybe not, but that's who she's been. I know that type. Debutante girls with all their charities and good works."

Elsa bristled. "Maybe you've forgotten that you're talking about my sister. My father was a steelworker—Tamsin was hardly debutante material."

He straightened. "I meant no offense. Just an observation."

"She's more than just beautiful, you know. She's an artist, a good one. She's very kind, and a good mother, and she loves beauty. She creates beauty in everything she does."

Deacon's mouth edged into the slightest smile. "Lady of the manor."

She rolled her eyes. "Whatever. You're being a snob, you know."

"Could be. You tend to know your place in the South." He pointed to where he wanted her hands on the post, and she followed directions. "You kind of have her on a pedestal, your big sister."

"No. I just know her. I'm proud of her. And she's going through a wretched, wretched time."

"Wouldn't argue with you there."

To change the subject, Elsa said, "What are you planning to grow?"

"Well, I've been debating. Garlic, 'cuz I love it. Tomatoes, of course, because they taste so good when they're hot off the vine. Mmm." He shook his head. "Cannot wait for that." He stapled down the length of the post, picked up the roll, and moved on, the staple gun loose in his hand.

Elsa trailed behind, and from nowhere, she imagined how his back would look without a shirt, how the muscles would move. For the space of a few seconds, the picture was vivid and compelling—the long spine, the muscles over it, his lean waist. A buried yen awakened, stretched, made a sharp yipping noise.

Startling. He wasn't her kind of man, all that brokenhearted charm.

Must be the sunlight. The spring. The fact that she'd not had sex in a while and human bodies were designed to indulge.

No.

He propped the fencing against the last post. "I want to grow collard greens, which you probably don't like."

"I love them," she said, "with hot pepper sauce."

"You don't say?" He paused to look at her. "Where'd you learn to like that?"

"My grandmother was Mississippi born and bred. We used to go down and spend summers with her until she died, when I was twelve. She taught me to cook, since my mother was the worst cook on the planet."

"On the planet?"

"Oh, you don't even want to know. She was absolutely tone

deaf and had no idea she was so terrible. Like somebody who sings off-key in church, very loudly."

He laughed.

"So I cooked for us a lot. And I cooked what my grandmother taught me to cook. Collards and beans and black-eyed peas. Hmm." She nodded. "Maybe I'll grow beans and peas, too. They keep so well."

"You're making me so hungry, sweetheart." He paused, holding the staple gun down. Every position his body took was graceful, easy. "You hear my stomach growling? There is no good southern food in this town."

"I guess I need to have you over for supper one of these days, then." She said it lightly, even as that blooming thing between them grew brighter. "Collard greens and black-eyed peas and cornbread."

"Oh." He put his gloved hands over his heart, faking a stagger. "I'd be your slave."

"Yes," she said.

"The sooner the better."

Elsa inclined her head. "That you become my slave?"

He smiled slowly. "You bet."

She ducked her head, surprised at herself. And pleased.

Tamsin's task for the day was to find a job. She not only needed the money, but she needed something to *do*. She was helping organize and set up the community garden, and had promised to be the "expert" on hand one afternoon a week, but that wasn't enough.

In her old life, the upkeep of the house and gardens took a lot of time, and she spent many hours a day on her quilts. She attended a book group and the quilting society, and volunteered at the library, which she supposed she should *still* do, but whenever she thought of going in there to face her friends, she couldn't breathe.

Her friends had been decidedly silent, actually. A couple of them had called when the news first hit, but nothing lately. It stung. Although, her two best friends weren't able to be seen with her, not now: Andrea's husband was a lobbyist, and Nancy's husband was planning a bid for Congress. Better to keep some distance from Scott Corsi's wife.

She twirled her long hair into a knot at the back of her neck. She stood back and surveyed herself—a crisp pink shirt tucked into gray slacks, a black belt and black shoes. The shoes were frankly awful, many years out-of-date, with their super-pointy toes, but they didn't have any scuffs at least. She wore a silver bracelet and her little opal studs. For a minute, she thought with longing of a blown-glass necklace in her jewelry box. Would they let her have those things, eventually—the sentimental ones that didn't have any real monetary value?

She had no idea, but it reminded her to pick up the phone and call the Sheriff's Office, as she did every morning. Things didn't get done by themselves, and she figured it was even worse at the station or any other place where bureaucracy held sway. The dispatcher answered in a bored voice. "Pueblo County Sheriff."

"Hello, this is Thomasina Corsi again. How are you?"

"Good, good. How are you this morning, Tamsin?"

"I'm fine, thank you for asking." She smiled to make her voice smile, too. "I'm just making my daily check. Don't suppose I can get my things?"

"Hold on, sweetie. Let me see."

Music came on the line. Tamsin leaned forward into the mirror and carefully applied a hint of berry lipstick. She smacked her lips together.

"Looks like a judge has ordered the department to accompany you to the house as soon as possible and supervise your claim on your possessions. You can come by and get the list, then somebody will go over there with you."

"Really?" She dropped her lipstick in the sink, leaving a curve of red against the porcelain. Using a tissue, she tried to wipe it off, but it only smeared. "Is there a time that's better than another? Do I need to get a truck or something, or is it just a little bit?"

"Probably best at around three p.m. Quieter then. The order says, let's see . . . 'Thomasina Corsi will be allowed to remove personal clothing and possessions, including quilting supplies and tools, but no quilts.' "

"What? Why did they say that?"

"Maybe the judge thinks the quilts are worth something."

"Mm. What about kitchen stuff?"

"That seems like it would be covered under personal supplies. You can also withdraw anything belonging to your child. I'm gonna tell you right now that there are no computers left, and once you leave today, they're going to seal the place."

Tamsin took a breath and blew it out. "Okay. You've been so nice. I really appreciate it. How long do you think I'll have?"

"If I were you, I'd plan on a couple of hours, no more, so bring whatever help you can get."

Tamsin smiled. "Thank you. From the bottom of my heart." Maybe, she thought, she would make her a quilt.

"You're welcome, Mrs. Corsi."

Since she was already dressed to impress and had a list of places with job openings, she decided to make the best of her time before going to the house. She had applied online for many of the positions, but she'd decided to also pop into the yarn shops and fabric stores in person. She had printed up copies of her newly written, neat little resume. Of course, she hadn't had a lot of experience to put on it, but she figured she'd make an impression with her charity work and quilt awards.

Actually, she *hoped* she would.

She also hoped no one would recognize her from the recent news stories.

Slipping out the back door, she walked down the block and around the corner, to where she'd left her car, out of sight. Nobody seemed to see her, and she prayed her invisibility held. Nobody would want to hire a woman dogged by paparazzi.

And she really, really needed a job.

The morning was disheartening. People took her resume, politely, but no one asked her to come back for an interview.

She hadn't had a dollar to her name in a week, and it was not only humiliating, but challenging. Not a dollar for a pack of gum or a bottle of water. She'd had to ask Elsa to fill her car up with gas, and it had cost over fifty dollars.

But she wouldn't give up. Maybe there would be things in the house she could sell on eBay, things the police had overlooked. She could have sold the quilts if they'd been released.

At just after three, she drove her Subaru over to the house, accompanied by Elsa, Deacon, and Father Jack. Deacon drove his truck. There wouldn't be a lot of room in Elsa's house, so Tamsin had gone through a mental list, trying to think of the most urgent things she needed. Her quilting supplies, of course, her wok and copper pots and pans, some clothes and costume jewelry, and everything she could get from Alexa's room.

But when she entered the house, the smell of it slammed her so hard that she swayed in the foyer, feeling as if she might faint. Beeswax and rotten bananas, dust and a thousand days of hard work. She looked upward at the stairs, following the golden light into her tower, and tears began to run down her face.

"Ma'am, you've only got two hours," said a woman deputy. "I'd suggest we get moving."

"You're right. I'm sorry." She shook off everything but the goal. "First my daughter's room. Deacon, you want to come with me?"

"On it." He grabbed some boxes and followed her.

"I'll tackle your room," Elsa said. "What do you want?"

"Just get as many of my clothes and shoes as you can. All my boots, especially. And the photos." She halted on the landing. "There's a trunk in the little room off the kitchen. It's filled with family photos and scrapbooks. We need to find that."

Deacon gently touched her shoulder, directing her up the stairs with his other hand. "Father Jack and I can find it in a little bit. Let's tackle one thing at a time."

Tamsin moved up the stairs, then whirled back. "And my spices! I have a lot of spices and staples."

"I'll get those," Father Jack said.

From this vantage point, Tamsin could see both the second floor and the first—polished wood spread out beneath her, adorned with antique Persian rugs she'd found at estate sales and antiques shows across the country. Light fell in golden pools, splashing over an armoire, and a giant fern she'd cultivated for two decades. Bavarian lace curtains hung over the long double-hung windows. She made a little sound.

"You don't have much time, honey," Deacon said behind her. She nodded and forced her heavy feet to move up the stairs, to Alexa's bedroom.

It was on the second floor, in the tower, and had windows on all sides. Alexa had fallen in love with it when she was six. "It's a princess's room!" she'd cried. They had furnished it with a canopy and hung gauzy curtains over the circle of windows, and held endless sleepovers and tea parties here.

The canopy was long gone, of course, but the shelves still held Alexa's dolls and stuffed animals and books from childhood. Alexa saved everything, a sentimental thread her mother shared, and Tamsin suddenly realized, urgently, that her most important task here today was to preserve as many of her daughter's childhood artifacts as possible. Nothing else really mattered, not even her quilting supplies.

"Let's get all the dolls and toys and books," she said, directing Deacon to the shelves. She pulled open the closet and started pulling out clothes and shoes, as many as she could stuff in. Other years, Alexa would have had her most precious things at school with her, but this semester, of course, she was living with a host family, and had taken only the barest of supplies—her laptop and MP3 player, some of her clothes, a camera.

Tamsin looked frantically through the drawers, wondering what was precious and what was only stuff. Bras and pretty underwear, pajamas of all sorts—she left them. She grabbed piles of journals, labeled by year, and tucked them into a box, took all the photos from the walls. Anything that looked vaguely memento-ish went into a box to be sorted later.

"I'll take these down," Deacon said, hefting two boxes. "You'd better move on and get your own stuff."

She turned in a circle, feeling both agony and a weird, lifting freedom. "What does any of this even mean?" she asked.

"You don't have time for existential questions," he said, and headed out of the room.

And the truth was, Tamsin wanted her fabrics. With one last glance over her shoulder, she raced downstairs, grabbed two good-sized boxes, and ran the three flights up to her studio, feeling in her quads the fact that she had been away from her exercise program—and all these stairs—for a few weeks.

The door to the room stood open—just as she'd left it. A beam of loss slammed into her chest, making her stagger backward for a moment.

This. Oh, this.

How much time had she spent here? Minutes upon hours upon days, weeks, months. *Years*. Through the windows, she could see clusters of seeds on the elm tree, green promise about to blow into the gardens and lawns of everyone in the neighborhood. The tree had always reminded her of a magic tree from a novel in her childhood, and she loved it as much as she did this house.

Oh, crap! She just loved it all, and this was maybe the worst day of her life, and if she wanted to cry, she was going to. She started pulling fabric from the shelves, all colors, all weights and threads, blue satin and white gauze and sturdy denim and clouds of silk. Over the years, she had found fabric everywhere, falling in love with patterns and colors—this, for example, this simple peach cotton, such an exquisite color. She put it in the box. All the fabric, squishing it down hard to make it fit. She filled another two boxes with notions, threads and buttons and plastic containers of beads, needles and pins and tape and scissors. She closed the little sewing machine and the longarm quilter, which was too heavy for her to carry down three flights of stairs. She took the small machine to the first floor, ran back up to get the boxes of fabrics.

For a long moment, she stood there, closing her eyes. "Thank you," she breathed, remembering thousands of hours of sewing and cutting, with music and color, and sunlight or starlight, flooding through her.

She ran her hands over the quilts, too. The most recent one she'd finished, the *Green Goddess*, which had been so highly praised, lay on the table, waiting to be sent to a studio for hanging. She put a hand on it, resentment rising in her. This was by far her best work! It wasn't fair that it should be sacrificed. The house and all of that belonged to Scott, but these quilts, everything she'd made all these years, belonged solely to her.

A wicked idea bloomed in her mind. What would happen if she crept back in here to get the quilts later? Maybe not all of them, but enough to sell to get a few hundred dollars on eBay?

What if she took some today? Glancing over her shoulder, she dumped one of the boxes of fabric and tucked two neatly folded quilts into the bottom of the box. On top of them, she shoved fabric scraps in tightly, covering the quilts. Her heart was pounding. She layered the rest of the fabric on top and carried the box downstairs, avoiding the gaze of the sheriff as she handed it to Father Jack.

No one even seemed interested. Maybe she should add a few more.

No, better not to press her luck. Instead, she headed for the bathroom on the main floor, where she closed the door and ran the water, to cover any sound. The window was tall and narrow, made of frosted glass. A bank of lilac bushes bloomed nearby, and would cast purple shadows into the room in springtime. She could fit through it okay, although it would be tight. Most important, it was reachable from the ground because the gas meter was right below it.

With hands shaking ever so slightly, she flushed the toilet and washed her hands and went back to the front. Deacon was coming in. "Can you and Father Jack get the quilting machine on the desk in my study?" she said.

"Quilting machine?" asked the female deputy. "That's not on this list of allowables."

"It's part of my livelihood."

The woman gave her a look devoid of sympathy. "I'd love to have a quilting machine. It's a luxury. It stays."

"But—!"

"You've got forty minutes. Finish up."

The back of Deacon's truck was filled with boxes. Where would they put them all in the little house? Tamsin went to the kitchen. Again that pang over the Viking range, the vast sweep of granite countertops, and the cool light coming in through the many windows. "I'll miss you, too," she said.

It didn't seem real, any of it. How could the life she'd lived for twenty-five years just be *over*, with no warning at all?

And yet, it appeared it was. Opening the cabinets, she made sure Father Jack had taken all the spices and condiments. She went through the drawers and grabbed a garlic press and three good knives, then knelt and took the wok out of a lower cupboard. Thinking of Elsa's mixed lot of dishes, she took out one bowl, one plate, one of her favorite iced tea glasses, and a knife, a fork, and a spoon. The rest . . .

She looked around. The framed art, the gleaming gadgets, the bread box and tall jars of rice, spaghetti, sugar, flour. All the antiques she had carefully collected . . .

Now part of her old life.

Outside, she saw the trunk had been wrestled onto the back of the truck. "I'm done," she said.

Elsa put an arm around her shoulder. "Let's go home."

With quiet urgency, she asked, "Did you get the earrings?"

A slight pause told Tamsin all she needed to know. "The jewelry was already confiscated."

Tamsin nodded. She did not allow herself to look back over her shoulder.

Chapter Fifteen

On the morning of the blessing of the fields, Elsa arrived early. She drove because she'd prepared food for the potluck, pie and vegetables and a main dish, bringing extra in case some people could not contribute. Sometimes, they ended up with a lot of bread or desserts, which was fine, but it was always good to have more solid food.

The church fellowship committee would set up tables outside for the potluck later, and she would help with that, but it was several hours before that would happen. She brought her food into the kitchen and put it on the counter.

This morning, she had heard from the board, who were indeed inviting Allen Tall Pine to be interim minister at her church. He wanted a three-month commitment, which was only a month longer than Elsa would have been away anyway. He would finish at the end of July. By then, Tamsin would be settled.

But the new development made her nervous, and all morning she had been trying to find ways to come to grips with her crisis of faith, so she could return to the ministry unburdened.

The first step would be to stop ignoring all of her spiritual practices. She had not meditated or said a prayer since December. That would be a good place to start.

After she put her food in the kitchen, she headed outside to the courtyard, which was cool and still and shadowy. Charlie pattered behind her, snuffling vainly around the bushes for the cat he'd flushed out before.

The statue of San Roque stood on a four-foot pedestal, his dog leaping toward him. The saint held a staff and his robe was lifted to show a suppurating wound. Beds of flowers grew to the right and left and behind him. Elsa sat down on one of the benches that faced him. Hyacinths bloomed along the edges of the path, and daffodils had sprouted their long straight leaves. Only two were blooming so far, bright yellow in the shadows.

Settling into a familiar position, hands loose in her lap, back straight, she took a long, slow breath and let it out. Even if it turned out that there was no God to hear her, she found comfort in the practice of breathing. In centering herself. Some people kept a journal. Elsa had always prayed.

For now, she let her hands lie loosely in her lap and looked up at San Roque, who was one of her favorite saints. Technically, he was called Saint Roch here, but she liked his Spanish name. He was a gentle priest who had fallen to plague or leprosy—the stories varied. Everyone deserted him but his dog, who not only stayed by his side, but healed his suppurating wounds by licking them. Ever after, the saint was known as the patron of dogs and pilgrims and plagues.

She was fond of him in part because she had not noticed him before the *camino*. But there, San Roque presided over many little churches, always with his dog at his knee. She knew his prayer, and parts of it floated through her mind as she sat there, breathing in the sweet softness of the spring morning, *San Roque, deliver us . . . from the scourges of God . . . preserve our bodies from contagious diseases and our souls from the contagion of sin . . . Assist us to make good use of health, to bear sufferings with patience . . .*

The words circled through her mind, easy, gentle, as she looked at the saint's face and his dog and the flowers. *Save our souls from the contagion of sin*. Despair was very much a sin in the Catholic Church. Even more so within the metaphysical movement, which proclaimed thought shaped everything.

By either measure, she had been in a distinctly unholy place for six months. "I don't know how to change this," she said aloud. "You will have to do it for me this time."

As if she'd just put down a very heavy suitcase, she felt relief drench her. C[illegible]die settled on her foot, a paw draped over her arch.

One habit of prayer she'd always practiced had been to ask for blessing on those in her world who were struggling. This morning, she began with her sister.

When they had returned to the house after dropping off most of Tamsin's things at a storage unit Elsa squeezed out of the budget, she had fallen onto the couch and lain there for a long time, not speaking, not sleeping, not crying. The boxes of her fabrics were piled in her small bedroom, and she had arranged her spices in the kitchen, along with the single plate, glass, bowl, and place setting of silver.

Elsa sat nearby, not speaking, a hand on her sister's ankle. Eventually, she got up and began to cook for the potluck, insisting at one point that Tamsin come have a small plate of bread and cheese and a glass of wine. She downed them dutifully, then went to her room and closed the door and stayed there the rest of the night.

The action caused an echo in the chambers of Elsa's memory. When they were children, Elsa had often been invisible in Tamsin's life. She was always closing her door on Elsa, shutting her out, keeping her at arm's length. Added to that, their parents had been weary of parenthood by the time Elsa arrived. It had been, in many ways, a very lonely house.

No wonder Elsa had found such pleasure in Joaquin's raucous household of what often felt like hundreds.

When Tamsin was a senior in college, Elsa a freshman in high school, their father died cleanly and suddenly, of a heart attack. Their mother, Helen, had never been one to fuss. She grieved quietly and simply, then found another husband within a year, a rancher from the northern part of the state. He, too, was widowed, with grown children, and he lived in relative luxury in a stone house on nine hundred acres in the foothills north of Denver.

Elsa had been a dutiful child, but she'd absolutely refused to move to a ranch in the country, 150 miles away from her high school, her boyfriend, her *life*. She was about to start her junior year of high school, and she could live on her own in the house. She had a job as a clerk at a bookstore. It couldn't pay all her bills, but her soon-to-be stepfather, eager to have his wife to himself, was more than happy to subsidize her.

And Tamsin, as it turned out. She arrived on Elsa's doorstep one rainy Saturday in October, all of her belongings piled into her car. She'd graduated with a degree in fine arts from CU Boulder, and had been working part-time at a small Denver museum when she found out that her boyfriend was married. Furious, brokenhearted, she fled the big city for home.

That was the year that the sisters had solidified their relationship. Tamsin was enough older that she could offer her sister some guidance, and Elsa was a steadying influence on her flyaway nature. They took turns cooking and cleaning and shopping, and kept each other company, and learned to respect each other's ways.

Tamsin did not mind that Joaquin slept over when he could manage it. Elsa did not mind when Tamsin met a man more than a dozen years her senior, who was smitten with her at first sight. Tamsin was cautious, but enjoyed Scott's attention, and made sure he was not married. He was a stockbroker and investment counselor. Over time, she'd fall in love with his big booming laugh, his tenderness toward her, his hunger to make a home and family. Within a year, Tamsin married Scott at a very fancy, upscale wedding in the Bahamas.

Sitting now at the foot of San Roque, Elsa frowned. She would have put a large sum of money down on the fact that Scott had *adored* Tamsin and Alexa. How could he have done this to them?

"If any saint is listening, please bless my sister. Bring a sense of meaning into her life, and heal this terrible wound." Elsa stood, plucked a hyacinth, and angled it delicately across San Roque's foot. It couldn't hurt anything.

She started violently when Joaquin said, "Good morning." He laughed gently and touched her shoulder. "I'm sorry. I didn't know you had not heard me. Were you praying?"

"Thinking, mainly."

He brushed away some dirt from the statue's podium. Touched the flower Elsa had placed on the saint's foot. "Tamsin?"

"Yes. Let's be sure she has plenty to do."

"She has the garden."

"She also liked serving food at the soup kitchen. We'll have her do something there." They fell into step, walking toward the end of the courtyard and into the sunshine, where they also stopped in sync. Each of them lifted an arm to shade their eyes from the sun. It made Elsa smile, how easily their bodies meshed into the old patterns.

"Look at that," she said. Plots had been measured and fenced, with a placard in front of each with a number, and soon, a name. "That's your doing, Father Jack. A trash heap into a garden."

"It is beautiful," he said. He looked down at her. "It was your doing, too."

"Mostly Deacon, I think. He's spent a lot of hours out here."

Joaquin nodded, looked back at the field. "You know he was in prison, don't you?"

She inclined her head. "Don't do that."

"What?"

"Try to discount him because you think he might be attracted to me."

He swallowed, giving himself away. "Are you attracted to him, too?"

For one long moment, she let herself admire her old lover's beautiful mouth, but it was the fantasy of Deacon's naked back that rose in her vision. "He's not my type."

Some of the tension left Joaquin's shoulders. "I agree." He turned toward the rectory. "Want some breakfast? We missed yesterday."

Elsa shook her head, taking a step back from him. "No thanks. I'm going to wander out and look at everything before we get started."

He paused for a single beat, regarding her. Then nodded. "See you after a while, then." He clapped his hands together and admired the sky. "It's a beautiful day for a blessing!"

Elsa raised her face to the blazing blue sky. "It is."

Joaquin did not go eat. Instead, he took his betraying flesh into the chapel and knelt before the Blessed Mother, squeezing his eyes tight, pressing his fists to his forehead.

It was not so easy to have Elsa around like this. He'd known that it would be this way, which was why he had resisted bringing her home, despite the prompts.

In many ways, he took pleasure in her proximity, especially the ease they felt in each other's company, in the unexpected and comforting way they fell into sync, as they had just outside. Her company for Friday morning breakfasts felt like one of the truest things in his life.

And yet, there was the trouble, too. He had not become a priest because he'd fallen out of love with her. He had answered a call so insistent that God had left him no choice.

"Blessed Mother," he prayed now, fiercely. Thick emotion came into his throat. "I had to bring her back here because you insisted, and it is true that she was broken and needed to come. But the struggle is much more difficult than I imagined. Help me. I have found joy in my work, but I am only a man."

When Elsa and Joaquin had parted ways after the *camino*, they had agreed that they would not speak for a year, to give both of them time to get used to the new order between them.

Joaquin had enrolled in seminary, while Elsa wandered in Europe. She never spoke much of that time, and he had not asked. He was afraid she had suffered badly.

One year later, she returned to the States and was admitted to the Unity ordination program. Their first contact was when she called to tell him the news, and it had shocked him deeply that she, who had been more devout than he at times, should turn her back on the Catholic Church. She said simply, "If I could be a priest, that's what I would do. Since I don't have that option, I'll be a minister."

Hope surged in him. "You could be a nun."

"No," she said firmly. "I will not. It is not the same thing and you know it."

Ever since, all these years, *all* these years, they had talked on the phone at least once a week. They shared their path through their religious educations, through their first assignments and roles in church leadership. Every now and then, they had seen each other for a couple of days, over the holidays, or if one happened to be close to the city where the other one lived.

Joaquin had settled, with more joy than he had suspected he'd feel, into the life of a priest. He was fulfilled. Devoted. Every morning when he awakened, he knew exactly why he was on the planet—to serve and help others, to ease their way, to shepherd them if he could, into more meaningful lives.

He thought that he'd released his carnal impulses. No other

woman had tempted him in the slightest, even when they were trying their utmost to do so. It was only Elsa who stirred him. Elsa who tempted him.

Her continued presence now underscored everything he'd given up for the priesthood—wife, love, family.

With a deep breath, he rose, and instead of fixing his breakfast, he went to his sparsely furnished bedroom, changed into his running clothes, and headed out, a rosary wrapped around his wrist. It was a good morning for a long run.

As he ran, he prayed. *Holy Mary, mother of God, blessed art thou among women . . .*

Elsa was helping to attach thin cotton tablecloths to the tables that were set up in the center of the field when Tamsin arrived. She looked wan and tired, but her hair had been washed and pulled off of her face, and she'd applied a little blush. She carried a pot of noodles and a box of doughnuts. She had borrowed the money for the doughnuts from Elsa, who gave it gladly.

"Where are the boys?" Tamsin asked.

Smiling, Elsa pointed. "You're going to be such a hero."

"I let them down before." She strode toward them, tall and lean and still gorgeous. Spying her and the box, the boys leapt forward, yelling. Calvin, dressed in a plaid man's shirt that hung down to his knees, flung his arms around her waist. Her hand went to his head.

Elsa nodded to herself. Perfect.

Deacon came over. "How's she doing this morning?"

"She's here," Elsa replied. "That's a lot."

"And you? How are you this fine morning, Miss Elsa?" He held the tablecloth while she attached a plastic clamp. "Excited?"

"I am." She couldn't help but grin at him. "I have the seeds and plan for the kids' garden, and they're so excited, and I have my personal packets of seeds, too. I can't wait to get started. How 'bout you?"

"I started seedlings inside, so I have actual plants. If you're real nice, I'll share with you."

"Well," she said, blinking with pretend innocence, "I did make pecan pie and collard greens for my contributions today."

He sucked his lower lip into his mouth. "Collards with *bacon*?"

"Of course. They are very good, if I do say so myself. I even brought some hot pepper sauce."

"Oh, hell, sweetheart, you can have all my bedding plants for that."

She laughed. "What did you grow?"

"Come see." He led her to his truck, where three flats of seventy-five plants were waiting. He pointed. "Onions, peppers—both sweet and hot—lettuce, and of course, collards."

"You must have started planting the minute we brought this up!"

"Pretty much." He jumped easily onto the bed. "I knew people would need them. Let's carry this over to the rest of the supplies." He picked up a flat and put it in her arms, pointing her toward the place where he'd set up rakes and shovels and seed packets, all for rent or sale at very low prices. "Your one-stop garden shop," he said.

"This is terrific! Where did you get all the tools?"

"Culled them from every Goodwill and Salvation Army from here to Denver. The handles are a little splintery on some, but they'll work."

She looked at all of the supplies, thought of all the work he'd done, the time he'd spent, and put a hand on his arm. "Thank you, Deacon. You've done so much. You're my hero, you know?"

He looked at her, and Elsa didn't turn away, wondering if there might really be something blooming between them.

A sense of anticipation skittered over the top of her skin, brushing the back of her neck, her elbows, her belly. His eyes were shaded by a baseball cap, so their color was a simple dark blue, and his mouth was very still. He put his hand over hers. "Thank *you*," he said simply. The words were craggy.

Yes, she thought, this was something possible. The thought made her smile. "Let's get this party started."

Together they carried the flats over and put them on a table. Deacon used a pair of heavy shears to cut the plastic trays into singles and ceremoniously handed Elsa a collard, a tomato, and an onion. "They'll go fast."

"Thank you," she said. "When I have a good harvest, I'll return your kindness by making you a nice meal. How's that?"

"I'll look forward to it."

By ten, the families were gathered in the field. Deacon's truck was parked at the north end, nearest the apartments. He stood in the bed with Joaquin, while the crowd gathered around them, young and old, children and parents, teens from the church looking scrubbed and shiny. Elsa stood next to Tamsin.

Joseph stood to one side with his drum, and as everyone gathered, he banged it once to get their attention. Faces turned toward Father Jack. He wore his vestments and his face was darkly handsome above them, his hair falling over his forehead, as ever, too straight and slick to stay in place.

"Good morning!" he called.

Elsa did not go to Mass, so she wasn't used to seeing Joaquin in his priestly attire. It made him look different. Powerful. With a cold little shock, she realized that she'd never heard him offer a sermon or a blessing or anything else. A tiny ripple of fear moved through her and she reached for her sister's arm and slid her hand around it. The sisters stepped closer together.

Joaquin said, "We are here this morning to ask a blessing on these fields, that they might be fertile and nourishing and life-giving, that they will offer us a chance to build community and relationships and bring more of God's love and light into the world."

His voice, Elsa thought, was booming and rich, just the right timbre to carry over the heads of the people. He spread his hands, palms up. His fingers were long and graceful. A woman murmured behind them, "We are so lucky to have Father Jack!"

"'Our help is in the name of the Lord,'" Father Jack said in invitation.

The crowd murmured, "*Who made heaven and earth.*"

"The Lord be with you!"

"*May he also be with you.*"

It had been more than sixteen years since Elsa had heard these words, since she had turned her back on the Catholic Church for the second time, in Santiago. The sound of them strummed a forgotten chord in her chest, and she found herself vibrating unexpectedly with it. She looked away from Joaquin, frowning a little, suddenly apprehensive.

Deacon stood with his arms folded, but Elsa saw him gesture to someone in the crowd. Then she spied the three boys, sneaking through the rows of people, tiptoeing with exaggerated silence toward some goal only they understood. Deacon shook his head. They halted, making gestures of protest. He pulled his brows together, pointed. Deflated, they slunk away.

Father Jack said, "Let us pray."

The crowd rustled, bowing their heads. Elsa watched, detached, and let the prayer glance over her.

"God, from whom every good has its beginning and from whom it receives its increase, we beg you to hear our prayers, so that what we begin for your honor and glory may be brought to a happy ending by the gift of your eternal wisdom; through Christ our Lord."

"*Amen*," said the crowd.

Across the field of Elsa's memory walked a girl, always one of the smallest in her class. Her hair was pulled mercilessly back into a braid her mother wrestled into place every morning, bemoaning the wild curls. It wasn't until junior high that Elsa had rebelled against the braid and realized that her scalp didn't have to ache all the time.

But this girl still wore the braid, and she wore modest dresses to church, even then preferring simple straight lines to fancier styles. She loved Mass. Loved the call, the invitation, the smell of incense, the bells. The church on summer mornings smelled of roses, of the Blessed Mother, with whom Elsa found much more acceptance than her own mother gave her. That devout, passionate girl stood in the nave, burning with the desire to serve.

Joaquin's voice drifted through the vision. "And at our lowly coming, through the merits and prayers of your saints, may demons flee and the Angel of Peace be at hand . . ."

The words strummed over the strings of the devoted young girl Elsa had been, and the emotions of long ago swelled in her woman's body.

"Ow," Tamsin whispered, pulling her arm away. "You're holding on too tightly."

"Sorry."

Elsa focused on Joaquin, who was now blurred into Father Jack, the two parts of him crossing like a hologram, first the priest, then the man standing in front. He held up a chalice of holy water.

"That you bless these fields," he said, and there was now a new, more powerful and commanding tone to his voice. As if he *did* embody something bigger than himself, and all those rituals that he'd partaken in at his solemn ordination—his hands rubbed with oil sanctified in mystic rituals on Maundy Thursday, the ancient Latin words spoken over his young head—had truly transformed him. Elsa found herself transfixed as she watched his familiar face become something new.

"*We beg you to hear us*," the crowd rumbled in response.

"That you bless and consecrate these fields!"

"*We beg you to hear us*."

"That you bless . . ." His voice seemed to amplify and deepen, spreading over the entire block. ". . . and consecrate and protect from diabolical *destruction* these fields."

"We beg you to hear us."

"That you mercifully ward off and dispel from this place all lightning, hailstorms, destructive tempests, and harmful floods."

"We beg you to hear us."

Elsa found she was trembling as the priest led the people in an Our Father, which she had learned to call the Lord's Prayer, the words so dear and old and powerful that she had to close her eyes. The people chanted it, each voice dear and sweet and true, one lower, one higher, all of them offering up themselves and their hopes and fears.

"And lead us not into temptation, but deliver us from evil. Send forth your spirit and all things shall be re-created, and you shall renew the face of the earth and the Lord shall manifest His goodness, and the earth shall yield her fruit."

Elsa became aware that she was shaking, and tears were rolling down her cheeks. In her ministry, she had met many, many refugees from the Catholic Church. Often a group of "recovering Catholics," as they called themselves, would share horror stories of what they had escaped—the fear and the inflexibility.

Elsa always wanted to say, "*But what about the beauty and the ritual? What about the Blessed Mother? What about confession and repentance, which on a purely practical level is a very powerful tool?*"

Standing in the field, with the sun overhead and the sound of the first Catholic ritual that she had heard in a very long time ringing through her body, Elsa admitted to herself that she missed Catholicism desperately.

The first time she turned her back on God, Elsa was fourteen. As a child, Elsa had burned with a dream of the priesthood for herself. Joaquin was an altar boy, a task that was closed to her. In some places, she had heard, girls were allowed to be altar servers, but there were none in Pueblo, not even any in Colorado that she had ever heard of.

None of the other girls cared, but Elsa burned to perform the rituals. She had begged her mother to talk to the priest, and lobbied Joaquin to put in a good word for her, had even written a shy letter to the priest to request his consideration.

He wouldn't even talk to her about it. The subject seemed to make him angry, and Elsa had learned to avoid it.

But every time Joaquin donned the robes and carried in the cross, she sat in the nave with the other parishioners, her blood so alive with jealousy that she feared sometimes her veins might suddenly burst into rivers of flame. She ached to wear the satiny robes, to carry the cross, to step into the holy space of the sanctuary and offer the priest water for his hands, and the chalice to be filled with the holy blood of Christ.

Oh, the honor of it!

For two years, she had been sick with this longing. She would overcome the sin of envy, confess it, and try to focus on the things that were open to her. Not being a nun, which everyone said she should be. Nuns always seemed so subservient in her eyes, only powerful when there were no priests to lord over them.

No, she didn't want to be a nun. She wanted to be a priest, a leader in the church. Surely, she thought, by the time she grew up things would be different. Why would God plant this fierce hunger for the priesthood in her if she wasn't meant to follow that path?

Over and over, week in and week out, she boiled with longing, fell prey to her jealousy, then confessed and started over.

One afternoon, her mother dropped her off at the church early. Later there would be a meeting of the Youth for Christ, but she was the first person there. She carried her potluck dish into the kitchen then, emboldened by the silence in the building, wandered up the hallway. The nave was empty.

Elsa slipped inside, telling herself that she was only going to sit and pray for a while, perhaps light a candle. On one side of the sanctuary reigned the Blessed Mother in her blue robes, her kindly face seeming to encourage Elsa to move forward.

She sat in the very first row, her hands in her lap. Candles flickered in petition on either side of the nave, to Mary and to St. Therese. There was no sound, not anywhere in the church, and it wasn't the sort of local spot where old ladies would come and sit and pray all day. They were home now, fixing supper. The priest was probably going to have his supper soon too, in the rectory.

She glanced over her shoulder, her heart pounding, and stood up. Before she could chicken out, she moved toward the sanctuary. At the foot of the stairs, she stopped, and looked around again to make sure no one else was about.

Then she climbed the steps into the sanctuary, her heart in her throat. She could feel the veil of holiness as she crossed into it, a hush of grace, as if Jesus himself held it in His embrace. She could feel it on her skin, and taste it in her throat.

Cloaked in awe, in joy, she turned and faced the pews. Standing there, she imagined herself resplendent in the robes of a priest, vestments shining over her shoulders, and she raised her arms, quietly reciting the priest's part of the call to worship: "Our help is in the name of the Lord."

She imagined the swell of voices returning, *Who made heaven and earth.*

"The Lord be with you!" she said, spreading her hands in priestly fashion.

Imaginary voices responded, *May He also be with you.*

A swell of joy moved through her body, almost lifting her feet off the floor, and she moved toward the altar table, still imagining she was the priest, forgetting that she was only a girl. She ached to ring the little bell, but did not dare. Instead she lifted the chalice, feeling the vibration of love and tradition and *God* in the very molecules of it, her head light as down, her heart swelling with the honor of it. *Oh, please,* she said to the heavens. *Please let me be a priest.*

The first blow caught her across the ear, and she fell sideways, dropping the chalice on the floor. "Stinking daughter of Eve!" the priest roared. "How dare you foul this sacred space with your fetid, unholy sin!"

Elsa scrambled to capture the chalice before it rolled down the steps. "I'm sorry—"

He hauled her up by her arms, his fingers digging into her flesh like pincers. His face only inches away from her, he screamed, "How dare you!"

Elsa yanked away from him, terrified, guilty, and cowered, tears rising in her eyes. "I'm sorry! I just wanted to know how it felt to be a priest!"

His face was purple with rage. "Women *cannot* serve! By their very existence they are the containers of all evil, the original sin. You have fouled this holy place!"

Elsa began to back away, and stumbled, falling to her knees. She picked up the chalice and offered it to him, ducking away as he released a howl of such fury that for a moment Elsa feared he might kill her.

"Get out!" he cried. "Get out! Get out, get out!"

Sobbing, she scrambled to her feet, snot running down her face. And there, at the back of the nave, were four of the boys who did serve. They had expressions of horror on their faces, and at first, Elsa mistook it for pity, that they were shocked that the priest should behave so badly.

But as she ran toward them, some of them her friends, boys she had known for years, one of them spit on her. "What were you doing?" Another pinched her, hard, on the upper arm.

She could feel the danger in them even before the priest screamed, "Out, Eve's whore!"

She fled. And she did not return for four years.

* * *

In the field, listening to the words she had so loved once upon a time, she could still feel the horror of that long-ago day. As an adult, she saw that the priest had been deeply wrong, but that didn't change what had happened.

As a high school senior project, Elsa had volunteered for a local political agency that provided shelter, food, and financial assistance to the immigrants, legal and illegal, who swarmed north from Mexico to work in the fields. It was led by a devoted and passionate nun.

Dorothy brought Elsa back to the Church. She led by example, providing the hands of God for the lost and hungry and lonely. She connected Elsa to the very best of the Church, the arm that served the homeless and hungry and poor, all over the world, in concrete ways.

So she returned to Mass. She studied comparative religions, trying to find her place in the Church and its place in her life. She walked the Camino as a pilgrim, an act of petition that had ended with punishment and loss.

Joaquin's voice, not Father Jack's, said with vast kindness, in the fields, "Almighty God, we humbly appeal to your kindness, asking that you pour out the dew of your blessing on these fields."

Elsa felt tears streaming, streaming, streaming down her face, and it suddenly made her furious. Abruptly, she turned and made her way blindly through the crowd. Joaquin's voice followed, filled with numinous power: "Wipe out any infertility from this land, thus filling the hungry with an abundance of good things, so that the poor and needy may praise your wondrous name forever and ever."

"*Amen,*" said the crowd.

She had no idea where she was even going, just that she needed to leave the crowd. She made her way to the courtyard, where bright sunlight now poured down over San Roque, and there was her own dog, asleep at his feet.

He leapt up when he saw her, big feathery tail wagging apologetically. She knelt and put her arms around his shoulders and let go of the tears. They were not noisy, but violent, silent heaves. Charlie made tiny whimpering sounds, and eventually shifted to lick her face, her neck, putting his paw on her shoulder to hold her still.

What was she mourning? The Church, Kiki, her own lost ministry? It was all a tangle, triggered painfully by the familiarity of the words she had so loved.

As she leaned into her dog's hot fur, letting him comfort her, she said to the universe at large, "Show me that you are really there. And where I'm meant to be. Where do you want me to go?" She squeezed her eyes tight. "I am so lost."

Then, aware there would be others drifting this way soon, she got to her feet and headed into the church. Charlie padded behind her in concern, even following her into the ladies' room, where she washed her face with cold water—very, very cold water—to ease the red around her eyes and mouth. She looked at herself in the mirror. "What the heck was that?"

Her sad eyes looked back at her. *He deserted you*.

Joaquin.

And God.

Quite a pair.

And yet, the people still needed to be fed. They still needed the help of those who would not judge them. Today she would help the children plant their garden, and plant the collards Deacon had given her, and give her sister a task to do. She would simply be present, for anyone. For all of them.

She did not need God to tell her that. "Come on, Charlie," she said, squaring her shoulders, pulling open the door. "Let's go plant some corn."

Everyone was headed toward their plots as she returned to the field. Elsa did the same. Tamsin was in their garden, gloves on her hands, looking at the soft open space with fierce intent. "Did you bring the map I drew?"

From her back pocket, Elsa pulled the folded map. "Yes. This is a sketch. We need to add collards."

"Okay." Tamsin pointed to the northwest corner of the plot. "Corn there. And beans. Sunflowers along that edge."

Elsa knelt in the earth, smelling the heady, damp fertility of it. Joseph and Joaquin were rounding the fields, drumming and dispersing holy water. Elsa ignored them when they paused by their plot, but a sprinkle of water touched her head. She glared at Joaquin, who had done it on purpose. He winked and moved along in his white satin vestments.

She thought of roosters crowing in the twilight of dawn, and smelled, briefly, the sweetness of churros frying in hot fat.

Long ago.

With her spade, she made a row. It clicked against something in the dirt. She paused, and put her fingers in the soil, fluttering around until she pulled out a string of beads. They were pale green quartz, carved like leaves. Even with dirt all over them, she could see they were beautiful.

Then she noticed the pale pink carved quartz roses between each decade of leaves. And the clear quartz cross at the bottom. A rosary.

For one long minute, Elsa held them up, shaking her head. Light touched the beads, setting them aglow, and she could see the rosary would be very beautiful once she washed it. "Good start," she said aloud, "but it's going to take more than that."

"Who are you talking to?" Tamsin said.

"No one," Elsa said, and tucked the beads into her pocket.

In a plot on the other side of the field, Calvin helped his mother. Paris had specially asked for the day off from the nursing home, and it was good to be outside with her son. She had too many seeds, she knew that, but when she'd found out she could buy them with her food stamps, she'd gone to the dollar store and picked out a bunch of things. Lettuce and peas, which they could eat early; potatoes, which she'd taken from old potatoes in the house, red potatoes growing eyes that she cut into pieces like her mama had always done, and now planted deep. "This is good earth," she told Calvin. "See how dark it is?"

He nodded seriously, and smelled it when she did, his big eyes always taking everything in. The sun sparkled over the top of his head and she could see his handsome daddy in him, but some of her, too, in his good cheekbones and his smile. "I still don't like peas, though."

"Maybe you'll like them better when they're fresh and you pick them yourself."

"How are y'all doing here?" asked Mario's Big Brother. She had to squint to look up at him, and he noticed and moved around to the other side. "Sorry about that."

"We're doing fine, thank you. Got the lettuce and peas in, and fixing to put in squash and corn."

"You've done this before, I think." His smile was kind, lighting up the sadness in his eyes. "You're a Southerner, like me."

"Kentucky," she said, and ducked her head, suddenly wishing that she could go back there, to her old town and her family. It had been rash, leaving. She picked up a packet of pumpkin seeds and shook it. The big seeds rattled inside. "How about you?"

"Mississippi, long time ago now."

"Deacon, look!" Calvin said, showing him a small cellophane package of beans. "These here are my magic beans. We got 'em in school. You know about magic beans? They grow to the sky!"

"You don't say!" Deacon admired the seeds. "I can't wait to see what happens!"

Calvin looked at the seeds very closely, his shy look. "Maybe a vine will grow all the way to heaven and I'll ask Jesus for a dog."

"Hmmm."

"Grown-ups never believe in things like that, but sometimes they're true. I know it."

"I reckon you're right, son. We need children to remind us that there's magic in the world yet. Thank you."

Calvin looked up. "You're welcome."

"Ms. Jennings, would it be all right with you if Calvin comes with Mario and me sometimes? And maybe it'd be okay if I took the little tyke on his own now and again?"

Paris raised her chin. She knew all about how somebody could seem to be nice and end up being not nice at all. "I'll think about it."

"That's fine, honey. Let me know." He straightened. "You have fun now, Calvin."

Calvin turned and looked at his mother. "If Jesus sends me a dog, you have to let me keep it, you know. It would be a sin not to."

She laughed softly, pretty sure nobody was delivering a dog. "I hope he sends bags of dog food, too, 'cuz we sure can't afford it."

Chapter Sixteen

Elsa had bought a dozen popsicle sticks from the church booth run by the teens, and now she stuck the last empty seed packet onto a stick and poked it into the corner of a square Tamsin had paced off with her feet, insisting it would be easier to grow the garden if it wasn't arranged in long rows. "There," Elsa said. "Done." She stood up next to her sister and slapped her gloves together. "What do you think of that?"

The squares were visible now. "We have to get something to mark the edges," Tamsin said. "Maybe string and spikes or something like that would be easy. Or rocks."

"Good idea. After lunch though. I'm starving." She took off her gloves and slapped one against Tamsin's arm. "How about you?"

She shrugged.

"Let's go wash our hands."

Walking through the middle of the field with her sister, Elsa peeked into the gardens, smiling at the other farm-holders, who smiled back. The sound of happy voices and laughter filled the air. Children chased one another through the pathways between plots, and not a few dogs trotted along behind them, Charlie among them. He spied Elsa and came running forward, his tongue lolling. "You look thirsty, big boy. C'mon, let's find a trough for all these dogs, shall we?"

In the kitchen, she found an old stainless steel bowl and carried it outside to the little bricked area by the statue of San Roque. Deep, cool shade grew behind him. She filled the bowl and put it down in the shade, and whistled for the dogs, who came racing and dove into the water with eager slurping, pushing one another out of the way.

Tamsin had gone ahead to wash her hands and she came out now with her hair loose down her back, her face and hands clean. A little sunburn gave her cheekbones some color. "You and your dogs," she said with a shake of her head. "It would never even occur to me to get a bowl and give them some water."

"It's not your job. You know how to make gardens grow in squares."

Tamsin smiled. "I'll meet you over there."

Once the dogs had been watered, Elsa refilled the bowl for the last time and headed inside to the ladies' room. She had it to herself. The first thing she did was pull the rosary out of her pocket, running it under warm water to wash away the dirt. It was a beauty, pale green leaves carved of what might have been jade, alternating with roses carved out of pink quartz, all strung on heavy string. Substantial.

She dried it and tucked it back in her pocket, taking a moment then to try to tame her hair and wash the dust off her face. The sun had kissed her, too, had made her look rested and healthy. Thinking of how lovely her sister looked, she plucked at her plain T-shirt, wishing she had a bit more chest, or *some* extraordinary feature, but she was honest with herself. Her eyes were an ordinary dark blue, her dark hair too curly, her face too full of angles to be pretty.

She plucked a few more curls from her tight bun, letting them frame her face a little, fall down her neck. Better.

When she returned to the field to join her sister at the tables that had been set up, Tamsin was already sitting with Deacon, making him laugh. "Hi, guys," Elsa said.

Deacon stood up. "We've been waiting for you so we can all eat together."

"Oh! Thanks." She didn't bother to sit down, because her stomach growled in earnest. "Let's do it."

But when they got to the food, the collards were gone, the bowl empty with a lone green leaf at the bottom.

"Poor Deacon," Tamsin said, her hand on his arm. "Look at that face."

He glanced at Elsa and she saw that he was truly disappointed. "I'm so sorry."

"I think I'm gonna have to beg for that dinner you keep promising."

Flustered, Elsa said, "Um. Yes. When?"

He leaned into her slightly. "Soon."

"Well, aside from Wednesday nights, when I'm busy with prep for the soup kitchen, we don't really have much on our schedule, do we, sis?"

Tamsin plucked a single slice of cucumber from her plate airily. "Speak for yourself. I have a job."

"You do?" Elsa laughed. "What? Where? When do you start?"

Tamsin unmistakably blushed. "Well, it's not exactly the Ritz. Fabric department at Walmart, thanks to the quilting list. Somebody there knew somebody in the fabric department and they called me this morning."

"Tamsin, that's great. You'll even like it."

She lifted one brow. "I guess. It's something."

Elsa spied a dish at the end of the row. "Look! There's one piece of pie left, Deacon. You want it?"

"Split it with me?"

"I can make me a pie whenever I feel like it," she said, leaning over to scoop up the lone slice. She put it on his plate. "You've worked really hard on this project. I appreciate it."

"It's you who's made it happen, Elsa." For one little moment, that vine twined around them again, binding ankle to ankle, as he looked at her. His eyes twinkled, but there was also something solid and real there. "But you're welcome."

"It was all three of you," Tamsin added as Joaquin joined them.

"What was?" he asked.

"Worked hard on the garden." Tamsin put a square of red Jell-O and fruit on her plate. It wiggled, still firmly set despite sitting on the table for a half hour. Anemic fruit cocktail grapes peeked through the gelatin. "Don't forget that Father Jack started the whole thing."

"Jeez, Tamsin, you are such a flirt."

She tossed her head with exaggerated coquetry. "Not everyone has such a handsome priest."

Joaquin grinned, and half the old ladies who were politely serving up food swooned. They urged him to try their special dishes. "Have a piece of my chocolate cake, Father," said a woman with clipped short black hair and hands gnarled by arthritis. "And my macaroni and cheese," said another. By the time he reached the end of the line, his paper plate was groaning.

They all sat together, though before Joaquin could actually take a bite, a man in his forties, dressed tidily in Clothes Purchased Just for Gardening, said, "Father, may I have a word with you?"

"Of course." Joaquin grabbed a cookie from the plate and walked away with the man, his head bent politely.

Tamsin asked, "Did they do that to you, Elsa? Talk to you all the time they need something?"

"Of course. That's the nature of the job." She took a bite of the macaroni and cheese; it really was quite good. "Did you taste this, Deacon?"

"No. Are you offering?"

She forked up a bite and put it on his plate.

"Didn't it drive you crazy, people needing you constantly like that?"

Elsa thought of the long line of people waiting to hug her after services, how some of them would have tears of illumination in their eyes, and how some would hold on hard for a long moment, conscious of the other people behind them, but unwilling to let go too fast.

She thought again, with longing, of the way the congregation had looked in her direction when she stood up to speak, their upturned faces expectant. "No." She took a breath. "I loved it."

"How long are you on sabbatical?" Deacon asked.

"It was supposed to be for six months, which meant I would go back in June. But there have been some complications."

"You didn't tell me that," Tamsin said.

Elsa waved a hand. "The man who took over for me had to have emergency knee surgery, so he's out. They've brought someone else in, and he wanted a three-month commitment." She speared a potato from the salad. "So, now I'm here through July."

"Are you going to go back?" Tamsin asked. "I thought you were done with it."

"I don't want to be. I just don't . . ." She didn't even know how to express her doubts. "I just have to figure some things out."

Deacon, sitting beside her, said quietly, "I told you my daddy was a preacher."

"Really?" Tamsin asked.

He nodded, still talking to Elsa. "He lost his faith for a time, struggled with it for a year or two, but in those days, there wasn't any way for him to say that out loud, that maybe he hadn't been called by a God that maybe didn't even exist. He had to keep preaching."

She knew he was trying to be helpful. In her pocket was the

rosary she'd found, a knot that was somehow hot against the fold of her leg. "It was a lot harder in those days."

"I don't know about that. It's always hard to . . ." He poked the potato salad. "Be an emissary. A person of God."

The press of emotion that had so overwhelmed her earlier rose again against the back of her throat, and she said, "I don't really want to talk about this."

"Fair enough." His blue eyes had the gleam of a pearly marble she'd had as a child. Such clear eyes seemed as if they could see too much. "About dinner—how's Friday evening work for you?"

She found herself smiling. "Friday is fine."

A murmur rose from the crowd gathered around the tables, coming toward them on a wave. Elsa heard the worry in it and looked up to see the three gang boys striding up the center path between the newly planted gardens. The tall one who had touched her neck with his knife was at the center, clearly the leader, a smirk on his face. They didn't do anything but walk through, snickering and jostling one another, looking down their noses at the people who turned their faces away, curled bodies around their small children.

Elsa asked, "Where's Joaquin?"

"What?" Tamsin said. "I think he was "

Elsa was already on her feet, jogging diagonally across the path, dashing down another, narrower aisle between plots. Joaquin stood on the west side of the field, his back to them as he talked to someone smaller than he was.

She grabbed his arm and he turned around, startled, and then spied the gangbangers veering around the church. The leader turned back and lifted his chin toward her, or Joaquin. Maybe both. A boy with a white cat in his arms came out of the courtyard, watching sadly. Elsa suddenly recognized him, by the rose tattoo on his face. He met her eyes.

When Joaquin's arm tensed, she simply stood there, holding on. "This is not a time for confrontation."

"They can't be allowed to intimidate people."

"True, but let's just let them go for now and come up with some ideas to address it in the next week or so, okay? There will probably be people here all the time and that will discourage them."

"Will it?"

With a firmness she did not feel, she said, "Yes."

Deacon found himself a little nervous as he parked his truck in front of the sisters' house on Friday night. It was a small place, like many of the houses in the area, a no-frills 1920's bungalow with a deep porch and a giant elm tree arching over it. In front were a small patch of grass and a strip of flower bed. Lilacs lined the driveway. When the flowers bloomed, they would fill the nights with a narcotic scent.

They had not drawn the curtains and as he approached, Deacon could see them through the picture window. Tamsin set the table, her long blond hair pulled away from her face into a braid that fell down her lean back. Once upon a time, she would have been his type. Lucinda, his ex-wife, was a tall, lean blonde like this. As his daughter, Jenny, would be, by now.

Loss ached in him for a minute, making him pause. Every time you put yourself out there, you might take a hit. Was he ready to take a chance as a sober man? He'd had his share of women since leaving prison, though not as many as he might've had when he was still drinking. He hadn't wanted to settle with any of them.

Tonight, he only had eyes for Elsa, with her small, taut body and black curls and unaffected face. If she wore makeup, he couldn't detect it. Not that he had anything against makeup, but she didn't need it. Her skin was smooth and olive, her eyes bright, her mouth a hearty rose that bloomed with good health. That was what it was, he decided as he climbed the steps. Her good health showed on her face.

He smoothed a hand over his own hair before he knocked. He'd brought a big bunch of sunflowers, sunny and enormous, and when Elsa opened the door and spied them, she gave a happy cry. "They look like sunshine!" She gestured him inside. "Come in, come in!"

"That's what I thought, too," he said, and stepped over the threshold. The scent of supper enveloped him, onions and pork and something sweet. "Mmm. Smells great."

"It will taste even better," she said with that saucy little smile.

He wasn't a man short on comebacks and flirtations. You could even say it had been one of his life pursuits. And yet all he could think when she gave him that grin was that he wished he was a better man. Not because she was a minister, which didn't unnerve him as it might have some others, but because that smile deserved to be met with the same sweetness with which it was given. A man who'd spent damn near twenty years in a whiskey bottle didn't have much sweetness left in him.

"Deacon, it's good to see you," the sister said, coming forward, her hand outstretched. "You remember me, right?"

And with her, it was easier. "How could any man forget you, sweetheart?"

"Oh, brother!" Elsa said with a laugh, and headed toward the kitchen, flowers in hand.

Tamsin tilted her head and accepted his homage as her due. She gestured toward the table. "Sit down. Can I get you something to drink? Wine? Beer, iced tea?"

"Iced tea, please." He appreciated the fact that Elsa had plainly not said, *Deacon, who runs the AA group, is coming over tonight. Hide the liquor.* Always excruciating.

As she fetched it, he looked around, not settling yet. The music was something he couldn't quite identify, a woman singer he thought he knew from the radio, not exactly what he would have expected from Elsa. Though now that he thought about it, he wasn't at all sure what kind of music he'd imagined she would like. And maybe she hadn't chosen the music anyway.

Noticing his thoughts chasing around like squirrels, he shook his head slightly. Crossed his arms. "Sure I can't help in there?"

Elsa, standing in view beneath an archway to the tiny kitchen, laughed. "There's not even room for two, much less three."

Tamsin reemerged with his tea. He nodded his thanks but still didn't sit down, instead going to lean against the kitchen threshold to watch Elsa at the stove. "This your music?"

She glanced up from stirring a thick gravy. "Yeah. You like it?"

"I do, as it happens."

"You strike me as a Lynyrd Skynyrd kind of guy. Allman Brothers."

"Are you stereotyping me?"

Her grin flashed, quick and elfin. "Maybe. Is it true?"

"Guilty." He sipped his tea. "But I like music in general. Just about all of it. No Death Metal, which I just can't understand, and no Rap, but the rest is good."

"Some Rap is pretty powerful, but I'm with you on the Death Metal. If there was such a thing as demons, that's what I think they'd sound like." She poured gravy into a waiting serving dish, and the steam curled in the air, carrying the smell of meat and salt and browned flour. Tucking hair behind her ear, she said, "What about Celtic, New Age? A lot of manly men don't like that kind of music."

She cut her eyes sideways at him, one eyebrow raised slightly, and Deacon's chest expanded the smallest bit, puffing up like he was a bird. The image of himself as a blue jay, fluffing up, seemed ridiculous, but true enough. "Manly men, huh?"

"You bet." She swept the gravy boat around and into his hands, and for one minute, her face was tipped up toward his, smiling, her eyes glittering. It had been ten thousand years since he'd felt anything real and true move in him, but he did now. He let it show in his eyes, then took the weight of the boat fully into his hands.

"Table?"

The corners of her lips seemed to turn up even higher. "Yes."

She followed him with a serving dish of fried pork chops and a bowl of greens, piled in flaky beauty, with a hank of bacon clinging to the top. A glass dish of cornbread steamed next to an old-fashioned butter dish with a glass hood. He hadn't seen anything like it since childhood. A thin bottle of peppers with a yellow lid sat next to the salt and pepper.

Deacon sat down and rested his hands on the table for a moment, letting the scents fill him with a powerful nostalgia. It had been many years since he'd had a meal like this. Decades. For a long moment, he tried to think when it could have been. Before his tumble, before his daughter was born, even before his marriage. Long before that.

"This," he said a little roughly, exaggerating his accent to cover, "is right neighborly, Miss Elsa."

"My pleasure." She picked up the dish of pork chops and offered them to him. "Dig in, sugar."

After dinner, Tamsin jumped up to clear the table. "I'll take care of the dishes."

"Would you like to take a walk?" Elsa asked Deacon. "It's a very pleasant night, and I'm sure Charlie would appreciate the chance to stretch his legs."

"Considering I ate enough for three people, that would probably be a very good idea."

She found the leash and a sweater and they set out, walking south beneath a bank of elms. Elsa was suddenly aware of herself, her head and her feet, her arms on either side of her body, a sense of space bordered by the big presence of Deacon. For almost a block, neither of them said anything. The air was cool, and scented with hints of moist earth and blooming flowers. They passed a yard neatly fenced with old-fashioned wrought iron, and an explosion of perfume enfolded them.

"Smell that?" Elsa asked, pausing. Charlie shuffled over to the gate to sniff the entire post. "Lilies of the valley." She peered through the gloom and spied them lining the edge of the porch, tiny white bells. "My aunt Rosalie loved them."

"They do smell great."

They walked on, arms swinging side by side. Deacon reached out and took her hand, giving her a little smile as he did it, as if he wasn't sure. She rounded her fingers around his big palm.

"Tell me a story, Elsa," he said. "About you. About your life."

Charlie planted his feet and intently smelled a shrub. When she tugged, he resisted. "A story, huh? What kind of story?"

"Tell me about your first kiss."

"You first."

"Fair enough." Charlie gave up with a sneeze and they walked on, slowly. Lights were on in the living rooms and kitchens along the way. Television flickered blue into the evening. Music and laugh tracks and an argument gave texture to the world. "I was ten. I mowed lawns around the neighborhood for extra money, and there was a pretty little eight-year-old who flirted with me all the time. I finally just got up my nerve and took her under a pecan tree in the backyard and kissed her." He held up a finger. "But I did it the right way, like I saw on TV, leaning her backward over my arm."

"You didn't!" Elsa gave a hoot of laughter.

He held up a hand in oath. "True story. Sealed my reputation as a ladies' man right then and there."

"I guess it would."

"Now you."

"My story is not that good. I was fourteen, and I'd had a very bad day, and my best friend followed me down to the park. I was crying my eyes out and he was hugging me and then . . ." She shook her head, remembering the way they had tumbled into the grass, pressing bodies together, only lips touching at first, then tongues. He slid over her, and they pressed their bodies together, and kissed for ages. ". . . we were kissing, like it was the most natural thing in the world."

"Gathering that must have been your old friend Joaquin. Is that right?"

"Yes," she said, and paused to look up at him. "But don't read anything into that. We returned to being best friends when he became a priest, and that was almost two decades ago."

He took a step closer, raising a hand and curling it around her neck. "This is our first kiss," he said, and leaned down to press his lips into hers, sweetly. Just lips, his rough palm against her skin, her breasts barely grazing his chest.

When he raised his head, she didn't move away, but instead rested a hand on his waist. Lightly. Gauging the ratio of flesh to muscle to bone beneath her palm, beneath his shirt. She thought again of her desire to see his naked back and now added his naked chest to the list.

His thumb traced her jaw and then he bent again, pulling her a little closer so that she could feel his whole body against the front of her whole body, and her mouth opened of its own accord, inviting him in, and as if she had never experienced such a thing before, she felt nearly faint when their tongues met. His arm slid around her waist, pulled them more tightly together, and his other hand was in her hair, and their mouths fit perfectly, perfectly. He knew how to kiss her, too, both delicately and hungrily, as if he had not tasted anything like this before and needed to take his time.

Kissing and kissing. He turned and pressed her against the tree, his hands sliding up her arms, down her sides. She explored the length of his back with her fingers, following the indentation of his spine, the muscles on either side of it.

Kissing and kissing, as if they were fifteen and he was dropping her off in front of her parents' house. Kissing and kissing, turning their heads this way and that way, taking time, hands moving but only in chaste ways.

He lifted his head at last. Brushed hair off her face. "I might be a little out of practice here."

She laughed softly. "That did not seem like out of practice to me."

"No?" He bent, kissed her again, sucking at her lips as if he couldn't help himself. "I guess I'd better stop now. Jesus, you have the sweetest mouth."

"Tamsin will wonder where we are." She suddenly realized that she still held Charlie's leash, and her poor dog had just sunk down on the grass, politely waiting. "And poor Charlie!" He swept his tail over the grass.

The walk back was only five minutes—they really hadn't been gone long, it had only seemed like it. Charlie spied someone going up the walk to the house and he leapt forward, ready to greet whoever it was with a big kiss. Elsa let the leash go, and he dashed ahead. When the visitor bent to speak to the dog, Elsa recognized Joaquin's voice.

He waited on the porch, a dish in his hand. "Hey," she said. "What's up?"

"I'm sorry," he said, looking from Deacon to Elsa. "Am I interrupting? I brought over a tarta de Santiago."

In the yellow glow of the porch light, he looked very much as he had when they were young and he would come to pick her up for something—a movie or an event at church or any number of other things—and for a single moment, she, too, was young. Seventeen and painfully in love with a good, honest man. She came up the steps. "Did you make it yourself?"

He gave an abashed nod and held it out. He'd even put the shape of the Santiago cross on the top with powdered sugar. "Don't tell the Gloriosa sisters. They'll be scandalized."

Elsa laughed, feeling buoyant, and kissed his cheek.

Deacon stayed on the lower step. "I'll leave you folks to dessert. I've got an early call."

Elsa turned. "You don't have to go! Come in and have cake."

"Thanks, but I really do need to run."

Elsa stood between the two men, a cake in her hands, the porch light exaggerating shadows and noses, painting more intent into each of their faces than could possibly be there. She took in a breath, smelling heat and salt and desire, twining red and purple in the air. Hers. His. Theirs.

"Good night, then," she said, and turned crisply away.

Chapter Seventeen

Tamsin sat cross-legged on the floor Monday evening, several lengths of fabric spread out around her. She'd worked her first shift at Walmart yesterday, six hours on her feet, with a single break of fifteen minutes. For seven dollars an hour. She'd been so tired when she returned home that she fell asleep waiting for water to boil for tea.

Today had been better, but she was embarrassed by everything she didn't know, things people took for granted, like how to punch a time clock, how to help someone figure out the notions for a dress pattern, and what shoes were best for a long day of standing. Her arches ached like the dickens; tomorrow, she would wear the tennis shoes in her gym bag. She hated the tedious aspects of the job, standing around under those ugly lights when there were no customers to wait on, tidying up over and over and over, and she lived in mortal terror of someone she knew showing up.

The saving grace of it was the fabric. Working with it, setting it out to be admired, cutting it for someone, guiding people to the right choices for whatever project they had in mind. And when she had a quilter, she was in heaven, talking batting and machines and stitching.

After such a long day, however, she wanted something creative to do. Elsa was off at San Roque, volunteering to help young mothers plant their gardens appropriately. It was the first time in a long while that Tamsin had been alone.

The newspeople had finally moved on to whatever breaking story was worth chasing now, leaving behind a pocket of quiet. She'd made a pot of coffee and now she sat in the middle of the living room amid spreads of fabric. Loreena McKennitt played in her ears. She'd found the iPod stuck in the side of her gym bag, and had accessed her iTunes account through Elsa's computer. Done! The wonders of modern technology.

The earliest part of a quilt was one of the best stages, when she simply let the fabric begin to speak, let it begin to arrange itself into a tale of many parts. A small scrap of blue and green paisley cotton sidled up to her knee, and pulled along a length of sea foam silk, which drew forth the gossamer aquamarine tulle. She ran her hand beneath it, admiring the airy thinness, then tugged it over the paisley and saw a clear ocean with fish swimming in it. She inclined her head, narrowed her eyes, scanned the fabrics for something that wasn't there. Sand? Sea? A hint of a wrecked ship?

On the floor next to her, her cellphone began to spin around in a circle, and she picked it up. Soon, this would have to be addressed, too, the fact that this was an expensive phone service and she was going to have to downgrade. It wouldn't be long before they turned it off, which was a problem, because it would kill Alexa's service, too.

Speak of the devil. It was Alexa calling. "Hi, honey! What's up?"

"Mom?" Her daughter's voice was shaking and Tamsin immediately sat straighter. "Some police just left here. American federal agents, looking for Dad. What's going on?"

"What?" Tamsin scrambled to her feet. "What did they say?"

"They wanted to know where he is. They grilled me for an hour and asked me about everything we talked about when he was in Madrid."

No matter how she approached the problem, Tamsin couldn't think of anything good to say. She thought of her daughter, alone in Madrid, on this side of a life-changing revelation. She stayed silent, letting her have one more minute before the world fell in on her head.

"Mom?" Alarm lit the word. "Mom? What's going on? Where's Dad? He gave me a bunch of money when he left, but I thought it was just one of those things he does, you know, but I—"

"He gave you money?"

"Mom, where is he? Where's Dad?"

She finally had to say it. "I don't know, Alexa. I haven't spoken to him since before he was in Madrid. He's disappeared." She bent closer to herself, curling around the phone as if she could protect her daughter. "He's wanted for a Ponzi scheme. They seized the house and everything in it, but I got as much as I could out of your room. Anything that I thought would matter to you, scrapbooks and things like that. We brought it all—"

"My *things*? What are you *talking* about?"

"He's wanted for racketeering. I didn't want to ruin your last month in Spain."

"This is crazy. Dad isn't a criminal."

"I know. It doesn't make any sense to me, either, but he is wanted. They closed his office, and our accounts are frozen, and the house—"

"Our *house*?" She gave a bitter little laugh. "What's it worth? A million, maybe? Not even that much, probably, in Pueblo. It's not like it's some penthouse overlooking Manhattan."

The buttery color of light pouring through the windows onto hardwood floors, the garden she had nurtured, her tower room, all welled up and punched Tamsin with a sense of acute loss. "Maybe not," she said quietly, "but it was my work of art."

"Oh, I'm sorry, Mom, I didn't mean that. I'm just not—this is so overwhelming, I can't even think. Where are you living?"

"I'm staying with Elsa in the house in the Grove."

"That teeny little rental?"

Tamsin looked around at the fabric spread over the floor and couch, the trees waving gracefully beyond the window. "It's not so bad. Elsa has been good to me."

The phone was so quiet, Tamsin thought she'd dropped the call until Alexa said, airlessly, "I have to go. I'll call you tomorrow."

"Alexa, don't! I'm going to worry about you."

"There's nothing to worry about, Mother. I'll be home in a few weeks anyway. I just thought . . ."

"What, honey?"

"Nothing. This is just . . . horrible. I can't even get my head around it, that he might be a criminal, that everything he ever said might be a lie, that—" She groaned. "This is impossible."

"Sweetheart, don't make it worse than it is. Give yourself some time."

"I have to go. I'll call you tomorrow, I promise."

"I love you!" Tamsin said, but the connection was lost before the words went through.

Alone in her flat, Alexa looked down at the sapphire on her finger. It wasn't as big and flashy as Duchess Kate's (but who would want the engagement ring of someone who had been so *cursed*, anyway?) but it was big enough that she turned it into her palm when she was out.

When her father had come to Madrid, he'd been in an almost hectic mood, but that was not all that odd. She'd taken him to eat *pulpo* and see the bar where Hemingway had written. He'd been very demonstrative, more than was usual.

Now it made sense. Usually she was proud of him, his urbane carriage, his funny asides. He was very witty and charming, and people always liked him. That night he seemed like he was on drugs or something, his cheeks flushed and his jokes a little forced. At the end of the evening, he walked her back home and pressed a thick manila envelope into her hands. "A present," he said. "Don't tell your mother. It will be our little secret."

He often did that, gave her extra cash or a bauble. He liked gambling, the thrill of it, and enjoyed slipping her some little something when he won big. She clutched it to her chest as he hugged her, feeling the particular softness of a wad of cash. "Be good, sweetheart," he said, and walked into the night, whistling.

Once inside, she opened the padded envelope to find two thousand dollars, all in hundred dollar American bills.

Over the years, she noticed that when he gave her something, he almost always gave her mother something, too. A new coat or a quick trip somewhere, Mexico or Hawaii or once Tahiti. He liked beaches and sunshine. Her mother just liked to travel. Anywhere, at the drop of a hat. Sometimes, Alexa thought her mom was a little jealous about her year in Spain.

Then there had been the flat. She looked around it now with a sense of airless disaster. The agents hadn't asked about it, perhaps assuming it was a rental.

Her heart beating too hard, she absorbed the sight of it. The floor-to-ceiling drapes floated on a breeze. She'd hung inexpensive posters on the walls for the time being, imagining a day when she would be able to furnish the flat properly, her own little pied-à-terre.

She loved it—something about it made her feel secure and powerful, owning a flat in a foreign city, a city she loved and felt comfortable in. It would also be her retreat if the demands of high society life became overwhelming. Hers. A center that was solid.

Now, turning her ring around and around on her finger, she

knew she would have to go home to her mother. She could not marry Carlos. It had been hard enough to win acceptance with his family (his mother) as an American. As the American daughter of a criminal on the lam from charges like this, she would be a pariah in Spanish society.

The fairy tale was over, as she must have always known it would be. A count did not fall in love with an ordinary girl and sweep her off her feet and then they lived happily ever after. It just didn't happen.

And now it wouldn't.

Squaring her shoulders, more her mother's daughter than she knew, she began to make a mental list of what would have to be done. The last thing was the ring. Which she would wear until the very last second.

April Showers, May Flowers

Many things grow in the garden
that were never sown there.

—Thomas Fuller, *Gnomologia*, 1732

Chapter Eighteen

Almost every morning, Elsa walked Charlie over to the garden so they could be there as the sun rose. It gave the day a special zest to spend the first hour admiring the little sprouts of life. She liked the frilly starts of peas and the unfurling corn poking up out of the dark earth, and the pretty shape of squash seedlings, looking so sturdy and stalwart, as if nothing could kill them. Her potatoes had sent sprouts into the sunlight, and it was much better than growing a potato in a jar on a windowsill, which she had done a lot as a child.

This Friday morning at the end of April was dark, the clouds low and pregnant. Elsa hummed under her breath and plucked bindweed from between the rows, and thinned tomatoes, even though it pained her to kill healthy tiny little plants. Charlie raced up and down the main aisle, tossing a plastic half-gallon orange juice container up in the air, then chasing it down.

Deacon ambled over, as he often did. He, too, came early, before the workday started for him. There were others, too. Now and then, she saw Joseph, flute or drum in hand, singing good spirits into the space, and there was an older woman who came once or twice a week.

"Good morning," Deacon said, and handed her a paper cup. "Tea, two sugars, and milk, not cream."

"Thank you." She tugged off the cotton gloves she wore and tucked them in her back pocket. Since the night he'd kissed her after dinner, there had been nothing else, only the friendship growing between them, as sturdy as the squashes at her feet. She tried not to mind that it wasn't more. Lifting her chin toward Charlie, she asked, "What do you think he's doing with that? Is he imagining it's prey?"

"Dogs like to work. He's a retriever, so if you were a hunter, he would go racing into the woods and bring back whatever you'd shot—your bird or squirrel or whatever."

"Squirrel?"

He shrugged. "Lots of people eat squirrels. Plentiful, and meaty enough."

"I guess they do. Arrogant of me to judge."

"Maybe a little." He rested his coffee cup lightly on the stake holding up the fence. "People do what they have to."

"Did you eat squirrel as a child?"

"No. Lots of neighbors did, but my father had his own work to do. He didn't have time to hunt for anything."

"Right, your daddy the preacher man."

His expression didn't lighten much at the teasing. "Yeah."

"Sorry, I hit a nerve."

He shook his head. Rubbed a hand over the back of his neck. "No, it's not you. I heard from one of my sisters that he's doing poorly. He's got Alzheimer's and congestive heart failure and diabetes and God knows what else."

Instinctively, she touched his arm. "Deacon, I'm so sorry. Are you going to go home and see him?"

"No. He disowned me long ago."

"I see." Elsa waited, feeling the tangle of emotions coming

from him, grief and anger and resignation. "No hope of reconciliation?"

"Trust me," he said, "no. And it wouldn't be that helpful, anyway. I'm not mad at him for dying. I'm mad at him for being such a bastard to his children and his wife."

Elsa took a sip of tea, listening, watching his face. He was the kind of man who'd learned to keep his feelings behind a mask, but his mouth gave things away. "Abusive?"

He looked out, into the past. "That's what they call it now, I reckon. Back then, it was just discipline. He used a switch on us, never his hands." His mouth twitched slightly, right at the corner. A freshening breeze blew hair over his forehead. "But mostly, it was his job to tell us what sinners we were, and try to beat it out of us." He shook his head. "My mama could never please him. She died trying, and left my poor sister there with the wreck of him. I should go, take some of the burden from her, but all I'd want to do is wrap my hands around his neck and twist it like a chicken."

She waited as he winced at his own words, but she also heard the truth in them. Gently, with some humor, she said, "Best to leave it alone, then."

His smile flashed. "Anybody you want to kill?"

"Oh, I don't think so." She inclined her head, thinking of family members. "My mother is a little clueless, but also ancient. My father is gone. I like my sister." Her imagination gave her a snapshot of Kiki's body.

He said, "You thought of somebody."

"A young girl in my congregation in Seattle was tortured and murdered. She was only fourteen. Charlie and I were part of the search party that was looking for her, and we found her. Body, I mean. Her body." The vision of Kiki's blue skin ran in front of Elsa's eyes, joined by her laughing eyes the day of the harvest festival, the emptiness of those eyes staring at the heavens. She took a breath, then met Deacon's gaze.

"I would kill the man who did it, slowly. Torturously. Fair is fair." She said it without apology, her voice solid. "Just one more thing I have to come to terms with before I can go back to the congregation."

He studied her face, his eyes a startling color even in the dark morning. "Do you? Have to get over that?"

"Maybe." She took a breath. "Unity teaches Divine Order, that everything, always, is in perfect harmony. Not feeling it right now."

He nodded. "Maybe you could start with forgiving yourself."

Her head jerked up.

"You're kinda hard on yourself, Sister Elsa. You're having a crisis of faith. Just be there with it."

"Do you believe in God, Deacon?"

He took a breath, looked at the sky, the plants. "I believe in something. Something good. Not sure what it's called, but I've had things happen I can't explain any other way except to believe there's something out there looking out for me."

She scowled. "Yeah, I hear people say that all the time. That grace and prayers saved them. All that. Joaquin has seen an angel. Twice!" She shook her head. "But where was God and grace and intervention when that fourteen-year-old girl was being tortured?" She raised her eyebrows. "Fourteen, Deacon." Her voice broke with fury. "Couldn't somebody have walked by? Couldn't God have sent a raven to peck out his eyes, that bastard?"

He put his coffee back on the fence post and opened his arms, wiggling his fingers to call her to him. Elsa moved into the circle, her cheek against his chest, his arms a solid comfort. For a long moment, he didn't say anything at all. It was such a *relief* to let go, to stand there and let somebody hold her.

"Maybe God tried," he said quietly, into her ear. "Maybe somebody was thinking about a walk and just decided not to take one, just for today. Maybe somebody was supposed to give that man some love before he got so twisted and lost that he could do such an evil thing."

She closed her eyes. "I know. I think about that, too. What happened to him to make him become the person who could do that? It had to be terrible." She clung to Deacon, her arms locked around his waist. "I still can't forgive it."

"Takes time." His voice rumbled in her ear through his chest, magnified and deep.

In her church, they hugged so much it was almost a joke, but she liked it. Loved it, loved the flow of energy between humans, the love. He smelled of coffee and laundry detergent and outside. He rubbed her back in a slow circle, right between the shoulder blades. "Oh, I have missed hugs like this," she said into his shirt.

"No hurry, sister," he said.

But there was that moment of shift, when the embrace slipped ever so slightly from platonic and comforting to something more. Elsa stepped back, her hands on his arms. "Thank you."

He nodded. "I didn't mean to stir up a can of worms."

"You didn't. The worms are always there, waiting to spill out." She winced. "Ew."

He laughed. His cellphone made a burbling noise, and he pulled it out of his pocket, glanced at the screen. "Yeah. There's my signal. I've got to get to work."

"I'm having breakfast with Joaquin." She widened her eyes. "And don't say anything about the angels. I don't know how much he tells people."

"No worries. He tells the story, or at least he told me. Once when he had the measles, and then again when he was on the *camino*."

Elsa looked at him for a long moment. "You must be close friends."

He ducked his head. Nodded. "That we are. I owe Father Jack quite a bit."

"I see." She lifted her cup. "Well, thanks for the tea and the hug and the ear. Have a good day."

"You, too, Elsa."

She turned to head toward the rectory, and he called her back. She looked at him.

"Would you like to join us, me and Calvin and Mario, for supper tomorrow night?"

"Not Tiberius?"

"He's got plenty of male relatives. He doesn't need a Big Brother."

For a moment, she hesitated, aware that there was more and more building here, and that she had other choices to make, other things to work out.

"Careful now," he added. "It's not just any old supper. We're going to the Passkey."

Elsa feigned a swoon. "Ah, the best grinder in the world. I haven't had one in twenty years, I bet. I'll be there. What time?"

"Six-thirty. I'd pick you up, but between boys and dog, there isn't a seat left."

She laughed. "I can drive myself."

"That's fine."

Elsa watched through the rectory windows as clouds moved over the sky. They were fat clouds, dark with rain. Lightning arrowed out of them, cracking and thundering. Charlie stuck close to her, lying on her foot if he could get away with it, moving when she moved, his body quivering every so often. "Weird to have lightning so early in the day," she commented, eyeing the sky from the table, where she sat with a mug of coffee clasped between her palms.

Joaquin stood at the old gas stove. A cast-iron griddle, a Christmas gift from Elsa a few years back, drew heat from two burners. He brushed the surface generously with melted butter, and glanced at the sky as he turned to pick up a plate of sliced peaches, lightly spiced with mace and cinnamon and nutmeg. "It looks like Kansas during tornado season." He'd lived there for a short stint as an undergrad. "Forecast is for serious rain."

As if to underscore the words, the first heavy drops splatted against the windows, as big as saucers. "I'm glad we don't get tornados here."

"Yeah. Not my favorite weather." He placed three slices of peaches in a circle, sprinkled them with brown sugar, and covered them with buckwheat pancake batter, a recipe he'd developed just for Elsa, who loved buckwheat as much as anything on the planet.

She smiled at his concentration, the comma of his body arched over the grill, his precision in placing the peaches and pouring the exact circle of the batter that surrounded each one. His face was nearly perfect in profile—the high brow and angled cheekbones, his aggressive Mayan nose and full lips. So very handsome.

And still too thin, she realized. His hands looked too big at the end of bony forearms, and his rear end had practically disappeared. "You're still not eating enough, are you? How much are you running, my friend?"

He finished the final pancake. "What? Running?" He put the bowl down and picked up a spatula. "I don't know. Eight or nine miles."

"Every day?"

With care, he used a kitchen towel to wipe away a spot of batter. "Yeah."

"That's a lot."

He shrugged. "I have a lot on my mind."

"Do you want to talk it out?"

He straightened and looked over his shoulder at her. "Not this morning, but thank you."

"You're not eating enough to compensate for all those miles. Maybe you need to have dinner with me and Tamsin more often. How about Monday evening?"

"Are you feeding all the unmarried men of the parish now?"

She raised her eyebrows at the tone in his voice. Outside, the rain splatted and spit, and in the distance were the first waves of thunder. Charlie edged closer to her leg, and she shifted to put one foot on either side of him. "It's all right, baby." To Joaquin, she said, "I am a nice person that way. I will cook your favorites, too. What do you want? I'll even cook paella."

He glanced at her, ever so slightly coy. "Really?"

She let a smile edge onto her face. "Really. Because I love you, and you are important to me."

"Promise?"

"Yes." She drew an X across her heart. "Cross my heart and hope to die."

His grin was true this time, and she fell back against the chair, glad to have jollied him away from . . . whatever it was that kept cropping up between them lately. "You need to eat more, Joaquin," she said firmly. "Or run less. Or both. I want you to gain ten pounds, *sabe*?"

"*Sí.*" He flipped the pancakes. "I promise."

As he reached into the oven for the plates warming there, a wild blade of lightning blazed over the sky, and before it had even stopped, a violent crack of thunder blasted the air.

Elsa jumped, giving an involuntary cry. Joaquin dropped the plates and they shattered on the linoleum floor. Charlie leapt up and barked frenetically, his whole body shivering.

As if the lightning had broken the sky, rain came pouring out of it, unbelievably loud, pounding so hard on the roof and windows it seemed like everything would fall apart.

"Wow!" Elsa cried, and fell to one knee to put her arms around Charlie. He wiggled and whimpered against her, inconsolable. To Joaquin, she called, "I need a blanket!"

He nodded, dashed into the adjoining living room, and tossed her an afghan. She wrapped it around her shoulders and sat on the floor, pulling Charlie into a tent made of her body and the afghan. He crawled, close to the floor, into her lap, and tucked his nose under her arm. She pulled the blanket down around him, humming a lullaby and rocking slightly.

Joaquin swept up the broken plates and threw them in the trash, then knelt beside Elsa. "What else can I do?" He put his hand on Charlie's hindquarters.

She shook her head. "Now we just wait it out."

"I'm going to take the pancakes off so they don't burn."

Overhead, the rain poured and poured and poured. Elsa rocked gently back and forth, singing softly "Alleluia," one of her favorite hymns. Joaquin turned off the stove and sat down beside them, joining in to sing the old words with her. His voice was deep and hers was an alto, and they had sung many many many songs together, but not for a long time.

Maybe because she had spoken to Deacon about it or maybe because the smell of rain and earth triggered her visceral memory, she was transported to another day, a day on the Camino, the week before they arrived in Santiago. The day that changed everything.

Everything.

She and Joaquin were nearing the end of their pilgrimage on the Camino. It had been raining for a couple of days. While they were not exactly used to walking in the rain, because it was never pleasant, they were also resigned to it. They'd been on the road for nearly two months, and rain was part of the game. They wore their ponchos and kept moving, drying out their shoes as well as they could at night, putting on fresh socks as often as possible. Twice, they'd taken a break for a day to dry out a little.

But at the end of the *camino*, with Santiago only six days away, they were exhausted in every possible expression of the word. In body, in mind, in spirit. It seemed to Elsa nearly impossible that they could keep walking for even two more days; conversely, impossible that they could ever *not* be walking. It was one of the reasons people undertook a pilgrimage—to reach that point of no return, to understand that life is only fleeting.

On that day, the rain came down hard, sudden and blinding. Lightning finally drove them to take shelter in a grim concrete shed, a gray little nothing thing—until you went inside.

A crude altar took up the entire back wall, and it was piled high with hundreds of offerings. There were pieces of paper with prayers written in a dozen languages, photos, and all kinds of other offerings—a barrette and a shoe, stones and feathers, even a branch from a tree, withered and old now. People had also written all over the walls and the altar itself.

As she ducked into the space, Elsa was shivering from the rain, but she shivered even more in the cold room, hearing all those whispers and pleas, a sibilant chorus giving texture to the quiet. Joaquin came in behind her, shaking himself off. His hair was long then, pulled back into a ponytail, and he barely had any beard at all; only wisps grew along his chin.

"This is amazing."

Elsa nodded, still shivering. She took a sip of water, and removed her poncho, shaking it out and then smoothing it on the ground so she could sit on it. She shrugged out of her backpack, which had been whittled down to practically nothing over the long miles. They had both begun with too much. Now they carried only the barest of necessities—three pairs of underwear and six pairs of socks, two sweaters, two T-shirts each, and the ponchos. One pair of shorts and one pair of long pants each. A hairbrush, two hats, lip balm, sunscreen, Band-Aids and moleskin and antiseptic and a small bottle of shampoo they alternated carrying. Joaquin carried a bar of soap and water bottles and any food they bought for the day—his shoulders were stronger, to start, and had grown powerful over the walk.

She dug her second sweater out of the pack and pulled it on over the first, hugging herself to keep warm. Last night had not been a good sleep—there had been young pilgrims partying all over the town, and the noises had gone on into the wee hours of the night. Elsa was usually too tired to worry about interruptions, but she had her period and couldn't sleep, tossing and turning and hurting. Maybe, she'd thought, they should take a rest day. But they were both anxious to get to Santiago, and a rest day would make it seven days instead of six, so they'd packed their gear, and Elsa had stocked up on supplies, making sure she had enough tampons to last between towns.

The skies were gloomy when they'd set out with a breakfast of rolls and meat and hot chocolate in their bellies. Elsa had popped a bunch of aspirin and they'd started walking in the dark day, donning ponchos just in case.

After a couple of hours, it started to rain. Harder and harder, until they were driven inside this cold shelter. Elsa huddled in her sweaters, leaning against the wall, her lower abdomen pulsing with low-grade pain. Joaquin moved around the room, looking carefully at everything, murmuring over one thing and another.

It had all started as such a lark, but both of them had been changed by their pilgrimage. The knowledge settled between them, unspoken as of yet, a quiet void of conversation they jumped over and around and sat on top of.

For Elsa, it was the people who had changed her, the pilgrims carrying their stories down the road to Santiago, the people manning the bars and restaurants and hostels along the way. She wanted to facilitate the journey of pilgrims, ordinary pilgrims in everyday life. Help the weary, comfort the bereaved, ease the furious.

She could not do that in the Catholic Church, not in the way she envisioned, so she would have to explore other options. She didn't relish telling Joaquin, who had been devout before they began their pilgrimage, and had grown more deeply so as they walked. His faith had always been one of the most appealing things about him. Now it glowed in him like a beacon, peaceful and encompassing. It drew people to him. As she watched him, sleepily, it seemed as if he was praying, his hand hovering over one of the lines written on the wall, and then another, sometimes adding his voice to the petitions that filled the room. Closing her eyes, she smiled softly, warming up now. A good man, her Joaquin. She dozed.

When she awakened, the rain had stopped, and she had fallen sideways, her head resting on a backpack. Joaquin was kneeling in prayer, but he didn't have his head bent. He was, instead, in an attitude of listening, his face turned upward to the altar. Blinking sleep away, Elsa thought she saw a woman sort of floating or sitting on the altar, a greenish light around her, and then she was gone.

Another violent crack of lightning, then thunder, shook the rectory kitchen, bringing Elsa back to this time. This room, with Joaquin again.

"Do you ever think of the *camino*?" she asked.

"I have been lately."

"Me, too." Overhead came a much louder racket. Hail began to clack against the windows. "Oh, this is bad, Joaquin. It's going to demolish the garden!" She wanted to jump up and look out, but Charlie quivered and whimpered under her arms. "What do we do?"

"Let's pray."

"Yeah," she said, snapping. "That always seems to work."

To her surprise, he laughed. "Cranky, cranky."

"What is so funny?"

"I don't know," he said, his shoulders still shaking. He bent his head, and laughter spilled out of him. "You. This. The dog. Prayers. All of it."

"Whatever. I'm not getting it, but you seem to be having a good time."

And he was. Still laughing, he fell sideways and then backward on the floor, his hands on his belly. He was laughing so hard that Charlie stuck his nose out of the afghan for a minute and stopped his quivering. Curious, he came out and licked Joaquin's face, which only made him laugh harder. And even though Elsa could see no earthly reason for the hilarity, she found herself laughing a little herself, just because he was, like yawning when someone else yawns.

Finally, he slowed and sat up, wiping tears off his face, then resting his long arms on his knees, hands dangling down. "Ah. Better now."

"What in the world set you off?"

He waved a hand. "It wouldn't make any sense to you." For a moment, he faced her, calm and easy in a way he hadn't been with her in a long time. Then he scooted forward, and with the dog between them, he took her hands. "Let's pray. It can't hurt, right?"

She shook her head. And closed her eyes and let him pray for the protection and survival of the garden, for the health of the people, and for hope.

"And finally, God, I ask a particular blessing on your daughter Elsa here, who has lost her way. Show her the path back to you so that she can continue her work."

Elsa raised her head and found him looking at her as himself, her friend Joaquin, instead of Jack the priest, and she accepted it in the spirit he offered it. "Amen," she said.

They sat on the floor, rubbing their hands over Charlie to keep him soothed. The hail slowed to a mild clatter, then stopped. The lightning ceased. Charlie fell on the floor and sighed, closing his eyes for a nap.

"Let's have breakfast and then we can go check the damage," Joaquin said.

Her stomach growled. "Good idea." She peered out the window to see San Roque covered with a shawl of tiny hail. She sighed and turned back. "Maybe we'll see an angel."

"You've never believed me."

"Yes I have, I do," she said, sitting at the table, and speaking the truth. "I'm probably just jealous. Why did God give you an angel and a calling and I got—" She had been about to say *a broken heart and a very bad year,* but that wouldn't be fair.

"You got a ministry of your own," he said, ignoring the unspoken. "And I'm sure, if you want to see an angel, you could ask for it."

She picked up her fork. "Or not."

He met her gaze and started to sing Joan Osborne's "One of Us," and said, "Because seeing would mean you would have to believe."

The rosary she carried in her pocket felt hot, and she only looked at him, wondering what it would take to believe completely, to be restored to the fullness of her faith, that deep and abiding love she had once felt.

"What if the pope were a woman?" she asked quietly, and took a bite of the perfect pancakes. "What would be different?"

Joaquin bent his head, his hands still beside his plate. Then he looked at her, and there was color burning over his cheekbones. "Everything," he said.

Because she had loved him in so many ways over the decades, she let it go and nudged his hand. "Eat, Skinny Man."

He picked up his fork.

* * *

Over breakfast, Joaquin had several phone calls from parishioners who were having problems as a result of the storm. The church secretary came in three times with pink slips filled with phone messages, and when two of the deacons arrived to examine the roof and church building for damage, he regretfully told her to check the gardens and get back to him.

So she and Charlie went outside alone. She stopped at San Roque and scraped away some clusters of hail that had piled up around his sandals and on his dog's snout, suddenly wondering what the dog's name was. She realized she didn't know.

"Watch over the gardens, will you?" she said to the saint. "I know it's not your realm, but we need help." She zipped up her hoodie against the hail-chilled air, and wandered into the field, bracing herself for what she might find.

They weren't alone anymore, she and her dog. A number of residents from the apartments were working their plots, plucking out twigs that had blown down from the fragile elms lining the space, bending in to examine the damage. The young man with the rose tattoo sat on the picnic bench at the center, and waved to her with a sunny smile. She waved back and made a mental note to have a conversation with him sometime soon. He seemed lonely.

Joseph, his black and silver hair falling loose down his back, used a hoe to gently scrape the rows between his plants. "Good morning!" he called, raising a gnarled hand in greeting. "Some storm, eh?"

She paused, looking over the orange plastic fencing. "How are your seedlings?"

"Oh, a little battered, but that's just the way it is in springtime. Not all the little ones survive, huh?" He shrugged. "It'll make the rest of them stronger."

"I guess that's the way to look at it." She lifted a hand and went to check her own plot. She and Tamsin had purchased some chicken-wire fencing and had nailed it to the supports, making it look more tidy and official. Deacon had made a gate for her out of old lumber and a screen of chicken wire, and hinged it to the post with a spring, so it snapped crisply back in place when it was opened.

A lot of hailstones littered the garden, along with branches and twigs and a hundred billion elm seeds, which formed a pale green blanket over the ground. Elsa grunted in annoyance. No matter how many she swept up, thousands would sprout—sturdy, hopeful little trees ready to take over the world. Someone had told her once that elms were not native to Pueblo. Their branches were too fragile for the heavy snows that fell in spring and fall. And yet they had settled nicely into a landscape that needed big shade trees. There was one in the yard of the house in the Grove that spread its arms over the entire roof and backyard, a relief in July when the desert temperatures could hit a hundred or better.

The largest hailstones were the size of marbles, and just as hard—translucent, tiny balls of ice—but most were much smaller. Gingerly, Elsa plucked the heaviest ones off the plants they were crushing, and brushed away the smaller ones. A swath of tomatoes had been wiped out, their delicate pale green necks broken, their bodies drowned in mud. The squashes that had looked so sturdy only hours before had been assaulted, their leaves shredded in places, a couple knocked over entirely. In a day or two, she would know which ones would make it, but in general, it didn't look as bad as she'd feared.

When she finished, she went to the children's garden, making repairs to the vines, cleaning out the fallen twigs, and then moved on to the church kitchen plot, which had taken the least damage, for no reason Elsa could pinpoint. Those done, she walked up the aisles, looking to see if there were any other repairs she could make on behalf of gardeners who were at work or otherwise unavailable. Joseph was doing the same, she noticed, tucking into this garden or that, shaking a rattle, singing in a voice that reached some knot in the back of her neck and untangled it.

Calvin's mother knelt in her plot, her long hair looped back into a scrunchie at the base of her neck. "Hello, Paris," Elsa said. "Did you get much damage?"

"Not too bad," she said, and sat back on her heels, resting her muddy gloves on her knees. "The corn took a hit, but it's early enough that I can reseed. And Calvin's beans are going strong, so that's the important thing." She gestured to a vine climbing up a stout branch stuck in the ground.

"Healthy!"

"He thinks it's going to grow up to heaven so he can ask Jesus for a dog." She picked up her spade. "I don't have the heart to tell him we couldn't afford one if God Himself delivered it."

Elsa sensed that Paris wanted to talk. "He does want a dog," she agreed. "Talks about it all the time."

"Don't get me wrong, now. I like dogs just fine, but I can barely keep us fed, much less an animal. And they have to go to the vet and get shots and all that." She poked the ground savagely. "It'd be good company for him, though. I know he's lonely."

As if to illustrate the companionship possibilities of dogs, Charlie raced up from some errand and dropped a stick at Elsa's feet. She chuckled and picked up the stick. "They are good company," she said, throwing it as hard as she could. "But you're right about the vet, too, and feeding him takes a lot." Some prompt made her add, "A small dog doesn't eat as much as Charlie, though."

"Oh, I don't know if I care for small dogs. My neighbor's got a Chihuahua and it's the noisiest little thing, and he always seems so *nervous*."

"Well. Not all small dogs are Chihuahuas."

Paris nodded politely.

"Where's your family?"

"Kentucky." Another poke at the earth. "Bunch of loud rednecks."

"All of them?"

She inclined her head in assent, as if Elsa could not know how deep that redneckedness could go. "I'm not stupid. I'd go home, where it would be easier, but they'd never accept my baby."

"Their loss."

The girl's face blazed as she met Elsa's eyes fully for the first time. "He's a good boy."

"He is," Elsa said. "Very charming, and very, very smart. He can be anything." Elsa smiled. "Anytime you need help with him, you can call me. We have a really good time together, and Charlie loves him."

"That's real nice of you. You're the minister, right? Father Jack's friend?"

Elsa nodded.

"Thanks. Calvin sure likes to be with you, and he thinks Deacon hung the moon."

"All the boys do. He takes time to pay attention to them."

"Rare." Paris brushed elm seeds away from a row of what looked like peppers. "You've got a good man there."

Elsa made a noise between a laugh and a protest. "Oh, no. He's not my—it's not like that. We're friends."

"Is that right," Paris said, not a question.

A voice cried from the other side of the field. "Elsa!" She turned, and Joaquin was walking their way, her phone in his hand.

"Whoops. I left my phone in the rectory again. Nice talking to you, Paris. I meant what I said. You can call me if you need somebody to watch him, or help with anything."

"Thanks, Miss Elsa."

Elsa hurried back to meet Joaquin. He gave her the phone, which had a live call on it. "It's your pal," he said.

Deacon's name was on the screen, and for the space of a second, Elsa found herself hesitating. *You've got a good man there.* Joaquin looked at her down his hawkish nose, lashes making a shadow over his eyes in the bright light. Holding his gaze, she put the phone to her ear. "Hello?"

"Hey, sweetheart, are you still over there at the gardens?" he said in his raspy voice.

"I am," she said, and turned from Joaquin, walking away so that she could listen to Deacon in peace. "What do you need?"

"Will you take a look at my plot and make sure it's not too wrecked?"

"I'll walk over there right now. Do you want to call me back or wait until I get there?"

"I'll wait, sugar."

"Oof!" Charlie slammed into her legs and dropped a stick. "Don't you ever get tired of fetch, dog?"

On the other end of the line, Deacon laughed, and she held the phone closer to her ear, pausing as all the nerves along her nape and spine rustled to life, as if that sound was a hand, brushing over her skin. "Good luck with that."

She flung the stick hard, and Charlie raced after it. Holding the phone to her ear, she walked toward the plot that Deacon had planted. He was quiet on the other end of the line, and then murmured a direction to someone: "Cut those bushes away there."

"Okay," she said, "I'm here." And the situation here was not as good as she would have liked. Fully half the plants were drowned or smashed. "Well," she said, kneeling, "the good news is that a lot of the babies are doing fine. Corn and collards look good. Tomatoes are a complete loss, though." She brushed half-melted stones away. "Oh, wait. There are some that look like they'll be fine."

"Bad, though, huh?"

"Not that bad. You don't have to start from scratch."

"All right, then. I'll try and get over there at lunchtime, see what I can do."

"No need. I'll knock the hailstones off and get the branches out, and you can come after work."

"You don't have to do all that."

"I don't mind, sweetheart."

He laughed again, and Elsa closed her eyes. "So, see you tomorrow?"

"Yes."

Chapter Nineteen

On Saturday morning, Tamsin opened the fabric department, arriving at seven to get everything ready for the busy day. She loved being there first, going through the bolts of fabric to be certain each one draped just so, sometimes rearranging bolts to create a more inviting display, and making sure that all of the little packets of tape and pins and various notions were where they should be. She wore a tape measure around her neck, and her reading glasses dangling from a cord. For three years, she'd been using the glasses only when no one else was around, but it was impossible to do this job without them—cut fabric and read prices and read the lists of notions on pattern envelopes—so she'd given up her vanity and let them hang around her neck like some old lady.

It was a challenging job, and for the first week, her back ached so badly that she soaked in the tub for an hour when she got home. It was also embarrassing to face where she was working. How could she be in her forties and have so few employable skills that she had to work at Walmart, as if she were a teenager?

But she was grateful for the money. One of her quilts had sold on eBay, bringing in two hundred dollars, yet that was just a drop in the bucket. It was a blessing that Elsa had the house, that they could live rent-free. Even in the short amount of time she'd been working at the store, she couldn't believe the struggle many of her fellow employees faced just trying to make ends meet.

It was humbling. Nobody here drank five-dollar coffee drinks. The first time she heard someone describe a twenty-dollar haircut as expensive, she nearly laughed, before she realized they were serious. "How much do you pay?" she asked.

"I can go to Cost Cutters for twelve dollars," the woman said.

Tamsin had regularly been spending close to seventy-five, not including the very expensive foil streaks she required every three months. It was the thing she probably missed the most. Not the gym or the fancy coffee drinks, but a good haircut and color. She'd been due for a cut and color just before her world fell apart and it was starting to look pretty gruesome now. She wasn't graying, thank heaven, but the base color of her hair these days was a very boring dishwater, not a sunny blond. The line showed badly, and she was going to have to ask Elsa to help her do a home color job.

It was like going back in time. How she had scraped and saved to look halfway decent in high school! She'd read magazines obsessively (at the library, of course) to stay abreast of fashion trends and beauty shortcuts.

But aside from all of the humiliation factors, Tamsin had to admit that she really, really loved the job. Helping people make good choices in fabrics, matching cloth to task. She loved wandering through the aisles of material, running her hands over them, as she was doing right now. She had her eye on a diminishing bolt of deep green velvet. She kept seeing trees on a cliff. Not pine trees, something else, more verdant. Putting her hand on the fabric, she rubbed her palm over the nap, seeing trees/cliff/sea.

A new quilt, growing. Between getting the little sunporch

room ready for Alexa's return and the forty hours a week she worked at the store, she had not had much time to work with the idea, but it tickled her daily, teasing her with the shape it wished to reveal. Soon, she thought. Soon.

A voice over the loudspeaker announced the opening of the store. Collecting two cardboard bolts that were nearly empty, Tamsin made her way to the cutting center and unwrapped the last bits of fabric, unpinning them from the cardboard. She smoothed the creases from the cloth, folded it neatly into a remnant, and set the empty bolts aside.

"Tamsin!" said a woman's voice. "Is that you?"

She turned, sticking the spare pins into a red strawberry she'd taken to wearing around her wrist. Standing there, in a crisp jacket over a tidy pair of trousers, was Cynthia Rhoades, the wife of a lobbyist who worked for the pharmaceutical companies.

Tamsin willed herself not to blush. She was wearing a simple pink button-down with a white skirt, and her uncolored hair was pulled into a French braid. "Hi, Cyn!" she said, taking a pin from her mouth. "How are you?"

"Are you working here?"

Tamsin straightened her shoulders. "I am. I'm sure you've heard about Scott. I had to do something."

"But the house! All your things—!" At Tamsin's expression, she halted, her own face going red. "I'm so sorry. The last thing you need is me making it worse." She came forward and wrapped Tamsin in a hearty honest hug that nearly brought tears to her eyes. "I know all about it. We all do, of course. I'm sorry I couldn't do more for you."

"Oh, please," Tamsin said, cheekbones burning. "I know."

Cyn straightened. "How is Alexa doing?"

"She's been in Spain." Tamsin thought of the pained phone calls they'd shared since Alexa had discovered her father's disappearance. "She'll be home on Monday."

"That will be good for both of you."

"Yes." Tamsin touched her friend's arm. "What about you? What have you been up to? How are the kids?"

"Everybody's fine. No grandchildren yet, but I keep hoping. I've been taking a painting class, and we're headed to Bali in two months. Hope there won't be any tsunamis or earthquakes. Right there on the ring of fire, you know."

Something brushed over her imagination, a niggling aspect she should notice, but Tamsin couldn't quite catch it before it flew away. "I'm sure it will be fine. Have you been before?"

"No. I'm really looking forward to it."

An awkward pause enveloped them, empty of the things they might have said to each other when both were busy with their book clubs and charities and fundraisers. "Well," Tamsin said, "it was good to see you, Cyn. I should get to work."

Cyn nodded. "You look . . . happy, Tamsin. Happier than you've looked in a long time."

Startled, Tamsin released a sharp hoot of laughter. "Happy? Really?"

"Yes," she said, frowning slightly as she studied Tamsin's face. "Really."

"Thanks. I guess."

A woman carried a bolt of yellow satin to the table. "I'd like seven yards of this, please."

Cyn raised a hand in farewell and Tamsin turned toward her customer, happy in *this* moment anyway.

Across the world, Alexa had never been more miserable in her life. She sat in the vastness of the Madrid airport waiting for her flight home, trying not to cry. This was not how she had imagined leaving. She had not imagined leaving at all, not anymore.

Her ring finger was empty now, the ring left with a servant at Carlos's home outside the city this very morning. She had written a letter to go with it, explaining that she could not marry him after all. Her family needed her. She asked him to respect her wishes, and not to contact her.

Staring at the dull skies, she relived every moment of their romance, from the magical time on the rooftop to the long walks they took through the plazas of the city, one folding into the next and the next, talking and talking. It was as if they had known each other in other lives. He told her later that his heart had stopped when he saw her across the room, because he could swear he'd seen her before, in a dream or on a plaza somewhere, drinking coffee.

Destiny, they both decided. She called him Count Chocula. He called her Azul. They were so very, very, very much in love.

In the Madrid airport, she began to weep again, helplessly. She covered her face with a pashmina that still smelled of her days with Carlos. A woman next to her patted her shoulder kindly, told her she would be all right.

Alexa accepted the touch but she knew she would never recover. Not from this, from finding her life and then losing it.

If she ever saw her father again, she would kill him.

On Saturday afternoon, Elsa received another email before she met Deacon and the boys for supper. They had been coming in a steady little trickle, every day or two.

Today's message was from a child.

> Dear Reverend Elsa,
>
> I know you're having a hard time, but I hope you come back. I miss you. I miss my sister and I miss your laughing, and I want to know everything is going to be okay.
>
> Love,
>
> Nick

Kiki's little brother, only seven. Too young, at least now, to understand what had happened to his sister. Elsa sat at the computer reading the words over and over, imagining someone helping him write it, a Sunday school teacher or relative. It was, she thought, a good sign. Maybe Tall Pine wasn't as much of a threat as she feared.

Not that it mattered. She couldn't leave Tamsin yet, especially with Alexa coming home

She sat in front of the computer for so long that she only had a few minutes to change her shirt and wash her face before her dinner with Deacon and the boys. Nearly everything was in the laundry, and she was down to one of her last T-shirts, a short-sleeved V-neck with a scene of beach life on the front. It was a good color, a little darker than turquoise, and she'd been getting plenty of sun on her arms and throat. At least with the tan she didn't really need makeup.

She made sure Charlie had water, and headed out.

As she got in the car, she caught sight of herself in the rear-view mirror, and heard her mother's voice: *It's too bad you're so small and plain.* As if she were a gnome.

A tired, familiar anxiety rushed through her. Why wasn't she trying to look her best tonight? Why hadn't she washed clothes in time to wear something a little less down-market? She *liked* Deacon. All day, she'd been lit with anticipation.

And yet, here she was, wearing an old T-shirt, her hair pulled back into a ponytail, not even a touch of lipstick on her mouth. Why?

Looking at herself in the little mirror, she saw the lines starting to etch themselves into her forehead and around her mouth. Her skin was not as luminous as it once had been. She would be forty in eighteen months.

What do you want? she asked herself. *Church, children, love, marriage, family, faith?*

Even knowing she would be late, she got out of the car and went back inside. In her closet was a delicate peasant blouse, embroidered with turquoise threads. She tugged it over her head and found a pair of silver hoop earrings to make herself look more feminine, and traded her shorts for a pair of worn-soft jeans that fit her very well. In the bathroom, she took down the ponytail, picked out the curls, and brushed on a tiny bit of lipstick and mascara.

When she stepped back to look at herself in the mirror, she saw a woman with her own style of beauty. She wasn't a swan like Tamsin, long-necked and graceful, but she wasn't a wren, either. She was a finch, smart and colorful and blessed with a gift of song.

Still, when she drove into the parking lot of the Passkey, she felt another swell of nervousness.

Deacon *was* beautiful. As a young man, he must have been impossible to resist, with that dark hair and those bright, twinkling eyes, his absolute assurance that you were going to like him. Even now, with crow's-feet at the outer corners of his eyes, his bone structure gave him power and beauty. He had a good mouth, smiling and sensual, and she often found herself watching him talk, watching his lips move.

She wanted him. It was hard to admit that after such a long dry spell. Hard to face her own desires, and hard to face the possibility of rejection.

But there it was, her desire, plain and clear as she spied him through the window of the restaurant. The boys were out of sight, below the level of the window, but Deacon was laughing, so they probably were, too.

That was the thing about him that kept drawing her in so insistently, besides his physical charms. He was kind. Vastly, deliberately, insistently kind. She saw it in the way he listened carefully to the old alcoholics who wandered in and out of the meetings on Thursdays, men so far gone, so *long* gone, that chances were good they'd never surface. If he ever felt that way, it didn't show. He welcomed them with coffee, with good words, with compassion. It was the embodiment of goodness and mercy on earth, the real thing.

What did she bring to this? A restless soul, a broken faith, a heart that had been so thoroughly shattered at Joaquin's hands that she had begun to wonder if it would ever be whole enough for genuine use again.

Stop thinking so much.

Right. She got out of the car, tucking a slim billfold with her ID and a little money into the back pocket of her jeans. On the way to the door, she finger-combed her hair. When she went into the restaurant, she spied the children and Deacon grouped in a corner booth. Deacon smiled, and he watched her all the way across the dining room. She slid into the booth, a little flushed. "Hi," she said, and her words came out breathless. "Sorry I'm late."

"Hey," he said, eyes glittering. "We weren't worried."

"How's it going, kids?" she said.

"Miss Elsa, look what I drew you!" Calvin said, and held up an exuberant drawing of flowers and bees and birds. In the middle was a boy who looked like Calvin and a lady with crazy black-crayon curls, presumably Elsa, holding hands and admiring a beanstalk that rose all the way to the sky.

"That's some beanstalk!"

He looked down at it, inclining his head. "I'ma climb it and get me a dog."

His hunger for a pet plucked at her again, but she said only, "Just like *Jack and the Beanstalk*." She leaned toward Mario, whose hair was braided tightly down his back. Around his neck was a medicine bag made of soft leather. "Did you make that?"

"My grandpa made it for me. He's teaching me stuff."

"Like what?"

"It's secret. To be a man, you have to know things."

"Ah." She finally felt grounded enough to look over the table at Deacon again. "There are a lot of things to learn, I guess."

"I would say so," he said. He wore a chambray shirt with pockets on the front, the sleeves rolled three-quarters of the way up, to show his lean, powerful forearms. He had a cup of coffee in front of him, black and steaming. "We waited for you to order. But some people here"—he bumped a shoulder against Calvin, sitting next to him—"might be getting impatient."

"That's 'cuz I can smell all the sandwiches right now and my stomach is growling, saying *Eat eat eat!*"

"Man, you is always hungry," Mario said with a grin.

Calvin bent his head and colored in the petals of a red flower. "I'm growing. A boy needs a lot of food."

She thought of Paris, kneeling in the garden yesterday, afraid she could not feed a dog in addition to her child. "Dogs need a lot of food, too, you know. Maybe that's why your mom doesn't want to get one just yet. She wants to make sure you have what you need."

"*I'll* feed my dog," he said stubbornly.

The waitress stopped by the table, dressed in a polo shirt and black pants. "You ready to order now?"

Elsa opened the menu. "I will be in two seconds. You guys go first and I'll figure it out."

The boys ordered cheeseburgers and French fries, and for himself, Deacon ordered the classic grinder, a flat patty of Italian sausage smothered in provolone on a toasted bun.

Elsa slapped the menu closed. "I know I should resist, but that has to be one of the all-time great sandwiches in the history of the world."

Deacon grinned.

"So you want the grinder?" the waitress asked.

"Yes. And tea, please, *hot* tea, with milk, not cream, on the side, and will you please make sure the water is very, very hot?"

The girl scribbled notes. "Sure. No problem. Be right back."

Deacon had a smile in his eyes. "Wouldn't have figured you for the picky type."

"At least I don't bring my own tea bags these days." She leaned back easily and explained, "I spent a year in England when I was young, and you get used to really good tea."

"I've heard that before. People pick up all kinds of things in foreign places, I guess. My ex had to have a particular kind of olives because she'd spent some time in Greece and said there was a big difference in good olives."

Under other circumstances, she would have asked a little more about that ex-wife. *How long ago*, for instance, but it wasn't appropriate in front of the children. "Have you picked up any exotic food tastes?"

"Not so much." He shook his head. "Farthest I've traveled is Mississippi to California."

Calvin looked up, excited. "My mom lived in California, too! Before I was born."

"Is that right? Whereabouts?"

"I dunno."

"How about you, Deacon? Where in California did you live?"

"L.A." His gaze went to the sturdy white cup that held his coffee, and he turned the handle by quarters—to the south, to the west, to the north. "Landscape architect to the stars." A rare bitterness gave the words a sour note.

"Movie stars?" Mario asked. "Like who?"

Deacon leaned forward, shame shuffled into the background. "Harrison Ford and Gladys Nones, which won't mean anything to you. But here's one you will know: Jack Black, who does the voices for the panda in those Kung Fu movies."

"No way!" Mario cried. "Whoa! Does he sound just the same?"

Deacon shot Elsa a glance. "Not exactly. But he's a funny guy."

Their food came, steaming piles of it, along with Elsa's tea. She helped Mario cut his burger in half, and passed the ketchup. Across the table, Deacon did the same for Calvin.

"You like that movie, Cal?" Mario asked.

"I never been to a movie," Calvin said, his mouth full of burger.

"It came on TV, too."

"We don't have no cable, stupe!"

"No names," Elsa said automatically, spreading a thick, loving layer of mustard over her bun, then smashing the bread onto the sandwich and cutting it in half. The smell of it made her stomach growl.

"You've never been to a movie theater, son?" Deacon asked gently.

The boy shook his head, swinging his feet hard. "I don't care. I got books from the libary. We go almost every week. My mama reads to me at night, and she loves to read. She can read like ten books in a week!"

"That *is* a lot. What kind of stories do you like?" Elsa asked, thinking it would be something like Captain Underpants or dragon stories.

"We just got done with *The Jungle Book*, by Rhubarb Kipling," he said, "and last night we started *The Lion, the Witch and the Wardrobe*."

Elsa suppressed a laugh over "Rhubarb," and noticed Deacon's lips twitching. "Did you like them?"

"I ain't heard too much of the new one, but I really, really loved *The Jungle Book*. It's the story of this boy who lives in the jungle and he has all these animal friends and stuff. It's kinda sad in places, but I liked it anyhow."

"I seen that cartoon," Mario said, and started singing a song from it, bouncing his head.

"You did?"

Deacon said, "They probably have it on DVD, kiddo. I'm sure we can find it."

Calvin's fork stabbed a French fry into a pool of ketchup, his face carefully neutral. "That's okay. I don't need to see the movie. I read the book already."

"You don't have a DVD player," Mario said. "You could come watch at my house."

Calvin shrugged, carefully not meeting anyone's eyes. Had she been sitting next to him, Elsa would have slipped an arm around him, discreetly touched his back.

"Your mom is pretty special," she said instead. "All that reading! She must be super smart."

He brightened. "She is. And she says I'm so smart I can even be president if I want."

"I believe that."

Mario said, "I'm gonna be a medicine man. It's in my blood, for many generations."

"That's a big responsibility," Deacon said. "I reckon it takes a lot of time and study."

"What's a medicine man do?" Calvin asked.

Mario put his fork down and drank a little milk. He leaned over the table, gesturing with his hands like a little man. "A medicine man knows how to talk to the spirit world," he said, "and he can see what's wrong with somebody when doctors can't."

"Like what?"

"Like a bad spirit. My grandpa said he has to keep singing in the garden because there are so many ghosts there."

Calvin gave an exaggerated jump. "No sir!"

Elsa put her hand on Mario's back. "Maybe not ghosts like we'd think of them, though, right? Calvin doesn't need to be afraid of the garden."

"What? No way." He picked up his fork. "You just have to know a medicine man if you get sick, 'cuz it might be a bad spirit."

"Lucky we know your grandpa," Deacon said. "Eat up, kids. We have a telescope waiting."

"A telescope?" Elsa asked.

"Yes, ma'am," he said. Calvin struggled with the ketchup bottle, and Deacon took it, shook it hard, handed it back. "I've got a telescope I'll set up in the garden, and we're going to look for Jupiter and the Milky Way and whatever else we can find." He looked at her across the table. "Want to come?"

"Maybe."

"Will you bring Charlie?" Calvin asked.

Elsa laughed. "That's exactly what I was thinking."

"He can play with Joe," Mario said in his husky voice.

"Joe, the dog?" Elsa asked. "Where is he?"

"Out in the truck," Deacon said, and raised a hand for the check. "Your moms and grandpa can come down, too, if you like."

"My mom is working," Mario said. "But my grandpa might if he's not asleep. He's kinda old, you know."

"My mom likes to read at night," Calvin said, shaking his head. "We shouldn't bother her."

Deacon studied Calvin's face for a minute, and Elsa studied his, seeing the fleeting worry about what might be going on there. She felt it, too, but another part of her loved the young, lost mother who read her child *The Jungle Book*.

Watch and see, she thought. And found she was admiring Deacon's tanned hands, long and elegant, with strong oval nails and flat, calloused palms.

Enough.

Elsa stopped by the house to add layers and pick up Charlie before heading back to the garden. Tamsin was fast asleep on the couch, in front of the television, an untouched glass of red wine sitting on the end table. She didn't stir, and Elsa bent over her. "Go to bed, sweetie. You'll get a crick in your neck."

Tamsin lifted her head, blinking hard, and wiped drool from her mouth. "What time is it?"

"Not quite eight-thirty."

Tamsin stood awkwardly, obviously aching. "I'm old," she said, and toddled off to her bedroom. "Don't forget we have to wake early to go get Alexa in the morning."

"I won't forget."

It was a mild night, but Elsa pulled on a pink wool sweater from her Seattle days. When she picked up Charlie's leash, he woofed once and wiggled over to her. "I know! I think it's strange to go out at night, too, but you'll like it."

He didn't really need a leash, so she tucked it into her pocket and loaded him into the car to drive over to the church. It was a very dark night, the new moon. Perfect for stargazing.

Not so great for walking the length of the field. She had parked on the street east of it and as she made her way to the middle, it was very dark, the entirety of the gardens lit only by streetlights on adjoining corners. Two of those were shadowed by trees. Tucking her hands in her pockets, she let Charlie run ahead. "Go ahead, baby." The voices of Deacon and the boys were clearly audible. She anchored herself on the path between two plots and took her time.

Overhead, the trees swayed in the wind. Little animals made rustling noises in the plants, and a white cat dashed across the path, freaking her out for a minute. A colony of feral white cats lived around the levee and the church, preying on mice and birds and snakes. They looked like ghosts, and Elsa was sure they had added to the field's reputation as haunted.

She'd always loved being outside at night, especially in a town or city, when others were tucked into their homes, lamps shining through the windows. Looking over at the apartment buildings, she could see bedroom lights and living rooms, and on the corner models, kitchens. A woman washed dishes. A girl sat at a table in front of a computer screen. Another window had battered miniblinds and red curtains.

Each house a life, she thought, thinking of the foods that were eaten for dinner, the music or television shows that might be playing. And this was just a trio of modest-sized apartment buildings in a small city. All over the city, all over the state, the nation, the globe, were little pockets of houses or rooms or tents where people carried out their lives.

Miraculous.

Like the stars. They were washed out a bit on the sides of the horizons tonight, but they shone more brightly toward the mountains. Far to the northwest a light shone on top of Pikes Peak.

As she reached her own garden plot, she suddenly smelled something rotten. Rotten apples.

Dread rushed over her skin, raising a trail of goose bumps, and she froze, so frightened she couldn't move. One hand went reflexively to the St. Christopher medal Joaquin had given her. She clutched it in her palm as she turned her body in a slow, careful circle, peering hard into the murky dark. In the distance were porch lights, and the softly lit courtyard of the church, and some windows pouring light out of the basement. Cats yowled at one another.

The smell thinned, disappeared.

"There she is!" Deacon said.

Charlie, who had run ahead, leaned against him, letting his head be scratched. Deacon and the boys had put on warmer clothes, too. Desert nights could be cold, even in April. Calvin had a long scarf wrapped around his body, and he peered into the telescope with dedication, his hands on his knees. "I can see it!" he chortled, pulling back. "Come see, Miss Elsa! It's Venus!"

Laughing softly, she went over and put her eye to the lens. It was a very good telescope, with powerful magnification and a sturdy tripod. When she looked through it, the stars popped vividly forward, with one glowing brightly in the middle. "I thought Venus was a planet."

"It is, silly," Calvin said. "But it's so far away it looks like a giant star."

"So pretty," she murmured, then stepped away and looked straight up to the sky, crossing her arms over her chest.

"Go ahead, Mario," Deacon said. "Your turn." Then he came to stand close to Elsa. "Amazing, isn't it? I never get over the night sky."

"No, me, either." Unbending her neck, she asked, "Do you know the names of the constellations?"

"Some. That's Cassiopeia, right there, and the Big Dipper, of course, and Gemini."

Elsa fell into the vastness of the darkness, the faraway-ness of the stars, the possibilities of so many stars lighting so many systems. "Do you think anyone lives up there?"

"God does," Calvin said.

"The Great Spirit," Mario said. "Or you could call him Father Sky."

"Whatever. It's all the same. Can we move it around, look at other stuff?"

"Sure," Deacon replied. "Take your time and really look, though, don't just spin it all around."

Elsa chuckled.

"Back to your question," he said. "I think there are all kinds of things living out there. How could there not be?"

"I wish we could travel to them and visit."

He brushed the back of her hand with his own. "Me, too." He let go of a sigh. "I used to look at the stars with my little girl."

She waited, hearing the hunger in his voice.

"You ever been married, Elsa?" he asked.

"No." She looked up at him.

"I was married for thirteen years, and I gotta tell you, my wife was as long-suffering as they come."

"Don't they call that co-dependent these days?"

He gave a rueful bark of a laugh. "They always have called it that, but in my opinion, she just loved me and thought she'd eventually see me turn my life around."

"That's a kind way of looking at it."

"Maybe. Maybe not. It's true that it took me a long time to hit bottom because she covered so much for me, but it's also true that she protected our daughter."

"How old is she?"

"Sixteen. And wants nothing whatsoever to do with me. Which I don't blame her for a bit. She's got a nice stepdad, a good life."

Elsa peered up at his face through the darkness. Poker face, which meant it wasn't showing anything he really felt. "How does it really feel, Deacon?"

"You see what I'm doing, don't you? Hanging out with two little boys who don't have dads of their own."

"Mario has Joseph."

"Yep." He lowered his voice, stepping a little closer so he wouldn't be overheard. "He's on again, off again, though."

"On what? He leaves?"

"He binge drinks. Sometimes he's sober for six or eight months, and then he'll fall off the wagon and disappear for a few weeks."

"That breaks my heart. He's such a great old man. I hate to think of him getting hurt or lost or something."

"Me, too."

Tucking her hands beneath her arms, she said, "I wish I'd thought to bring a thermos."

"I did bring one. Want some hot chocolate?"

"Yes! That's a great idea."

"Come on over here. There's a blanket." He walked toward the telescope and picked up a big thermos and paper cups. "You boys want some hot chocolate?"

"Not right now," Mario said, engrossed in the sky. "Lookit that, Calvin! It's red!"

Calvin traded places with Mario. "Whoa!"

Elsa followed Deacon to the blanket and sat down. He passed

her a cup fragrant with chocolate and cinnamon. "Mmm, smells good."

"It's the Mexican kind, the one you get in little tablets?"

She sipped it. "Perfect. What a good idea."

"I have my uses." He rubbed Joe's back. "I am a Grade A dog rescuer, for one thing."

"Do you have others?"

He flashed a grin. "Uses?"

"Dogs."

"At the moment, also an incontinent terrier. And the most adorable little Shih Tzu you ever saw. I want another one . . . or two, depending."

"On?"

"How much attention each one needs. How far gone they are, if they need a lot of medications or generate a lot of vet bills." Joe lifted his chin and made a low, happy noise. "But there's the love, right there."

"I used to think that's how God must love us, with blind devotion, and that he just put dogs down here to help us remember."

"I believe that," he said. "Did you stop thinking it was true?"

In the darkness, the weariness in his face was erased, and she saw only the kindness. A shepherd of children and dogs and lost old men. She wanted to touch his wrist, visible beneath the sleeve of his coat, but it had been too long, and she might have misread him. She sipped her chocolate, vividly aware of her entire left side. "I have no idea what I think or believe right now, that's the truth."

As if he sensed her need for him, Charlie dashed out of the darkness and plopped down, panting. She chuckled and scrubbed his side. "All tuckered out, are you?"

He made a talking noise, looked into the darkness, and jumped up, bowed, and danced in a circle, giving a playful yip. He raced in a circle, dashed toward the edge of the clearing, danced back. "What is he doing?"

Deacon said, "He sure acts like he's playing with somebody." He looked at Joe. "What do you think?"

The old dog only panted in a smile, uninterested in anything but Deacon and getting his head scratched.

Charlie barked, and bowed again to the empty space, then ran in the peculiar racing way of a dog happily being chased. Elsa laughed.

So did Deacon. Charlie kept playing with his invisible friend, and the boys noticed and started laughing until all four of them had tears streaming down their faces.

At last, Charlie, worn out, came over and fell beside Elsa, panting hard and very pleased with himself. He leaned on her thigh and she rubbed him. "What were you playing with, you silly dog?"

Calvin and Mario came over and sat down. "We want hot chocolate now, please."

"You got it. Then I think it's time to head home, boys. It's getting late."

"Oh, not yet!" Calvin said. "I want to look at more stars!"

"They're not going anywhere."

"Maybe," Elsa said, "you can ask your mom to help you find a book about the stars the next time you go to the library."

He nodded, and only then did she see how sleepy he was. Tenderly, she ruffled his curls. "You're a sleepyhead."

To her surprise, he leaned into her, and she put her arm around him, pulling him close. His frame was slim and strong, and he smelled of the outdoors, of wind and sunshine and play.

I want this, she thought fiercely, surprising herself. A boy to read to, a girl to sing to, a child to tuck under her arm, to bake cookies with. To love. She thought of the day Kiki had painted her face, and the little girls played with her hair. She had breathed a prayer of longing as their hands patted her face. *This, please.*

In everything that had happened afterward, that simple prayer had been lost, but now she looked at Deacon over Calvin's head.

Deacon, who had lost his daughter and now filled the emptiness with little boys and old dogs.

He was perfectly still, watching her. Next to him, his dog gazed up at her, too, a smile on his snout.

The night air began to smell of roses and possibility.

They loaded the telescope into the back of Deacon's truck and helped Joe into the cab, then walked the boys home. Charlie tagged along quietly, as ready for his bed as the boys were for theirs. Mario let himself in, and they peeked around the corner to see Joseph sleeping in his recliner, hands tucked over his belly.

Paris opened the door to Calvin, smiling when she saw Elsa. "Did y'all have a nice time?"

"The best," Calvin said, and turned to hug first Elsa, then Deacon, who was taken aback a little. "Good night!"

Which left Deacon and Elsa to walk back down the stairs together. The halls were lit with harsh halogen bulbs, but the stairways were dark, the lights broken out, and it gave her the creeps. "Why doesn't the landlord fix this?"

"Absentee. I hear he's trying to sell." He took her elbow, guiding her, and let it go again when they left the building. "Where's your car?"

She pointed. "East side." The depth of the shadows struck her again. "What happened to the lights?"

"Knocked out with rocks. I have to get screens to cover the fixtures."

"It really is dark without them."

"Are you scared?" He reached for her hand. The calloused palm and long fingers engulfed hers. She laced her fingers through his, and he tightened his grip ever so slightly.

"Maybe a little."

Just before they reached the pool of light spilling over her car, Deacon stopped. Elsa stopped with him and looked up, aware of her body again, all of it, her breasts and thighs that had not been touched in so long, the length of her spine, rippling with the desire to be stroked. He smelled of hot chocolate and cinnamon, and she could tell he was nervous, which was touching in some strange, human way.

She raised her hand to his face, a finger tracing the high angle of his cheekbone, her palm against his cheek. His jaw was smooth, and the idea of him shaving before he came out tonight gave her a sweet swelling tenderness. He lifted his hand and covered hers, his calloused palm rubbing against her knuckles. Without breaking eye contact, he pulled her palm over his mouth and kissed the very center.

Charlie had been leaning against her leg, and now he barked suddenly. Fiercely. Elsa and Deacon broke apart, startled. Charlie growled, low and menacing, at two youths sauntering along the sidewalk. One of them smoked a cigarette, blowing smoke out in a gust illuminated by the streetlight.

"Evening," Deacon said.

Neither of them said anything, just stared as they walked by. Charlie kept rumbling, and as they passed, he leapt up and gave a deep, businesslike warning, barking savagely. Elsa reached for his collar.

"He's never done that before."

Deacon inhaled. "Maybe he never had reason before."

She looked after them. "Maybe not."

"Let's get you to your car," he said, and just like that, the moment had passed. He opened the door and stepped back. Charlie jumped in and Elsa paused for a moment, wondering if she should do . . . something. But neither of them did.

"Good night, Deacon," she said finally, and got in the car.

"Good night, Elsa," he said, and snugly closed the door.

At home afterward, Deacon eyed the box of paper on his table. It was a stationery set he'd bought at Hallmark, light blue paper with matching elements. Classy, he thought, and the simpleness made it masculine. Over the past three years, he'd written a lot of letters on that paper. All to Jenny.

Who didn't want his letters.

Now he took out the lined guide he'd made to keep his handwriting straight and put a sheet of the thin blue stationery over it. Using a fountain pen he'd bought specially for this purpose, he began to write, concentrating on keeping his letters clean and legible.

Dear Jenny,

I'm sitting here tonight with a couple of old dogs begging for scraps. Last night, I made scrambled eggs with cheese and jalapeños and pimentos, and I couldn't help thinking of you.

You won't remember, but we used to make that sometimes when you were little. You always liked the hot stuff, even when you were a bitty little thing. We'd make the eggs and some toast with butter and raspberry jam, then read a book or twenty together.

You don't want my letters anymore, and I get that. I'm not mad or anything. I just like writing them, thinking about you reading them, putting your hands on this very same piece of paper I'm touching right now. It's like we're still connected somehow.

When you grow up and have babies of your own, I reckon you'll get how much I love you. Or maybe you won't. I'm pretty sure my daddy never really loved any of us at all. I wish I could let you know that I do love you, and always did. You are the finest thing to ever show up in my days, ever. I didn't deserve you when you were born and did a lot to deserve you even less, and that's not a pity party, it's just God's own truth.

I love you. I let you down. You deserved better and it sounds like you got it.

But I'm realizing that these letters are partly what's been keeping me together. I guess maybe you are my Higher Power, Jenny. Wish I could have seen that sooner, but it is what it is. In your honor I try to do things better now. I pay attention. I try to listen. I don't drink. Someday, maybe, you'll come see me. Whenever that is, even if it's when we're both old and gray, that's okay with me. I will always be here. Waiting. Loving you.

Dad

He folded the letter, put it in its envelope and carried it over to the stove. He flipped on the gas burner and stuck a corner of the letter into it. When it caught, he swiveled to hold it over the sink, letting the carbon curls fall to the old porcelain.

Eased, he could finally go to bed.

Solstice

If a June night could talk, it would probably boast it invented romance.

—Bern Williams

Chapter Twenty

Elsa and Tamsin waited for Alexa at the center of the Denver airport. Midday sunlight poured through the high windows. They had been lucky enough to snag a bench, and they drank coffee out of paper cups.

"Why doesn't Starbucks recycle more?" Tamsin said, frowning at her cup. "They're supposed to be so hip, and yet how many cups do they go through in a day, do you suppose? Ten million? Not to mention these little finger protector thingies. Why don't they have recycling bins in every single Starbucks in the country?"

Elsa had been thinking of Deacon again, reliving that moment when she could have invited him to bend in and kiss her. She had wanted it. Why hadn't she?

Why hadn't *he*?

"They should definitely have recycling," she said.

Tamsin gnawed on a plastic stirrer. "This is so weird. The last time I saw my daughter, absolutely everything in my life was different. Everything. It's kind of bizarre, how everything can flip over in a second."

"Like a tsunami."

"Yeah. Or a tornado." She sipped her latte, eyes trained on the door from which exiting passengers would emerge. "It's funny how we expect things to be stable and they never really are."

"Yeah."

Tamsin looked at her sister. "You aren't listening to me at all, are you? Where's your head this morning?"

"I don't know. Maybe I'm just sleepy." She wiggled a foot, thinking of Deacon's wrist, a flat rectangle with scatters of dark hair. She thought of the shape of his mouth.

Let it go.

She took in a breath and blew it out. To redirect the conversation, she said, "Honestly, Tamsin, you are so much less—wrecked—than I would have expected."

She puffed out a bemused laugh. "I know. Me, too. I saw a friend of mine yesterday and she said I looked happier than I had in years."

"Were you unhappy in your marriage?"

"No," she said, slowly. "But I'm not sure I was happy either, you know? He was gone all the time, traveling for work, for pleasure. I—" She pursed her lips. "I think I was lonely. I think I've been lonely for a long time." She gave Elsa a perplexed little smile. "How is that possible, that you live with someone for all those years and you don't even know them, really?"

"I don't know. There's only one person I know like that, and, honestly, he probably is exactly who he seems to be."

"Joaquin, you mean."

"Who else?"

Tamsin took a breath, blew it out. "Yeah, that's true." She shook her head. "You were always his only weakness. Still are, if you ask me."

A memory floated through her, Joaquin kneeling in the gold-drenched cathedral at Santiago. Her body had still smelled of his lovemaking as he declared his intention to be a priest. "No," she said. "He loves God."

"How did that all happen, anyway?"

"It doesn't matter, Tamsin. It was a really long time ago. We're different people now." A trickle of people began to emerge from the international terminal. "Here they come."

A long line of people poured through the doors, their faces wearing the glazed and greasy mask of an overnight flight. It was more than five minutes before Alexa emerged.

"Oh, my God," Tamsin said, covering her mouth. "She looks awful!"

"Don't tell her that," Elsa said.

But it was true. Alexa had the wan look of a terminally ill patient. Her eyes were ringed with purple and her lips had been bled of color, and she'd dropped at least fifteen pounds from her already slender frame, making her collarbones and cheekbones too prominent, her arm bones awkward. She spied her mother and broke into a run, dashing through the crowd unerringly. "Mommy!" she cried, dropping her pack and flinging herself into Tamsin's arms. She burst into tears. "I just want to die."

Tamsin grasped her daughter powerfully, putting a hand on her hair, the other around that tiny waist. She gave Elsa a look of alarm over Alexa's shoulder. Elsa stepped forward and put her hand on her niece's back and leaned into her from the other side, making an Alexa sandwich. "We love you," she said, putting her cheek against the bony back. "We love you."

"We love you," Tamsin repeated. "You're home now. We're going to take care of you. Everything will be all right."

"No," Alexa gasped. "Nothing is ever going to be okay again." Her body shook with sobs. "It's all ruined."

After a time, Tamsin said, "Let's go home, baby. You can get some sleep."

Alexa curled into her misery in the backseat, covering her head with her sweater so she could sleep. How she hated this long drive down I-25 to Pueblo! It was bright and sunny and the landscape could have been Spain in some ways, the mountains and the yellow plains and the bright blue sky. But there were no tumbles of villages or ruined castles in the distance or British tourists with their apple-red cheeks. Only shopping malls and subdivisions.

And until they drove up in front of the house where her mother and Elsa had grown up, it didn't really sink in that she wouldn't be going *home,* to her pretty bedroom in the tower of the red sandstone Victorian with its blooming poppies and peonies that her mother had coaxed out of the earth.

Instead, they drove through a working-class neighborhood with frame houses all built in the twenties. Little houses, with two-foot spreads of lawn in front of them, and porches to sit on to wave at the neighbors. It was all neat enough. Flowers were blooming in the beds, tulips mostly, a few more exotic things.

She got out of the car feeling like her limbs would not carry her, and it finally occurred to her that she hadn't eaten in . . . well, a really long time. "I need food," she said.

"Done," her mother replied, getting Alexa's bag out of the trunk. "You go ahead. I'll get these things."

Elsa rushed ahead to open the front door. At the picture window, her dog barked cheerfully, his paws on the windowsill, making him seem very tall. He was big, with a shiny black coat, and a wagging tail. "What kind of dog is he?"

"This," Elsa said, opening the door to let the dog come greet them, "is Charlie. Sit." He obeyed, but his whole body wiggled with excitement as he looked from Elsa to Alexa, his mouth in a toothy smile. "He's flat-coat retriever for sure, but something more than that, too. I don't know what. Maybe Newfoundland."

"He's beautiful," she said, holding out her hand so he could smell her. He made a low noise of longing and looked at Elsa.

"Okay, baby," she said. "Greet."

He stood up and came over to Alexa to sniff her all over, curiously. She ran her hands over his fur, and it was as soft as it looked. "I've never had a dog."

"He's a good one." Elsa put her keys down on a table by the door. "Come in, sweetie, and sit at the table. I'll start some lunch. What would you like?"

The living room and dining room were one long rectangle, with windows down one side and a little archway opening into a tiny hallway. At the far end was another archway leading into the kitchen, where she could see a stove and a sink, and another window. "Where will I sleep?"

"Back here," Elsa said. "Follow me."

Alexa followed her through the kitchen to a room lined with windows that ran the width of the house, though it was only about ten feet wide. Pine paneling covered the walls and ceiling. White curtains, crisp and starched, hung at every window. Her mother's doing, Alexa was sure. She had probably even sewn them. A double bed with a cast-iron headboard, clearly ancient, took up most of the space at one end. A white chenille bedspread covered it, and someone—her mother—had piled bright-colored pillows over it, along with the stuffed animals from her childhood. A simple chest of drawers, a small end table beside the bed, and the backdoor heading into the garden. That was it.

"Your mom thought you'd want to put your things around you, so they're in the boxes right there. The room faces west, so it's hot in the late afternoon, but with all the windows, you'll have a nice breeze, and it won't be too bright in the morning."

"It's pretty," she said without feeling.

"Good. Your mom worked hard on it."

"I can tell." She put a hand over her middle.

"Come on, let's eat. I have some cheese and bread and soup. What would you like? Eggs?"

A thousand choices danced over her imagination. *Pulpo*, and fish and *churros y chocolat*. "I wish you had churros," she said.

Elsa laughed, touching her arm. "Me, too. At least you can get them here. When I left Spain, I went to England, and they had no churros at all."

A breath of something green moved through her. She had forgotten that Elsa had felt this homesickness once, this longing for the place left behind. "Did you miss it when you came home? Spain, I mean?"

"Yes," she said, and took one of Alexa's hands. "Yes, I did. Eventually it gets better."

Alexa thought of Carlos and tears began to well up in her eyes again, but she was too tired to cry anymore. She was dizzy with jet lag and hunger and grief, and she needed to eat and have a bath and go to bed, in that order. "I hope you're right," she said. "I guess I'd like some eggs."

"I can do that."

Wednesday afternoon, Elsa stopped by the church to drop off the supplies she'd gathered from various sources for the soup kitchen—a local butcher had contributed bacon scraps and ham bones; Safeway had offered day-old doughnuts and mixed cookies, which were always popular, and a bag of expired produce that included wilted celery and carrots, and some collard greens that were wilting but not yet spoiled.

Perfect. She would make caldo gallego, a Spanish peasant soup, with beans and chorizo. Using the small budget that the church provided for the soup kitchen, she purchased mixed navy and pinto beans, big fresh onions, and some dinged canned tomatoes, half stewed, half chopped. All good. As summer ripened, they would be able to harvest a lot of these things themselves. Fresh, wholesome produce! She could hardly wait.

From her own pocket, she bought a fat chicken fryer, and left it in the car when she ran everything else inside. The beans went into a bowl for soaking overnight, and the celery into an icy bath to revive it.

St. Martha gazed down benevolently from her niche in the wall. Elsa put a cookie on her foot, then headed back out. She poked her head into the church office. Mrs. Timothy sat primly at the desk, typing into her computer. "Is Father free?" Elsa asked.

Mrs. Timothy shook her head, mouth tight. "Busy all afternoon," she whispered.

Elsa waved, strangely relieved, and headed back home with her chicken. Tamsin was at work. Alexa sat on the couch, television remote in hand, flipping channels through soap operas. "Why don't you take a walk, sweetheart? Take Charlie and get outside. It's beautiful."

Alexa barely moved, flipping again. "I don't feel like it."

Her color was better, but barely, and she still couldn't seem to summon any appetite, picking at the scrambled eggs her mother had cooked, nibbling a taco, a section of tangerine. It had only been three days, but Elsa wanted to see Alexa get moving. She reached over, plucked the remote from the girl's hand, and said, "Go sit on the porch, then."

"I don't feel like it."

Elsa carried her canvas bag into the kitchen and put it on the counter. "I don't care. Do it anyway. You need some fresh air to clear your head."

"My head isn't going to clear. My life is over."

Torn, Elsa looked at the chicken, then put it away in the fridge. Grabbing Charlie's leash, she said to Alexa, "Go put on some shoes. You're going for a walk with me, like it or not."

"Whatever." She shrugged, as limp as any Victorian heroine, and shuffled off to find her shoes. Her hair was lifeless and greasy, and she had chapped lips from biting them constantly. It made Elsa think of Marianne in *Sense and Sensibility*. Maybe they should watch that movie, the one with Kate Winslet as Marianne.

It was tempting to be exasperated with such fainting despair. The adult who had weathered so much of life wanted to say, *Come on, pull up your bootstraps, kiddo, and get on with it. You have your health, your brain, your life. I know a girl who was tortured to death. She'd love to be in your shoes right now.*

But once, Elsa had been twenty-two and shattered by a broken heart. That girl lived within her, too. She remembered the needles of sorrow sticking out all over her as if she'd fallen in a patch of prickly pear cactus, the hair-fine needles excruciating whenever anything brushed them, and everything did. Clothing, sights, sounds, songs, food, and drink. Anything that reminded her of her lost love.

Alexa had not said much about what had happened, except that she couldn't be with Carlos anymore because of her father's criminal behavior. They had broken up.

The girl came out with flip-flops on her feet, and her hair tied back in a ponytail. "Ready."

"Good."

It was the kind of day that made the hot Pueblo Augusts worthwhile. The lilacs were blooming in full force, their scent filling the air, and the flower beds around the neighborhood bloomed with tulips and budding poppies. Not even a breath of wind disturbed the air. The day was quiet, with children still at school, adults at work, and they walked along the old sidewalks at an easy pace. For a long time, neither of them spoke.

From her pocket, Elsa took the rosary beads she'd found in the garden and slid them around her wrist, cool and solid. She'd been carrying them in her pocket every day. She had also been wearing the medal Joaquin had given her.

"I went to England," Elsa said. "When my heart was broken like yours is."

"Why?"

"I don't know, honestly. I just couldn't bear to come home and go back to everything being the same as it was before we left."

"Well, at least I don't have that problem."

"You've lost a lot, Alexa. Don't make light of that. Your home, your father, your boyfriend."

"My life," she said, and there was such exhaustion in the word that Elsa wanted to stop and hug her on the street. Instead, she kept walking.

"What do you mean by that? Carlos?"

Alexa's mouth worked. "I don't want to talk about all this. Okay? Please?"

To each her own. Elsa would take it as a victory that Alexa walked with her. Breathed the fresh air. "Okay."

"How far do we have to walk?"

"Just around the next block and back home, okay?"

When they got back to the house, Elsa wouldn't let Alexa turn the television on, so she went into the long bedroom they'd created, drew all the curtains, and crawled into bed with her MP3 player.

Elsa, too, found her player and stuck the buds in her ears, sliding through playlists until she found one that was a good mix of indie rock and blues and her favorite female vocalists of the moment, Pink and Sheryl Crow.

Long rays of deep gold light slanted through the kitchen window as she unwrapped the chicken, sturdy and fat, with clean pink-white skin. She washed it under cold water, and then cut it into pieces, legs and thighs first, then wings and back, which she set to one side. The breast she cut carefully in two plump pieces.

It was for Deacon. An offering. She had not stopped thinking of him since Saturday night, and although she had seen him a couple of times since, in the morning or evening at the gardens, he seemed to hold himself a little apart from her. Maybe, she thought, she had been mistaken about the attraction she sensed from him.

And yet, that kiss under the tree. The way he held her hand. Since Saturday night, she remembered over and over the way he had held her gaze and pulled her hand over his mouth. Over and over she remembered the movement of his lips against the heart of her palm. Over and over it replayed in her imagination.

In her ears, Sheryl Crow sang an entreaty. *Are you strong enough?*

As she patted the chicken dry, Alexa's sorrow floated through her. The emotion was dark purple, as thick as smoke, obscuring all that was real and true about life. Elsa let it move in her own chest, accepting it, as she measured Crisco into a heavy cast-iron skillet. She paused for a moment, closing her eyes, imagining the smoke dispersing, thinning down until her niece was bathed in a warm golden light that spilled over her in her bed, soaking into her body, all the way into her bones.

A face came into Elsa's meditation, a man bent over, weeping desperately. It startled her with its clarity. He wore a white shirt and his shoulders were broad and straight in the way of young men, and his hair was thick and curly. *Alexa!*

Elsa did not move, waiting for more. But that was all there was, Alexa in her bed, soaking in sorrow and light in equal measures, the picture of the young man weeping.

She opened her eyes and went to the door of the bedroom. Alexa lay in a pile of skinny limbs. She was fast asleep, a real sleep, a healing sleep, and Elsa let it be. Later, she'd find out more.

In the meantime, Pink's husky voice spilled out of the earphones, singing about a man in a garden, a man who called her Sugar, and in response, Elsa's skin rippled all the way up her arms and back, into her hair. She thought of Deacon's big hands and of her own hand on his face the other night.

A fever flushed her as she mixed flour and salt into a bowl, then added pepper, then a little more, until it speckled the flour. The last ingredient was nutmeg, a solid pinch. The flame beneath the skillet began to melt the fat. She imagined Deacon's mouth on her own, imagined the slow heat of his tongue, and thought of his hands moving over her skin. She dredged chicken pieces in the flour mixture, coating them thoroughly, and putting each piece on a clean plate to set, thinking of her and Deacon's limbs tangled, his raspy voice in her ear.

When the fat was hot, she lowered the chicken into it carefully, letting it swell up in bubbles over the edges. The breasts went in last, flesh down. Elsa covered the pan and set the timer. The smell filled the kitchen, heat and seasoning and simmering skin.

She wiped her brow and her neck and sat down to wait.

Chapter Twenty-One

Elsa couldn't sleep. She awakened every half hour or so, thinking of Alexa and the weeping man, or Deacon holding her hand against his face, or for some bizarre reason, Joaquin running along the levee. She half thought, half dreamed of her congregation back in Seattle wandering like loose sheep in a meadow, and she saw Kiki there among them, eating a taco. Elsa hugged her. "I thought you were dead," she said, in relief. Kiki said, "You know better than that."

The words lingered as she awakened, looking up into the darkness. *You know better than that.*

Finally, just after four, she got up and took a shower, washing away all of the half thoughts and hungers and losses as well as she could. Her neck was tired and it would be a long day at the soup kitchen, but a good walk in the cool morning would be a tonic to her soul.

Before she left, however, she pulled out the tortilla España she had made for her niece last night, eggs and fried potatoes cooked together with onions and salt. Ordinary. Comforting. She wrote a note that said,

Microwave on medium for 1:30. EAT! Love, E

And propped it against the dish.

Tucking the wrapped fried chicken into a backpack, she headed out with Charlie just as the sun began to brighten the eastern horizon. They made their way to the levee, and met the sun just beginning to rise, as if emerging from the Arkansas River. On her right, the water turned topaz and opal, shimmering against the sand and the industrial clutter of the landscape. Birds twittered in the trees to her left, and she was nearly on a level with their nests. A pair of muscular Rottweilers barked warnings from someone's backyard.

Coming toward her was a runner, backlit so that his features were obscured. It was only as he nearly overtook them that she realized it was Joaquin, looking not at all like a priest in his bike shorts and a zippered performance top that left his throat exposed. She rarely saw it. The shorts showed off his beautifully muscled thighs and calves, and she wolf-whistled playfully. "Looking good, Father Jack."

He grinned, and stopped. "Yeah?" He touched his lean middle. "Not too skinny?"

"No, Father. I think you've been putting a little weight on, haven't you?"

"It's not hard with this parish, let me tell you." He blew out hard, put his hands on his hips. Sunlight burnished his black hair with a copper gloss. A part of her, the part that was grieving along with Alexa, remembered how much she had loved touching that hair. It was a wistful emotion, a husk of longing.

"I can imagine." She shook off her thoughts and looked at him, her oldest friend, her brother. "Hey, we might need your help with Alexa. She's not really eating. She has a terrible broken heart. She's pining . . . for Spain, for her lover, for everything she lost."

He closed his eyes, hands still on his hips, and took a breath. His tongue touched his lower lip and then he looked at her, cheeks burning. "The circle turns, doesn't it?"

"I didn't mean it like that."

"I know." He swallowed. "It's me. It's all the things I've been thinking about since you've been back."

She waited, feeling the roles between them shift, as they often did—one the mentor, one the mentee, and then the other way around. He needed Reverend Elsa right now. "My being here is bringing things up, isn't it?"

His nostrils flared. "I've questioned everything."

"We never have dealt with it, really. It was over so fast. One day we were engaged and in love and the next we were finished." She took a breath, letting it cool the heat in her throat. "We were together for a long time. We should have taken some time to bury the old relationship."

He said, "I still love you, you know."

"Of course."

"No," he said, stepping forward, that dark intensity in his eyes. "I mean, *love* you. Those feelings didn't change at all."

"I knew what you meant, Joaquin." That sorrow that had been swirling around Alexa now engulfed them, obscuring the bright shining sun, the sound of the birds.

And then the church bell began to ring, signaling six a.m. Joaquin raised his head and smiled ruefully. "I've always loved how the sound of bells carries the power of exorcism. We can all use that once or twice a day."

Relieved, she laughed. "Let's get to work, Walking. I've got bellies to fill and you've got souls to minister." They took the path down the hill off the levee. "I dreamed about my congregation last night," she said. "They were wandering around a pasture."

"A flock without a shepherd?"

"Maybe." She reached level ground. "Maybe it's starting to feel like I might go back."

"You know I'll miss you, but I hope you will."

As they neared the church, she turned off toward the kitchen, Joaquin toward a shower. "It's all going to work out the way it should," she said.

He smiled, both sadly and wisely. "Yes."

When he was out of sight, Elsa ducked around the back of the church to see if she could spy Deacon's truck. It wasn't there, and she went inside, putting the chicken away in the fridge before she got to work on the soup.

Having started so early, she was alone for quite some time, thinking about the people who would come to eat the soup today. It was the end of the month again, so there would be more children and mothers, along with the usual suspects. She cut the bacon ends into pieces and browned them in a heavy pot, rendering the fat she then used to soften chopped onions, diced carrots, garlic, and celery over low heat. The fragrance began to fill the kitchen, easing the tension she'd been feeling. The ham hocks and beans went into the pot, and she brought it all to a full rolling boil, then covered it and turned it down to a simmer.

As she cooked, she thought of Joseph, and Deacon's comment that he sometimes fell off the wagon. What would help strengthen an old man? There was an old, old herbal in the basement, an encyclopedia of ways to use herbs in healing and in cooking. She dashed downstairs to get it. When she came back up, Deacon was pulling the big coffeemaker out of the pantry.

Her moist thoughts of his body rushed through her and it suddenly seemed as if the chicken was a fool's offering, silly and girlish.

"Hey, Deacon," she said. Even in her own ears, she sounded false.

"Hey, Elsa. How's it going?"

She nodded, not looking at him, wondering if her neck was as red as it was hot. She gave the soup a good stir, then leaned against the counter, flipping the book open. He carried the coffeepot over to the sink and started filling it.

"How's your niece?" he asked.

"Wrecked. Her entire life was just turned completely upside down."

"Poor kid."

She flipped through the herbal, reading lists and recipes here and there. Tea for high blood pressure. Tea for weight loss. *Ah, alcoholics.*

"Is everything all right, Elsa?" Deacon asked.

She met his eyes. "Yes. Just a minute." She went to the fridge and pulled out the package of foil-wrapped chicken. "I made you something."

His eyes crinkled. "Well, well, well. For me? What is it?"

"Fried chicken. You can take it home with you."

He slipped open one end and stuck his nose inside to smell. "Have mercy," he murmured, closing his eyes. An absurd sense of pleasure moved through her.

He straightened. "You cooked for me."

She nodded. In the distance, she heard two women's voices approaching. Her volunteers.

"Does this mean you like me?"

She smiled. "Yes."

He pushed the chicken into her hands and turned toward the coffeemaker. "You want to help me carry this all downstairs?" he said as the two women came around the corner.

"Sure. Viola, will you check the bread dough? I'll be right back."

"No problem."

Deacon led the way. Elsa fixed her gaze on his blue shirt, tucked in at his belt, feeling a honeyed charge in her limbs. When they reached the basement, he put the coffeemaker on its table and took the chicken out of her hands. She stepped back, but he caught her hand. "I'm too old for you."

"Yes, you are," she agreed. "You must be at least seventy, right?"

"May as well be," he rasped, and put his hand around her neck, beneath her hair, and pulled her close.

And kissed her. Elsa leaned into him, tilted her head, opened her mouth to let him in. He tasted clean, and smelled of shaving cream and a spicy deodorant, and Elsa let herself fly into the moment, really tasting him, touching him, her hands on his arms, his chest, his waist, every inch of him lean and muscled from the work he did.

After a moment, he hauled her closer, one hand on her face, the other roaming over her back. She arched upward, luxuriously, imagining how it would feel to be bare chest to bare chest. A hungry little sigh rose in her throat.

"Sweet Jesus," he whispered, raising his head for a moment. Their eyes met, and Elsa fell into that, too, dizzy with the intimacy of looking so closely at him, seeing the flecks of green and gold in his irises, the strong arch of his brows. Holding her gaze, he bent to kiss her again, and she was the first to lower her lids, afraid of what might be written in her expression. His hands, those big hands, hauled her bottom closer to him. She pulled his shirt out in the back so she could put her hands on his skin, feeling as if there was a sizzle when flesh met flesh.

Naked.

The thought, so vivid, sent a bolt of such lusty heat through her that she wanted to have sex right there, right then, on the floor if necessary. It burned from groin to belly to breasts and made her want to bite him, growl. He sucked sharply at her lower lip, his hands tightening hard on her bottom. It was all she could do not to rub against his thigh, put her hand on him, too.

Abruptly, she pulled back. "We—I—um—" She clapped her hands to her overheated cheeks. "Someone is going to be down here any second. We have to stop."

He nodded, his eyes sober as he reached for a lock of hair that stuck to her face. His pupils were dilated, his face as flushed as her own must be. He took a step back. "Here's the thing, Elsa. He's my friend."

"Who?"

"Father Jack."

She scowled, stepping away from him. "You're misunderstanding our friendship. That's all it is."

"I'm not misunderstanding, Elsa. It's pure, and platonic, I believe that, but that doesn't change some realities." He ran a finger down her arm. "You move like a married couple. Right in sync."

She yanked her arm away from his touch. "He married the church instead of me," she said, and had to lift her chin hard to avoid showing too much sorrow. "He was the love of my life, I won't lie. It just about killed me when he"—she held up her hands and flung them to the heavens—"answered the call from his own very special angel. He left me, and frankly I don't give a *damn* what he thinks of my love life. He's my friend, and that's it."

"Elsa—"

She sidestepped his reach, backing away. "No. I don't really want to talk to you right now." She whirled and went upstairs to finish the soup.

Most evenings, Joaquin had parish duties. He visited the sick at home and in hospitals; he had dinner with families who invited him over; he visited the elderly. His was a full life, and so he treasured his solitary moments. He liked his Mondays off, and used the time to read, to drive to the mountains to hike, to have dinner with friends and relatives. His was a large clan, and he was glad to live in his hometown again. His older relatives, especially, were delighted that there was a priest in the family. He knew they sometimes speculated over his career possibilities. Maybe he'd be a bishop someday! Even . . . who knows, he's smart and devoted . . . a cardinal!

A rich life, even without adding his devotion to God, which was true and deep and kept him company throughout all his other duties. It gave him joy to be the face of God for those who needed him—an old man who could not speak for the tubes in his throat, a grieving widow who couldn't accept her husband's death, the lonely and old and poor and forgotten.

But every so often, there was this reality, too.

Eating alone, a little too late, in the rectory kitchen on a Thursday night. The overhead fixture cast a greenish light over the old linoleum, and the fluorescent buzzed faintly, all the time. He had been on his feet nearly all day, taking sacraments to one of his deacons, attending a business meeting at the cathedral, participating in a committee meeting about the beautification of the grounds. He had avoided the soup kitchen, embarrassed at his impassioned confession to Elsa.

His body was tired when he took the foil-wrapped packet of fried chicken Deacon had given him this afternoon and a grapefruit soda from the fridge and carried both to the table. Inside the foil were a hearty-sized breast and a thigh. Beautiful. He was very hungry.

It was perfect chicken. The skin crispy, not greasy, the meat perfectly tender. His stomach growled, like an animal grabbing a prize. Aside from the faint buzz of the overhead light, his world was utterly silent—the rooms above and around him, the church and its warren of rooms and basement and offices. All empty. Quiet.

Save for Joaquin, sitting alone eating perfectly fried chicken some woman had made for Deacon, angling to capture his heart. Women cooked for Joaquin, too, lots of women, and he knew their hearts were not always completely innocent. The stories he could tell of women trying to seduce him were legion, but a priest did not tell. And he was immune to their coaxing. They were lonely or ignored or unhappy in their lives. He stood in front of them week after week, offering the face of God, the hands of God, and they spun their fantasies around him. It was how things were.

He peeled away a perfectly crisp layer of skin and put it in his mouth, tasting salt and a spice he could not name. He sucked the flavor from his fingers and lifted the moist flesh to his mouth and sucked the juices there, closing his eyes, thinking of Elsa's smooth olive throat, her breasts, her tiny, tiny waist. The only woman in his life. The only one he had ever wanted.

The second time he'd seen the angel, Joaquin had been exhausted from walking the Camino. Weeks and weeks and weeks they'd walked, in the rain and the blistering sun. He had not taken it seriously, but he should have. Before they left, he had dreamed he was swallowed whole by a monstrous bird with fierce bright wings.

The angel came to him in the same green light and gown she'd worn before. This time, he was not sick. He was not feverish. He was not afraid. He was only cold and tired, and ready to be finished with this crazy undertaking that he'd done largely for Elsa's sake. They would go home and be married.

He'd been uncomfortable and restless for days, haunted by dreams full of whispers, and a sense of impending doom. Each time they passed a church, he had ducked within and dropped a coin into the bucket to pay to light a candle. *Keep us safe*, he'd prayed. *Keep us safe*.

Twice, they had been trailed by a black dog, a big shepherd mix of the type that was so common on the road, and Joaquin had wanted to run away from it. Elsa left it food.

They had taken shelter in the concrete hut, alone, which was a miracle in itself, so close to the finishing mark. The rain poured down with rare intensity, driving everyone off the Camino, into friendly bars or hostels. Elsa curled up into a ball and went to sleep. Joaquin watched over her, and he moved along the walls, reading the petitions and prayers and graffiti. It was always so touching to think of what they carried, the pilgrims who'd walked this road—the offerings they had made so that God would take away their pain or cure a child or bring back a lost wife. He found himself touching the words, praying on behalf of the writers, one and another and another, whispering with them, however long it had been. After a time, he fell into a meditative state, apart from the rain and his body. His nose was cold and his arm began to ache, but he kept touching the petitions.

He saw the light first, that spill of palest green, which he had come to believe over the years was just something his childish brain had filled in for him. It softly glowed in a corner of the room. Joaquin turned, feeling both dread and piercing excitement. There was the angel, so startlingly familiar and beautiful, wearing a green gown. Her eyes were clear and large and very dark. "It's time, Joaquin," she said.

He frowned at her, the fingertips of his right hand still touching the wall. He shook his head, denying her or the moment or what she was about to ask.

"You will be a priest. When you leave Santiago, you will leave your old life behind."

Again he shook his head, gesturing toward Elsa. "I'm to be married."

She gazed at him steadily and in her eyes he saw what eternity might look like, vast and beautiful.

A third time, like Peter, he shook his head in denial. But his eyes filled with tears as he knelt on the cold hard floor and felt the angel surround him, filling him with light.

All these years later, alone in the rectory kitchen, he knew he could not have denied her. It was the greatest joy and the greatest sacrifice of his life.

Deacon had the option of choosing one of the women who brought him plates of food. A woman to be his partner and listen to his problems and random observations. He would lie with her at night, and when he awakened in the darkness, she would be there, and he could put an arm around her and hold her close.

Grief rose in Joaquin. This was the suffering that was his to bear, the loss of this simple, ordinary thing—a wife to keep him company and bear witness to his life. He longed for it, longed for Elsa. To make love, yes, of course. It was a simple, cornerstone pleasure in life, and they had been well matched. But more, he longed for her face at breakfast, for her comfort in the middle of the night, for her hand on his head when he was overcome with human suffering.

The loss of it welled in him, filled him like a dark smoke, and he bent his head to his arms. Would it really have made him a lesser priest if he had married? What would have been lost if he had children to fill the rectory? To bring him his slippers when he was tired, as he had brought his own father's?

He wept, ashamed of his weakness and longing, but so filled with it that he could not help it. *What would it have cost you,* he asked the silent heavens, *to let us have wives?*

He fell asleep just like that, his head on his arms, chicken bones spread around him.

Deacon, too, had chicken for supper. It was dark by the time he made it home, and he was dead tired. He was getting too old to dig in the dirt and haul 4 x 4's and manhandle bags of peat. He'd be fifty in three years, and he felt it in every bone and muscle in his aching back.

He tended the dogs, filling the water dishes and food bowls, giving each dog a good dose of loving. He'd diapered Sasha before he left, and now he took it off and shooed her outside. The others, smelling chicken, had no intention of leaving him. Joe made his laborious way to the table and plunked down, waiting with sad eyes for Deacon to join him. Mikey, the Shih Tzu, skittered forward and back, eagerly looking up at Deacon for the possibility of a treat, until Deacon finally got fed up with it and barked out, "Go lie down."

The chicken was perfectly golden brown, the batter speckled with pepper and something reddish. Each piece was just right, the crust not too thick or too thin or falling off. He debated heating it in the microwave, but feared the breading would go soft.

Still, he wanted hot food, not cold. He'd give it a try with a lesser piece, see how it worked. Choosing a thigh, fat and battered, he wrapped it in waxed paper and heated it in the microwave for a minute, then let it sit in its own grease for another minute while he opened a can of beans and put them in a pot to heat.

When he unwrapped the chicken, it steamed. When he bit into it, the skin was crisp, but hot juices burst out and spilled down his chin, salty and delicious. He closed his eyes, chewing. Perfect.

Elsa came into his mind. Elsa, Elsa, Elsa. He'd thought of little else for days. Weeks, really, since that first day when they'd planted the garden. He'd seen her slip away, weeping over the blessing, and then come back with her little fierce face, determined to be present, even if it was hard.

Grit. He liked that about her. In fact, he had yet to find anything about her he didn't like. She was good with the kids, and a no-nonsense organizer who pulled off the feat of the soup kitchen every week as if it were coffee for her sister. Her newest venture was to organize Saturday night potlucks in the garden, giving the gardeners a chance to share recipes, trade secrets, and generally cement the place as a community center. Smart.

He wrapped the rest of the chicken pieces individually and put them on the plate to heat in the microwave, then returned his attention to the thigh in his hand. Thighs, breasts. He liked those things about Elsa, too, physical things. Her hair, especially, caught him every time, those dark glossy spirals. It was such healthy hair, the evidence of good living. He wanted to undress her, taste her, shake that composed exterior into a frenzy of—

The trouble was Father Jack. Who loved her even if he never said so. Deacon owed him. A lot. A good man didn't steal a woman his friend loved.

But if that friend was a priest? Didn't that change things?

He wiped his fingers and put the chicken bones in a bag in the sink—if he didn't get them outside, one of the dogs would find them and choke to death. The microwave dinged. He dished up the beans, and took them to the table, where he turned on his iPod, connected to a small dock. The music looped out, quiet blues tunes, and it eased the tenseness in his neck.

He had met Father Jack when he was in prison in Cañon City, so full of anger and shame he was like a whirling tornado. He'd been chosen to participate in a program for recovering alcoholics to take some training in anger management and prayer, and despite his upbringing, he'd gone for it. Father Jack and a Protestant minister of some kind led the sessions once every other week.

Deacon liked Jack immediately—his earthy sense of humor, his realness. He seemed less a priest than a man who had happened to run into God somewhere at a watering hole and had become good friends with him.

Even now, Deacon envied him that relationship. He sometimes thought he might have a glimmering of the Divine, and he sure had long talks with his Higher Power, because a drunk like himself wouldn't stay sober long without them.

But he didn't know God like Jack did.

Or Joaquin, as Elsa called him.

He rubbed his face and tried to shake it off. Elsa, Jack, Joaquin, God, angels, the garden, all of it. The chicken waited, hot and salty and juicy, and Deacon began to eat. Slowly. Savoring it. Hot juices, tender flesh. He thought of Elsa's mouth, plump and succulent and eager, thought of her hands on his lower back this morning, moving in little circles, and the press of her pelvis against his.

He closed his eyes, half-dizzy, and took a breath. His libido gave him a vision of her naked on his bed, that black hair scattered over his white pillowcases. He would begin at her forehead and kiss every inch of her body. He would not let her move until he had done that, covered her with his mouth and tongue. And then—

A scratching at the back door startled him out of the fantasy, and he stood up, adjusting himself like a teenager. He let the dog in, and his craving moved with him, on the back of his neck and the small of his back, in his belly and his knees and his mouth.

She deserved to be more than the surrogate wife of a celibate priest.

But what did Jack deserve?

And Deacon supposed that he, as a man who'd already lost a perfectly decent family, and the killer of a mother, didn't technically deserve anything at all.

A strange, ancient desire rose in him then, a remembrance of whiskey, the way it blotted out dilemmas like this one. He could taste it on the back of his throat, the fire and relief, the letting go.

Dangerous, that. Maybe it was a sign that he wasn't ready for anything as intense as this might be. Wiser to stay away, keep her at arm's length.

If he could.

Chapter Twenty-Two

In the dead of night, Alexa snuck into the living room to check her email on Elsa's laptop computer. She used a web-based service and logged on, finding a long line of messages from the same address. Clenching her teeth, she highlighted the whole list and put her finger on the delete key.

At the last minute, she couldn't resist just the smallest glimpse of him, the small pleasure of hearing his voice through his written words. Bracing herself, she opened the first.

> Azul, Azul, Azul! Where have you gone? I am bereft. Your ring is on a chain around my neck, close to my heart. I will wear it until you return.

It was like shards of glass slamming into her heart. She thought of his chest, covered with silky black hair, thought of her beautiful ring lying against his heart. She punched the button to read the next one.

> Where have you gone? Every day I wake up thinking that today is the day you will call me. Or knock on my door. I know there must be some explanation for this terrible disappear-

ance, but I cannot think why you could not talk with me about it. Cara, cara, cara, please. I am bereft without you.

Tears began to leak from her eyes, blurring the screen. She should not have started reading them. She could hear his voice clearly, feel his touch. But now she couldn't stop.

Cara, Azul, I cannot eat, I cannot sleep. I pace all day, going to the roof to see if I might catch sight of you coming closer. Where are you? Why will you not respond? My heart is bleeding.

And another.

The world is bled dry of color without your eyes. There is no music I can bear without your laughter. I can barely breathe the air if it does not have your perfume in it.

Where are you? Why have you run away?

And the last one:

I am losing faith, my dearest love. I fear you will never return, and I will die if that is so. You think I jest, but this is true and real, this love between us. I will *die* without you. My life is draining through my fingers, into the earth. Without you, I am nothing.

Alexa crumpled into a fetal ball, covering her ears with her hands to banish his voice. She was dying, too, she could feel it. Without him, there was no reason to live.

Tamsin found her daughter asleep on the living room floor, her magnificent hair spread around her. For a moment, she looked dead, and Tamsin pressed her hands over her heart, feeling like Lady Capulet. Then she saw Alexa breathe, and realized that she was only asleep.

The girl looked so wretchedly miserable. Her cheekbones

stood out like hawk wings, her skin was as pale as chalk. Tamsin sank down beside her, touched her hair, brushed it away from her face. "Wake up, sweetie. You're going to get a crick in your neck."

Alexa stirred, rolling over to rest her head in Tamsin's lap. "Why did he do this?"

"Carlos?"

"No, Dad. How could he be so cruel to us when we were supposedly the center of his world? How could he do something so terrible?"

Tamsin drew her fingers through her daughter's hair, thinking of the pat answers, that Scott had a disease, a gambling disease, and he couldn't help it. But Tamsin didn't feel the truth of that herself, and her daughter needed more. Deserved more. "Sometimes people take a wrong turn, baby. A really, really bad turn. He loves you. I know that. I know he would have tried to spare you." Against her body, Alexa tensed a little, or maybe only came to attention. "I think it must have just gotten out of control and he didn't know how to get off the merry-go-round."

Alexa pushed herself to a sitting position. "You shouldn't let yourself get into a position like that in the first place. He can't be the person I thought he was."

"No," Tamsin agreed. "Probably not."

Alexa hung her head. "What am I going to do?"

"The next thing. And the one after that." Tamsin thought about reaching for her daughter again, but she kept her hands in her lap. "Today, you need to take a shower. And get dressed, and take a walk."

"And go where? Do what?"

"I don't know. That's up to you. What you have to stop doing is only sleeping and crying. Now you have to get up and get dressed."

"Whatever." She pulled herself upright, a collection of bones.

Tamsin half expected to hear skeletal clattering as she walked to the back room. "You don't understand."

"Elsa does," Tamsin said. "And so will Father Jack. Go talk to him."

"What does a priest know about a broken heart?"

"He wasn't born a priest, you know. He's still a man. He can help you. He helped me."

"I don't want to talk to anybody." She slipped into the other room.

Tamsin made herself a pot of coffee and some oatmeal and toast, trying to be quiet. Instead of getting dressed, Alexa had gone back to sleep, snoring quietly through her congested nose, and since Elsa still had nightmares, Tamsin hated to wake her when she was sleeping in apparent peace.

She carried her breakfast into the dining area of her childhood home, feeling oddly content. Safe, in this little pocket of time when crisis had thrown her together with her sister and her daughter, the two people in the world she genuinely loved. Calamity had brought her a measure of company, revealing just how lonely she'd been before.

But this time would not last. Alexa would heal. Elsa would find out if she still believed in God, and would return to her church or find something else to do. What would Tamsin do? Work in the fabric section of Walmart forever, living in her childhood home until she became an old woman?

Maybe she needed to start thinking about her own future. How to live, what to do, what kind of work she might want to pursue.

She took a bite of toast and oatmeal together, and slid her finger over the center of the tracking square on the laptop. Alexa's email account was on the screen, showing a list of emails from the same person, Carlos Galíndez. *Please!* one subject line said. *I love you, please call me*, said another.

Tamsin scowled, sorely tempted to open just one of the emails to find out what was going on. All this time, she had assumed that Carlos had broken up with Alexa, not the other way around. But before she could follow through with her snooping, she clicked to sign out.

What was the breakup about? Was Alexa ashamed? Was it about money?

Maybe Tamsin should send Alexa back, to work things out or at least give it a try.

A cold slap of reality doused that idea. A trip to Spain would cost more than a thousand dollars. Tamsin didn't have two hundred, and even if she sold all the quilts she'd taken out of the house, she wouldn't have very much. The best quilts, the ones she could sell for real money, were still locked up there.

For a moment, she felt the unfairness of her situation again. After so many years of comfortable living, she had nothing now. Not even a thousand dollars for a plane ticket for her brokenhearted daughter.

The burn rose and Tamsin slid her finger over the track pad to bring up the screen again. She signed on to her quilting boards, needing the distraction of her compatriots to blot out the heavy questions of the morning. The questions of what to do with her life and how to save her daughter were too big to answer just this moment.

What could she do *today*? She could quilt. She could make something beautiful. She might not have much control over her life right now, but she could have control over those scraps of fabric. She could create order out of disorder.

And then it hit her. The earrings Scott had given her. The giant diamonds she'd tucked into the secret stash in her bread box last fall and completely forgotten about.

Holy cow. She laughed, and then clapped her hands over her mouth. Beautiful!

She'd left that window open. She would sneak back in and get the earrings, and while she was at it, she'd steal the rest of her quilts, too. She would steal back her own property and then she would sell them on eBay.

But the earrings. The earrings could make a big difference. Energized, she finished her breakfast, gulped down her coffee, and headed for the shower. She had to be at work soon, but she'd go by afterward.

And tonight over dinner, she'd get to the bottom of what had happened between Carlos and Alexa.

Which reminded her to leave a note for Elsa.

> *Hey, sis, will you make sure Alexa gets up and takes a shower and goes for a walk today, please? Maybe set up a counseling schedule w/Fr Jack. See you after work.*
>
> *Xoxox, Tamsin.*

Humming quietly under her breath, she headed for the shower herself. It was only as she stuck her head under the spray that she realized that the tune was "I'm in the Money." She laughed aloud. Oh, life could be so sweet!

It was Friday morning, almost time for Elsa's standing date with Joaquin. She was half-tempted to skip it, and the thought rolled around in her mind as she roused Alexa and made her take a shower, then sat with her while she ate some scrambled eggs. "You're making me eat and you're not having anything?" her niece asked.

"I have plans for breakfast." She sipped her coffee. "In fact, I want you to come over to the church in about two hours and find me in the rectory. We'll do some gardening."

"I don't feel like doing that."

"Well, I'm sorry. You have to come anyway."

"How will I get there?"

"Walk."

"It's miles!"

"Maybe two miles, I guess. It will be good for you."

"No." She shoved her plate away. A small pile of eggs remained on it. "I'm not walking."

Elsa pushed the plate back. The point was fresh air and exercise, which they would find in the garden. "Eat the rest of your eggs and I'll leave you the keys to my car."

For a moment, Alexa scowled. Then she picked up her fork. "Fine."

Elsa stood and kissed her head. "My keys are on the hook over there. See you in two hours."

Alexa nodded.

"Promise?"

"Yes," she said with exasperation. "I promise."

Elsa had not actually spoken with Joaquin after the odd moments on the levee yesterday. The conversation had been strange enough, but then Deacon had followed it with his weird . . . what? Accusation? Insight? Skewed loyalty?

Whatever. She was irritated with men in general, and it was good for her to walk. She and Charlie wound through the sleepy, morning-lit streets. She could suddenly taste summer in the air. The trees were no longer clothed in the delicate pastels of spring, but had donned the vigorous palette of summer. Roses and peonies had replaced lilacs in the yards along her route. She passed a stout woman in a housedress, waving a hand sprinkler back and forth across the beds. "It's gonna be a hot one today," the woman called.

"That's what I hear." It had been a long time since she'd spent summer in Pueblo, and she looked forward to it. The long evenings alive with crickets and the calls of children, the afternoons so hot and bright you found the coolest spot in the house and curled up for a nap.

The door to the rectory was standing open, and Elsa called through the screen door, "Knock, knock."

"Come in," Joaquin called.

She pulled open the screen door, a sturdy wooden one, and let Charlie run in ahead, but he looked over his shoulder and whined. "Okay," she said, "you go run in the field." She unleashed him and he took off with a happy little yelp, as if he were off to meet a buddy. "Funny dog."

Joaquin stood at the sink, filling the coffeepot. He had not yet changed out of his running clothes. "Sorry," he said, "I'm headed for the shower right now. Just fell a little behind this morning."

His shirt was an old turquoise running tank, so old the letters were worn off across the front. It showed the long length of his throat and his arms, the color of pecans. He must smell sweaty, but to Elsa he just smelled like Joaquin, heady and sharp and real. "Go," she said, waving her hand in front of her nose as if he stunk. "I'll take care of getting things started. What's on the menu this morning?"

He backed from the sink, not quite meeting her eyes. "Hadn't really thought about it yet. What are you in the mood for?"

"I don't care. Did you run a long time? Maybe you want pancakes?" She poured water into the coffeemaker. "Are there some frozen berries?"

"Yeah, okay, that sounds good." He still had not met her eyes, and she was suddenly aware of a thick awkwardness between them.

"Is everything okay?"

His head came up. "What do you mean?"

"I don't know. You're just acting kind of weird."

A flush of color touched his cheekbones—embarrassment or secrets or something—and she inclined her head. "Walking? What's up?"

But he just shook his head. "I'll be back down in five minutes."

"Pancakes?" she called after him.

His voice was muffled as he dashed up the stairs. "Fine."

So Elsa turned the radio on to the local pop station and started taking out the ingredients and utensils they would need—flour and eggs and milk and berries, the scarred electric griddle, pancake turner, and a glass bowl, blue with red and yellow stripes, that had probably been there since the second world war. As she turned the griddle on, a thought tickled her imagination, and as she stirred the ingredients together, she spun a scenario of what this place might have been like seventy years ago, when there had been two priests and sometimes a seminarian for the summer, and a flock of nuns who lived in the convent across the street who taught in the old school. Bustling, busy, vital.

It still was. Sunlight splashed through the windows, and she could spy San Roque in the courtyard. Roses grew up a trellis behind him, sending their scent into the air, and a big white cat sat nearby, grooming himself in the sunshine. His fur was glossy and beautiful. On impulse, she went to the door. "Here, kitty kitty," she called.

He lifted his head, his pink tongue still sticking out the tiniest bit, which made her laugh, and put his paw down. She didn't think this was the same cat she'd seen before. There was a gaggle of them, a pack of feral strays who lived on the smaller creatures who populated the riverbanks. "Come on," she called. "Come here, kitty, kitty."

He thought about it, then decided she might be all right, and sauntered over, a big healthy male. Elsa stepped into the courtyard and he bumped against her leg with an arched back. She bent down to pet him, finding his fur thick and silky. "What's your name, baby?" she cooed. "Do you want some breakfast?"

He chirruped, his tail high, and she said, "Just a minute. Let me find you something."

She dashed into the kitchen, looked in the pantry and found

a can of tuna, and opened it. The cat stood on the other side of the screen door, tail waving back and forth across the ground like a snake, but his posture was otherwise patient. "You're so pretty," she cooed, spooning half the can onto a plate. He bent over it with delicate intent.

"Are you feeding that cat?" Joaquin asked from behind her. He'd tucked himself into his clerical clothes. His collar was tightly in place against his neck. Even his hair was slicked back from his face. "He'll never quit now."

"Is he a stray? He seems well tended."

"I think somebody abandoned him."

She gave him a sideways smile. "Ah, so this is not the first time he's been fed at this door."

"Maybe not." He clapped her on the arm. "Come on, let's get breakfast going. I have a busy day."

"Anything interesting?" She checked the heat of the griddle with a few drops of water. They danced across the surface, so she ladled out pancake batter.

He poured coffee for both of them, splashed milk into hers and set it beside her. "Not really. Or not more or less interesting than most days. Just a lot going on. Wedding season is upon us."

"Ah." She sipped her coffee, and spilled some onto one of the pancakes. "Dang it. I'm so clumsy this morning! I stubbed my toe stepping up to a curb." She scraped up the bad pancake and stepped on the lever of the trash can to lift the lid. It was quite full. Right on top were the remains of a chicken breast and drumstick, along with a tangle of foil. "Chicken for dinner?" she asked, feeling airless.

"Yes. Deacon brought it to me. Some woman made it for him, I think."

Still holding the spatula, she looked back at him. "Is that what he said?"

Joaquin had been sorting through a stack of mail, and now

raised his head to look at her. For a long, long moment they were silent, knowledge passing between them, back and forth, back and forth.

At last, Joaquin said, "Not exactly. I made the assumption. Women are always bringing him things. Food, socks they've knitted."

Elsa carefully, precisely, flipped a pancake. "I see."

"Did you make it for him?"

For the first time in their entire relationship, Elsa lied, too humiliated to say yes. "No. Who has time for that?"

After breakfast, Elsa headed to the garden. Alexa would be there soon. They could do a little weeding, then she'd let the girl off the hook to go hibernate. Elsa didn't know what she would do with herself, though. She felt restless—irritable, even.

The cat had curled up beneath a rosebush at San Roque's feet. She stopped to pet him, and he purred but didn't open his eyes. A pink climbing rose curled around the saint's pedestal. Absently, Elsa plucked one and laid it at his feet, thinking, *A dog for Calvin, home for a stray cat*.

It was beginning to dawn on her that she didn't have enough to do. For more than a decade, she'd been involved in a demanding career, part counselor, part teacher, part shepherd. The variety and constantly shifting roles of the job had appealed to her most of all. For a minute, she looked up at San Roque, his kind eyes. "You have any thoughts on this?"

But he didn't speak, not like Joaquin's angel. "That's another thing," she said, pulling the leaves and flowers rosary out of her pocket as she sat down. "Joaquin gets an angel and I get nada? And you let Kiki be killed." She rubbed the flat part of the leaf, feeling the tiny engravings of veins. "Not you, you, of course, but *You*. That You. I get that you need us to do your work, so why didn't you just nudge *me?*"

It was the first time she'd been able to articulate that thought.

Elsa had been right there, not even a half mile from where Kiki was being tortured and raped. It haunted her. What had she been doing during the hours Kiki had prayed and cried and dreamed of rescue? Washing dishes, complaining that the pantry was a mess again, writing an email.

She bent her head. *Why not me?*

The sun was surprisingly hot against the top of her head. It made her think of Spain, of childhood sunburns, of sitting in a field somewhere with Joaquin when they were barely teenagers, trying to best each other with stories of wounds and illnesses.

It made her sleepy, and she closed her eyes, letting the sunlight turn the back of her eyelids red.

And just like that, she fell sideways into the vastness. The bigness. The everythingness of meditation. All boundaries dissolved entirely and she was no longer contained by human arms and legs, but could swim between the molecules of everything, outward into sunlight and the liquid scent of roses hanging in the air and thorns and cat and galaxy and back through her own body, into the deep red muscles of her heart, the blue rivers of her veins, and then again outward, to all things in all universes here and all through time, everywhere. It was the opposite of fear, the absence of loss, the soft wave of time and history and love and—

She jerked herself back to real time. To the solid concrete bench beneath her, to the beads in her hand, so hot she yanked them off her wrist. Her cheeks were wet with tears.

The cat had emerged from under the roses and he blinked a smile at her, his tail switching over the earth. If he were a cat in a fairy tale, he would be San Roque come to life, or a messenger of the saint. Instead, he was only a stray cat, healthy and very much a flesh and blood being.

Who needed a home.

In sudden decision, she scooped him up and carried him, unresisting and purring loudly, back into the rectory. Joaquin was in his office, guarded by Mrs. Timothy, but Elsa waved a hand. "This is important," she said, and breezed by. The cat was so big he completely filled her arms, and his outstretched paws bounced.

Joaquin was doing paperwork and he looked up in surprise.

"San Roque is giving you a present. This is your cat."

"He's white!" Joaquin protested, indicating his black shirt and pants. "He'll shed all over me."

She nodded. "That's why they invented lint rollers." She put the cat down on the couch where parishioners often sat for counseling. He promptly lay down and curled his front paws under him, blinking up at Elsa. "You're welcome," she said.

"What are you doing, Elsa? I've never had a cat."

"I don't know," she said honestly, looking at him. "We have to be the hands of God sometimes, don't we? He needs a home and you need"—she broke off, then inclined her head and finished—"a companion."

Joaquin swiveled around, his big hands flat on his thighs. "Is that true?"

The cat blinked.

Elsa laughed. "His name should be Buddha."

Joaquin laughed, too. "Yeah. But we might have to come up with something else." He looked at her. "Have you been in the courtyard all this time?"

"All this five minutes, you mean?"

"No," he said with a quizzical smile and pointed at the clock. It had been nearly an hour since she'd left him.

"Huh," she said.

"Were you—"

She held up a hand, touched her index finger to her lips.

He smiled.

Alexa waited in the car, parked in the shade of an elm tree. She wore shorts and a T-shirt, her hair braided away from her face. "Where have you been? I've been waiting for you for an hour."

"Sorry. I got distracted. Let's go find Charlie and do some weeding."

"You just let him run? Aren't you afraid he'll get hit by a car?"

"No. He stays in the garden. He likes to play with sticks and visit all the gardeners."

As they headed into the fields, Elsa again saw summer taking hold. Vines crawled up trellises and flowers bloomed in borders. The earth had sprouted hair from every pore—verdant and fertile and exuberant.

A lot of gardeners were tending their plots, no doubt getting their chores done before the heat settled in. "Morning," Elsa said to a middle-aged man wearing a hat to protect his face. He nodded in return.

"What's the old guy doing?"

Elsa saw Joseph walking the perimeter with a rattle in his hand. The sound of his singing reached them easily in the still air, a low monotone in a language Elsa couldn't identify. "He told me at lunch yesterday that the spirits have been warning him that bad things are coming. He's singing to protect the land within from whatever it is."

Alexa made a little face, but said nothing.

As they walked toward her and Tamsin's plot, Elsa saw Deacon's truck, but not the man himself. Charlie spied her and came dashing over, his muzzle dripping from a drink of water. "Come on, silly. Ew. Don't get me all wet!" She opened the gate and waved Alexa into the garden.

She entered, and stood there, hands akimbo. "What should I do?"

Elsa gave her a pair of cotton gloves printed with rosebuds. "We need to weed." She squatted and pointed out the crops. It was all growing vigorously, squashes spreading over the ground with their beautifully shaped hairy leaves, the corn shooting like rockets out of the earth. "We need to water, too," she said, poking the soil. "It's not getting quite enough for these hot days. Start with the weeds and I'll go get the hose."

Alexa nodded, and squatted like a peasant, already pulling out the starts of sagebrush and goat heads. Noticing her niece's pale pink skin, Elsa asked, "Did you put sunscreen on?"

She gave her aunt a pained look. "Will you stop treating me like I'm six?"

"Sorry." She exited their plot and headed for the center pump, where hoses had been attached, long enough to reach most of the gardens.

As she connected a red hose, she spied Deacon helping Paris set stakes for her tomatoes and beans. She said something and he laughed, that rich low chuckle carrying easily, and Elsa flushed, thinking of the way she'd been awash with lust as she fried the chicken, fully expecting she'd have him in her bed before long.

Screwing the hose in tight, she turned the water on and stalked away, finding the end to drag into her plot.

He'd given the chicken away. Directing the water into the rows between the plants, she glanced over her shoulder. He had straightened and was looking at her without so much as a twinkle. After a moment, he raised a hand in greeting. Elsa returned it and put her attention back on the watering.

A little while later, he drove away in his blue truck, without even stopping by to say hello.

Chapter Twenty-Three

When Tamsin got off work at two, it was raining, which somewhat complicated her plan to break into her house to steal the earrings and quilts. She didn't want to park in the driveway; she had planned to use the alley, then carry the quilts out the back door. Few people in the neighborhood would be home in the middle of a weekday afternoon, but it was better to be careful.

However, the alley was clay, and muddy, and she didn't want to track a bunch of mud through the house or risk ruining the quilts.

As she turned onto her street, she tried to decide where to park, and realized that her heart was racing with either nerves or excitement or both. She pulled over halfway down the block, behind the house, and peered at the street through the swish of the windshield wipers. Rain, swipe, clear, rain, swipe, clear. She didn't have an umbrella. It wouldn't hurt her to get wet, but she didn't want the quilts to get damp. Surely there were still trash bags in the kitchen.

No one was around. It took two professional incomes to buy a house in this neighborhood. Unless you happened to be a crooked hedge-fund manager, of course. Her blue Subaru was so ordinary it was practically invisible. Leaving it unlocked, she stepped out into the rain and dashed down the sidewalk toward her house. The mailman was coming up the street, so she ducked into the backyard quickly, entering her sacred space, closing the white picket gate behind her.

Oh, her garden! She stopped, stricken. The peonies had not been staked, and had fallen over, dying on the grass that was too long and going to seed. Dandelions starred the lawn, bright yellow and ridiculously healthy, and she had a vision of Scott attacking the plants with a spade, as if they were his worst enemy. It had always made her laugh, how virulently he hated the weeds, as if it were personal, as if they bloomed just to thwart him.

Surely no one would care if she came in and removed the peonies, the striped irises, the perennials upon which she had lavished a fortune in time and money? She could replant them at the church or at Elsa's house. Somewhere she could still see them sometimes.

Rain dripped down her face. Another day. She headed for the window she'd left cracked and stood on the gas meter to reach it, trying to ease it up. The window moved without effort, but even standing on the meter, the reach was much higher than she'd expected. Grabbing on to the window ledge, she tried to pull herself up, but after a couple of minutes, she realized it was never going to happen. It was just too far to pull herself.

She jumped down. Her hair was dripping, and her shirt was stuck to her body, but she was here now, and by damn, those quilts belonged to her. Heavy padlocks covered the front and back doors, which were flanked with signs that screamed warnings from the feds saying the house was part of an investigation and trespassers would be prosecuted to the full extent of the law.

The full extent of the law. What would that mean in this case? Surely it wouldn't be much more than a ticket or a fine or something. Not that she had the money to pay a fine, of course.

Flinging her hair out of her eyes, she rounded the house and ducked behind a bank of lilacs that grew higher than her head. They offered a fence in the summertime, and cast green shadows into the dining room. Alexa had played magic castle along the house here, pretending an entrance into another world was hidden within the bushes.

A wooden door lay against the earth, an old coal slide. Tamsin yanked it by the ring, and it creaked open, the old wood protesting the movement. Spiders scurried away, leaving their long white webs floating in the air, and Tamsin shuddered, nearly dropping the door. She personally had never gone through this entrance, for just this reason. Spiders.

Could she do it now?

It wasn't just spiders, it was black widows. Shy, giant spiders that had a virulent bite. She had never been bitten, nor had anyone she knew, and you didn't die of it, anyway, just got really sick, and that wouldn't even happen to her because she would know what was wrong—

Ugh. Staring down the concrete stairs, she saw that there were leaves and dust piled up, but no actual spiders on the stairs themselves. Rain soaked her ever more thoroughly, and she shivered in both dread and cold. Turning around, she broke off a branch full of leaves from the lilac bush and brushed away as many webs as she could see, then held it out in front of her like a sword, moving it back and forth as she rushed down the stairs before she could chicken out.

The basement was gloomy, but enough light shone through the door and the old glass windows with their chicken wire that she could make her way to the steps leading into the main house. Boxes and cast-off furniture sat in shadowy sorrow, but she ignored them all and ran up the stairs.

The door opened into the kitchen. It smelled stale, like something had rotted in the drains. Tamsin stopped at the bread box, slid open the secret drawer, and there were the earrings. Bezel-cut diamonds in a platinum setting, each diamond at least a karat and a half. Maybe two. Enormous. Beautiful. Expensive. How had she forgotten about them?

The truth was, because she'd others at the time. Many of them.

Her hands shook as she admired them, thinking how much her life had changed since the day he'd given them to her. With a sudden, fierce wave of pain, she thought of Scott leaning out the window, thought of making love to him and then eating together later in bed, laughing when Scott spilled wine onto the pillows.

Had it all been a lie?

She looked at the diamonds in her palm, the sheer enormity of them. They had to be worth thirty or forty thousand dollars. Less on resale, of course.

She thought of the strange expression that had crossed his face that day, just that slight shadow that had made her worry.

He had known.

If he had left her money or property or anything that could be construed as part of the joint estate, Tamsin might have been implicated in the scam. But he'd wanted her to have something. These earrings were an offering.

With a lump in her throat, she removed the opals she'd been wearing since the seize and placed them on the counter. She slipped the diamonds in her ears, and felt tears stream down her face. She wished he had not done this. She wished she could talk to him. She was angry about what he'd done, and confused about her future, and furious on behalf of her daughter, but she had also loved him. She had been so afraid over the past few months that everything she'd believed to be true about her marriage was a lie. Now she knew it was not. Scott had loved her. He had protected her. Tried to provide for her—

And with a blast of insight that almost knocked her sideways, she knew where there was more. Grabbing a couple of trash bags from the pantry, she ran upstairs to her tower room.

The loss hit her again in the solar plexus. She'd always loved to work in here when it was raining, the panes of the windows running with gray, the lightning flashing all around. She could get lost for hours and hours in this room.

Pushing past the pinch of longing, she yanked open a deep narrow closet that she'd rarely used. It was creepy. But in the back was a secret door, left over from Victorian times. Tamsin had thought it quaint, but of course, there were sometimes spiders in there. No way she'd wanted to reach her hand inside.

Now, when she slid the little door sideways, there was a thick envelope. Heart pounding in her ears, she wrestled it out sideways. Her name was on the front, in Scott's hand. She opened it.

A thick wad of bills was inside, along with a single white sheet of paper.

Dear Tamsin,

I'm sorry. I love you. It just got out of control. Scott

The bills were hundreds, and there were a lot of them. A stack as thick as a hardcover novel. Stunned, she flipped through them, hands shaking in fear and anger and relief.

God! What to do with it? Where to hide it?

Awash with a sense of urgency, she yanked open the closet where her quilts were stored carefully, between layers of tissue paper. She took several of them out and shoved them into the bags, then wrapped the money in a square of fabric still lying on the desk. She tucked it into a bag. Layered another quilt on top.

No. She took out the money and peeled three bills off the stack and tucked them into her jeans, then dashed down the stairs. Her feet clattered on the wooden steps, and skittered over the polished floor at the top of the cellar stairs. She dove through the cellar, and back out into the rain, down the alley to her car. Urgently, she shoved the money under the front seat, locked the doors, and looking around at the empty street, rushed back into the house, her heart pounding. She realized when she was back in the tower room that she'd gone through the creepy spidery basement twice, and her hands were shaking violently.

Breathe.

Planting her hands on her hips, she took in several long slow breaths, and felt herself calm down.

Sweating now, and feeling scared, she decided it was time to cut her losses. She started taking more quilts from the shelves and layering them into the two trash bags she'd brought upstairs with her. They were bulging by the time she finished, and she realized she couldn't even lift them. Sweat dripped into her eyes as she ran back down the stairs, all three flights, grabbed two more bags, and tried to run back up. *Ha.*

She walked back up, then painstakingly divided the contents of two bags into four. The weight was manageable now, and she hauled two down the stairs, leaving them by the basement steps, then ran up and grabbed the final two. With one last look over her shoulder at the room she had loved so much, she began to drag the bags downstairs. Her breath was becoming ragged now.

Almost there, she told herself.

Just as she reached the landing on the second floor, she heard the front door burst open. She had enough time to glance out the window and see the flashing lights before two uniformed policemen appeared in front of her, guns aimed at her chest.

"Drop the bags and put your hands up," one said. He looked about thirteen, and that somehow made her want to laugh.

She said, "This is my hou—"

"Hands up!" he shouted, wiggling his gun.

Tamsin obeyed. "These are my quilts," she said as the other officer rushed up the stairs. The first one took her right wrist in his hand and slapped a handcuff around it. Then he grabbed her other hand and pulled it around her back and slapped the cuff onto that one, too.

"Ow!" Tamsin protested. "You don't have to yank my shoulder out of joint."

"You are under arrest for breaking and entering," the baby said. "You have the right to remain silent—"

It dawned on her, finally, that she was being arrested. "Wait!" she cried, pulling free. "You don't understand. This is my house."

"Ma'am, this house has been seized by federal authorities. Everything in it belongs to the courts." He took her arm, firmly. "I would advise you to stop talking now."

Tamsin caught sight of the bags. "They're mine," she said, and let herself be led down the front steps and back into the rain. "Can I get my purse, my phone? They're in the car down there."

"No, ma'am."

When Tamsin called, Elsa was on the sunporch, shelling peas. All day she'd been feeling a sense of unease, of things gathering in the distance. Sitting with the bowl of peas in her lap, she tried to tap into whatever that darkness was. She cracked the pods and slid the peas from their casings with a fingernail, *pop pop pop*, taking pleasure in the rhythm, the color of the peas, their fresh green smell.

The unease stuck with her, though, a low-level hum. She looked off into the horizon as if it had an answer, but there was only the cool, life-giving rain. It had been an odd day, between Joaquin and Deacon and the lost hour in the courtyard with San Roque. Around her wrist lingered the marks of the rosary, pale red as if the little leaves had been scorched into her skin. The beads were in her pocket still. She should remember to put them away. She had no idea why she was carrying them around with her all the time. She wasn't Catholic and hadn't been for a long time.

Charlie snored at her feet, exhausted from his long day of play, and she rubbed a foot over his side. She'd tried to enlist Alexa in the shelling, but the girl had rolled her eyes. "No."

But now she came outside. "My mom's on the phone," she said, holding out the sleek iPhone she used. "She said she tried calling you on yours, but you didn't answer. She sounds kinda weird."

Wiping her hands and taking the phone, Elsa said, "Hello?"

"I need to be bailed out of jail," Tamsin said. "Don't tell Alexa where I am. And don't make a big fuss because I know she's listening."

"She's in jail?" Alexa said, making a face.

"She heard you," Elsa said. "What happened?"

"I went to the house to get some of my quilts." She sighed. "It was stupid, okay? Just please come get me."

"Right away, sis," Elsa said. "Don't worry."

As she handed the phone back, Elsa probed the disquiet, wondering if the arrest was what she'd been sensing. But no, it was still there, dark and gathering weight. She rubbed her belly irritably. Why, she wondered, as she had wondered all of her life, give a warning without giving some direction along with it?

Even as a small girl, she'd had these washes of knowledge. A sense of death lurking, or danger. Once she'd shied away from a side street, later learning someone had been kidnapped from it that same day. Another time, she awoke screaming about a car accident and learned that afternoon a classmate had been in one very near that hour.

The advice she'd been given was to pray at those times, that her hunches were like a smoke alarm going off. The world needed prayers.

Because she had no other way to address the warnings, she now found herself taking the rosary out of her pocket and looping it around her wrist, a habit she'd picked up as a child. All through the drive to the police station, she mentally chanted the rosary, flicking the leaves through her fingers one at a time.

"Are you praying?" Alexa asked.

"Yes."

"Do you think she's in a lot of trouble?"

"No," Elsa answered honestly, parking the car. "It feels like something is out of sync, but it's not your mother."

In the station, Tamsin was bedraggled, her hair tangled and knotted, as if it had been wet and then dried without being combed. She'd clearly been crying. "I'm so sorry," she said as she walked out with them, her head bowed. She climbed into the front passenger seat.

"Why did you *do* that?" Alexa asked.

"I guess you really don't need two criminal parents, huh?"

"It's not that. It's just kind of crazy. It's not like you."

"I wanted to get the quilts. They're mine. I made them. I should be able to sell them so you can get back to Spain and work things out with Carlos."

"Mom! Nothing is going to work out with us. He's part of the royal family. He can't marry the daughter of a criminal. I love him, okay? It's just this very careful world he lives in, and they will *never* let him marry me. I needed to make it a clean break so that he—" She set her jaw, pressed her thumbs to her eyelids. "I don't want to talk about this. I don't want to cry anymore. It's just done."

Elsa touched her sister's hand. "I think your daughter means that what you did was a grand gesture."

"I do, Mom," Alexa said, and she leaned forward to put her head on her mother's shoulder. "Thanks for trying. Only, don't have any illusions, okay? He's lost to me now."

"What about all those emails? I didn't mean to read them. But you left your account open on the laptop, and I saw them. He loves you."

"I didn't tell him what happened. I felt so . . . ashamed."

Elsa looked at her niece in the rearview mirror. There was

something a little off about her tone. Something she was hiding. "Do you know anything? Like where your dad might be?"

"No!" The word was vehement. "If I did, believe me, I would track him down and make him pay for ruining our lives."

"Revenge doesn't solve anything," Elsa said, stopping at a traffic light. In the mirror, Alexa was chewing on a thumbnail, worrying it. She might not know where her father was, but she was definitely hiding something.

"Oh, I don't know," Tamsin said. "I bet it would solve some things for me."

Elsa glanced at her. "Are you finally angry? It's about time."

"Don't," Tamsin snapped. "Just don't be the wise one. I'm sick of it."

"Somebody has to do it," Elsa snapped back. "Maybe I'm tired of it, too. *You're* the older sister!"

"As if you'd ever listen to anything I might have to say!"

"I do listen to you!"

"No, you are the supercilious know everything, never in trouble, always with the same guy—"

"Who left me, remember!"

"Yeah, for God! You can't really say, 'No, sorry, God, I'm not doing that.'"

A light went red in front of her and Elsa stepped on the brake a little too hard. "Oh, yes, you can. You can walk away. I've done it, three times, and no bolt of lightning has knocked me down yet. I seem to be doing just fine!"

"Oh, yeah, you're doing great," Tamsin said sarcastically. "Hiding out in your hometown, playing wife to the priest—"

"Stop!" Elsa yelled, slapping her.

The car went deadly silent. Tamsin's mouth dropped open and she raised a shaking hand to the red mark on her face. Alexa was as still as a statue. Elsa gaped, her fingertips stinging from the contact.

Behind them, someone honked. The light was green.

"I'm sorry," Elsa said. She drove through the intersection, and on the other side parked at the curb. "I can't believe I did that."

Tamsin grabbed Elsa's hand and pressed it to her own face, on the other side. "I'm sorry, too. I should never have said that. I'm just in an evil, evil mood."

"You're right, though. I mean, there's a lot that rings true in that."

"Wow," Alexa said from the backseat, and her voice was stronger than it had been since she arrived home. "I don't even have to watch TV to get a Hallmark moment."

Both sisters laughed.

"I think we need ice cream," Tamsin said. "I'll buy." She reached into her pocket and fanned out three one-hundred-dollar bills. Wiggling her eyebrows, she said, "I found some money."

"They didn't confiscate it?"

"Nope."

"I want a banana split," Alexa said from the backseat.

Elsa glanced at her sister. "Let's feed the girl."

They drove to Dairy Queen. Alexa ordered her banana split, and Tamsin got her favorite, an Oreo Blizzard. Elsa chose a hot fudge sundae. The clerk was annoyed over the hundred-dollar bill, but he broke it.

They carried the sundaes to a table by the window and watched it rain.

Tamsin said, "You should see how bad my garden looks. It's totally overgrown and the peonies bloomed without anyone noticing." Her voice broke. "How stupid, right? But it breaks my heart that no one saw them bloom, that they're just invisible. They're so beautiful!"

"That is sad," Alexa said. "I'm going to miss our bathtub for the rest of my life."

"It was a pretty good one."

"What happens next, sis?"

"I have to go to court on Monday."

"Wow, that's fast."

"It's just an arraignment or something. To see if they'll press charges or not. I'm worried it'll be the same lady judge I got before. She didn't like me one bit."

She slapped her hands over her face. "Argh! I can't believe I even have conversations like this!"

Elsa laughed.

To her surprise, so did Alexa. "You're such a bad girl. Maybe you should get a tattoo."

"Maybe I will. Maybe I'll pierce my nose."

"No," Alexa said firmly. "Tattoo yes, but I will not let you pierce your nose like some pathetic middle-aged divorcée."

Tamsin gave a belly laugh. "You mean like the pathetic can't-get-divorced-because-her-husband-has-disappeared middle-aged mom I am?"

"You are not like that."

Tamsin asked Elsa, "Would you ever get a tattoo?"

"I don't know. Maybe, under the right circumstances."

"What would you get?"

She thought for a minute. "A shell. On my foot."

"For the *camino*?" Alexa asked.

"Yes." She swirled hot fudge around the ice cream. "It was very important."

"How about you, Mom?"

"I don't know. I've had kind of a boring life." She laughed again. "Until lately, that is."

Elsa said, "How about you, Alexa? Would you ever get a tattoo?"

She stared out the window. "Yes," she said, and her brooding face came back.

Tamsin said, "Do you notice anything different about me?" She tucked her hair, still messy, behind her ears and blinked in exaggerated innocence. In her ears were enormous diamond solitaires.

"Whoa," Alexa said.

"The police didn't notice?" Elsa asked.

"They only put me in a holding cell. They didn't take my stuff."

"Lucky."

"Shhh," Tamsin said, and looked around the empty room. "The walls have, hmm, ears." She laughed.

"Where did you find them?" Elsa asked quietly.

"In the secret drawer in the bread box."

Alexa laughed. "Get out! Perfect." She high-fived her mother.

"I have no idea how to exchange them, so to speak, but in the meantime, I have some money, baby."

"Good job," Elsa said. "Even if it was crazy."

After they came back from Dairy Queen, the women scattered. Alexa retreated to her bedroom, leaving the windows open to the rain-cooled air. Tamsin got on the computer. Elsa and Charlie went out to the porch. She thought, briefly, about a cigarette, but it was too dangerous with both Alexa and Tamsin at home. The rain had stopped, but leaves still dripped, making a tapping noise. Crickets began to whir.

Elsa curled up in a sweater and held her phone in her hand, thinking about calling Joaquin. Often, before she returned to Pueblo, Friday evenings were one of the times they would have long chats, after the evening Mass. They'd talk about their sermons and sticky issues that had come up, and problems they faced as shepherds of a congregation.

But Tamsin's words had struck a reverberating note. Maybe she was using Joaquin as a crutch to avoid facing her life.

Maybe she was hiding out here, hoping the storm would blow over, rather than taking steps to figure out what her life should look like.

Her phone rang in her hand. Joaquin's name flashed over the screen.

Of course. She answered. "Hey, is everything okay over there?" she asked, pulling the sweater sleeves down over her hands.

"I think so. Should I be checking?" She'd experienced the warnings since childhood, so he understood.

"Yes. There's something amiss. I don't know what it is. But it's something."

"I'll make the rounds after we talk." He paused. "I just wanted you to know that I have a cat on my lap. I'm completely covered in white cat hair, which is going to give the Gloriosa sisters fits."

Elsa laughed. "I can imagine."

"He is a really nice guy, I gotta say. He purrs and he likes his belly to be rubbed." He sounded slightly surprised and very pleased. "It's kinda nice."

"Did you name him yet?"

"Yep. He's Santiago."

Elsa felt a whisper of stillness move through her. "Good name."

"So. Tell me about your meditation this morning, Elsa."

"Am I talking to Father Jack now?"

"Is that who you need?"

She swallowed a fierce, sudden rush of emotion. "Yes. I love my friend, but things are strange between us right now. I need a shepherd."

"I'm listening."

"I miss my work," she said. "I don't know who I am without it."

He made a soothing noise.

"That seems like a sign I should go back."

"Are you avoiding the subject of the meditation, Reverend?"

"No. I just don't know what happened, exactly. I didn't really intend to meditate. I sat down in the sunshine and just dove over to the other side. You know how that is, when you dissolve into . . . whatever it is. God. The universe. San Roque, maybe."

"So if there's no God, where are you going when you meditate?"

She sighed. "I don't know what it is."

"But it's something, right? A different place, a different state, a different something."

"Yes." And she spoke her own truth. "It's impossible for me not to do that, not to seek that communion. When I got the warnings tonight, I started to pray."

"You say that like it's a bad thing."

She laughed softly. "I know."

"I think you're asking a question we all ask at times, Elsa, and that's 'Why?' Why do terrible things happen? Why doesn't God intervene?"

"Yes. That's it. And please don't give me any platitudes. You know it's a difficult question."

"It is. And I don't know the answer. What I do know is that God is good. God is wise and He uses even evil to further His own ends."

The cold evil of Kiki's body, lying exposed to the elements, flashed through her memory. How could any good come of that? Any good at all? She closed her eyes. "I have to figure this out."

"Yes."

"It's driving me crazy to be so adrift. I have no anchor, no harbor. That was always my faith, and I don't have it now."

"You've lost faith before."

Elsa wished for a cigarette. Took a deep breath of cool air instead. "Yes."

"How did you get it back those times?"

She knew he didn't expect a full answer. "I've been thinking about that."

"As Father Jack, I suggest that more prayer is a good step. If you don't show up, how can there be any communication?"

She thought of sitting with San Roque today, the peace that had overtaken her, the sense of the eternal rightness of things. "Maybe," she said. He was quiet, which was one of the best things about him.

She was quiet, too, and for a moment, she slid sideways again, into the silence between crickets, the space between the scent of earth and rain. She yanked herself back.

Why? Why keep running? "Do me a favor, as my friend?"

"Anything."

"Let me have some time in the courtyard in the mornings this week. When you go for your runs, leave the rectory through the front door."

"Absolutely."

"Thanks, Walking."

"You need to stop running from God, Elsa, and turn around and face him. There is nothing to be afraid of."

"Isn't there?"

"One thing I know to be absolutely true is that God is good. Whatever happens in the world that's evil is the opposite of God."

"It's lonely, without that connection."

"You know what to do."

"Yes." She rubbed the dull worry at the base of her solar plexus. "Check the gardens, will you? Just take a look, and then text me."

"Will do."

She was brushing her teeth when the text came in:

It's 9 o'clock and all is well.

Thx!

As she climbed into bed, Charlie slumping down with a sigh at her feet, she felt the warning double, triple. There was nothing to be done but pray. Whether it was real or not, whether anything or anyone could hear, it was the only thing she knew to do.

Mainly it was a prayer of protection, for all of her loved ones, for Tamsin and Alexa, who honestly seemed much better this afternoon. For Joaquin, engaged in his own struggles, for Deacon and the boys, for the garden and her congregation and whoever might need it.

She prayed, even though prayers had not made any difference for Kiki. She prayed, even though God had taken her fiancé away and seemed disinclined to replace him, even after all these years. She prayed for her congregation, and something pinged, hard, in the middle of her chest.

More of this.

So she offered more prayers for them. Protection for whatever was coming.

Chapter Twenty-Four

It was Joaquin who found Joseph.

He had been running, going the reverse of his usual direction to give Elsa the privacy she had requested. The morning was cool after last night's rains, and clouds still hung low over the trees, turning the river a dark silver.

When he'd told Elsa the night before that she needed to stop running from God, the words seemed to lodge somewhere in his own chest. He was only a man, after all. Called to be a priest, but not called to be perfect. In the still morning, alone, he murmured aloud to God and San Roque and the angel who had never returned. He asked for forgiveness and guidance. He asked for help in mastering his hungers. And even in the asking, he felt a great weight fall away.

He was not alone in this.

As he ran along the levee, the church came into view, first the bell tower and the roof, surrounded by the graceful arms of elms, their leaves thick and green now, offering shade from the hard summer suns. Scores of birds twittered in them, blue jays and sparrows and robins; magpies with their magnificent long tails and patterned wings; the odd owl and bullying ravens. Their mingled calls seemed loud beneath the blankets of clouds.

The building came into view, and then the wide expanse of the garden, the width of a full city block. At first, it only looked as if the rain the night before had knocked some branches out of the trees, for there was a lot of litter strewn across the paths. Then he realized that fences had been knocked down.

Yanked down.

He detoured, dashing sideways across the steep bank to investigate, and stopped dead.

It looked like a herd of buffalo had torn through, trampling fences and the carefully tended plots. Plants were smashed, tossed into piles. A scatter of squash leaves and blossoms lay in a clump in the middle of the path, and much of the sturdy knee-high corn that had been looking so vigorous had been snapped at the base.

Wanton destruction. Rage rose in him as he strode down the middle path.

Here was Elsa's warning. Almost all the fences had been torn down, almost every plot had some damage, but it was capricious, like a tornado. Some gardens had been trampled and yanked up badly. Others had only sustained wounds from the toppled fences. He started counting. Three very badly damaged plots. One of them was the church soup kitchen's, which was better than if it had belonged to a family. He picked up a fence, shoved the support in the ground, tenderly knelt and propped up a listing tomato cage. Within, the tomato plant had a broken arm, but Joaquin pinched it off.

A handful of others had taken a hit, with broken plants, footsteps in the middle. Toward the far end, the damage was very minimal, as if the vandals had been chased away.

And that was where he found Joseph, lying facedown in one of the narrow alleys between two plots. A drum had been smashed near his head, and a gourd rattle lay near his knee, a hole stomped through it.

Joaquin knelt urgently. "Joseph!" He touched the old man's back, the frail bones beneath his cotton shirt. He was breathing. Joaquin pulled the long hair off the old man's face, and saw that he'd been beaten. A cut with matted blood and dirt marred his left eyebrow and his eye was purple and swollen beneath it. As Joaquin murmured, the old man groaned.

"Be still," Joaquin said. "I'm going to get some help. Don't move."

He ran toward the church, dashed into the courtyard, and halted, torn. Elsa was sitting on the bench, hands folded in her lap, her face utterly serene. A rosary made of green leaves was looped around her wrist.

"I'm sorry," he said, touching her shoulder. "I need you. Joseph has been beaten."

Her eyes popped open and she was on her feet. "Where is he?"

"All the way at the other end of the garden. I'm going to call 911."

"I'll go sit with him."

"Elsa," he called, walking backward. "The gardens were trashed, too."

Something fierce crossed her face. "I'm going to sit with Joseph."

Elsa ran, barely taking in the damage all around her, at least not consciously. By the time she reached the old man, tears were already streaming down her face, and she didn't bother to stop them. Kneeling at his side, she gently placed her hands on his shoulder. "Can you hear me, Joseph? Help is coming."

He tried to stir, and she said, "No, just be still. I'm so sorry you were hurt."

He reached for her hand. "You . . . got to . . . drum. Somebody."

"Shhh, Joseph," she said, stroking his head. "You can tell me later."

"No." His voice was raspy, and he struggled to sit up. Elsa heard an ambulance in the distance. "Spirits need our help. He . . . bad . . ." He coughed, and there was a wet sound to it she did not like. "Bad evil. Bad spirit."

"We will drum. I promise. I'll find somebody."

"Broke my drum." He closed his eyes.

The paramedics arrived with an electronic whoop and two big guys in dark blue uniforms carried a stretcher toward her. Joaquin directed. "This way!"

Elsa stepped back to give them access, crossing her arms as they took the old man's vital signs and called in statistics. Tears still poured from her eyes, unchecked, as if from some untapped well.

People started to drift over from the apartments, the word spreading. Joseph was taken away, his daughter in the ambulance with him, her hair scattered down her back. Mario had been sent to Calvin's apartment.

The gardeners surveyed the damage, faces masked with rage and shock and sadness. "Who would do this?" one older woman asked, lifting a decapitated cabbage. Another tried to brace her torn fence, but it kept falling over again.

Elsa pulled her phone from her pocket and called Deacon. He answered gruffly, and Elsa said without preamble, "We need you at the community garden. There's been some vandalism."

He swore. "How bad?"

She looked over her shoulder. Paris was running down the center path toward her plot, Calvin and Mario in tow. "Bad. They beat up old Joseph, too."

"Bastards."

"We need fencing and tools to start the repairs. Can you help with any of that?"

"You bet. I'll be there as soon as I can."

"Thanks," she said, and jogged up the side of the garden to reach Paris and the two boys, just as they arrived at their plot. All three of them stared at the torn-down fence with blank expressions.

Calvin went immediately to his bean plant, which had been twining up a stake, and made a roaring noise. "They wrecked my beanstalk!" he cried, and his mother, who'd been looking at the destruction with a murderous expression on her face, wrapped her arm around him.

"No, baby, look," she said, kneeling. "The stake is gone, but we can tie the bean up again."

The plant was distressed, but didn't appear to be broken. Elsa spied the stake and carried it over to him, her eye on Mario. He stood in the bright morning, wearing a dirty T-shirt, his hair loose down his back. His mouth trembled. Elsa went to him.

"How are you doing, honey?" she asked, and slid an arm around him.

He shrugged. "Somebody beat up my grandpa."

"I know. I talked to him, though, and he was really worried that he wasn't going to be able to do the drumming. He said the spirits need that. Do you have a drum?"

"Yeah." He swiped an angry tear from his face. "I don't know how to do what my grandpa does, not just like him."

"I think the spirits will understand that you're a medicine man in training. They'll just be glad you're doing it."

He chewed on his lip. "Will I get beat up, too? I'm scared of those guys."

"You won't be here by yourself," she said. "I promise. Let's go take a look at your garden, too, see what we can fix. Deacon will be here in a little while."

"Good." He shrugged off her arm. "I gotta go to the bathroom first."

Elsa nodded, then turned back to Paris, who was carefully tying the beanstalk back to the stake. Calvin patted the earth at the base. "You think Father Jack would sprinkle some holy water on it?" he asked.

"You can ask him."

Calvin jumped up. Hopeful. "I'll be right back, Mama."

Paris nodded. "Stay in sight."

Elsa knelt in Paris's garden and plucked leaves from a sunflower, and removed some broken bits of a tomato. The carrots and potatoes would be fine, hidden as they were under the earth. A swath of corn was crushed. Paris yanked out the little broken plants with fury. Elsa put a hand over hers. "I think if you leave those alone, they'll be okay in a week or so."

Paris tossed the shoots aside, and Elsa saw that her hand was shaking violently. "My whole life, all I've been trying to do is have a little bit of comfort, to make things a little bit nicer than rock-bottom hillbilly shit." She wiped at her jaw. "Just a *little*. And every time, some man takes it away, stomps on it, or gets himself killed, or ruins it. I'm tired of that." Her blue eyes, so young and so old, met Elsa's. "So tired."

"I know," she said quietly, not looking away. "It's evil, and it's painful, and it doesn't seem fair. But you are good and strong and smart and real." Paris leaned toward her, soaking up the words. Elsa continued, "You're also raising a boy who will grow into a man who will make the world better, not worse. I believe in you, Paris."

The girl stared at Elsa for a long moment, too ferocious, too angry. "I could just kill those boys. What were they thinking? They're just as poor as we are. This is *food*."

"I know." Elsa stood. "They've been damaged, too, somehow, or they wouldn't want to do this. We can't fix them, but let's see what we can do about this fence."

All day, Elsa helped in the gardens. Her sister came and went, taking Charlie back home with her. Joaquin and Deacon worked, too, hauling rebar out of Deacon's truck and patching the fences and digging out sections of damaged crops. A church member went to a garden shop and brought back three flats of mixed bedding plants to help replace those that had been lost.

In the late afternoon, Elsa sank down at the picnic table in the center of the gardens, took off her gloves and slapped the dust from them. Her hands were shaking and she realized she had not eaten since breakfast. Someone had brought doughnuts and bananas and gallons of water. She'd gobbled down a strawberry-frosted doughnut, and poured a big paper cup of water. As she gulped that down, too, she thought again how efficient the volunteer system was in Joaquin's church. Absently peeling a banana, she looked around for him, wondering how he kept the machine running. He was nowhere in sight. The bells began to ring, calling the faithful to Mass.

Of course. It was Saturday afternoon. A couple of men in the garden looked up, dusted themselves off, and wandered toward the church.

It had been like that in medieval times, *before* medieval times, with the same bells, the same Mass, the same words. That was something she missed about Catholicism, one of the many. There was all that time and history and ritual already in place, the weight and solidness of it a pattern to hold on to.

Would she have been a priest if she could have? If it had been allowed? Would she have made the sacrifice Joaquin had made?

"Hey, stranger," Deacon said, sitting down next to her. He had two cups in his hands, steaming hot. "I thought you could use a little more substance. Tea for you. Two sugars and milk, not cream, right?"

She grinned up at him. "Right. Thanks."

He faced the church, as she did, and they each drank in silence for a time. "I don't think I've thanked you for the fried chicken," he said. "It was delicious."

She smiled sadly. "You don't have to lie, Deacon. Joaquin told me you gave it to him."

"I gave him half," he said. "Not all of it."

Elsa turned.

He looked at her, then looked down and put his hand over hers. "I'm struggling a bit with my loyalties, Elsa." His fingertip traced the curve of her nails.

She waited.

He raised his head, looked at her mouth, at her eyes. "Joaquin saved my life." His drawl seemed deeper, softer. His hand was hot and it pulsed over hers with a clear burning energy. A scent of grass came from his skin. Elsa had a clear and perfect wish to move closer and taste his mouth. Her heart was beating a little faster.

"I was in prison and lost and he came into that place like—" He made a clicking noise. "Hope. Just hope. He spread it around all of us like fresh soil."

She forced from her mind all of the reasons they shouldn't be together and looked up at him directly, letting her heart open to him. She sensed in him the things he needed, saw them in his pupils, and the beauty of his mouth.

And she allowed herself to acknowledge her own wishes, too. "I think you should take me somewhere for dinner."

He hesitated still, but at last he gave in, and leaned forward and kissed her. Just a brush of his mouth on hers, but Elsa caught the back of his neck before he could draw away. She pulled him back to her. On his lips she tasted the future—music and laughter, things they would do. Places they would go.

With a soft sigh, he pressed his forehead to hers. "What do you feel like eating?"

She straightened. "A lot. I'm starving. Pizza?"

"Let's go." He poured the coffee onto the ground and turned around to hold out his hand. With a sense that she was stepping across an invisible line, Elsa took it. Something like glitter seemed to burst in the air. She hummed under her breath and danced a little beside him.

* * *

They went to the Riverwalk and found a table downstairs on the patio at Angelo's, where their dusty clothes wouldn't be noticed. It was darker on the lower patio, close to the river flowing through a man-made channel. The sidewalks and paths along the river were busy on a Saturday afternoon, and the sound of fountains cooled the air. They ordered a pizza and root beers, and chips and salsa to tide them over.

"The Riverwalk always amazes me," Elsa said. "It's so beautiful and it really has changed the look of this area, hasn't it?"

"I never saw it before. I only got here about four years ago. I was living in Denver when I got the DUI, and only came to Pueblo when I got out of prison. The Riverwalk was already here. Maybe not as developed as it is now, but they'd built the channel."

"Ah. Well, it used to be a pretty run-down area, and the river was over behind the levee. Safely, so it couldn't flood." She gestured with a chip, encompassing the entire area. "In 1921, there was a massive flash flood. Wiped out downtown, and this whole area was so deep underwater that you could only see the tops of those buildings."

"I've always kinda wondered about that. It's a pretty small river by southern standards, but that's a *serious* levee."

"Right. That's why. This was the original channel of the river, but as you see, only a little bit of the water is allowed to come through."

"It's pretty. I like it down here." He leaned back and stretched out his long legs, then inclined his head and looked at her for a long moment. "I was watching you today. You were really in your element."

"What do you mean?"

"You were just tireless, and everybody looked to you for help and advice. You have a real gift for ministry, Elsa."

She shook her head ruefully. "It's funny how that kind of event or need just"—she made a circle in front of her heart—"pulls me in. I feel like I'm a much better version of myself." To her surprise and embarrassment, tears pricked the back of her eyes. She blinked hard. "I miss it," she said honestly. "I was telling Joaquin that last night. I have to figure things out. This drifting is not what I'm meant to do. What any of us are supposed to do."

"You don't have to be in a church, you know. There are a lot of ways to help people. You could work with the Red Cross or take up nursing or . . . a thousand things."

Before she could stop them, words came pouring out of her mouth. "But I love being a minister. In a church. I love church, period. All churches, pretty much, but especially when I have one of my own, a flock to look after."

He smiled. "Sounds like you have your answer."

Their pizza came and Elsa, ravenous to her very bones, picked up a slice. "We can keep talking about that in a minute, but I have to eat first."

They both dug in. Elsa concentrated fully on the pizza, with its Brooklyn-style crust, the salt and tang, the onions and greasy pepperoni. Across the river channel, a woman drifted out to a balcony to water pots of petunias. Elsa wiped grease from her lips, and gestured toward the woman. "That would be a nice place to live."

"Pretty," he agreed, and pointed north. "You can see Pikes Peak."

"Imagine how gorgeous the world looks from up there."

"I'm sure you have to pay for the privilege."

"No doubt." She admired his jawline against the light, the length of his neck, and thought of putting her mouth there, nestling in to smell him. Her skin rippled, like a cat's, hungry for stroking. Beneath the table, she kicked off her sandal and put her foot on his.

He cocked an eyebrow, very slightly, and that charming half

smile flickered. He reached for her hand, tracing a circle on her inner wrist. His expression was bemused. "Are you coming home with me after this?"

"I would like to."

He nodded, put down his pizza. Wiped his lips carefully. "I need to ask you a question, point-blank, and I need a clear answer."

"Okay."

"If Father Jack suddenly were not a priest, would you be his wife?"

"No," she said with some amusement and leaned forward so that she could speak quietly. "I have done everything I can think of to let you know that *you* are the one I'm interested in. No," she said, interrupting herself, "'interested' is way too small a word. I was just sitting here thinking how much I'd like to bury myself in your neck and smell you. I keep imagining how you'll look without your shirt on."

"That's what I wanted to hear," he said gruffly, and leaned over to kiss her, just once, with promise. "Finish up your pizza, sugar."

"I love it when you call me sugar."

"I thought you hated it."

"I don't like the casual endearments you use for everyone. I want 'sugar' to belong only to me. Can you save it for me?"

He chuckled. "That I can do."

"I have a question for you, too." She picked up another piece of pizza. "I might well go back to my church, you know."

He nodded, meeting her eyes.

"They need me, and I need to be busy again. Until I've sorted everything out, I won't be the teacher they need, but it feels like I might be getting there."

"That's good."

"You know what church life is like. Could you ever live around that again?"

He leaned forward and picked up her hand. "I reckon I could, for the right woman."

The pocket of tension in her chest dissolved. "What do you believe in, Deacon?"

He looked toward the west. The sun had fallen behind the mountains, leaving a jagged blaze of gold light on the horizon. "I don't feel the need to be that specific. There's something up there, out there, all around us, but I don't necessarily know what to name it." He lifted a shoulder. "I like it when Joseph says 'Great Spirit.' That seems as close to what it feels like to me as anything." He took another piece of pizza in his long-fingered hand and looked at her with a level gaze. "You reckon you might be a touch too hard on yourself?"

Elsa laughed. "*Moi?*"

As they ate in companionable silence, she kept her bare foot on his arch, touching his ankle with her big toe. Anticipation, bright yellow and edged with heat, brewed between them, circling, tightening, sweetening. The water shimmered. It seemed that all of Pueblo was out enjoying the day, eating ice cream as they walked by, having a beer at Angelo's, strolling along the walkways.

Elsa became aware of a man behind her speaking in urgent Spanish into a cellphone. The accent pricked her—Spanish from Spain, not Mexico or Latin America—and then his words caught her attention. Her Spanish was rusty, and she listened shamelessly, translating laboriously. *I cannot find her. The house is closed up. You need to find the address of her aunt.*

She turned. There in the corner, taking out a cigarette, then putting it back, was a young and very handsome man. He was dressed well, casually but expensively. For a long moment, she tested her recognition. Could it really be? He hung up the phone and flung his head into his hands, the curls tumbling in glossy, glorious disarray around his golden fingers. Fever rose around him in an orange cloud.

It was the man she had seen in her vision, weeping over Alexa.

"Carlos?" she said.

He raised his head. "Do I know you?" he asked in English, beautifully accented.

Elsa smiled. "You will," she said. "Please, join us."

As he stood, a puzzled expression on his face, Elsa picked up her phone and dialed. When her sister answered, she said, "Bring Alexa to Angelo's. We're on the lower level."

Chapter Twenty-Five

Before the phone call, Tamsin was working on a new quilt. She had the base spread over the dining room table. It was an emerging landscape of a tall cliff overlooking a clear aquamarine sea. Bougainvillea tumbled in pink and salmon swaths down a craggy, dangerous cliff. She had only just begun to piece the flowers.

She'd rescued her car and the money, but it made her jumpy. What if someone had seen her? What if the police found out about the cash? Her fear kept her from telling Elsa or Alexa about it. It also made her change the hiding place for the stash about every three hours.

She did not have the nerve to be a criminal. And maybe it wasn't right, having that cash when so many others had lost everything, but she . . .

Well, she was keeping it anyway.

Quilting helped. At this stage, the work was blurry, just big areas of color and a few layers and shapes. She could see in her mind's eye what the finished piece would look like, but to the uninformed eye, it was nothing much.

A song kept weaving through her mind as she cut hot pink paisley fabric into triangles, a French folk song, "Dominique," a lively little tune that looped through her mind every time she started to work on the quilt. Something about the song nagged her. As if she should remember something about it.

But whatever it was swirled away every time she tried to catch it. She would just keep working on the quilt. Eventually it would come to her.

Her phone buzzed in her pocket. Tamsin saw that it was Elsa calling, and she picked up. "Hey, what's up?"

Alexa had only joined her mother reluctantly. She yanked her hair back into a ponytail, stuck her feet into flip-flops, and climbed in the car. Her mother drove.

"Why are we doing this?"

"She didn't say. You haven't been down there in ages—you might be surprised by how lovely it is. And anyway, it's good for you to get out."

"I helped in the garden." Alexa leaned back. "Never mind. I get that you're both trying to make me feel better." She watched the shops pass by, the storefronts with their small-town feel, clean and tidy. "I hope you know that I really am trying."

Her mother patted her hand. "I do."

They parked by a fountain and crossed the street, then wound around the path to the restaurant. A lot of people were sitting on the patios. Alexa wished, suddenly, that she'd taken a little more care with her appearance. It was something that mattered and she should be respectful of others. Not that a ponytail was so terrible, or her yoga pants and tank. But no makeup, the floppy shoes—she really should get her act together.

She saw her aunt Elsa and her boyfriend, or whatever he was, sitting on the deck. And maybe because she'd just been thinking of him, she saw a man who looked just like Carlos. That thick hair. His beautiful face. He was standing up, almost in slow motion, and suddenly Alexa heard a roaring in her ears.

He cried out, "Azul!" and dove around the tables, running toward her.

Alexa spun around and ran down the Riverwalk, as fast as she could. He couldn't see her this way. She couldn't face him with so much disgrace piled upon her family. He thought he could be romantic and fix it, but romance and love couldn't fix *anything*.

She nearly tripped on her flip-flops, and kicked them off. One landed in the water, and she didn't care—she kept running in bare feet. People moved out of her way, and she leapt over a skateboard. Carlos was a strong sailor and lacrosse player, but she thought she could outrun him, and he didn't know the neighborhood. Her breath came in ragged gasps—and then she tripped over the hem of her yoga pants and tumbled into the grass.

He tackled her, crying out her name. "Alexa, my Azul, stop! Stop." He used his body to hold her down, and suddenly, Alexa realized how foolish it was, running away. The smell of his skin overwhelmed her, and with a cry, she turned in his arms and kissed him, tears running sideways over her temples. She grasped the back of his head and kissed him deeply, and he kissed her back, murmuring, "Why did you go, Azul? Why did you run away? What happened?"

He held her and they both wept, overwhelmed and clinging to each other. "I'm sorry," Alexa said. "I wanted to make it easier for you."

"Easier? I don't understand any of this." He took her hands, kissed her fingers. "Tell me what happened."

Alexa raised her head, and shook it slowly. "I love you," she said. "And this is the most beautiful, romantic thing I've ever even heard of. But I can't marry you. My father—" Her voice broke. She took a breath. Spoke firmly, so he would understand. "My father has disappeared. He stole a lot of money. Like, millions. The police have frozen all of my mother's accounts. They took our house. He's gone and I'm poor and have nothing."

"Your father has disappeared?"

"He's wanted by the federal police. Your family—" She broke off, shaking her head.

He was, in addition to being passionate and beautiful and rich, very intelligent. She did not have to explain it twice. His breath left him as if he'd been punched—*ooff!*—and he bowed his head over her hands. "That is bad," he agreed.

Gently, she extracted her hands. "So that's why I left. So you didn't have to make a choice between me and your family." She stood, wiping tears from her face with resignation. It was done.

"Azul."

She turned, and he got to his feet, moving his hands to his neck. He lifted a chain from beneath his shirt, and on it was the ring he'd given her. "I have made my choice." He took the ring off the chain and held it in his palm. "I choose you." His eyes burned brighter than a noonday sky, so blue and intense that she wanted to melt. In that fierce gaze, she saw his devotion, his love, his passion. And she saw that she had wounded him. "Do you choose me?"

"Yes," she said, and took the ring and put it back on her hand, and flung herself into his arms, weeping with relief and love. "I'm so sorry," she choked out. "I didn't know what else to do." He hugged her back, tightly.

"Do not," he said, "ever leave me again."

"No," she promised.

He pulled away and held her hands in his own. "We may not be able to marry properly. I don't know how to make that happen. But from now until we are dead, I am your husband and you are my wife."

Alexa nodded solemnly. "I am your wife and you are my husband."

They kissed once more, to seal it.

She tugged his hand. "Come. It's time you met my mother."

Elsa watched the flight down the Riverwalk with her heart in her throat. They all did—not just Deacon and Tamsin and Elsa, but everyone on the patio, and the people out walking their dogs, and the romantic couples. When Carlos tackled her, one man looked ready to get involved, and then Alexa turned and hugged him.

Tamsin said, "That has to be one of the most romantic things I've ever seen in my life."

Elsa wiped away a tear. "I hope they can work it out."

Deacon took her hand, raised it, and kissed the palm. She looked up at him. "I'm not going to try to top that," he said, leaning in to speak quietly, "but I hope you won't let this . . . distract you."

She smiled, a very small smile. "From?"

"Me."

She slid an arm around him and leaned into his body. "Not a chance."

Carlos and Alexa came up the hill hand in hand. Both had tear marks on their faces. The diners broke into spontaneous applause, and Carlos lifted their clasped hands into the air.

"Sometimes you've gotta run 'em aground," said a craggy voice.

Carlos bowed, then gave a little wave, and Alexa led him to the table where her mother waited. "Mom, this is Carlos. Carlos, my mother, Thomasina Corsi."

He bent over her hand with courtly grace. "I am honored to meet you."

"I'm so glad you're here," Tamsin said.

Alexa introduced Elsa and Deacon, and then it was plain they wanted only to escape. "I will return her to you soon," Carlos said, and they walked off, into the gloaming, heads twining like swans.

Tamsin touched her chest. "I've never seen a couple so madly in love."

"Me, either," Elsa agreed.

Deacon put his hand on Elsa's lower back, lightly. The heat moved from his hand to the base of her neck, spread in radiating waves around her ribs. She said, "I'm sorry to desert you, Tamsin, but I have plans with Deacon."

Tamsin waved a hand. "Go."

Deacon pulled her toward the parking lot and they climbed into his truck. Before he even closed his door, Elsa leapt on him, laughing, and buried her face in his neck, kissing his throat and chin playfully. He slid away from the steering wheel a little and pulled her closer, putting his hands in her hair, shivering under her rain of kisses.

Her playfulness fell away as she lost herself in the smell of his skin, the taste of it against her lips. "You better drive us home," she said.

"Yes," he agreed, and turned the key in the ignition.

Deacon awakened in the soft gray gloaming on Monday morning to find himself wrapped around Elsa like a limpet. She was fast asleep, her naked back pressed against his chest, her bottom nestled into his genitals in the classic spooning pose. Her hair spilled over his arm.

A powerful sense of gratitude poured over him. Her tiny body was so small that his arm, angled across her chest, almost completely covered her. Her skin was smooth and clear and olive. She smelled of some fruity shampoo and garlic and sex, and he wanted to begin again, kissing her from head to toe and every nook and cranny in between, but there was a day to get going.

He didn't want this weekend to end. She had stayed with him Saturday night and all day Sunday and Sunday night, too.

Flashes of their lovemaking moved through him, her hair flung out on the pillow, the earthy sound of her coming, the pulse and heat of it around him. He thought of the long hours they'd spent talking, and the midnight snack he had scrounged out of his kitchen.

It was a miracle that he could feel this way after so many years, filled with possibility and hope and a sense of honor. He held himself still so as not to disturb her and let it all move through him.

Love. Love, love, love. He'd maybe thought he was too old for it, had made too many mistakes, and yet, here she was, curled up like a kitten against him, her hands tucked under her face like a child. She had confessed she wanted children. She had confessed she wanted a husband.

His old self, the self he had been yesterday, might have said he didn't deserve any of those things. The self he had become under her ministrations knew that he would give as much as he would take.

She moved a foot against his shin, and he tucked his hand close around her breast. "I have to get to work, sugar," he said.

"I know." She turned in the circle of his arms, lifting her face to be kissed. He obliged and rubbed his nose over hers.

"I really don't want to leave this weekend behind," he said.

She gazed up at him seriously, lifted a hand to his face. "Me, either." Flinging a leg over his thigh, she clasped his hand on her breast and gave him a coquettish blink. "Would you like to come to supper tonight?"

"I've got a long day," he said with regret. "Tomorrow?"

"Tomorrow it is."

"Good."

Suddenly, she tossed the covers off her body. "Oh, crap! I forgot I promised I'd go to court with Tamsin. I have to get going, too." She picked up the phone from the night table and punched in a number. Waited for the call to be answered. "Hey, Tamsin.

What time is court?" She listened, nodding. "Good. I'll spend an hour at the garden and then head home.

"Whew." She clicked the phone off and set it aside. Deacon lay where he was, admiring her compact nakedness, her small breasts and flat belly, her generous thighs and that wild hair.

"Come here," he said, and flung back the covers himself.

Laughing, she leapt on him, covering and kissing him, and they made love one more time.

Elsa had gone by to pick up Charlie early on Sunday. Tamsin had been asleep, and Elsa had felt a little guilty taking the dog when Alexa obviously wasn't home, either, but he was ecstatic to see his mistress.

Now Deacon dropped them off at the church gardens. Charlie bolted joyfully straight down the center aisle while Elsa ambled behind him, lost in postcoital juiciness. She was sloshing with satisfaction, leaving behind bright red footprints of pleasure, her joints loose and easy beneath her thoroughly explored skin.

Deacon, do-dah, do-dah. She wanted to sing his name, do somersaults, skip across the paths.

The family garden plot she shared with Tamsin had clearly been weeded and tended the day before. Elsa connected the industrial hose to the pump in the center of the field and dragged it to her garden. She watered the tomatoes and sprinkled the beans. Daydreamed in the warm morning.

"Good morning," Joaquin said.

She startled a little at his sudden appearance. "Hey. How's it going?"

"Fine."

She waved the water over the patch of squash. "How's Joseph?"

"He's all right. He's out of the hospital, back at home."

"That's good. Have we come up with any new ideas for security?"

He shook his head. "Trying. I gave a pretty fierce sermon yesterday on the responsibilities of the community." He glanced at his watch. "A couple of neighborhood men came by yesterday afternoon to offer their help in organizing watch crews, and I'm going to meet with them in a couple of days. We'll see if it works."

"Good start."

"Yeah. I wish—" He broke off, his jaw tight. "I feel responsible for Joseph. I should have stepped it up sooner than this."

"Things begin where they begin," she said. "It isn't like this was a safe spot before the garden went in."

He shrugged and changed the subject. "I saw Tamsin and she told me about Carlos showing up."

Elsa smiled in memory. "Walking, it was the most romantic thing I ever saw. It was beautiful."

He stood there, not moving or talking, and finally she really looked at him. "What's up?"

"You were pretty scarce yesterday."

Elsa raised an eyebrow. "And?"

"Did you spend the weekend with Deacon?"

She stiffened. "Don't, Joaquin."

"You're my oldest friend. He killed somebody, you know that?"

"Yeah, years ago. And he's a lot more loyal to you than you are to him, Mr. Priest." She flung the hose aside. "What is *wrong* with you?"

"I just can't believe you'd sleep with somebody like that. It's immoral."

She gave a deep belly laugh. "Oh, it was okay for us, but not for me as an adult, right?" She shook her head. "Give me a break. You're just jealous. And I can't help you with that."

His cheeks flamed. "I'm not—"

"You are." She took a step closer. "Look, it hasn't been easy for me, either, being here like this. I've had a lot of unresolved stuff to deal with, too."

"Have you?"

"Yes. Not just this, either. I've been thinking about you and God and the Church and where I fit." She shook her head. "And I can talk about a lot of things with you, Joaquin, but not this. Not love and sex and all that goes with it." She took another step toward him. "When that priest knocked me off the dais of the church that day, and you were the one who comforted me, and our romance started, it felt like God had a plan for me. I could forgive the priest for narrow-mindedness—"

"You didn't forgive him. You left the Church."

She raised a hand. "Let me say this."

"Sorry."

"Dorothy helped me overcome my anger and hurt over that, but it also felt like we—you and I—were destined to be together. So when you decided to be a priest, I was absolutely shattered." She sighed. "You have no idea."

He bowed his head. "I know. I'm so sorry."

"But you see, I didn't want to be bitter and hard and mean-spirited, so I worked really hard to get myself back together. To make peace with you and a god who could call you and leave me in a million little pieces—"

"Elsa—" He had tears in his eyes.

"Wait." She raised a finger. "I grieved you and me, us, and all the things that we would never do or be or have. I grieved for the lost children, for the lost perfection. I found a vocation, and my place. But I also really want a family and children and all that goes with that."

He ducked his head. "Strange twist of fate, isn't it?"

"What?"

"That because the Church would not allow you to become a priest you will probably end up with everything—a vocation and a spouse and children." He met her eyes, and there were tears flowing down his face. She wanted to go to him and knew she couldn't. "It's so ironic."

"You don't have to remain a priest, Joaquin. You have free will."

"I have said vows," he said, his jaw tight. For one more hot minute, he stared at her, his dark eyes burning into her face. Then abruptly he turned and walked away, his shoulders stiff.

She was going to have to leave Pueblo. What she had believed to be water under the bridge was flooding over that bridge now. She could not bear to lose her friend Walking, but she would have to if he couldn't make peace with their past.

And what about Deacon? Would he want to leave? Would it even be appropriate to ask? Or would they suffer through some long-distance connection that would be doomed to trickle into nothing? It was so very new and fresh and tender. How could it possibly stand up to such weighty questions so soon?

"Argh!" she cried. "Couldn't just let me have one good day, huh?"

She stomped over and turned off the water. She might as well go home.

That was when Charlie came to her, limping dramatically on his forefoot. "What happened, baby?" He whimpered softly and lifted his paw. Something had sliced right through three of the pads, and it was bleeding profusely. Forgetting everything, Elsa whipped off her sweater and wrapped it tightly around his wound. She dialed Tamsin. "I need you to come take me to the vet."

Charlie needed six stitches. Probably, she thought with a thunderous scowl, something left over from the gang boys' trash-and-destroy mission the other night. She'd like to crack their heads together.

What was wrong with them, anyway? This was a neighborhood project. Some of their mothers and brothers and fathers and little sisters were invested.

Because the paw had to be bandaged, the vet gave Elsa a cone for Charlie's head. When he saw it he turned baleful eyes on her.

"I won't do it unless I have to," she promised him. "I'll keep him leashed, Doc, right by my side. I'll put the cone on at night, and when he's alone."

On the way home, she pushed his face away from the bandages three times. "Charlie, you'll hate it if I have to do this."

"I'm going to drop you off so I can get to court," Tamsin said.

"I'm still planning to come with you, sis."

"Don't be silly. I can handle it on my own. If you leave Charlie, he'll have to wear the cone. Just hang out with him and I'll be back in a couple of hours. But if you see my daughter, will you ask her to call her mother?"

It took much longer than Tamsin had expected to get her turn with the judge. When it finally arrived, she willed herself to stand up straight next to her court-appointed lawyer, who looked to her like a boy, barely old enough to be out of law school. But he had a commanding voice and a presence that belied his age—and he was donating his time.

As he made the argument for leniency, the judge looked bored right to the tips of her streaked hair. All Tamsin could think about was the peonies lying on the grass, with no one to appreciate their beauty, and her quilts stacked in trash bags, and the empty rooms echoing with no one in them.

She had nothing left to lose. "Your Honor, may I say something?"

Her lawyer leaned over. "Not a good idea."

"I need to speak for myself," she said quietly. "I'm not going to be obnoxious or anything."

"Very well," the judge said, "step forward."

Tamsin clasped her hands together. "I know it was wrong to break into the house, but I just wanted my quilts, and I'm asking you to let me have them, to release them. They're my own work and they're all I have. My husband had nothing to do with them. It's wrong that his actions should take away my life's work."

"He took a lot more than that, Mrs. Corsi, from a lot of people," the judge said, looking over her reading glasses. "Allegedly, of course."

Tamsin paused for a moment, thinking of the best way to phrase her reply. "I agree, it's terrible. A lot of people have lost a lot, but so have I. I've lost my home, my gardens, everything I've worked for for the past twenty-five years. And so be it—but I want the quilts and the machine. That's it. Taking them from me isn't going to give anybody else anything. It will give *me* a lot. I need to be able to support myself."

The judge said nothing for a moment. "Very well. I'll release the quilts and dismiss the breaking and entering charges, but if you come within thirty feet of that house again, I'll throw you in jail. Got it?"

"Yes, ma'am." Tamsin thought of the peonies—and let them go. Somebody, someday, would love them just as she did. "Thank you."

As she left the courtroom, she felt a sense of jubilation and excitement, relief, and more than that. She felt free. As if she had moved over some invisible threshold. To what? she wondered. Her new life, maybe?

Or maybe, she thought, ducking out of the rain into her car, she had crossed a threshold to herself.

A most intriguing idea. For a moment she sat with her hands on the steering wheel, staring at the rain. She was in her mid-forties. Her daughter was grown and her husband had disappeared. She had virtually nothing of her own.

She laughed. How many people were handed such a clean slate, such a sweet chance to start over?

Elsa found herself restless and irritable on that rainy afternoon. The encounter with Joaquin made her realize that she really needed to make some decisions.

To do that she had to either walk or cook. Since it was a rainy afternoon and she could not leave poor Charlie alone, she decided to cook.

Not that there was much food in the house. In the crisper, she found a package of carrots and a couple of forgotten bags of sun-dried tomatoes. There were potatoes and onions, a box of chopped, frozen celery. Carrot soup, then. And bread. She looked for yeast and found there was none. She would have Tamsin bring some bread home.

She called Alexa on her cellphone and said, "Bring Carlos to dinner."

"I'm kind of embarrassed," Alexa said in a low voice. "How can I bring him there? It's so . . . working class!"

"Alexa," Elsa replied with exasperation. "Don't be so shallow. I'm cooking dinner, and your mother wants to spend time with you and your beloved. He's Spanish and he will understand that. Bring him."

"Okay."

She texted Tamsin and left a message asking her to bring home two loaves of some hearty bread. Keeping an eye on Charlie, who was sleeping in the dining room after the trauma of his cut foot and trip to the vet, she turned her iPod to a meditative playlist that included flutes and some medieval chant and women singing in Latin.

The first step was to scrub and peel the carrots, a big pile of them. Letting the music and the repetitive hand movements soothe her turbulent mood, she rolled her issues around the back of her mind.

Until this morning, she hadn't realized that she could lose her deep, long friendship with Joaquin if she stayed in Pueblo. When she had returned to the States after they broke up, they'd picked up their platonic relationship by phone, and it had evolved over the years into a rich braid of support for them both, encompassing their shared childhood, their devotion to spiritual matters, and their history as a couple. Joaquin had been witness to her life, as she had been witness to his.

Or so she had believed. She sharpened a knife and began slicing carrots into wheels, carefully and methodically. But in fact, they had not witnessed each other's transformation into spiritual leaders. She had not, until the blessing of the fields, seen him as *priest*. He had never seen her teach a sermon or lead a class.

But the rest . . . the rest was real and true. She loved him deeply as a friend, as if he were a brother. Dispassionately, she remembered their love affair and the connection they had shared, but she did not want to re-create it.

Nor did he. She understood that. It was only because he had so easily managed his bodily hungers until now that the surprise of his carnal desire for Elsa had startled and unsettled him.

Far in the distance, thunder rumbled. Charlie lifted his head, but when it didn't repeat, laid it back down again. The vet had given him a pain medication. Would it work to keep him calm during storms? She'd tried a couple of things over the years, but they only seemed to make him dopey and crazed, which was worse than terrified and sober.

Just now, he snored deeply, and his paws twitched with dream running.

The carrots finished, she pulled out a heavy pot and poured olive oil into the bottom, and let it begin to heat. She diced a big yellow onion, wincing at the strength of it, then scraped it from the cutting board into the pot. While they softened, she crushed three cloves of garlic, chopped them, and added them to the slowly heating onions. Two ribs of celery, roughly chopped, went into the pot, the leafy tops set aside. After another minute, she dropped the carrots in, too, and let all the vegetables gently warm and soften in the oil.

A part of her did not want to leave. She had loved this time with her sister, with the gardens, with the boys and Deacon, and the daily contact with Joaquin. All of it had come together to provide her with rest and ease and love. Given a choice, she would have stayed a little longer, asked Unity to give her another couple of months, to the end of the summer at least, to give her relationship with Deacon a chance to grow, to harvest the garden, to see how the community solidified.

Do what is yours to do.

The edict had guided her through her studies, into the ministry, into her daily work. Even here, she had taken on the soup kitchen because it had given her an outlet to directly serve the community, as the garden did.

But she was bored. She stirred carrots and celery and breathed in the heady scent with pleasure. As lovely as it was, it wasn't enough. She needed much more.

What was hers to do?

Immediately she thought of the little church in Seattle, the cool dampness on winter mornings as she unlocked the doors and came into the sanctuary. The memory of it filled her, covered every inch of her mind and heart for a moment, and she closed her eyes, feeling transported.

Under her care, the church had grown from a congregation of 70, most over the age of fifty, to a sturdy, artistic body of 250. They had created programs to attract young families and children and young people, and there were a number of GLBT members who felt at home in the liberal environment. The disenchanted came to them from a wide variety of backgrounds and religions, and they welcomed discussion, offered a spiritual home for the lost and needy and broken, without judgment.

A piercing sense of longing burned just above her heart, and Elsa put a hand to it. "I miss it desperately," she said aloud.

What had she come to believe during this sabbatical? What did she believe *now*?

In the back of her mind ran the Apostles' Creed, the declaration of faith made by Catholics.

> I believe in God, the Father Almighty, Creator of heaven and earth; and in Jesus Christ, His Only Son, our Lord: Who was conceived by the Holy Spirit, born of the Virgin Mary; suffered under Pontius Pilate, was crucified, died and was buried . . .

The onions were completely translucent. Elsa added four quarts of chicken broth from paper cartons, and waited for the liquid to come to a boil. Outside, thunder rumbled again, a little bit closer, but Charlie still didn't stir.

When the soup reached a full, rolling boil, she turned down the heat, added a bay leaf, thyme, and coriander she found among her sister's spices, and the celery tops.

What did she believe in? One of the things that had startled her during this time was how deeply Catholicism ran through her blood. She had wanted to abandon it, reject it as it had rejected her, a mere woman, but she could not, not entirely. She still longed for the rosary and the rituals and the Blessed Mother and the rituals of praying to saints.

Taking a sweater from the back of a chair, she went to the picture window and looked out into the street. Rain always made the street fill up, side to side, and now it was running almost as fast as a river. Her sister would not be foolish enough to drive into that mess. She was probably waiting it out somewhere.

What did she believe in?

She believed that humans were basically good, that they could be encouraged to better things. She believed that if each person found the work they were meant to do, the world would be a happy place. She believed in an action-based spirituality—it was fine and good to talk, but people needed food and community and medicine and help, and that meant other human beings had to step in and do the work.

She believed in alleviating loneliness whenever possible, whether through kindness or listening or teaching people to talk to Spirit.

Behind her, Charlie snored. Elsa smiled. She believed in dogs. And friendships and family.

She also genuinely believed Joaquin had seen an angel. She could not deny there was something when she prayed and meditated. She absolutely believed in the warnings she got. If that was not Spirit, what could it be?

There was something. Something, capital "S."

Behind her, Charlie jumped up and then yipped in pain when he landed on his wounded paw. "Oh, baby," she cried, and rushed to his side. "Lie down. It's okay." She sat on the floor and let him put his head in her lap. She sang to him, thinking of Deacon and his three rescues, his gentleness with the boys, his tireless attention to the garden.

To her body, to her mouth, to her—

She shivered in memory, touching her mouth as she thought of kissing him. What a surprise he was!

And that was the other part of leaving, of course. Deacon. What would she do about Deacon, about the nascent connection growing there?

Do what is yours to do.

As she rubbed Charlie's sides, she suddenly caught the scent of rotten apples.

Chapter Twenty-Six

All afternoon, Joaquin could not be still for ten seconds. His belly burned with warning and discomfort, and not only from his tangled emotions. Something was afoot. Something cloudy and dark, blowing in from the river. He kept peering out the windows, looking for a sign, but nothing was there.

Finally in the late afternoon, there was a break in the weather. The sun came out and heated up the air. Joaquin prepared himself, then took a bottle of holy water to the garden. He walked the perimeter, chanting a blessing, asking for protection for all involved and for the earth itself. Calvin, Mario, and Tiberius saw him, and they ran over to him, asking if they could help.

"I could get my drum," Mario said.

"I got a rattle my mom made from a gourd," Tiberius said.

"That's fine."

As they ran to get their instruments, Calvin pouted. "What about me?"

Joaquin gave him a small bell. "Ring this."

"What's a bell do?"

"It's another way to bring God into the garden, just like the holy water and our prayers."

"And the drum brings good spirits. Mario tole me that."

"How's his grandpa doing?"

"Grouchy!" Calvin said. "He say his head hurts."

"I bet it does."

Mario rushed back with a small hide drum. Joaquin led and the boys followed, drumming and ringing. It felt urgent to do this, and he wondered if they should have someone in the garden tonight. The meeting had gone well this afternoon, with two men stepping up to organize a volunteer watch group. One man was a cop, and he thought he could recruit some other members of the force to participate when they were off duty. The other man, who had lost a grandson to gang violence right in this neighborhood five years before, wanted to name the group for that lost boy.

But nothing was in place yet.

As if his ritual had called them, a cluster of gang boys walked by on the sidewalk. Joaquin straightened, and met their eyes directly. "Good evening, gentlemen."

The leader of the trio smirked, but one of the others said, "Evening, Father." His friend shot him a look over his shoulder, warning. Behind the trio trotted another young man, wearing a blue hoodie. A rose tattoo marked his face, and Joaquin remembered seeing him around a lot lately, often with a cat. He hurried after the others now, a little too fat to be quick.

Joaquin returned his attention to his task. Eventually, the garden would either create new unity and peace in the neighborhood or it would fall to ruin. If it was the latter, he believed that the spirits of those who had planted their hopes here would fall into darker despair than they had known before. He gave particular ferocity to his prayer.

When he had finished, the boys ran off. Joaquin saw Deacon's truck pull up at the far end of the block, and although he knew he should speak with him about the sense of trouble he was feeling, he simply could not face his friend. Not yet, not with the fresh hell of imagining Elsa with him so new a wound.

Instead, he took his thorny jealousy into prayer. He and Santiago the cat wandered into the courtyard and sat on a bench. A few birds were still twittering here and there, and a wave of cool air washed upward from the grass. San Roque stood over the square with a benevolent and patient expression. The air smelled of roses.

Someone was busy in the basement of the church, a youth group, he thought, and their laughter echoed into the evening every so often.

Dear Father in Heaven, he prayed, *I am a lost sheep instead of the shepherd I should be. I am riddled with doubts and sorrows and regrets. I am tortured by hungers I thought I had forgotten. Please help me. Lead me. Show me the way.*

It came to him that if he was so miserable as a priest, he could simply walk away. It was done all the time. He could refuse the call, leave behind his flock, and pursue a different life. That was, after all, what Elsa was doing. She questioned her call.

And now she had taken a lover. The knowledge burned a hole right in the middle of his gut. She had done everything he struggled with, and God had not spit her out, had He? She had even turned her back on the Church, taken up another faith, and she still had not been smitten.

He bowed his head. "Oh, God, I am only a man. I am lost. Help me."

But no angel came to anoint him in his very human struggle. No light filled the courtyard. His cat wound around his feet and birds sang in the treetops and Joaquin came as close to despair as he ever had. That, too, would be a sin.

At last he picked himself up and let the cat into the rectory. The nave was quiet, though candles burned in two stations, before the Blessed Mother, clothed in her Virgin of Guadalupe mode, before St. Francis.

He knelt in supplication before the crucified Christ. The room was still and holy, filled with the love and hungers of the parishioners who had brought their souls and hearts here to worship over the years. He could sense their spirits now, the prayers they had whispered. He knew a hundred prayers, a thousand perhaps, and he sorted through them to think what would most serve him.

Through the centuries monks and priests had faced their mortal selves to rise above them.

"Dear Jesus," he prayed aloud, "in the Sacrament of the Altar, be forever thanked and praised. Love, worthy of all celestial and terrestrial love! Who, out of infinite love for me, ungrateful sinner, didst assume our human nature, didst shed Thy most Precious Blood in the cruel scourging, and didst expire on a shameful Cross for our eternal welfare! Now illumined with lively faith, with the outpouring of my whole soul and the fervor of my heart, I humbly beseech Thee, through the infinite merits of Thy painful sufferings, give me strength and courage to destroy every evil passion which sways my heart, to bless Thee by the exact fulfillment of my duties, supremely to hate all sin, and thus to become a Saint."

When he finished, he was overcome with a staggering exhaustion, one so vast that he nearly could not stand. He managed to make his way to his bed, where he fell, fully clothed, into a profoundly deep sleep.

When the rain stopped, Elsa opened the door to the cool breezes, letting them blow away the cloud of rotten apple that followed her around.

She had begun to set the table when the first crack of thunder shot through the heavens. The storm was circling back from Kansas, where it had spawned a dozen tornadoes. This time, the lightning was not distant. It boomed and cracked right at the tops of the trees.

Charlie leapt to his feet and made a howling noise, lifting his paw up to protect it. Elsa made a dash toward him, but as she reached for him, a bolt of lightning struck so close that the resulting thunder sounded like the gods had taken an ax to the roof. Elsa felt his fur beneath the tips of her fingers before he bolted—straight out the screen door into the rain.

Elsa bolted right after him. "Charlie!" she cried. "Come here, baby!"

He ran at full speed, even favoring his paw. She could barely keep him in sight through the rain. All around them, lethal flashes of lightning slammed into the earth, knocking down trees and power lines. "Charlie, baby, stop!" she cried. "Come here, sweetie."

Charlie, out of his mind with terror and drugs, ran. So fast, so far, she couldn't see him, couldn't catch him. She was soaked, her clothes dragging at her, her hair dripping in her face, and her breath coming in raggedy gasps. Still she kept going, running the route they usually walked, circling, looking into gardens.

"Don't let him get hit by a car," she prayed, starting to weep in fear. "Don't let him get hit by lightning. Keep him safe, keep him safe, keep him safe."

The storm moved so fast that in ten minutes the lightning was in another part of town and the rain had slowed to a drizzle. Gasping for breath, freezing, soaked, Elsa made it to the garden by the church, sure she would find him there. "Charlie!" she called. "Charlie! Come back, baby!"

She whistled, and jogged up the center aisle, unable to see much in the gloom. The ground was sloppy with mud and she was starting to shiver with cold.

When she first saw Paris, she was so focused on her fear over Charlie that it took a long moment to make sense of the scene. It looked most like a fabled beast of some kind, a multi-limbed beast.

Then Paris screamed. Elsa spied her on the ground, in the midst of a trio of gangbangers. Her legs and arms pumped as she tried to escape and she cried out again. She slipped out of their grasp, but was immediately hauled back, and Elsa saw her shirt being stripped away.

"Stop!" Elsa cried, and ran toward them. She picked up a rock and aimed it at the boys' heads. She threw it with as much force as she could muster, and it slammed into the shoulder blades of one of them, hard enough to make him stagger sideways. He turned with a roar of fury. Elsa saw that it was the leader, Porfie, with his long eyelashes. She thought, for one hopeful second, that he would run. Instead, he said, "Get that bitch, too."

Time slowed, one frozen frame to the next. Elsa saw Paris, smeared with mud and fighting the hands grappling with her slippery arms, scramble to her knees and yank herself free of the boy holding her. Porfie reached out like some kind of supernatural being and snatched her by the hair, hauling her back down. He hit her, and she went still.

Elsa thought of Kiki, still alive, fighting. Instead of running away to find help, she ran hard for Porfie and leapt on him, yelling at the top of her lungs, "Leave her alone! Leave her alone! Leave her alone!"

He reared, trying to reverse positions with her, but Elsa had an arm around his neck, a hand locked in his hair, and he couldn't quite grab her.

"Get this bitch off me!"

Her hair snagged hard in something, and she found herself falling. Then she was flung sideways, her neck whipping painfully, and she caught sight of a foot. Someone laughed.

Elsa went cold, realizing that her hair hadn't caught in something, it had been grabbed. By the time that sank in, she was on the ground, splatting against the mud. She yelped, pushing against the hands holding her ankles and waist, reaching for the hands in her hair. "Don't do this," she cried, panting. "It's only going to make it worse."

"Shut up, bitch," her main captor said, and punched her in the face.

It was so shocking, so painful, so incomprehensible, for the space of seconds Elsa couldn't move or even breathe. She smelled the sulfurous scent of rotten apples, clouding the air, making her heart squeeze painfully with fear.

"No!" she cried, pushing frantically at them, yanking her feet, moving anything, everything she could. Arms, head, body twisting, legs scissoring.

He hit her again, his fist like an anvil. And again, and her eye stung with stars. She tasted blood. Boots slammed into her ribs, her back, her legs. She curled up, her hands over her head, but someone yanked them away and started tearing at her shirt. She fought against them, grabbing a wrist and biting it, and he stood up and kicked her in the ribs. "Bitch!"

"Hold her fucking hands."

Somebody grabbed her wrists and yanked them over her head and somebody else had her feet, and hands tried to skin her pants from her body. She squeezed her knees together, brought one up to his belly, and he yelled, "Fucking hold her still!"

He pushed an arm over her throat, leaning hard, gagging her.

Out of the corner of her eye, she saw another figure, the boy who wore a dark blue hoodie. He held his white cat, his expression calm and sad at once.

Help! she screamed in her mind, at the top of her voice, and again she felt a punch and something gave over her eye. She thought, urgently, and irrationally, of Charlie. *Keep him safe, keep him safe.*

The third time he saw the angel, Joaquin awakened in the cold dark from an almost unnaturally deep sleep. She was the same, her dark eyes, the green light, but there was no smile on her lips. She said, "Go to the garden and find Elsa, now."

He did not hesitate, but ran down the stairs as fast as he could, shirtless and barefoot, out the back door of the rectory. It was just past twilight, and gloomy with the storm that still had rain leaking out of the sky. In the middle of the garden, he thought he could see a soft light, and ran for it, dread building in his gut, so powerful he did not cry out at all.

There was light on the scene, that was the only way he could have seen what he did. A swarming, surging tangle of humans—gangbangers, two—no, three—and a young woman, soaking wet, swinging her hands, kicking at the attackers, yelling, crying, and at the center of the mass, Elsa splayed out in the mud, her body muddy and white. Still. "Stop!" he cried. "What are you doing?"

He grabbed the shoulders of the one on top, hauled him away with almost superhuman strength, and the teenager tumbled sideways.

The other two scattered, falling backward, putting their hands up in front of them. One scrambled to his feet and ran away into the darkness. The other one crouched in fear. Joaquin collared the leader, the would-be rapist, and hauled him up by his neck. Rage filled Joaquin, mighty and punishing, and he felt the power in him to snap the youth's neck. Porfie fought him, but it was a foolish contest, flailing hands, his pants around his ankles.

"Don't," Elsa said in a craggy voice. Her face bleeding, she rolled to her side, covering herself. "You will hate yourself. His mother will hate you. It will just keep going."

Joaquin subdued the youth, one hand behind his back, and barked to the cowering boy, "Take his pants."

"He'll kill me, Father."

"I'll kill you if you don't."

The frightened one crept across the mud, staying low to the ground, and yanked at the other boy's pants. Porfie kicked at him, struggling against Joaquin's stranglehold, but the boy managed to get his leader's pants off.

"Elsa, can you walk?"

She did not answer, and he saw now that she was lying very still on her side, her back smeared with blood or mud or something else dark. He raised his eyes in terror and saw Paris standing there in her bra and jeans, her hair stuck to her neck. "I tried," she said. "She stopped them from raping me."

"It's all right," Joaquin said. "Cover her up. And you"—he lifted his chin at the terrified youth at Elsa's head—"call 911."

The boy was sobbing. He fished in his oversize pants and brought out a phone. Paris knelt tenderly beside Elsa and tucked her torn shirt over her chest. "Stay with us, Elsa," she said, brushing hair from her white face.

"He'll kill me," the weeping boy said. "He'll kill me. Father, protect me, I can't go to jail with him. He'll kill me."

It seemed to Joaquin there was too much light, that he could see too much. The gang leader in his grip struggled again, fighting against the arm across his throat, the hand that held his wrist. Joaquin held him easily, as if he were a giant and Porfie was only a ragdoll.

"Call 911," Joaquin said, "and then run. But if you don't come back to see me at the church in two days, I will hunt you down myself. *Sabe?*"

The boy did as he was told, and then ran.

Paris wept at Elsa's side, pressing her palm to her cheek. "Don't die," she cried. "Don't die."

Elsa could hear Joaquin and Paris, but it was a strangely disconnected feeling, and she realized abruptly that she was sitting up, a few feet away, watching the scene. She could see Joaquin's back, and the pantless gangbanger, and Paris kneeling over her form on the ground.

The boy with the rose tattoo stood next to Paris, a cat in his arms contentedly purring. He looked directly at the Elsa who was not in her body, his eyes grave. Elsa thought there was something she should be doing, something she needed to remember, but she was filled with a sense of extraordinary quiet, as if she was not just in meditation, but had become part of the fabric of it, that quiet, that space between all things.

And she grew aware that she was not alone in the garden, in this strange place between places. Small blue lights bounced through the plants, and when she looked closer, she saw that they were cats, most of them white cats, frolicking with one another, leaping on bugs and hiding beneath leaves to ambush. It made her laugh, that the blue lights everyone talked about were cat ghosts.

There were not only cats, but human-shaped lights, too. Old and young, some of them standing around her body, weeping and wringing their hands, only parting like water to let the EMTs through. Others drummed and sang, and it seemed to Elsa that their song gave light to the plants themselves. Everything was limned with blue light, the leaves and the trees and the cat ghosts. She held out her arms and saw the light shape her arms and legs, herself but not herself. When she turned in a circle, she saw the glow of life in the trees, rivers flowing upward through the trunks and branches and into the leaves, then changing form and floating into the air, where the humans breathed it in.

The boy with the rose tattoo stood beside her and gestured toward the stretcher, with her on it, moving away from the garden. *You have to go with them.*

I want to keep these eyes. See the world this way always.

Then all was darkness.

Tamsin was worried sick by the time Charlie came up on the porch and barked outside the screen door. He was panting and muddy and soaked.

She'd arrived home with two loaves of bread to find the door standing wide open, soup scorching on the stove. The table had been halfway set. What the hell had happened here?

Carlos and Alexa arrived only a few minutes later. Tamsin kept telling herself that Elsa would have a good explanation when she got back. Charlie had been injured earlier. Maybe . . .

Maybe what? Elsa's car was still in the driveway. The leash was still on the hook.

"Where's Elsa?" Alexa asked. She looked like another person entirely. Her hair was shiny, tumbling down her back in a clean wash, and she wore a simple blue summer dress that highlighted her eyes. On her hand was the ring.

"I have no idea." She lifted Alexa's hand. "May I see it?"

Carlos put an arm around Alexa. "We do not know if we will ever be able to have a public wedding, but we are engaged nonetheless. We will be together, and this is my promise."

The ring was an enormous rectangular sapphire with an antique cut and diamonds on either side. "It was his great-grandmother's ring."

"It's beautiful. You are beautiful." She kissed Alexa's forehead, and turned to Carlos. "And I am so happy to finally know you. Let's all sit down and have a glass of wine. I'm sure Elsa will be back soon."

But a half hour passed and there was still no sign of her. Tamsin was about to call the rectory when Charlie showed up. His fur was wet and his bandage was tattered, but still intact. When Tamsin urgently inspected the paw, she found the stitches were still okay, too.

"What have you been doing, Charlie-Man?" she said, calling him Elsa's pet name. "Where is your mama?"

He whined and looked at the door, as if she would be coming in at any moment.

"What happened to poor Charlie?" Alexa asked.

Tamsin explained everything. "I think I need to get him cleaned up a little and rewrap this paw." She sighed. "We're going to have to postpone dinner."

"This is weird. Charlie wouldn't leave Elsa."

"You're right," Tamsin said. "Why don't you call the rectory while I look after his foot."

"Do you have the number?"

"Look it up." Tamsin led Charlie into the bathroom. As if he were apologetic for all the trouble he'd caused, he followed meekly, with his head down.

Tamsin found a roll of bandages in the medicine cabinet, along with a bottle of alcohol—no way—and some hydrogen peroxide. Better. She dried him off with an old towel, then sat on the side of the tub and gently lifted his injured paw into her lap. "You're going to be really sore in the morning, Charlie," she said, taking away the shredded, muddy bandage. He panted hard, looking at her patiently. "Where'd you get to, honey? Were you afraid of the storm?"

He whimpered again softly.

"It really is terrible that we can't explain lightning to you." She positioned the paw over the toilet bowl and poured peroxide over it. It foamed, but not terribly, and she did it again. "Good dog."

Alexa appeared at the door. "No answer at the rectory. Do you want us to drive to the church? Or maybe Deacon will know something."

A slow burn started in Tamsin's gut. Something was very wrong. "Go by the church and see if you can find Father Jack. If you can't—" She scowled. "Crap. I don't know how to get ahold of Deacon."

Her hands were shaking as she wrapped Charlie's paw.

Alexa came into the room and put her hand on Tamsin's shoulder. "Why don't we stay here with Charlie and you go look for Aunt Alexa?"

"Okay."

In the dining room, Elsa's phone began to ring.

Tamsin picked it up. "Hello? Elsa?"

"It's Father Jack, Tamsin. You need to come to St. Mary Corwin. Elsa has been injured."

"Injured? How? What happened?"

"Just come. I'll explain everything when you get here."

Chapter Twenty-Seven

The first time she saw an angel, Elsa awakened to the slow beep of machines. For long moments, she could not get her bearings. The room was not well lit, but she could make out shadowy figures around her.

Clearly, it was a hospital, but what was she doing here? There was something she should remember, something that lurked—

The boy from the garden stood by her bed, holding his cat.

What are you doing here? she asked.

Watching over you, he said. *My name is Rafael.*

Are you alive?

He shook his head sadly. *They killed me. Threw my body into the river. Everybody thinks I ran away.*

Are you an angel?

"She's talking." She felt someone take her hand. Tamsin, she thought. "Can you hear me, Elsa?"

Charlie! she thought urgently, and tried to sit up. But she didn't even move her head before everything exploded. "*Charlie!*" she cried, but it came out as a mewling sound, hardly words at all, and she couldn't figure out why that would be.

"He's safe," Tamsin said. "He came home. Alexa and Carlos are with him."

Relieved, Elsa slid away again into the muffling darkness.

"Are you going to be okay, Mom?" Alexa asked. When it became clear that Elsa's condition had stabilized somewhat, Joaquin, Deacon, and Tamsin agreed on a rotating schedule so there would always be someone with her.

Paris, thankfully, had only experienced minor injuries, yet she was devastated by the incident and the fact that Elsa had been injured trying to defend her. Seeing how distraught she was, Tamsin insisted that Paris and Calvin come home with her. They were now settled in and sleeping.

Tamsin nodded wearily at her daughter. "I'm just going to get some sleep." Alexa and Carlos hugged her, and left to head back to his hotel, hands entwined.

She was absolutely exhausted, and thought about a glass of wine, but decided against it. Instead, she brewed a cup of herbal tea and pulled out the quilt she'd been working on. As soon as she spread it over the table, the insistent sound of "Dominique" started to play in the back of her mind. Exasperated, she turned the radio on, very quietly, to a classical station.

Again she admired the bougainvillea, coming along so beautifully, and the dark green tree standing on the cliff. She still wasn't quite sure what kind of tree it was, but knew that it could be quilted in, layered with lighter and darker fabric once she figured it out.

More than any other part of it, she was pleased with the way the layering of the sea was turning out. The gossamer aquamarine tulle over darker blue cotton and sharp white sand and paisley tropical fish darting about and—

Suddenly, she knew exactly where Scott was. She had been making this quilt of that spot since he'd disappeared.

* * *

The next time Elsa awakened, there was more light in the room, which she could see through the small slits created by her barely opened eyes. Any wider than that and her head felt like a rocket was blasting through it. She heard the beeping of a monitor, slow and steady, and voices somewhere beyond her, brisk and worldly. Greenery waved arms at the window.

Then she felt her body. Left hand throbbing. Left shoulder. Right eye. Mouth. *Face*.

More. Right ankle, abdomen. And oh, sweet mother of God! Left little toe.

She made a noise.

"Elsa?" Joaquin's face swam in her vision, and his hand circled her wrist. "Can you hear me?"

She grunted a sound like "yes," discovering her throat was utterly raw. "Water."

He disappeared from view, returned, and positioned a straw between her lips. She sucked, and cool water poured through her mouth, down her throat. She swallowed, and tried opening her eyes a little more, but they didn't move much. "Car accident?" she guessed.

"You don't remember?"

"No." There was something about Charlie, and she bolted upward, sending fresh waves of pain through her head. "What happened to Charlie? Something happened to him."

Joaquin gentled her, a hand on her shoulder. "He's fine. Tamsin is babysitting him."

"Good," she said, and closed her eyes, diving back into velvet.

It was Deacon who was with her when she next opened her eyes. This time she could open them a little better, and it wasn't quite so brutally unpleasant. He was sitting in the armchair by her bed, reading a thriller. A pair of black reading glasses perched on his nose. The sight sent a rippling wave of love through her. "Hey," she said.

He leapt to his feet, whipping off his glasses. His expression told her how desperately worried he'd been. "Hey," he said gently, leaning over the bed. "How you feeling?"

"Headache," she said, and swallowed. "How long have I been here?"

"Do you want some water?"

"Yes, please." She thought she'd asked a question, but couldn't remember what it was, and suddenly it didn't matter. "Good drugs," she said. "Godzilla could be sitting here and I'd be friendly."

He smiled and held the water to her lips. She drank a little, and struggled to surface a little more clearly. To talk to Deacon. "You look good."

He touched her face, a thumb to her cheek. "You look like crap, but I've never seen anything better than you opening your eyes."

Again she reached for something, a thing she couldn't remember. "What happened?"

He lifted her hand and pressed a kiss to the palm and she saw that there were tears in his eyes. "Time enough for that."

She remembered lying in his bed, with his body curled around hers, his hands on her body. "We made love," she said. "I remember that."

"Yes." He put her hand against his face. "We did."

"And Carlos came to find Alexa." There was something about that, something she should remember, and she couldn't. Her stomach rolled and she skittered away from it. "The Riverwalk."

"Yeah, it was damned romantic."

She felt her body going lax, her brain drifting away. "I think I'm falling asleep again."

"You go ahead. One of us will be here when you wake up."

She grabbed his hand. "You, please. Can you stay?"

"I'll be here," he said, his voice breaking. "I'll be here."

She dreamed that her room was filled with saints. She recognized them easily. San Roque was handsome in the way of the aesthete, his eyes large and extraordinarily bright. He wore a brown pilgrim's robe and had a little dog at his side. She'd always imagined that his dog was large, like a husky, or Charlie.

There were others, too. St. Martha and Ganesha and St. Therese. The Virgin of Guadalupe wore a purple dress and her long black hair flowed over her voluptuous body like a glorious cape. In the chair sat Jesus, wearing a pair of jeans, his hair pulled neatly back. He was astoundingly handsome, but then, she supposed that he would be. He smiled, as if he could hear her thoughts.

"What are you all doing here?"

A woman spoke from her other side. "You wanted to see an angel."

Elsa sat up straighter, wishing she had a way to comb her hair, and be more presentable.

"It's all right," said Guadalupe. "You are beautiful just as you are."

It seemed odd and wonderful that they were all here, just as she'd wished so many times, just to talk to them and have them talk back. She knew it was a dream, if only because she didn't think San Roque would wear Tevas. It made her laugh. "Can I ask a question?"

"Yes."

She thought about it. Why did God punish her instead of rewarding her for the long, difficult trek to Santiago? Why hadn't God intervened in Kiki's death? What—

"Is she all right?"

Guadalupe stepped closer. "She is happy."

"I don't know why you couldn't save her."

The woman on her other side, a woman with large dark eyes and a green gown, said, "There is evil in the world. You know that now. You have looked it in the eye."

That lurking memory sucked at her, something about rain, about mud—

The angel placed her hand on Elsa's heart. San Roque stepped forward to touch her feet, and Jesus stood at her side. Their voices murmured over her, rising and falling, offering encouragement, love, affirmation. *You are valuable. You are doing good work, and will do more. Thank you. The world needs you. Believe.*

Their hands and their light swirled into her, all through her, touching broken places, sore places, aching places. As if from far away, Elsa saw her body on the ground on the field, and she remembered the way the world looked when she had been outside of her mortal form, everything alive with soft blue light, the energy of Spirit, flowing through all things, everything.

She remembered how peaceful she had felt, looking at her own body, and realized that Kiki, too, was made of light, energy. A forest light now, perhaps, or a saint helping someone else.

Surrounded by angels and saints, Elsa slept.

When she awakened, it was morning. She smelled coffee. Her stomach growled and she sat up, starving. Joaquin was in the room, and she said, "I need breakfast."

His smile blazed. "You've got it. I'll be right back."

If she'd had her way, she would have wolfed down pancakes and coffee and eggs and bacon. They let her have thin oatmeal and some orange juice and—when she begged—a cup of coffee.

"I had the most amazing dream," she said to Joaquin, and told him about the saints and Jesus putting their hands on her. "And I think I saw your angel. She wears green and has big dark eyes."

Joaquin stared at her. "Yes."

She took a breath. "I saw her, too, that day on the road. She looked at you so tenderly, and when I saw your hands on those prayers, all those things people had written on the walls, it was like there was light coming from you, going out into the world." She touched his hand. "You are such a good priest."

Tears welled up in his beautiful eyes. "I have been foolish since you've been back, Elsa. I am sorry."

She shook her head.

"My vocation gives me great joy," he said. "To feel the power of God moving in me . . . it is the most beautiful thing in the world."

"Don't wear her out," said a nurse, coming in to take vital stats. "Why don't you go get a cup of coffee, Father, and let me tend to our patient here."

He stood. "I'll be back later." The nurse moved the tray aside and took Elsa's pulse, looked at her chart, asked if she thought she might be strong enough to go to the bathroom on her own. Elsa told her she was willing to try.

But as she put her feet down, she remembered everything. Not at a distance, but as a woman. She crumpled into a heap on the floor, weeping in fear and reaction and relief. She was alive. Alive.

The nurse helped her into bed. "Pour it all out, honey. You've been through a lot."

Elsa did just that, cried and cried and cried. She wept for the assault and for Kiki and for the very real fact that evil could arrive so easily when people didn't do the work they were meant to do. It was not the evil of demons, but the evil of despair and neglect and loneliness. Finally, she let go of the burden of her grief.

And this time when she slept, it was the normal sleep of a very tired woman.

Chapter Twenty-Eight

Tamsin went to a great deal of trouble to find the right materials for her letter. This very hot July afternoon, Elsa, Paris, Calvin, and Alexa had gone to the movies. Elsa was almost as good as new three weeks after she'd been released from the hospital, and she was frankly irritated with all the fussing. She was returning to her Seattle church at the end of the month. Tamsin would miss her, but for the first time, she had plans of her own.

Just now, she had a letter to write. She'd searched high and low for airmail paper and an old-style envelope to match, both very thin paper with blue banding. She'd purchased a blue fountain pen, as well, and practiced so she would be able to write elegantly with it. Now the trick was to be clear without being specific.

July 7, 20—

Darling Jim,

I have been working on a marvelous jigsaw puzzle, made up of a delicious set of clues. There was a secret drawer with jewels inside, and a hidden closet right under my nose filled with piles of valuable paper, and a posh flat in a foreign city that I really must visit. In my leisure time, I have been working on a quilt, a lovely thing of a cliff overlooking a vast, clear sea with fishes swimming around in it. I'm quite pleased with the water and the bougainvillea, which I will quilt this evening, but the damnedest song kept running through my head as I worked. That strange little song we tried to forget, do you remember? "Dominique"?

That was the last clue, of course, though it took me a little while.

The fair child is well. Her mother is well, too. Thanks to solving the puzzle, I have some time, perhaps a year, to travel. My first destination is Africa, where I will be volunteering with a teaching project designed to give young women marketable skills. I was required to commit for six weeks, and there are those who are not at all sure I am up to the task, but that Fair Child is not privy to all the internal changes that have occurred over the past months. I am deeply looking forward to the work. My life has often been shallow and has lacked focus aside from the art of the quilts. Perhaps in giving some time to women who have had so much fewer advantages than I have, I will learn more about what the next chapter of my life should be.

After I am finished in Mozambique, I will travel to the Continent, where a friend has a flat her father bought for her, and stay there for a time. I've never lived abroad, and Spain seems agreeable.

Hope this letter finds you well.

Lisl

P.S. Please do not mistake mercy for forgiveness.

When the letter was finished, she sealed it, stamped it, and then she addressed it to *Jim Bond, c/o General Delivery, Taiohae,*

Marquesas Islands, French Polynesia. The return address was *Lisl von Schlaf, c/o General Delivery, Pueblo, CO 81003.*

For a long while, she only looked at it, recognizing that she was on morally thin ground here. The authorities would be very pleased to know that she'd figured out where Scott had fled. For the first couple of days after her realization, she'd tussled with herself—should she call them? Not call them?

He was undeniably a criminal. And yet, even in his darkest hour, he'd tried to take care of his wife and daughter. He was not a monster, only one more misguided human being on the planet. And after decades of loving him, she found she could not turn him in and live with herself.

Thus the letter.

Before she could change her mind yet again, she took it to the post office and dropped it into the mailbox.

Feast of San Roque

Patron saint of dogs and pilgrims

August 15

AUGUST 15

Chapter Twenty-Nine

The day of the blessing of the dogs was overcast and threatening rain, and Elsa eyed the sky as she loaded the last of her things into Tamsin's Subaru. "Think it'll hold off?" Tamsin asked, carrying out a suitcase.

"No. But it will put me in the mood for Seattle."

Tamsin turned her lips down at the corners. "It's going to be so lonely after we've been together all this time!"

"I know. I'm really going to miss you." She put a hand over the hollow spot in her belly. First Alexa had left, and now she was leaving, too. Life was taking another turn.

As life did.

"But you'll be off on your own adventure in two weeks, so you'll have plenty to do."

"I know." Tamsin rubbed dust off the window, a hand in her back pocket. Her eyes were full of tears when she looked up. "It's funny how sometimes you think life is going to be terrible and it ends up being something you'll remember forever, isn't it?"

"Oh, don't cry yet!" Elsa said, blinking hard.

"It's true, though. We both started out so miserable, and now . . . well, I think we're happy."

"I am." Elsa brushed hair from Tamsin's forehead. "Are you happy, sis?"

"I'm not sure what the word is, exactly. Excited? Scared?" She shrugged. "I feel like I'm getting ready for college."

"Miss Elsa!" Calvin called from the porch. "You want this, too?" He carried a small box.

"Yes, please. Bring it down. We'll put it on the front seat. It holds treats and poo bags for Charlie."

"He isn't gonna like being in that car all that time!"

"No, it won't be his favorite thing, but he'll be okay." The back was packed with boxes and suitcases and she'd filled the space between the backseat and front seats, too, and then covered it with a thick mattress of blankets for Charlie.

Paris and Calvin waited on the front porch. They were going to live in the house during Tamsin's travels. Elsa had offered to rent it to them at a much reduced rate, on two conditions—that Paris take one class per semester toward her nursing degree, and that she allow Calvin to get a dog. Deacon had taken the boy and his mother to the Humane Society, and helped them choose a dog that would be right for them. It was a three-year-old mutt with the coloring of a German shepherd, the size and pretty fur of a springer, and the kind, devoted heart of a golden retriever. She sat calmly at Paris's feet, her pink tongue hanging out. Paris had tied a silky white scarf around the dog's neck.

"You guys all ready?" Elsa asked.

Tamsin came out onto the porch, her blond hair cropped short in preparation for her Africa trip. Elsa was still startled each time she saw her sister—the cut made her look strong, no-nonsense.

"Let's go," Tamsin said.

This morning was the blessing of the dogs. It was too hot for Calvin's seven-year-old legs to walk so far, so they piled into two cars and headed over to the church. Tamsin drove Elsa's car.

"When do you think you'll hear from Alexa?" Elsa asked.

"She said it could be a week or two. They're moving ahead with their plans to be married, with or without his family's approval."

"That's a better answer than eloping, in the long run."

"Carlos's mother is the stumbling block, but his father is on board." She blinked suddenly. "What if I don't want my daughter to live in Spain and have her children there? What if I want them to be in Pueblo? Or at least Colorado?"

"It's not your life to live. Be thankful that she grew up to be so self-aware."

Tamsin nodded. "I do like him. He'll be a good husband."

"Yes."

They parked at the far end of the garden and walked down toward the church, and as she had every time since that night, Elsa remembered the blue light infusing every single thing. Now, in August, the corn had grown over her head, the squash apparently hoped to take over the world, and in their garden plot alone, there were enough roma tomatoes to feed twelve counties.

"Look at all of this!" Tamsin said.

"Good thing Paris knows all the homely arts. She's been giving canning lessons, did you know that?"

"No, that's perfect."

"I still don't know why we aren't doing the blessing outside. It sure seems like it would be easier." Elsa saw people carrying their dogs or leading them by leashes. Charlie trotted along beside her and Tamsin, cheerfully sticking close, as if he sensed something was in the air.

"It's always inside," Tamsin said. "I think Father Jack secretly likes having all that chaos in the sanctuary."

Elsa laughed. "Speak of the devil." He was coming toward them in his clerical clothes, his hair freshly cut, so it was out of his eyes for once. "Hey, Walking. Don't you have a Mass in a little while?"

"I was looking for you, Reverend Elsa. I wonder if you might come with me. I have a little favor to ask of you." He held out his elbow.

She glanced at her sister, but she only shrugged. "Sure. What do you need?"

"I'll show you." He led her inside, but instead of heading toward the rectory, he led her into the bowels of the nave. The smell of it—incense and sweat and beeswax—brought back a thousand memories, and Elsa stopped, inhaling it. She closed her eyes and breathed it in deeply. "I love that smell."

Joaquin took a gold satin robe from a row of them. It was a simple thing, with a zipper and long full sleeves. He held it up to her. "That will fit. Will you put it on?"

"Because . . . ?"

Joaquin took a sash from a wooden dowel. "Because I would like you to be the altar server today, if you would not mind."

For a long moment, she only looked at him. He gazed back at her kindly, dark eyes knowing. She could not manage the words, so she simply nodded.

She put the robe on over her clothes and pulled her hair back as if she were going to be giving a lesson. Her hands shook a little as she adjusted the sash around her shoulders. "I don't actually know what to do," she said.

"That's all right. I do. And I'll tell you." He donned his vestments, red for love on this day of celebrating dogs and the people who loved them. When they were both dressed, he stepped forward. "I won't see you before you leave," he said, taking her hands. "I kept trying to think of priestly things to say to send you off, but it isn't Father Jack who is going to miss you. It's Joaquin."

She covered his big hands with her own. "My old friend."

"I want you to be happy," he said. "Have a lot of children you can share with me."

"I would be honored." She squeezed his fingers. "The way I

have loved you over the years is different, Joaquin, but I hope you know that I will always love you, and our friendship is one of the best things in this life for me."

He looked down, touched her ring finger. "Yes," he said, in a whisper.

"I want you to be happy, too, Joaquin. Promise."

"I promise." In the church, music began to play, and he lifted her hands to his mouth, kissed them, and gestured for her to follow him.

And so it was, that twenty-four years after the first time she had turned her back on God, sixteen years after the second, and nine months after the third, Elsa Montgomery stood on the altar wearing satin robes. She poured the wine into the holy chalice and washed the priest's hands and rang the bell and looked into a sea of faces, human and dog. Her heart expanded outward, upward, filling the sanctuary itself, and she whispered her thanks.

It came to her that there would always be evil in the world, that there would be error and doubt and loss and things that could not be explained, but there would also be hope and goodness and kindness and love.

Joaquin met her eyes over the chalice and smiled.

Goodness.

After the Mass, Elsa found Deacon waiting, as they had arranged, at the house. The bed of his truck was enclosed with a camper shell. Dogs stuck their noses over the top of the back gate, tails wagging, and Joe kissed Elsa as she came up. Sasha turned in a circle, then barked cheerfully. Her bottom was swaddled in a diaper. Toby, the little Shih Tzu, would ride in the front.

"Hey, Rev," Deacon said with his slow, beautiful smile. "You sure looked good up there. I can't wait to hear you preach."

She took the hand he offered and stood on her toes to kiss him. She smiled. "We call it a lesson."

"I'll get the lingo, don't you worry." He slapped the side of his truck as if it were a horse. "You ready for this? Our big adventure?"

"Are you?"

"I can't wait." He touched her tummy. "Let's have some babies, huh?"

"You bet." She noticed a little bag hanging around his neck. "What's this?"

"Medicine bag. Mario made it for me."

"Is he all right?"

"He'll be fine."

Elsa looked over her shoulder at the house, feeling a pluck of nostalgia. "I'll never forget all this."

"Me, either."

"But," she said, whistling for Charlie, "I'm looking forward to the next chapter, too." When Charlie showed up, she opened the back door of the Subaru and he leapt in. "Let's hit the road," she said.

"Right behind you, sugar," Deacon said, climbing into his truck.

As she headed for the highway, Elsa glanced back and saw Deacon singing as he drove, his old dogs in back, and she suddenly thought of Kiki, shining with blue light.

Good choice, don't you think?

Goodness all around, she thought, and began to sing.

Recipes

Chicken and Dumplings

Split Pea and Barley Soup

Tarta Santiago

Caldo Gallego

Chicken and Dumplings

—Elsa—

This is one of those comfort foods that fill the hollowness left by a grief or a loss or a worry. Choose a good quality chicken and let it simmer a long time. The smell alone will cure many ills.

1 4–5 lb. stewing chicken, whole, giblet and neck removed
2 T olive oil
1 large yellow onion, diced
3 ribs celery, sliced
3 carrots, diced
1 bay leaf
1 tsp thyme
1 tsp sage
1 tsp salt
½ tsp pepper
Water

Wash chicken inside and out. Pour the oil into a large, heavy pot and add onions, celery, and carrots. Cook gently for 5 minutes, just to release the flavors. Add chicken, whole, and cover with water. Add seasonings and bring water to a boil, then turn heat down to medium low and let simmer for several hours.

When the chicken is falling off the bone, strain the liquid into a clean bowl, and then return to pot. Let the chicken and seasonings cool, then pick out the bones, loose skin, and bay leaf. Return mixture to pot and return to a low simmer.

Dumplings

Dumplings of this sort are really just biscuits poached in the stewing liquid, which is what gives them such lovely flavor. They absorb the fat and seasonings from the broth, and taste like pure love.

2 cups flour
2 tsp baking powder
½ tsp salt
1 tsp sugar
2 T cold butter
1 cup buttermilk

Combine flour, baking powder, salt, and sugar. Mix well. Cut in butter using a pastry cutter or two knives. Add buttermilk and blend quickly, then knead just ten times on a floured surface. Roll out the dough to about 1 inch thick, then cut it into triangles about 2 inches wide. Gently drop the dumplings into the simmering broth and cover the pot. Let cook for about 10 minutes. (You can test one by taking it out and cutting it open—the inside should be fluffy, like bread. If it isn't, let them simmer a little longer.) Serve in bowls with plenty of chicken and broth.

Split Pea and Barley Soup

—Elsa—

SERVES 10 EASILY.

TO SERVE 100, MULTIPLY ACCORDINGLY.

This is a hearty soup with a surprisingly dense flavor.

Olive oil
1 large yellow onion
3 stalks celery, sliced
5 carrots, sliced
2 cloves garlic, minced
2 quarts vegetable broth
1 lb. split peas, picked over and thoroughly rinsed
2 cups pearl barley
1 15-oz. can chopped tomatoes
2 tsp salt
1 tsp pepper
1 bay leaf
Water as needed

Pour olive oil into a heavy, large pot and add onion, celery, and carrots and let them brown slightly. Add garlic and cook for about 3 minutes. Add broth, then peas, barley, tomatoes, and seasonings. Bring to a boil, then cover and turn down heat to medium low. Cook for 2 hours, checking often to add water as necessary. When peas and barley are fully cooked, correct seasonings and serve with bread and butter.

Tarta Santiago

—Joaquin—

It is true that the Gloriosa sisters, who keep house for me, would be scandalized to find a priest cooking for himself, much less for others. This is an almond cake that you find on the Camino de Santiago. Not too sweet, not too complicated, and very good with a cup of tea. Elsa loves all the foods we ate on the road, but this is her favorite of all.

2⅔ cups ground almonds
1 stick butter at room temperature
4 eggs
1¼ cups sugar
¾ cup flour
½ tsp baking powder
½ cup water
Zest of 1 lemon
Powdered sugar to decorate

Blanch the almonds, then using a grinder or a food processor, grind them until they are fine. Set aside.

Heat the oven to 350°F. Grease a round 8-inch pan and cut a piece of paper to cover the bottom of it. Grease that, too.

Beat together eggs and sugar, then add butter and mix again. Add flour, baking powder, and water, and beat well.

Stir the almonds into the batter. Grate the lemon and add the zest and stir until thoroughly mixed.

Pour batter into cake pan. Bake in oven on the middle shelf for approximately 45–50 minutes. Check doneness after 45 minutes. Cake is done if a toothpick inserted into the center of it comes out clean.

The final step is the marker of the traditional cake. Cut out a cross of St. James (a sword that looks like a cross) from a piece of paper. Place the paper on the center of the baked cake, and dust the cake with powdered sugar. Remove the paper and you have the traditional cake.

Caldo Gallego

SERVES 10 EASILY

A hearty peasant soup to hold you over many days of walking. Plus, how can any soup with bacon be bad? Don't skip the turnip: It's full of things that are good for you and no one ever knows it's there.

1 lb. bacon ends and pieces
1 large onion, chopped
3 cloves garlic, minced
4 quarts vegetable or chicken stock
1 lb. mixed beans, white or brown or red, doesn't matter
1 large turnip, diced to 1 inch
2 potatoes, peeled and diced
¼ lb. chorizo sausage, skinned
1 lb. collard greens or other fresh greens, thoroughly washed and torn into small pieces
Salt and pepper to taste

Brown the bacon in a heavy soup pot, and let drain on paper towels. Pour off the fat in the pan, leaving 2–3 T in the pan. Add diced onion and cook 5 minutes over medium high heat, then add garlic and cook for another 2 to 3 minutes. Add bacon, stock, and beans, and cook until beans are tender, 2 to 7 hours, depending on the type of bean you use. (If you like, use two 15-oz. cans of white and/or pinto beans instead.) Add turnip and potatoes and cook until tender. Add diced chorizo and greens and cook until greens are wilted. Add salt and pepper to taste.

Serve with bread and butter and no one will go hungry.

PHOTO © BLUE FOX PHOTOGRAPHY

BARBARA O'NEAL fell in love with food and restaurants at the age of fifteen, when she landed a job in a Greek café and served baklava for the first time. She sold her first novel in her twenties, and has since won a plethora of awards, including two Colorado Book Awards and six prestigious RITAs, including one for *The Lost Recipe for Happiness*. Her novels have been widely published in Europe and Australia, and she travels all over the world presenting workshops, hiking hundreds of miles, and, of course, eating. She lives with her partner, a British endurance athlete, and their collection of cats and dogs, in Colorado Springs.

About the Type

This book was set in Goudy Old Style, a typeface designed by Frederic William Goudy (1865–1947). Goudy began his career as a bookkeeper, but devoted the rest of his life in pursuit of "recognized quality" in a printing type.

Goudy Old Style was produced in 1914 and was an instant bestseller for the foundry. It has generous curves and smooth, even color. It is regarded as one of Goudy's finest achievements.